WILLOWEND

THE JOURNEY CONTINUES

ROBERT GRIFFITH

GRACE AND TRUTH PUBLISHING
P.O. Box 338, Gunnedah NSW 2380 Australia
www.graceandtruthpublishing.com.au

ISBN: 978-1-7642635-7-3

1. WHEN THE CROWD LEAVES

The heat returned to Willowend without asking permission. It arrived early, settled heavily over the town, and lingered in a way that made even small tasks feel deliberate. Mornings offered little relief, the air was already warm before the sun had fully climbed, the promise of another long day carried on every breath.

From the outside, very little appeared different. The town still moved at its familiar pace. Shops opened when they always had. Neighbours exchanged greetings in passing, unhurried and polite. Life, as far as anyone driving through might notice, had resumed its usual rhythm.

But Pastor Caleb Merritt had learned over the years that change rarely announced itself.

Sometimes it came quietly, not as disruption but as a subtle shift - the kind that altered how people listened, how they spoke, how they waited. You noticed it not in crowds or noise, but in pauses that lasted a moment longer than they used to.

He had sensed it over the past few weeks, not as momentum, but as something settling - like ground that had been disturbed and was now finding its shape again.

He unlocked the church early on Tuesday morning, earlier than he needed to, drawn there by habit rather than necessity. The building smelled faintly of polish and dust, the familiar scent of old timber warmed by a rising day. The sanctuary was empty, the chairs back in their neat rows, the lectern centred again after weeks of being nudged and adjusted to suit different voices.

He stood for a moment at the back, taking it in.

There was a temptation - subtle, but persistent - to assess the season that had just passed. To measure it somehow. To decide whether it had been successful, or fruitful, or worth the quiet disruption it had caused. He resisted that instinct, knowing where it led.

Counting had never helped him listen better. Instead, he walked slowly down the aisle, running his hand lightly along the edge of a pew, feeling the smoothness where generations before him had done the same.

He thought of the people who had come and gone in recent weeks - some returning home changed in ways they might not yet recognise, others leaving simply grateful for a place where they had been allowed to rest.

And then there were those who had stayed.

The midweek gathering the night before had been small. Smaller than it had been at the height of the retreat momentum. Caleb had noticed that - not with disappointment, but with curiosity. Those who came had not come out of excitement. They had come because they wanted to be there.

That mattered.

He switched on the kettle in the small kitchen beside the hall and waited for it to boil, listening to the building settle around him. The church made sounds when it was empty - quiet clicks and sighs as the temperature shifted, the sort of noises that felt like breathing if you paid attention.

Howard arrived just after eight, as he often did on mornings when he knew Caleb would be around. He let himself in without knocking, calling out a greeting that echoed briefly through the hall.

"Thought I'd find you here."

Caleb smiled. "You usually do."

Howard filled a mug and leaned against the bench, studying him for a moment in that way he had - not intrusive, just observant.

"It feels different," he said at last.

Caleb nodded. "It does."

"Not quieter," Howard added quickly. "Just… steadier."

They carried their mugs into the sanctuary and sat near the front, the sunlight beginning to creep through the high windows. Howard rested his elbows on his knees, staring ahead.

"I've been thinking," he said. "About what comes next."

Caleb waited. He had learned not to rush people through their own thoughts.

Howard continued, "There's no pressure, is there? No sense that we have to keep producing something."

"No," Caleb agreed. "At least, not unless we decide to put it there."

Howard smiled faintly. "That's what I was hoping you'd say."

They sat in companionable silence for a while. Outside, a truck passed by slowly down the street, its engine fading into the distance. Somewhere nearby, a door closed.

"I've noticed something," Howard said eventually. "People are listening to each other differently. Not all of them. But enough that it's noticeable."

Caleb thought of the conversations he'd had over the past few days - not dramatic, not confessional, but honest in a way that felt newly possible. He thought of Mary's careful questions, Graham's long pauses, Amelia's quiet attentiveness.

"Yes," he said. "I've seen that too."

"And it's not coming from you," Howard added.

Caleb glanced at him. "Is that a complaint?"

Howard laughed. "It's an observation. And a relief."

They both knew what he meant. For years, Caleb had carried the unspoken expectation that if something meaningful happened in the life of the church, it would somehow be traced back to his initiative, his insight, his leadership. That expectation had loosened lately - not because he had withdrawn, but because others had stepped forward without being asked.

That, more than anything else, unsettled and steadied him at the same time.

Later that morning, Caleb walked through town, as he often did when he needed to think. The streets were quiet, shops open but unhurried. He stopped briefly outside the bakery, exchanging a few words with Sheila, then continued past the post office and along the road that led toward the edge of town.

At the park, two women sat on a bench, heads bent together in conversation. They looked up as he passed, smiling in greeting, then returned to what they had been saying without the self-conscious pause he would once have expected. He noted it and kept walking.

This, he realised, was the work that followed the opening.

Not momentum. Not growth measured in numbers. But a shift in posture. A willingness to stay with questions longer. A freedom to speak without needing to be impressive.

It was also more fragile than the excitement which had come before. Fragile things always were.

As he turned back toward home, his phone vibrated in his pocket. He stopped and checked the screen.

Ruth.

He hadn't expected that, not mid-morning on a weekday. They spoke regularly enough, but usually in the evenings, when her world slowed enough to make space for a call.

He answered, stepping into the shade of a gum tree.

"Hello," he said.

"Hi, Dad."

Her voice was warm, steady. Familiar in a way that went deeper than sound.

"Is everything all right?" he asked.

"Yes," she said quickly. "Nothing wrong. I just… had a bit of time between meetings and thought I'd call."

Caleb smiled to himself. "That's a novelty."

She laughed softly. "You have no idea."

They talked for a few minutes about ordinary things - her work, the city, the weather. She asked after Rachel, passed on her love, then hesitated.

"I've been thinking about Willowend," she said.

"Oh?"

Just… hearing bits and pieces. Mum mentioned the retreats. And I saw something online - not much, just people talking about how helpful it was."

Caleb listened, careful not to fill the silence.

"It sounds good," Ruth continued. "Encouraging. I'm glad for you both."

"Thank you," he said.

There was another pause, longer this time.

"I might come up for a visit. I have some long service leave, and I would like to spend it in Willowend." she said finally. "If that's all right."

Caleb felt something shift inside him - not alarm, not excitement, but awareness.

"Of course," he said. "We'd love that."

"Good," she replied. "I just thought I should check with you."

They said goodbye soon after, neither of them rushing to end the call, neither quite saying what else might be sitting behind her words.

As Caleb slipped his phone back into his pocket and continued walking, he became aware of a quiet convergence taking shape. The life of the church settling into a new rhythm.

The first questions beginning to surface beyond Willowend. And now, his daughter turning her attention back toward the place she had once left behind.

What remained when the crowd left, he suspected, was more demanding than what had come before. And far more revealing. Caleb did not mention the call straight away. Not because it unsettled him, and not because it felt secret, but because he had learned that some things needed time before they were named.

Ruth's voice lingered with him as he continued walking, not the words she had spoken so much as the attentiveness behind them. She had not rung out of obligation or nostalgia. She had rung because something had stirred her curiosity in a way she had not yet put into language.

That mattered.

By the time he reached home, the afternoon heat had deepened, the air pressing close against the walls as though unwilling to be kept outside. He opened the windows and moved through the house quietly, aware of how accustomed he had become to stillness. Ministry had once filled every spare corner of his attention. Now, space seemed to be part of the calling.

He made tea and sat at the kitchen table, the late light stretching across the floor in long bands. Outside, the town moved at its unhurried pace - a car passing, a door closing, someone calling out a greeting that carried easily in the warm air. Willowend did not announce its days. It allowed them to unfold.

Ruth's life felt far from this place now. Her world was shaped by meetings, deadlines, decisions made quickly and defended confidently. She had grown into it well. Caleb and Rachel had never worried about her capacity or her resilience. If anything, they had worried about whether she allowed herself to rest.

And yet, despite the distance - geographic and otherwise - she had been paying attention.

When Rachel came in, she set her bag down and leaned briefly against the bench, pausing as if to mark the transition from one part of the day to another.

"You look thoughtful," she said.

"I am … Ruth rang earlier."

Rachel's expression softened immediately. "How is she?"

"Good," Caleb said. "Busy. Settled."

"And?"

"She's got some long service leave and she wants to come and stay with us."

Rachel nodded slowly, absorbing it. "That makes sense."

"Does it?"

"Yes," she said. "She's been watching for a while now."

Caleb looked at her. "You think so?"

"I do," Rachel replied. "She asks very careful questions when she calls. Not about details. About people. About tone."

Caleb smiled faintly. "That sounds like her."

"But she won't come looking for answers," Rachel added. "She'll come looking to see if what she senses is real."

They both knew what that really meant. Ruth would not arrive impressed by stories or language. She would notice what people did when no one was directing them. She would see whether kindness lingered once enthusiasm faded.

That evening, Caleb returned to the church alone. He hadn't planned to, but the pull had been there all afternoon, quiet and persistent. The heat had softened by then, the air still warm but no longer heavy.

Inside, the building held the day's warmth in its timber and stone. He moved through the familiar space without turning on the lights, letting the shadows lengthen naturally as the sun slipped lower outside.

Howard's mug sat neatly washed and set aside near the sink. Caleb noticed it and smiled - a small sign of shared ownership that would once have gone unremarked.

He sat near the front, hands resting loosely in his lap, not to pray in any formal sense but just to be present. His thoughts moved easily, unforced, from Ruth to the town, from the conversations of the past week to the silences that had followed them.

The renewal that had begun in Willowend had not arrived with declarations or demands. It had come without a name, carried forward by people who did not yet realise they were leading. That was what made it both hopeful and fragile.

He thought of Graham's slow honesty. Of Mary's quiet clarity. Of the way people had begun listening to one another without rushing to fill the space. None of it required explanation. All of it required care.

By the time he locked up and stepped back outside, dusk had settled across the town. The street was quiet, the shopfronts dark, the heat finally beginning to lift. He walked home slowly, aware of a growing convergence he could not yet define.

The church was learning to hold what it had been given without trying to own it.

The town was adjusting to a deeper attentiveness it had not sought but now recognised.

And soon, his daughter – very thoughtful, capable, unconvinced - would walk these same streets and see Willowend with eyes unclouded by familiarity.

That, Caleb knew, would matter more than any review, any gathering, any carefully chosen words. Because what was being shaped here did not belong to him. And because love, when it paid attention, often revealed what leadership could not.

The next morning arrived quietly, without the sharp edges of urgency that used to define Caleb's weeks. He woke early, as he always had, but there was no sense of being pulled immediately toward a task.

Instead, he lay still for a few moments, listening to the house breathe around him - the soft creak of timber as the temperature shifted, the faint sound of birds beginning their day beyond the open window.

This, he thought, was what steadiness felt like.

Following his breakfast, Caleb walked into town again, not with appointments in mind but with attentiveness. Willowend revealed itself best to those who moved slowly. He passed the old mechanics' shed, now permanently closed, its faded sign hanging at a slight angle.

Further along, he saw Mrs Kline's curtains drawn back earlier than usual, sunlight spilling across the lace. He made a mental note to check on her later in the week, not because anything was wrong, but because noticing mattered. Outside the bakery, Sheila was propping the door open with a crate of bread, the smell drifting out into the street.

"Morning, Pastor," she called. "You're early."

"Habit," Caleb replied.

She smiled. "I like seeing people out walking again. Feels… friendlier."

He nodded. "It does."

She hesitated, then added, "I've been thinking about joining the Thursday group. Not to talk much. Just to listen."

"You'd be welcome," Caleb said simply.

She nodded, satisfied, and returned to her work without further discussion. That was becoming the pattern. No persuasion. No convincing. Just space being offered - and accepted.

Later, Caleb stopped near the park, where two men sat on a bench, coffees in hand, their conversation unhurried. They greeted him, then continued talking without lowering their voices or changing their tone. He walked on, quietly grateful for the trust implicit in such small gestures.

By midday, the heat had returned, settling heavily over the town once more. Caleb retreated home, where Rachel was already working at the table, papers spread out in loose order. She looked up as he came in.

"You've been out walking again," she said.

"Yes."

She smiled. "I thought so."

He poured a glass of water and sat opposite her. "People are choosing things carefully."

Rachel nodded. "They're listening to themselves."

"And to each other," Caleb added.

"Yes."

She gathered her papers, setting them aside. "That will bring questions."

"It already is."

Rachel leaned back in her chair. "Are you ready for that?"

Caleb considered the question carefully. "I don't think readiness is the point anymore."

She watched him. "What is?"

"Faithfulness," he said. "And restraint."

Rachel smiled. "Those have always been your strengths."

"Only because I've learned what happens when I ignore them."

They sat in comfortable silence, the kind that did not need to be filled.

That evening, Caleb received another message - brief, polite, from someone outside the region. A pastor, curious about what had been happening in Willowend. Not requesting a model. Not asking for some formula.

Just wondering if they might talk sometime. Caleb read it twice before replying. He did not answer immediately.

Instead, he set the phone down and stepped outside, letting the fading heat wash over him. The sky above the ridge was clear, the colours softening as evening approached. The land looked settled, as though it had exhaled after holding tension longer than it realised.

This, he thought, was how most good things began - not with certainty, but with attention.

Later, as darkness settled and the town quietened, he and Rachel sat on the veranda, chairs angled slightly toward one another. Somewhere nearby, a dog barked once, then fell silent again.

"Do you think this will last?" Rachel asked.

Caleb did not answer straight away.

"I don't know," he said finally. "And I think that's the wrong question."

She waited.

"What matters is whether we can tend it without trying to own it," he continued. "Whether we can let people grow without shaping them into something recognisable."

Rachel nodded slowly. "That will be uncomfortable for some."

"Yes."

"And freeing for others."

"Yes."

They sat together as the last light disappeared from the sky.

Before going inside, Caleb checked his phone once more and typed a brief reply to the earlier message. Nothing elaborate. Just an openness to conversation, without promise or agenda. He sensed, even as he sent it, that the path ahead would widen in ways he could not yet see.

Willowend would remain his place - of that he was certain. But the work unfolding there would not stay contained by its borders. Nor he suspected, would it remain uncomplicated.

As he turned off the light and prepared for bed, Ruth's voice returned to him again - attentive, measured, quietly curious. She would come soon. He did not know what she would make of what she found, or what her presence would stir in him.

But he trusted that her questions, like the season itself, would arrive without malice. And that, perhaps, was the truest sign that something new was taking root.

Not certainty.

Not clarity.

But the courage to remain open - together - to whatever God was shaping next.

2. LEARNING WHO SPEAKS NOW

Caleb noticed it first in the pauses.

They were the subtle and almost imperceptible moments when a conversation did not immediately rush to find its conclusion. Someone would ask a question and then stop. Someone else would begin to answer, hesitate, and try again. Words were weighed, not withheld, and that difference mattered.

It happened during a small gathering midweek, nothing formal. A handful of people sat in a loose circle, chairs pulled closer than usual, the windows open to the evening air. No one had been assigned to lead. Caleb had said as much at the start, and then resisted the urge to correct the silence that followed.

Eventually, Mary spoke.

Not loudly. Not with authority. Simply with clarity.

"I keep thinking," she said, "that we're learning to listen again. And that makes us nervous."

No one contradicted her.

Graham shifted in his seat. "Listening to who?" he asked.

Mary smiled slightly. "That's the question, isn't it?"

The room stayed quiet. Caleb watched as people leaned forward, not physically so much as inwardly. He felt the familiar pull to guide the conversation, to shape it gently toward something manageable. Instead, he waited.

Amelia spoke next and said carefully, "I don't think it's just God … I think it's each other."

There was a murmur of agreement.

"And maybe that's much harder," Sheila added. "God doesn't interrupt. People do."

A few smiles surfaced, but the truth beneath the humour landed.

Caleb said nothing.

He was learning - again - that restraint was not absence. It was participation of a different kind.

Afterward, as people lingered in small clusters, Caleb overheard fragments of conversation that would once have unsettled him. Questions without immediate answers. Disagreements handled without defensiveness. Reflections that did not end with neat conclusions.

It was healthy.

It was also risky.

On Thursday morning, Caleb met with Howard as usual, the two of them sitting across from one another in the small office off the hall. Howard had a notebook open, though he had not written anything in it yet.

"I've been thinking about leadership," Howard said, tapping the pen lightly against the page. "About what it looks like now."

Caleb nodded. "And?"

"And I don't think it's as obvious as it used to be," Howard continued. "I'm not sure who people are looking to anymore." "That could be a problem," Caleb said gently.

"Or a gift," Howard replied.

Caleb smiled. "That sounds like something Mary would say."

Howard chuckled. "She's rubbing off on me."

They sat quietly for a moment.

"There's a difference," Howard went on, "between everyone speaking and everyone being heard."

"Yes," Caleb said. "And between guidance and control."

Howard met his eyes. "So are you comfortable not being the clearest voice in the room?"

Caleb considered the question honestly. Years ago, the answer would have unsettled him. Now, it felt like a test he was willing to sit with.

"I'm learning to be," he said. "Though I don't always enjoy it."

Howard nodded. "Fair enough."

That afternoon, Caleb walked through the church again, noticing details he had overlooked before. A notice pinned to the board that he had not approved. Chairs rearranged slightly from their usual alignment. A whiteboard with handwritten notes from someone else's discussion.

None of it was careless. None of it was disorderly. But it was no longer centrally curated.

He stood for a long moment, hands resting on the back of a chair, aware of the tension rising quietly in his chest.

This was what shared discernment looked like.

Not chaos.

But relinquishment.

Later that day, a letter arrived from the regional office. Nothing official. Just an update about upcoming gatherings, a reminder of expectations, a brief note of encouragement.

Caleb read it once, then again more slowly.

There was no criticism in it. No warning. But there was an assumption threaded through the language - that clarity came from alignment, and alignment came from consistency. That leadership was something you could describe cleanly and reproduce carefully.

He folded the letter and set it aside.

That evening, Rachel listened as he spoke about the day, about Mary's comment, about Howard's question. "I don't think anyone's trying to take over," he said. "But I do think people are beginning to trust what they're sensing."

Rachel nodded slowly. "That's not the same thing as trusting themselves."

"No," Caleb agreed. "But it's close enough to make some people nervous."

"Who?" she asked.

"Everyone," he replied. "Including me."

She smiled softly. "That's usually where discernment starts."

He looked at her. "You're quieter lately."

"I'm watching," she said. "There's a difference."

He nodded. He had noticed.

Before bed, Caleb sat alone for a while, the house quiet around him. He thought of Ruth again - of how she would read these rooms differently. She would not be impressed by sincerity alone. She would notice who carried weight, and why.

He wondered, briefly, whether he would recognise his own voice in this new season - or whether it would sound unfamiliar even to him.

Learning who speaks now, he realised, was not about authority.

It was about trust. And trust, once given, reshaped everyone who touched it.

By the weekend, the conversations had begun to surface beyond the walls of the church.

Not loudly. Not publicly. But in the places where people spoke more freely - at the counter in the bakery, near the shelves at the hardware store, along the fence lines that marked properties and long-held habits.

Willowend had always been a town where news travelled quickly, but interpretation travelled slowly. People preferred to decide for themselves what something meant.

Caleb became aware of it on Saturday morning, standing near the post office as two men he knew well enough nodded to him and continued their discussion without lowering their voices.

"I'm not saying it's wrong," one of them said. "I just don't know how you tell when it's God and when it's just… people."

"That's always been the question," the other replied. "We just used to pretend it had easier answers."

Caleb did not interrupt. He walked on, letting the words settle where they had landed.

That afternoon, he received a call from Margaret Ellis. Her voice, usually brisk and self-contained, sounded tentative.

"I don't want to be a bother," she said, as though the phrase itself had been rehearsed.

"You're not," Caleb replied. "What's on your mind?"

"Well," she said slowly, "people have been asking if I'd teach.

Not formally. Just… share."

Caleb waited.

"I've never thought of myself as someone with anything particular to offer," she continued. "I've attended Bible studies for years. Listened. Taken notes. But teaching?"

"How does it feel when they ask?" Caleb said.

She paused. "Like something is being noticed."

"That's often how it starts," he replied.

There was relief in her exhale. "I was hoping you'd say that."

After the call, Caleb leaned back in his chair, the conversation replaying quietly in his mind. For years, he had worked hard to encourage participation, to draw people into service gently, patiently. Now, invitations were being extended without him. It was both gratifying and disorienting.

Sunday came without any drama. The congregation gathered as usual, not significantly larger than before, not noticeably smaller. The singing was steady rather than exuberant. The prayers unadorned. Caleb preached briefly, resisting the urge to explain what was happening among them. Instead, he spoke of the importance of real attentiveness - of recognising the difference between noise and guidance, between urgency and faithfulness.

He noticed, as he spoke, how people were listening. Not with expectation, but with engagement. Some nodded. Some frowned thoughtfully. A few wrote notes, though he suspected they were not writing down his words so much as their own reflections.

After the service, people seemed to linger longer than usual, conversations unfolded without any hurry. Caleb found himself pulled into small exchanges rather than central ones. Questions came, but they were careful, unassuming.

"How do we stay grounded?"

"What if we get it wrong?"

"How do we stop this becoming about personalities?"

He did not answer them all. He answered some with questions of his own.

On Monday morning, Howard appeared at the office door, expression thoughtful.

"I've had three phone calls," he said, settling into the chair opposite Caleb's desk. "None of them angry. But all of them cautious."

"About?"

"About who decides what's appropriate now."

Caleb nodded. "And what did you say?"

Howard smiled wryly. "That I wasn't sure there was a single answer anymore."

Caleb laughed softly. "That probably didn't help."

"No," Howard admitted. "But it was honest."

They sat quietly for a moment.

"There's a concern," Howard went on. "Not unreasonable. That we could drift. That without clear direction, people might mistake enthusiasm for discernment."

"That risk has always existed," Caleb said. "We've just managed it more tightly before."

Howard leaned forward. "Do you think we should start doing that again?"

Caleb considered the question carefully. "I think the question is why we would."

Howard nodded slowly. "Because letting go feels irresponsible."

"Yes," Caleb agreed. "And sometimes it is."

"But?"

"But sometimes," Caleb said, "holding too tightly does more damage."

Howard exhaled. "That's what I was afraid you'd say."

That afternoon, Caleb met briefly with Mary. She sat opposite him, hands folded in her lap, eyes clear.

"You're carrying a lot quietly," she said.

"I'm aware of it," Caleb replied.

"You don't need to resolve everything," she continued. "But you do need to keep naming what matters."

"What matters?" he asked.

"That this is about faithfulness, not novelty. About obedience, not experience."

Caleb nodded. "I know."

"Good," Mary said. "Because some people will confuse the two."

She stood to leave, pausing at the door. "And some will want you to stop this because it makes them uncomfortable."

"Yes," Caleb said. "I know that too."

That evening, as he sat at home, Caleb thought again of Ruth. She would hear these conversations differently. She would not frame them in theological terms. She would hear the human dynamics underneath - the fear of loss, the uncertainty of change, the relief of being seen.

He wondered what questions she would ask.

And whether he would be ready to answer them without retreating into explanation.

Learning who speaks now, Caleb was discovering, also meant learning when not to.

And that, he suspected, would be a much harder lesson.

The question followed him into the next week.

Not as a challenge, and not as a doubt, but as a presence - steady, insistent, refusing to be rushed away by activity.

Who speaks now? It was no longer an abstract concern. It had now taken on faces, voices, pauses. It had also begun to shape the atmosphere of rooms.

Caleb felt it most clearly during a meeting he had not planned to attend. It was a small gathering, organised by a few people who had begun meeting on their own initiative - nothing secretive, nothing defiant. They had simply chosen a time and place and told others they were welcome to join if they wished.

He had found out about it only because someone had mentioned it casually in passing, not as a request for permission but as a statement of fact.

He went along quietly, slipping into a chair near the back, just content to observe.

The discussion was unstructured, at times uneven, but earnest. Scripture was read slowly, without commentary at first.

Then people spoke - not all at once, not competitively, but with the hesitancy of those learning to trust their own discernment.

One person spoke of a conviction they had carried for years but never voiced. Another admitted uncertainty, unsure whether what they sensed was wisdom or simply preference.

There were moments of clarity, and moments of confusion. Nothing was resolved neatly.

And yet, Caleb noticed something that stayed with him long after the meeting had ended.

No one looked to him for approval.

Not once.

They acknowledged his presence politely, warmly even, but their attention remained with one another - with the shared work of listening and responding. He was not excluded. But neither was he centred.

As he walked home afterward, the evening air cooler than it had been in days, Caleb felt the familiar mix of humility and unease that often accompanied genuine growth.

It would have been easier, in many ways, to step back into a more directive role - to offer clarity, to tidy loose ends, to give shape to what felt amorphous.

But clarity imposed too early had a way of silencing voices before they were fully heard.

Midweek, the first disagreement surfaced openly.

It happened during a discussion about how the church should respond to new interest from outside Willowend. Some felt cautious, wary of attention.

Others sensed an invitation to hospitality, even partnership.

The conversation was respectful but firm, lines of difference clearly drawn.

Caleb listened, intervening only to slow the pace when voices rose slightly, or to invite quieter members to speak. He noticed who deferred and who persisted. Who spoke easily, and who only spoke when directly invited.

At one point, an older man who had rarely spoken in any gathering cleared his throat. "I don't know if this is helpful," he said, glancing around, "but I feel like we're asking the wrong question."

The room stilled.

"We keep asking what we *should* do," he continued. "But maybe we need to ask who we're becoming."

No one responded immediately. The question settled, heavy and unavoidable.

Caleb felt a quiet surge of gratitude - not because the comment was particularly eloquent, but because it had emerged without prompting.

This was what it meant for voices to surface naturally, shaped by trust rather than permission. Afterward, as chairs were stacked and people drifted away, one of the elders approached Caleb, his expression thoughtful.

"I'll be honest," he said. "This feels risky."

Caleb nodded. "It is."

"I don't mean spiritually," the man added. "I mean structurally."

"Yes," Caleb agreed. "That too."

The elder sighed. "I suppose I'm wondering when you step in."

Caleb met his gaze. "I am stepping in."

The man frowned slightly.

"Just not in the way you're used to," Caleb continued.

"I'm watching for patterns. Listening for alignment. Naming concerns when they matter. And holding space when they don't."

The elder considered this. "And if it goes wrong?"

Caleb did not answer immediately. "Then we'll deal with what's real," he said finally. "Not what we fear."

At home that night, Rachel listened as he described the meeting, the disagreement, the question that had silenced the room.

"They're growing up," she said simply.

"Yes," Caleb replied. "And that's harder than growth in numbers."

Rachel smiled faintly. "It always is."

He thought again of Ruth - of how she would read these dynamics with clarity and without sentiment. She would not be impressed by consensus or disturbed by disagreement.

She would notice whether people were allowed to speak honestly without being corrected too quickly.

In that sense, her presence would be both gift and test.

Later, alone in the quiet of the house, Caleb opened his notebook and finally wrote.

Not an outline. Not a plan. Just a single line.

Guard the space.

He stared at it for a long moment, then closed the book.

That, he realised, was his work now. Not to define every outcome, but to protect the conditions in which discernment could grow.

To resist the urge to rush towards clarity, even when uncertainty felt uncomfortable.

Learning who speaks now was not about volume or authority.

It was about courage - the courage to listen without controlling, to guide without dominating, and to trust that God was as present in the hesitations as in the convictions.

As he turned off the light and prepared for sleep, Caleb felt the weight of the season settle around him - not oppressive, but substantial. The kind of weight that asked for steadiness rather than strength.

Tomorrow would bring more questions. More voices. More moments when silence spoke louder than words.

And he knew, with a quiet certainty that surprised him, that he was not meant to answer them all.

3. A GIFT NO ONE ASKED FOR

The call came late in the afternoon, at the point where the day had already decided what it would be.

Caleb had finished the last of his visits and was standing at the kitchen bench, rinsing out his mug, when the phone vibrated against the timber. He glanced at the screen, half-expecting it to be one of the usual names. Instead, it was unfamiliar - a number from outside the district.

He answered cautiously.

"Caleb Merritt."

There was a brief hesitation on the other end, as though the person had not quite expected to be connected so quickly.

"Pastor Merritt," the voice said. "My name is Helen Ward. I was given your number by someone who attended one of your gatherings a few weeks ago."

Caleb listened, his posture shifting subtly. "All right."

"I hope this isn't intrusive," she continued. "I'm not ringing to organise anything. I just… needed to talk to someone."

He leaned against the bench, giving the call his full attention. "I can listen."

There was another pause. Then, "I don't belong to your church."

"That's all right," Caleb said gently.

"I don't really belong anywhere at the moment," she admitted. "Spiritually, I mean."

He said nothing.

She went on, words gathering confidence as they were allowed to surface. She spoke of a long season in ministry - not pastoral, but adjacent - years of volunteering, supporting, teaching children, coordinating programs.

And then, without drama, she described how it had ended. A quiet falling-out. Misunderstood intentions. A slow withdrawal that had never been named as departure.

"I didn't leave angry," she said. "I left tired."

Caleb closed his eyes briefly. He had heard this story before, though never from this voice, never in this cadence.

"I listened to a recording someone sent me," Helen said. "Not a sermon. Just a conversation. People talking. You didn't say much."

Caleb smiled faintly.

"That was the first time in a long while that I felt… permission," she continued. "Not to do more. To stop."

They sat with that for a moment, the distance between them bridged by shared recognition.

"I don't really know what I'm asking," she said finally. "I just wondered if we could talk sometime. Not formally. I'm not looking for answers."

Caleb thought of the note in his notebook. *Guard the space.*

"Yes," he said. "We can talk."

When the call ended, the house felt unusually still. Caleb stood at the bench for a moment longer, hands resting on the cool surface, aware that something had been offered without request. This, he realised, was the gift.

Not growth. Not affirmation. But trust extended from beyond the boundaries of Willowend.

That evening, Rachel listened as he described the call, her expression thoughtful.

"She didn't ask you to fix anything," Rachel observed.

"No," Caleb said. "She asked me to hear it."

Rachel nodded. "That's different."

"And heavier," he added.

"Yes," she agreed. "But also truer."

They sat together, the quiet between them unstrained.

Later, as darkness settled, Caleb returned to the church, not out of necessity but out of instinct. He unlocked the door and moved through the building, switching on only one light near the front. The sanctuary felt unchanged yet subtly altered by the stories it had begun to hold. He sat in one of the front pews, thinking of Helen's voice, of Graham's pauses, of the way questions were now being asked without expecting resolution.

The phone buzzed again.

This time, he recognised the number.

"Hi, Dad."

"Hi, Ruth."

"I've booked the time off," she said without preamble. "I'll come up next Thursday, if that works."

Caleb felt the moment settle around him. "That works."

There was a brief silence, then, "I'm not coming to inspect anything," Ruth added lightly. "Just to see you. And Mum."

"I know," he said.

"And," she continued, her tone shifting slightly, "I'm curious." He smiled. "About Willowend?"

"About you," she replied. "About what you're carrying now." Caleb leaned back against the pew. "You might find that harder to define than you expect."

She laughed softly. "I usually do."

They spoke a little longer — about travel, about the heat, about nothing in particular. When the call ended, Caleb remained seated, phone resting loosely in his hand.

A gift no one asked for.

That was how it was unfolding.

Not through initiative, but through recognition.

Not through clarity, but through attentiveness.

And now, with his daughter's arrival approaching, the season which was ahead promised to reveal not only what Willowend was becoming - but what it would require of him to remain faithful in it.

He turned off the light and locked the door behind him, the night air cooler now, the town quiet.

Some gifts, he was learning, arrived already carrying weight. And wisdom lay in knowing how to receive them without trying to shape them too quickly.

The days leading up to Ruth's arrival passed with an unspoken attentiveness that Caleb found difficult to describe, even to himself.

Nothing outward changed. The rhythm of Willowend held steady. People gathered, spoke, listened, returned to their lives. And yet beneath the surface, he sensed a quiet tightening — not of anxiety, but of awareness. As though the town, and the church within it, were learning to hold something gently without yet knowing its shape.

On Wednesday morning, Caleb met with Graham again, this time not at the farm but at the small table near the back of the church hall. They sat with mugs of tea between them, the windows open to let in what little breeze there was.

"I nearly didn't come," Graham said, without preamble.

Caleb raised an eyebrow. "Why's that?"

"Didn't want to say the wrong thing," Graham replied. "Didn't want to sound foolish."

Caleb nodded. "What changed your mind?"

Graham looked down at his hands. "I realised I've been quiet most of my life because I thought only certain voices counted."

Caleb waited.

"I don't think that's true anymore," Graham said. "But I'm still learning what my voice sounds like."

"That's a good place to start," Caleb said.

Graham smiled faintly. "It doesn't feel like a gift."

Caleb thought of Helen Ward's voice on the phone, of Ruth's careful curiosity. "Some gifts arrive disguised as discomfort," he said.

Graham considered that. "Then maybe this one's worth paying attention to."

Later that day, Caleb sat at his desk responding to a handful of messages. None of them were urgent. A question about timing. A reflection shared quietly. An invitation to coffee that carried no firm agenda. He answered each one slowly, resisting the temptation to be efficient at the cost of presence.

Efficiency, he was discovering, had never been neutral.

In the afternoon, Mary stopped by, settling into the chair opposite him with the ease of someone who knew she belonged there.

"I hear your daughter is coming," she said.

Caleb smiled. "News travels fast."

"In a town like this," Mary replied, "it doesn't need to travel far." She studied him for a moment. "You're aware she'll see things others don't."

"Yes," Caleb said. "I'm counting on it."

Mary nodded. "That's wise. Familiar eyes grow kind. Outside eyes stay honest."

She leaned forward slightly. "Don't ask her to understand. Let her observe."

"I plan to."

Mary smiled. "Good."

That evening, Caleb received a message from Helen Ward. It was brief - just a thank-you for listening, and a note that she had slept well for the first time in weeks.

He read it twice, then set the phone aside, aware again of the weight such trust carried.

No one had asked him to take this on.

And yet, here it was.

On Thursday morning, Rachel busied herself around the house with quiet purpose. She did not say much about Ruth's arrival, but Caleb noticed the care with which she prepared the spare room, the small touches she added without comment.

"She's grown into herself," Rachel said once, smoothing a crease from the bedspread. "But she still notices whether a place feels ready."

Caleb smiled. "You always did."

Rachel met his gaze. "So did she."

When Ruth arrived that afternoon, it was without drama. Her car pulled into the drive, dust rising briefly before settling again. She stepped out, sunglasses perched on her head, her expression open and composed.

"Hi," she said, as though she'd only been gone a week.

Caleb hugged her, feeling the familiar mix of tenderness and pride that never quite faded. Rachel followed, holding her a moment longer.

Inside, Ruth took in the house with quick, perceptive glances — nothing intrusive, just attentive. She asked about neighbours, about the heat, about the drive up. Ordinary questions, asked with genuine interest.

Over dinner, conversation flowed easily. Work. Travel. Stories shared without embellishment. Ruth listened more than she spoke, her questions thoughtful but unforced.

Later, as the evening cooled, the three of them sat on the veranda, the sounds of the town drifting up around them.

"So," Ruth said eventually, turning to Caleb, "tell me what's changed."

He considered how to answer.

"Not what you're doing," she clarified. "What feels different."

Caleb smiled. "People are listening to each other more carefully."

"And you?" she asked.

"I'm listening more carefully too," he said.

She nodded, satisfied.

"I don't know what I think about all of it yet," Ruth said. "But it feels… unmanufactured."

Caleb felt something ease inside him. "That's probably the best description I've heard."

She smiled. "Good. Because anything else would make me suspicious."

They sat in silence for a while, the air cooling, the stars beginning to emerge.

Later, as Ruth settled into the spare room and the house quieted, Caleb lay awake longer than usual. He thought of Graham finding his voice. Of Helen's unasked trust. Of Ruth's steady, discerning gaze.

A gift no one asked for.

It was becoming clearer now what that meant.

Not affirmation.

Not expansion.

But responsibility - to hold what had been given without shaping it into something safer or smaller than it was meant to be. And that, he knew, would require more of him than any role he had carried before.

Ruth did not rush her observations.

Caleb noticed it the next morning as they walked together into town, the air already warm but still bearable. She matched his pace easily, hands loose at her sides, eyes moving from place to place without lingering too long on any one thing. She did not ask questions straight away. She watched.

That, Caleb realised, was the difference between curiosity and scrutiny.

At the bakery, Sheila greeted Ruth with an enthusiasm that surprised neither of them. Introductions in Willowend were rarely formal, and Ruth accepted the warmth easily, smiling, exchanging a few words, listening more than she spoke.

"You must be proud," Sheila said, glancing between them.

Caleb felt the familiar tightening in his chest, the reflex to deflect praise. Before he could respond, Ruth spoke.

"I am," she said simply. "They've built something steady here."

Sheila nodded, pleased. "That's the word for it. Steady."

As they left, Ruth said nothing for some time. They walked on in comfortable silence, past the post office, along the edge of the park where a few people sat talking quietly.

"It's interesting," Ruth said eventually.

"What is?" Caleb asked.

"No one's performing," she replied. "There's no sense that people are trying to convince each other of anything."

Caleb smiled. "That's new."

She glanced at him. "Does it scare you?"

He considered the question carefully. "Yes," he said. "And no."

She nodded, satisfied with the honesty.

Later that morning, Caleb excused himself for a meeting, leaving Ruth at home with Rachel. When he returned, he found them at the kitchen table, cups of tea cooling, conversation evidently deep.

Rachel stood as he entered. "We were just talking about expectations," she said lightly.

Ruth smiled. "Or the lack of them."

Caleb raised an eyebrow.

"It feels," Ruth continued, choosing her words carefully, "like people are being allowed to arrive without being directed."

"Yes," Caleb said. "That's exactly it."

Ruth leaned back in her chair. "That's rare."

Caleb knew she wasn't talking only about churches.

That afternoon, Caleb met with Helen Ward for the first time in person. She had driven in from out of town, arriving early and waiting quietly in the hall, hands folded, expression calm but guarded.

Ruth was there too, sitting near the window, unobtrusive but present.

Helen spoke slowly, carefully, as though testing each word before releasing it. She spoke of exhaustion, of years spent giving without replenishment, of how difficult it was to admit weariness in spaces that prized faithfulness above honesty.

"I didn't come looking for permission to leave," Helen said quietly. "I came looking for permission to rest."

Caleb listened, saying little. Ruth listened too, her gaze steady, her posture open.

When Helen finished, the room stayed silent for a moment longer than expected. Then Ruth spoke.

"That sounds lonely," she said gently.

Helen looked at her, surprised, then nodded. "It was."

Ruth didn't offer advice. She didn't spiritualise the experience. She simply named what she heard.

Caleb felt a quiet confirmation settle in his chest. This, he realised, was part of what Ruth carried - not answers, but clarity of presence.

When Helen left, thanking them both, Ruth turned to Caleb.

"You didn't try to fix her," she said.

"No," he replied.

"That's harder than it looks."

Caleb smiled. "It took me years to learn."

That evening, the three of them sat on the veranda again, the heat finally easing, a soft breeze moving through the trees. The town settled into its familiar quiet, punctuated by distant sounds that felt companionable rather than intrusive.

"I can see why this matters to you," Ruth said after a while. Caleb looked at her. "In what way?"

"It's not about growth," she said. "Or success. It's about integrity. About letting people be honest without penalising them for it."

Rachel smiled. "You always did notice those things."

Ruth returned the smile. "Someone had to."

They laughed softly.

As darkness settled, Ruth grew thoughtful. "You know," she said, "from the outside, things like this can look vague. Unstructured. Even irresponsible."

Caleb nodded. "I know."

"But from the inside," she continued, "it feels… brave."

Caleb let the word sit with him. Brave. He had not thought of it that way.

Later, after Ruth had gone to bed, Caleb remained outside a little longer, the stars sharp against the dark sky. He thought of Graham, finding his voice. Of Helen, reclaiming rest. Of Ruth, seeing clearly without demanding certainty.

A gift no one asked for.

He understood it differently now.
It was not the gift of affirmation, or influence, or momentum.

It was the gift of being trusted - by others, and by God - with something fragile and unfinished.

That kind of gift could not be managed.

It could only be tended.

As he turned toward the house, Caleb felt both the weight and the grace of that responsibility settle more firmly around him. The season ahead would require patience, humility, and a willingness to be misunderstood.

But it would also, he sensed, reveal depths of faithfulness he had not yet imagined.

And that, perhaps, was the truest gift of all.

4. WHEN SCRIPTURE OPENS A ROOM

The first sign that something was different came not in what people said, but in how long they were willing to stay with a passage of Scripture without moving on.

Caleb noticed it on a warm evening when a small group gathered in the church hall, chairs pulled into a loose circle that resisted neatness. Someone had opened a window, and the sounds of the town drifted in - a car passing slowly, a door closing, the murmur of voices somewhere down the street. Nothing about the setting felt especially reverent, and yet there was an attentiveness in the room that had not been there before.

Caleb read the passage slowly, without preface or explanation. He resisted the old instinct to frame it, to offer context or direction, trusting instead that the words could stand on their own for a while. When he finished, he closed the Bible and waited.

The silence that followed was not awkward. It was expectant, but not urgent. People shifted in their chairs, some glancing down at the text in their own Bibles, others staring into the middle distance as though listening for something that had not yet fully formed.

Eventually, Amelia spoke.

"I've heard that before," she said carefully. "But tonight, it feels like it's asking something of us."

No one responded immediately. Caleb felt the familiar pull to clarify, to ask a follow-up question that might shape the conversation. Instead, he let her words settle.

Graham leaned forward, elbows on his knees. "I keep thinking about the part we usually skip over," he said. "The bit that doesn't sound encouraging."

Mary nodded. "That's often where the room opens," she said quietly.

Caleb watched as people returned to the text, not to extract meaning but to try and dwell within it. They were not debating interpretation. They were inhabiting the words, allowing them to press gently against their assumptions.

"This feels risky," someone said softly.

"Yes," Mary replied. "But Scripture has always been risky. We just learned how to manage it."

That line hung in the air, unchallenged.

Later, as chairs were stacked and people lingered in small clusters, Caleb found himself approached not with questions about meaning, but with reflections about impact.

"It stayed with me," Sheila said, gathering her bag. "I didn't feel like I had to understand it straight away."

"That's all right," Caleb said. "Understanding often comes later."

She smiled. "Or not at all."

"That's possible too," he agreed.

On the walk home, Caleb felt the weight of the evening settle around him. Not heaviness, exactly, but substance. The kind that made him aware of responsibility without pressing him toward action.

At home, Ruth was sitting at the kitchen table, laptop open, a mug beside her that had long since gone cold. She looked up as he came in.

"How was it?" she asked.

"Different," Caleb said.

She smiled faintly. "That's becoming your default answer."

"Yes," he replied. "Because it's true."

He sat opposite her, watching as she closed the laptop and turned her full attention to him.

"I sat in on part of it," she said. "Not the whole thing. Just long enough to get a feel."

Caleb nodded. He had known she would, and he had not discouraged it.

"What did you notice?" he asked.

Ruth thought for a long moment. "No one was trying to be insightful," she said. "They weren't performing spirituality."

"That's new," Caleb said.

"It's rare," she corrected. "And it makes a difference."

She hesitated, then added, "But it also removes the safety net." Caleb smiled. "Yes."

"What happens when someone says something that doesn't fit?" she asked. "Something uncomfortable. Or wrong."

"That depends," Caleb replied. "On whether we're more committed to being right or to being faithful."

Ruth nodded slowly. "That's a costly distinction."

"It is," he agreed.

The next morning, Caleb found a note slipped under the office door. No name, just a few lines written carefully.

I don't usually speak in groups. But last night, I felt like I was allowed to be quiet without disappearing. Thank you.

Caleb folded the note and placed it in his notebook.

That afternoon, he met briefly with Howard, who had been hearing similar things from different corners of the church.

"There's appreciation," Howard said. "But also concern."

"About?" Caleb asked.

"About Scripture," Howard replied. "Or rather, about what happens when people start encountering it without a filter."

Caleb nodded. "That's understandable."

Howard leaned back in his chair. "Some are worried that without clear teaching, people might take things too far."

"That's always been the fear," Caleb said. "The question is whether control has ever actually prevented that."

Howard smiled wryly. "You're asking dangerous questions lately."

Caleb smiled back. "I think the questions have always been there. We're just not avoiding them anymore."

That evening, Ruth joined Caleb on a walk along the edge of town, the air cooling as the sun dipped low. They walked in silence for a while, the road stretching ahead, the paddocks glowing softly in the fading light.

"You know," Ruth said eventually, "for someone who's not sure what she believes anymore, this place feels surprisingly safe."

Caleb glanced at her. "Safe how?"

"To not pretend," she said. "To not rush answers. To let Scripture unsettle rather than reassure."

He nodded. "That's what it's meant to do."

She smiled faintly. "I can see why some people would resist that."

"Yes," Caleb said. "It disrupts certainty."

"And certainty," Ruth added, "is comfortable."

They continued walking, the town quiet behind them.

When Scripture opens a room, Caleb reflected, it does not tell people what to think. It invites them to stay. And staying, he was discovering, was where the real work began.

The resistance did not announce itself all at once.

It arrived quietly, disguised as concern, often framed in the language of care.

Caleb recognised it for what it was not because it was hostile, but because it was familiar. He had heard its tone before — in other churches, other seasons, even in his own thoughts at different times.

It surfaced first in private conversations.

One person stopped him after a gathering, lowering their voice instinctively. "I'm glad people are engaging," they said. "I really am. I just wonder if we're giving enough guidance."

Another rang midweek, apologetic before they had even finished their first sentence. "I don't want to sound negative," they said. "But I worry that people might misunderstand Scripture if it's left too open."

Caleb listened carefully to each concern, never dismissing them outright. He knew they were not born of cynicism. They were born of fear - the fear that something precious might slip out of reach if it was not held firmly enough.

"What would misunderstanding look like to you?" he asked one afternoon.

There was a pause. "Well… people drawing conclusions that don't align with what we've always believed."

Caleb nodded slowly. "And what if the alignment comes later? After the questions have had time to breathe?"

Another pause, longer this time. "That feels risky."

"Yes," Caleb agreed. "It does."

He found himself returning often to the same inner tension: how to honour the genuine desire for faithfulness without surrendering the fragile openness that was beginning to take root. Control could always be justified as protection. The challenge lay in learning to discern when protection became suppression.

On Thursday evening, the group gathered again, slightly larger than the week before. Not dramatically so, but noticeably.

A few unfamiliar faces sat near the edges, alert but reserved. Caleb greeted them quietly and took his usual seat, resisting the instinct to position himself at the centre.

The passage that evening was shorter, but no less demanding. It spoke of obedience, of trust expressed not through certainty but through action taken without full knowledge of the outcome. Caleb read it once, then again more slowly, before closing the Bible and setting it aside.

The silence stretched.

This time, it was broken by a man who had not spoken in any gathering before. His voice was steady, but his hands trembled slightly as he rested them on his knees.

"I'm not sure how to say this properly," he began. "But this makes me uncomfortable. And I think that might be important."

No one laughed. No one rushed to reassure him.

He continued, encouraged by the absence of interruption. "I've always liked Scripture best when it tells me what to do. When it settles things. This feels like it's asking me to trust without that."

Mary nodded gently. "That's often the invitation," she said.

"But how do we know we're not just projecting our feelings onto the text?" he asked.

The question was not defensive. It was sincere.

Caleb leaned forward slightly. "We don't always know," he said.

"That's why discernment is communal. Why we listen together. Why no one voice carries the whole weight."

The man nodded, relief evident in his posture. He had not been corrected. He had been accompanied.

As the evening unfolded, Caleb noticed something else emerging - a willingness to name uncertainty without apology. People spoke more freely about what confused them than about what they felt sure of.

The room felt less like a classroom and more like a shared workbench, tools scattered, progress uneven but honest.

Afterward, Ruth lingered near the doorway, watching people leave. She said little, but her eyes followed interactions closely - a hand on a shoulder, a quiet word exchanged, a smile offered without expectation.

"This is where it gets complicated," she said quietly as they walked home together.

"Yes," Caleb replied. "It already is."

She considered that. "You're trusting people with more than ideas. You're trusting them with responsibility."

"That's the hope," he said.

"And the risk," she added.

They walked in silence for a few moments.

"At work," Ruth said eventually, "we talk a quite a lot about empowerment. But it usually comes with parameters. Metrics. Safeguards."

"And does that work?" Caleb asked.

She smiled wryly. "Sometimes. But it rarely produces maturity. Just compliance."

Caleb nodded. "Faith doesn't grow well under compliance."

The next day, Caleb met with Howard again. This time, the conversation was more direct.

"I think we need to be prepared," Howard said, closing the office door behind him. "Not everyone will stay."

Caleb exhaled slowly. "I know."

"There are people who liked things predictable," Howard continued. "Who felt secure knowing exactly how things were meant to run."

"And now they don't."

"No," Howard agreed. "And some will interpret that as loss rather than growth."

Caleb leaned back in his chair. "Then we need to grieve that honestly, not rush past it."

Howard studied him. "You're willing to lose people over this?"

Caleb met his gaze. "I'm willing to lose certainty over it. Losing people is something I hope we avoid. But I won't trade integrity to prevent it."

Howard nodded slowly. "That's a hard line."

"Yes," Caleb said. "But a necessary one."

That evening, Caleb sat alone for a while, the house quiet around him. He opened his Bible again, not to the passage they had discussed, but to another - one that spoke of wisdom crying out in public places, calling to those willing to listen.

Wisdom, he thought, was not loud.

It did not force its way in.

It waited to be received.

When Scripture opened a room, it did far more than invite reflection. It exposed motivations, unsettled loyalties, and revealed where trust truly lay.

Caleb closed the book and sat back, aware that the season ahead would not allow him the comfort of neutrality. Choosing openness was itself a choice - one that would shape the future of Willowend in ways he could not yet fully see.

But for the first time in a long while, that uncertainty did not feel like failure.

It felt like faith.

The shift became unmistakable the following Sunday.

It wasn't visible in attendance numbers or in the order of service. Nothing about the morning would have seemed remarkable to someone unfamiliar with Willowend.

The hymns were familiar, the prayers unadorned, the Scripture reading read plainly without commentary. And yet, Caleb sensed it almost immediately - a collective attentiveness that carried weight.

People were listening differently.

Not just to him, but to the silences between words, to the cadence of Scripture itself, to the subtle ways meaning surfaced without being announced. When he preached, he spoke more slowly than usual, aware that clarity did not require completion. He allowed ideas to land without resolving them, trusting that the congregation could hold what was unfinished.

After the service, conversation spilled out into the sunlight in a way that felt less performative and more genuine. People did not cluster around him as they once might have. Instead, they lingered with one another - sharing their reflections, voicing their questions, listening without rushing to respond.

Caleb watched from a distance, resisting the urge to insert himself. This, he knew, was the work of trust.

Later that afternoon, a letter arrived by post, handwritten and carefully addressed. It was from someone who had not attended church in years - a name Caleb recognised, though he could not remember the last time they had spoken.

The letter began: *I don't know if this belongs with you, but I felt compelled to write ...*

The writer described sitting at home on Sunday mornings, listening faintly to some church bells in the distance, feeling both comforted and excluded. Recently, they had heard through neighbours that something had shifted — that the Baptist church felt less like a place you had to "get right" and more like a place you were allowed to arrive honestly.

I'm not ready to come back, the letter continued. *But it matters to know the door isn't closed.*

Caleb folded the letter slowly, aware of the quiet significance of such words.

This, too, was what it meant when Scripture opened a room. Not everyone entered. But many noticed the light.

That evening, Ruth joined him on the veranda, her expression thoughtful.

"I keep thinking about boundaries," she said. "Not the physical ones - the emotional ones."

"In what way?"

"You're letting people sit with Scripture without telling them how to resolve it," she continued. "That's generous. But it also means you're trusting them not to weaponise it."

"Yes," Caleb said. "And that trust can be misplaced."

Ruth studied him. "Are you prepared for that?"

He considered the question carefully. "I'm prepared to respond if it happens. I'm not prepared to pre-empt it out of fear."

She smiled faintly. "That's a difficult line to hold."

"Yes," he agreed. "But I think it's the right one."

The following week brought its first real test.

A conversation erupted during a midweek gathering, sparked by a single comment that landed awkwardly in the room. It wasn't overtly harmful, but it revealed an assumption that went unchallenged in earlier seasons. The atmosphere shifted subtly - a tightening, a collective hesitation.

Caleb watched closely.

Before he could speak, Mary leaned forward.

"I think we need to slow down," she said gently. "That sounded certain. And I'm not sure certainty is what we're being invited into here."

The speaker flushed, clearly unsettled, but not defensive.

"I didn't mean it that way," they said quickly.

"I know," Mary replied. "That's why this matters."

The conversation paused, then continued with greater care. No one was corrected publicly. No one was shamed. The moment passed, but not without leaving its mark.

Later, as people gathered their belongings and prepared to leave, the person who had spoken approached Caleb quietly.

"Thank you for not stepping in," they said.

Caleb met their eyes. "You didn't need me to."

They nodded. "I don't think I realised how quickly words can harden when they're not held gently."

Caleb watched them walk away, struck again by the quiet power of shared discernment. This was what it meant to trust the community - not to avoid mistakes, but to address them without fear.

At home that night, Rachel listened as he recounted the moment.

"You didn't rescue anyone," she observed.

"No," Caleb said. "I trusted the room."

Rachel smiled. "And the room held."

"Yes," he replied. "Barely. But it did."

They sat together in silence for a while, the weight of the season pressing gently rather than heavily. Outside, the town rested beneath a sky scattered with stars, the air cool and still.

Caleb thought again of the phrase that had lodged itself in his mind weeks earlier - *guard the space.*

He was beginning to understand what that meant.

Not guarding outcomes. Not guarding reputation. But guarding the conditions in which Scripture could do its work - unsettling, inviting, opening rooms that had long been kept closed.

That kind of guarding required patience. And courage. And a willingness to let go of control in order to remain faithful.

As he prepared for bed, Caleb felt a quiet resolve settle within him. This path would not satisfy everyone. It would not always feel safe. But it was honest.

And honesty, he was discovering, was fertile ground.

When Scripture opened a room, it did not promise comfort.

It promised encounter.

And Willowend, for the first time in a long while, was learning how to stay present when that encounter came.

Enthusiasm arrived in Willowend quietly at first, then all at once. It showed itself in small ways - an extra chair pulled into a circle, a longer conversation after a gathering, someone volunteering to help without being asked. None of it felt forced. In fact, that was what made it compelling. Energy was emerging naturally, unprompted, as though something that had been dormant had finally found permission to move.

Caleb noticed it most clearly on a Sunday morning when the service ended and no one seemed in a hurry to leave.

The hymns had been sung with more confidence than usual, not louder, but fuller. People stood straighter. A few smiled at one another mid-verse, as though sharing a private recognition. When the benediction was spoken, it felt less like a conclusion and more like a pause.

Afterwards, the foyer filled quickly. Conversations overlapped. Laughter rose and fell. Someone brought out a plate of biscuits without being asked, setting them on the small table near the door as though it had always been there for that purpose.

Caleb stood near the edge, observing rather than directing. He felt genuine, deep gratitude – but also a quiet unease he did not immediately name.

By midweek, the momentum had gathered further.

A group that had once met fortnightly asked if they might meet weekly instead. Another suggested extending their time together rather than rushing off once the formal discussion ended. A few people began sharing insights they felt had been given to them during prayer or reading, offering them tentatively, then with growing confidence.

Much of it was thoughtful. Some of it was clumsy. All of it was sincere.

"This feels good," Graham said one afternoon as they walked the boundary of his property. "Like something's finally moving."

"Yes," Caleb replied. "It does."

Graham glanced at him. "You sound cautious."

Caleb smiled faintly. "I'm attentive."

They stopped near the fence, looking out across the dry paddocks shimmering in the heat.

"I've seen this before," Caleb continued. "Not here. Elsewhere. The energy is a gift. But it's not the destination."

Graham nodded slowly. "What happens when people think it is?"

"That's when things get complicated," Caleb said.

The complication arrived sooner than he expected.

On Thursday evening, a group gathered that was noticeably larger than usual. The atmosphere was buoyant, conversation lively even before the passage of Scripture was read. When the text was shared, several people spoke almost at once, eager to contribute, eager to be part of what felt like a shared discovery. Caleb watched carefully.

At first, the energy was helpful. Ideas built on one another. Reflections deepened as different perspectives were offered. But gradually, something shifted. The pace quickened. Voices grew more confident, less tentative. Where there had once been listening, there was now anticipation - people waiting for their turn to speak.

One comment landed heavily, delivered with enthusiasm but little care. Another followed, sharper than intended. The room did not fracture, but it tightened.

Caleb leaned forward slightly, ready to intervene if needed. Before he could, Ruth, seated quietly near the wall, spoke.

"I might be wrong," she said calmly, "but I'm finding it hard to hear what's being said because we're moving so fast."

The room stilled.

No one challenged her. No one rushed to respond. The honesty of the observation settled where enthusiasm had been running ahead.

Mary nodded. "Thank you for naming that."

The pace slowed. Conversation resumed, this time with greater care. When the gathering ended, the energy was still present, but tempered - less effusive, more grounded.

As people left, one man lingered near the door, his expression uncertain.

"I hope I didn't come on too strong," he said quietly.

Caleb met his gaze. "Your eagerness isn't the problem," he replied. "We just need to learn how to carry it together."

The man nodded, relieved.

Later on that night, Caleb sat with Rachel at the kitchen table, recounting the evening.

"It's happening," he said. "The enthusiasm phase."

Rachel smiled gently. "It was always going to."

"Yes," Caleb agreed. "And I don't want to dampen it."

"But you also don't want it to run unchecked," she said.

"No."

She reached for her mug. "People often confuse feeling alive with being mature."

Caleb nodded. "And correcting that too early can often feel like resistance."

Rachel met his eyes. "And correcting it too late can often feel like betrayal."

They sat quietly for a moment, the weight of that truth settling between them.

The next day, Caleb received an email from someone beyond Willowend - appreciative, affirming, curious. They spoke of what they had heard, of how encouraging it sounded, of how refreshing it was to see people "on fire" again.

Caleb read the phrase twice.

On fire.

He closed the email without replying immediately.

That language, he knew, carried expectations. Heat. Momentum. Expansion. It assumed that enthusiasm was the truest measure of life.

But he had learned otherwise.

Life, sustained over time, required rhythm. Breath. Restraint.

Enthusiasm could ignite a season.

It could not sustain it.

As the afternoon wore on, Caleb walked through town, greeting people who seemed lighter, more animated than they had been weeks earlier. He was glad for it. Truly glad. And yet, beneath the gratitude, he felt the familiar pastoral responsibility rising - the call to shepherd not only energy, but direction.

The limits of enthusiasm, he reflected, were not found in its absence, but in its excess.

The work ahead would not be to suppress it, nor to indulge it, but to shape it - gently, patiently - into something that could endure long after the initial spark had faded.

And that, he knew, would require wisdom that did not rush to speak, and courage that did not fear slowing the pace.

The conversations that followed were more revealing than the enthusiasm itself. They surfaced in fragments - half-finished thoughts offered at the end of gatherings, questions asked quietly in doorways, reflections shared over cups of tea rather than in the room where the energy had been strongest.

Caleb noticed that while some people left meetings buoyant and encouraged, others departed thoughtful, even unsettled.

Both responses mattered.

He became aware of it one morning at the bakery, where Sheila was serving a steady stream of customers, her movements brisk, her expression thoughtful rather than cheerful.

"People are talking," she said as she handed him his change.

"About what?" Caleb asked.

"About whether this is something we're meant to lean into," she replied, lowering her voice slightly, "or something we're meant to be careful with."

Caleb nodded. "And what do you think?"

She considered the question. "I think it depends on how much space there is for people who aren't keeping up."

That stayed with him long after he left.

By midweek, Caleb sensed a subtle divergence beginning to form - not a division, but a difference in pace. Some people were very eager to move forward, to explore, to name what they were experiencing with confidence. Others preferred to observe, to test the ground slowly, still unsure whether the enthusiasm represented depth or simply relief.

Neither posture was wrong.

The danger, Caleb knew, lay in allowing one to dominate the other.

He saw it clearly during a midweek gathering when a suggestion was made to formalise one of the newer practices - to schedule it, promote it, give it a name. The proposal was offered with good intentions, framed as a way of "making space" and "inviting participation."

But as the discussion unfolded, Caleb noticed shoulders tighten.

A few people shifted uncomfortably in their chairs. Someone who had spoken freely earlier grew quiet.

Mary spoke at last.

"I'm wondering," she said gently, "whether naming it too quickly might change it."

The room stilled.

"How so?" someone asked.

"When something is named," Mary continued, "it is often claimed. And once it's claimed, it starts to carry expectations."

Caleb felt a quiet surge of gratitude. This was discernment at work - not opposing enthusiasm but asking it to slow down.

The suggestion was set aside, not rejected, but held. The group moved on, the conversation less animated now, but more thoughtful.

Afterward, as chairs were stacked away, a younger man approached Caleb, his expression earnest.

"I don't want to be difficult," he said. "I just feel like things are finally alive. And I don't want us to miss the moment by hesitating."

Caleb met his gaze. "What do you think we'd miss?"

The man hesitated. "Momentum."

Caleb nodded. "Momentum can be helpful. But it can also carry us somewhere we didn't intend to go."

The man frowned slightly. "So what do we do instead?"

"We learn to notice," Caleb replied. "And to ask whether what feels urgent is also what's faithful."

The answer did not fully satisfy him, but it did not offend him either. He nodded slowly and moved away.

That evening, Caleb and Rachel sat together after dinner, the windows open to the cooling air.

"I'm hearing different things," Rachel said. "From different people."

"So am I," Caleb replied.

She looked at him. "Some are afraid we'll lose what we've found if we slow down."

"And others are afraid we'll lose ourselves if we don't," Caleb said.

Rachel smiled. "That's the tension, isn't it?"

"Yes."

They sat quietly for a while, listening to the sounds of the town settling for the night.

"I keep thinking about responsibility," Rachel said eventually. "About who carries it now."

Caleb nodded. "That's shifting too."

"And you're letting it," she added.

"Yes."

Rachel studied him. "That's not nothing."

He smiled faintly. "It feels like less doing. But it costs more."

The following day, Caleb received another message from outside the region. This one was more direct, more eager. The sender spoke of what they had heard, of the excitement it generated, of the possibility of gathering others to "see what God was doing" in Willowend.

Caleb read the message carefully, then set it aside.

That afternoon, he took a long walk along the edge of town, the paddocks stretching out under the wide sky, the heat softened by a light breeze. He thought of the word that kept surfacing - *enthusiasm* - and of how easily it was mistaken for depth.

Enthusiasm, he reflected, was like a spark. It could illuminate, or it could scorch. Its value depended not on its intensity, but on what it was allowed to become.

Back at the church, he found a note waiting for him, handwritten and left on his desk:

I'm grateful for the freedom to speak, but I'm even more grateful for the freedom to stay quiet.

Caleb folded the note carefully.

That, he realised, was the measure he needed to keep returning to.

Not how many people were speaking.

Not how animated the conversations felt.

But whether people were still free - free to speak, free to question, free to remain silent without being sidelined.

The limits of enthusiasm were not meant to restrain life.

They were meant to protect it.

And the work ahead would be to hold that line - gently, faithfully - even when the pressure to move faster grew stronger.

The pressure to move faster did not come as a demand.

It came as a suggestion. As a possibility. As the quiet implication that something good might be missed if it was not seized while it felt warm. Caleb recognised the pattern easily enough. He had lived through it before - in other places, other seasons - when momentum had been treated as a moral good rather than a temporary condition.

What unsettled him now was not the enthusiasm itself, but how quickly it began to seek justification.

He saw it one afternoon in a conversation that began innocently enough. Two people stood near the noticeboard, discussing whether the recent gatherings should be mentioned more prominently on Sunday mornings.

Not announced as a program, but "acknowledged," as one of them put it.

"So people know it's important," the other added.

Caleb listened without interrupting.

"Important to whom?" he asked eventually.

They exchanged glances. "To… everyone," one replied, though without much conviction.

Caleb nodded. "And what happens if it's not important to someone yet?"

There was a pause.

"I suppose," the first said slowly, "they might feel behind."

Caleb smiled gently. "That's what I'd like us to avoid."

The conversation did not end with agreement, but it softened. The suggestion was not withdrawn, but it lost its urgency. Caleb walked away aware again of how easily enthusiasm turned into expectation without anyone meaning it to.

Later that evening, Ruth joined him on the veranda, her feet tucked beneath her on the chair, her posture relaxed.

"I've been thinking," she said.

Caleb waited.

"At work," she continued, "we often confuse energy with clarity. When people feel energised, they assume they know where they're going."

"And when they don't?" Caleb asked.

"We tend to fill the gap quickly," she said. "With language. With plans. With goals."

He nodded. "To reduce anxiety."

"Yes," she said. "But it also reduces listening."

They sat quietly for a moment, the town settling around them.

"I can see why you're cautious," Ruth added. "This isn't about stopping people. It's about not rushing them into something they haven't yet chosen."

Caleb smiled. "That's a generous reading."

She shrugged. "It's an honest one."

The following Sunday, Caleb addressed the tension without naming it directly.

He spoke briefly, not about enthusiasm, but about pace. About how growth that lasted often looked slower than growth that impressed. He spoke of seasons - of sowing, tending, waiting - without assigning Willowend to any particular one.

"What matters," he said, "is not how quickly something takes shape, but whether it can bear the weight of time."

He noticed how the words landed differently across the room. Some nodded. Others looked thoughtful. A few appeared disappointed, though not hostile.

After the service, a woman approached him, her expression earnest.

"I hope you're not worried," she said. "About people being excited."

"I'm not," Caleb replied. "I'm grateful for it."

She hesitated. "It sounded like a warning."

Caleb considered her words. "It was an invitation," he said. "To stay attentive."

She nodded slowly. "That's harder."

"Yes," he agreed. "But worth it."

Midweek brought another test.

A gathering that had been scheduled informally drew more people than expected. The room felt crowded, conversation animated, the energy unmistakable.

Caleb arrived late, having been delayed by a visit, and stood near the door for a few moments, taking it in.

The discussion was lively, but he sensed something different this time. The eagerness to contribute had edged more toward competition. People spoke quickly, building on one another's comments without pause. A few voices dominated the space.

Caleb moved toward an empty chair, prepared to intervene if needed.

Before he could, Graham cleared his throat.

"Can we slow this down a bit?" he asked. "I'm finding it hard to keep up."

The room quieted.

Graham continued, his voice steady. "I don't want to stop what's happening. I just don't want to lose it by rushing."

There was a brief silence, then a murmur of agreement.

The pace shifted. People began to pause between comments. Someone suggested taking a moment of quiet before continuing. The change was subtle, but real.

Caleb felt a quiet surge of relief.

This was what he had hoped for - not that enthusiasm would be managed from above, but that discernment would emerge from within.

Afterward, as people left, one of the more vocal participants lingered, looking unsettled.

"I didn't realise how much space I was taking," they said quietly.

Caleb met their eyes. "You weren't wrong to speak," he said. "You were just early."

They smiled faintly. "I'm learning."

"So are we all," Caleb replied.

That night, as he and Rachel talked through the day, Caleb felt both weary and grateful.

"It feels like I am walking a narrow path," he said. "Between encouraging life and restraining excess."

Rachel nodded. "That path never widens, no matter how long you walk it."

He smiled. "That's comforting."

She smiled back. "It should be."

Before bed, Caleb sat alone for a while, notebook open on his lap. He did not write much. Just a few words, written slowly.

Enthusiasm reveals desire. Maturity reveals love.

He closed the notebook, aware that the season ahead would continue to test that distinction.

The limits of enthusiasm were not boundaries to be enforced.

They were invitations - to patience, to humility, to the kind of faith that trusted God enough to move slowly even when faster options beckoned.

As the house quieted and the town settled into sleep, Caleb felt again the familiar weight of responsibility - not as burden, but as calling.

To guard the space.

To honour the energy without being ruled by it.

To trust that what was taking root in Willowend did not need to be hurried in order to be real.

And that, perhaps, was the hardest work of all.

6. WHO BELONGS WHEN THE DOORS STAY OPEN

Belonging had always been assumed in Willowend.

Not questioned. Not debated. It was shaped quietly by years of shared history - who had grown up together, who had stayed, who had buried parents in the same ground and remembered the same stories. The church reflected that rhythm. It was welcoming, certainly, but its boundaries were understood without ever being written down.

Lately, those boundaries had softened.

Caleb noticed it in small, almost incidental ways. A newcomer lingering after a gathering without anyone ushering them toward a membership conversation. Someone free in attending midweek discussions without appearing on Sunday mornings. Familiar faces sitting beside unfamiliar ones without explanation or awkwardness.

No one had announced a change.

And yet, something had shifted.

The question of belonging surfaced for the first time in a conversation that felt more observational than confrontational. Caleb had been standing near the side of the hall, gathering his notes, when one of the long-standing members approached him, her expression thoughtful rather than concerned.

"I'm just wondering," she said, lowering her voice instinctively, "how we know who we're responsible for now."

Caleb paused. "What do you mean?"

"Well," she said, "there are people coming who don't seem to want to join anything. They're not against the church. They're just… present."

"Yes," Caleb said. "I've noticed."

She hesitated a little. "I don't mind that. I just don't know how to hold it."

That, he realised, was the heart of it.

Belonging, when it was assumed, did not need to be explained. But when it became fluid, it asked for discernment rather than rules.

Later that week, the question surfaced again, this time more directly. A man who had attended several gatherings but rarely spoken waited behind after most people had left.

"I hope this doesn't sound strange," he said. "But I don't know what I am here."

Caleb waited.

"I'm not a member. I'm not even sure I believe everything that's said. But I feel… welcomed. And that makes me uneasy."

Caleb smiled gently. "Why uneasy?"

"Because I don't want to take something I haven't earned," the man replied.

Caleb shook his head slowly. "Belonging isn't earned."

The man looked unconvinced. "That's not how most places work."

"No," Caleb agreed. "It isn't."

They sat for a moment in the quiet hall, the weight of the conversation settling around them.

"You don't have to decide anything right now," Caleb said. "You're allowed to be here while you work out what this means for you."

The man nodded, relief evident in his posture. "That helps."

As he left, Caleb felt the familiar mix of gratitude and caution. Open doors invited honesty, but they also exposed assumptions - about commitment, responsibility, and identity.

That evening, Ruth raised the question from a different angle.

They were walking along the edge of town, the light fading, the heat finally easing. She had been quiet for most of the walk, observing, listening.

"It feels," she said eventually, "like people aren't being asked to define themselves straight away."

Caleb nodded. "That's intentional."

She glanced at him. "Is that sustainable?"

He considered the question carefully. "It depends on what we mean by sustainable."

Ruth smiled faintly. "You're good at that."

"What do you think?" he asked.

She slowed her pace slightly. "I think it lowers the cost of entry. Which is good. But it raises the cost of leadership."

Caleb smiled. "That's perceptive."

She continued, "When people don't have to sign on immediately, someone has to carry the ambiguity."

"Yes," Caleb said. "And that someone is usually the one with the most visible responsibility."

Ruth nodded. "You."

They walked in silence for a few moments.

"I'm not criticising," she added. "I'm noticing."

"I know," Caleb said. "And you're right."

The next Sunday, the question of belonging took on a more communal shape. During a time of open prayer, someone prayed aloud for those "who are finding their place among us." The words were offered simply, without agenda, but Caleb noticed how several people looked up at the phrase.

After the service, a small group gathered near the back of the church, conversation unfolding naturally. One woman spoke quietly.

"I don't know if this is where I'll stay," she said. "But I'm grateful I don't feel rushed to decide."

Another nodded. "Me too."

A third added, "It feels like there's room to breathe."

Caleb listened, aware that such freedom would not feel equally reassuring to everyone. For some, clarity equalled care. For others, space was the greater gift.

Later that afternoon, Caleb met briefly with Howard, who had been hearing similar observations.

"We need to talk about responsibility," Howard said. "Not in a restrictive sense. But in a realistic one."

Caleb nodded. "I agree."

"When people belong loosely," Howard continued, "it's not always clear who we're accountable to - or for."

"That's true," Caleb said. "And it means leadership has to be more attentive, not less."

Howard leaned back. "Some will interpret this as a lack of structure."

"Yes," Caleb said. "And some will experience it as care."

Howard smiled wryly. "We can't control which it will be for each person."

"No," Caleb agreed. "But we can be honest about what we're offering."

That night, Caleb sat alone for a while, thinking about the word that kept returning to him.

Belonging.

It was tempting to define it narrowly - to attach it to attendance, commitment, alignment. But the season unfolding in Willowend seemed to invite something more patient, more spacious.

Belonging, he was learning, was not a gate to be guarded.

It was a field to be tended.

And fields, by their nature, did not belong only to those who arrived ready to build.

They belonged first to those willing to stay.

Who belonged when the doors stayed open was not a question to be answered once.

It was a question to be lived - carefully, faithfully - day by day.

And Caleb knew the days ahead would test how much openness they were truly prepared to carry.

The tension around belonging did not surface in conflict. That was what made it harder to address.

No one raised their voice. No one threatened to leave. Instead, the questions appeared in sideways comments, careful phrasing, and well-intentioned concerns that were difficult to dismiss without sounding dismissive in return.

Caleb became increasingly aware that people were watching him - not anxiously, but attentively - for cues. Not instructions, exactly, but signals. How he spoke about newcomers. How he referred to commitment. How quickly he moved to clarify what was still deliberately unclear.

One morning, as he was arranging chairs for a small gathering, Margaret Ellis arrived earlier than usual. She moved slowly, leaning on her walking stick, but her eyes were sharp, taking everything in.

"You've got more people coming through these days," she observed.

"Yes," Caleb said. "We do."

She lowered herself carefully into a chair. "Some of them don't stay long."

"No," he agreed. "Some don't."

Margaret tilted her head. "Does that worry you?"

Caleb considered the question. "Sometimes. But not for the reasons people assume."

"And what reasons are those?" she asked.

"That they might leave without settling," Caleb said. "I worry more that they might settle too quickly, into something they don't yet understand."

Margaret nodded slowly. "That makes sense."

She sat quietly for a moment, then said, "I remember when this church was smaller than it is now."

Caleb smiled. "That's saying something."

"It is," she replied. "Back then, belonging was simple. You turned up. You stayed. You helped when help was needed. No one asked you to explain yourself."

"And now?" Caleb asked.

"And now," she said gently, "people are asked to explain themselves everywhere. I can understand why it feels like a relief not to have to do that here."

Her words stayed with him.

Later that week, a situation arose that brought the issue into sharper focus. A woman who had been attending sporadically asked whether she could help with a particular activity. She did not frame it as volunteering, but as offering - something she could do, rather than something she wished to join.

The request unsettled a few people. Not because she lacked capability, but because she existed outside the usual categories. She was not a member. She had not attended long enough to be known. She had not been part of the shared history that often underwrote trust.

Caleb listened carefully as the concerns were raised.

"We don't really know her yet," someone said.

"That's true," Caleb replied. "But we'll never know her if she's not allowed to contribute."

Another added, "What if she doesn't stay?"

Caleb smiled gently. "Then she'll have helped us for a while. And that will still have mattered."

The matter was settled without formal vote, but not without discomfort. The woman was welcomed into the task, and she carried it out thoughtfully, without fanfare. Some noticed. Others watched cautiously.

Afterward, Caleb overheard a quiet exchange near the door.

"She didn't overstep," one person said.

"No," another replied. "She just… fitted."

Caleb said nothing, but felt a quiet gratitude.

That evening, Rachel raised a related concern as they prepared dinner.

"People are learning how to belong in a new way," she said. "But some are grieving the old way without knowing it."

Caleb nodded. "Belonging used to be predictable."

"And predictability feels safe," Rachel added.

"Yes," he said. "Even when it's limiting."

They worked in silence for a few moments before Rachel spoke again.

"You're asking people to trust something they can't yet name."

"I know," Caleb said. "And I don't want to pretend that's easy."
The following Sunday, Caleb addressed the issue obliquely, as he had learned to do. He spoke about hospitality - not as politeness, but as posture. About how welcome was not an event, but a sustained attention to others.

"Hospitality," he said, "doesn't ask people to prove they deserve space. It asks whether we are willing to share it."

The words landed unevenly. Some nodded. Others shifted in their seats. A few looked relieved.

After the service, a man approached him, his brow furrowed.

"I don't disagree," he said carefully. "I just don't know where the line is."

Caleb met his gaze. "Neither do I," he said honestly. "But I know we'll find it better together than by drawing it too early."

The man considered that. "So you're saying we learn as we go." "Yes," Caleb said. "And we stay humble enough to adjust."

That afternoon, Caleb walked through town, greeting people who were slowly becoming familiar faces. He noticed how easily some of them blended into the life of Willowend - not as members, but as participants. He also noticed those who stood at the edges, uncertain, grateful but cautious.

Belonging, he was discovering, was not a single movement inward.

It was a rhythm - approaching, retreating, returning.

That evening, Ruth joined him again on the veranda.

"It's interesting," she said. "Watching people negotiate space."

"How so?" Caleb asked.

"At work," she replied, "belonging is transactional. You contribute, you belong. You stop contributing, you don't."

"And here?" Caleb asked.

"Here it's relational," she said. "And that makes it messier."

Caleb smiled. "Messier, yes. But also more honest."

Ruth nodded. "It asks more of everyone."

"Yes," he agreed. "Especially of those who've always felt at home."

As darkness settled over the town, Caleb felt the weight of the season pressing gently but persistently. Keeping the doors open was not a neutral act. It required discernment, patience, and a willingness to absorb uncertainty.

Belonging, when allowed to remain spacious, demanded trust - not only in God, but in one another.

And Caleb knew the coming weeks would reveal how much of that trust Willowend was truly ready to carry.

The uncertainty did not resolve itself. Instead, it settled in - not as anxiety, but as a quiet, persistent awareness that the old markers no longer worked as reliably as they once had.

Caleb began to notice how often people spoke in questions rather than statements.

"Do you think it's all right if…?"

"I'm not sure whether this is the place for…"

"I don't know if I belong yet, but…"

The language of certainty had softened. In its place was a cautious honesty that felt both fragile and brave.

One afternoon, Caleb sat in the church office with a small group who had gathered to talk through some practical matters. The agenda was simple, almost mundane, but the conversation kept circling back to the same underlying concern.

"How do we explain what we are now?" someone asked eventually.

Caleb looked around the room. "Why do you think we need to explain it?"

There was a pause.

"So people know what they're walking into," another replied.

"And what are they walking into?" Caleb asked gently.

Silence followed - not uncomfortable, but searching.

Mary spoke at last. "They're walking into a community that's learning how to listen."

Caleb nodded. "That sounds right."

"But listening to what?" someone asked.

Mary smiled. "To God. To one another. To themselves."

The simplicity of the answer did not satisfy everyone, but it slowed the conversation. Caleb sensed again that the temptation was not toward clarity, but toward reassurance - a desire to remove uncertainty before it asked too much.

After the meeting, Caleb walked with one of the group toward the door. The man hesitated, then spoke quietly.

"I've always known where I stood here," he said. "That used to feel comforting."

"And now?" Caleb asked.

"And now," the man replied, "I'm not so sure. It feels like the ground has shifted."

Caleb nodded. "Sometimes that's because it has."

The man stopped. "Do you think this is temporary?"

Caleb considered his answer carefully. "I think the discomfort is temporary. The openness may not be."

The man absorbed that, then nodded slowly.

That evening, Caleb received a message from someone who had attended briefly and then stopped coming. It was very polite, thoughtful, and unexpectedly candid:

I just wanted to say thank you. I'm not sure this is the season for me, but it mattered that no one pressured me to decide. That made leaving feel honest, not like failure.

Caleb read the message twice before setting it down.

Not everyone who passed through Willowend Baptist Church would stay. He had known that intellectually. Now he was learning what it meant pastorally - to release people without needing to interpret their departure as loss or rejection.

That, too, was part of keeping the doors open.

On Sunday, the issue surfaced again, this time indirectly. During a shared reflection, someone spoke about feeling "at home but unfinished." The phrase lingered in the room, unchallenged, as though many recognised themselves in it.

After the service, a woman approached Caleb with tears in her eyes.

"I don't know why," she said, embarrassed. "But that phrase — unfinished - it felt like permission."

"To be where you are," Caleb said.

"Yes," she replied. "Without pretending I'm further along."
Caleb smiled gently. "That's not something you need to outgrow."

Later that day, Ruth joined him as he walked the perimeter of the church grounds. The grass was dry underfoot, the air warm but not oppressive.

"I can see why this is hard," she said.

"For whom?" Caleb asked.

"For you," she replied. "And for them."

Caleb smiled. "That's accurate."

"At work," Ruth continued, "we talk a lot about inclusion. But it's mostly procedural. This is different."

"How so?" Caleb asked.

"This asks people to tolerate ambiguity," she said. "Not just structurally, but internally."

"Yes," Caleb agreed. "It exposes where we draw identity from."

Ruth nodded. "And not everyone likes what they find."

They walked in silence for a moment.

"You're changing the culture," she added. "Even if you're not announcing it."

Caleb smiled faintly. "Culture always changes quietly first."

As the week unfolded, Caleb became more intentional about naming what he *would not* do.

He would not rush people into clarity. He would not equate presence with commitment. He would not measure health by speed.

These decisions did not make his role easier. If anything, they made it heavier. Ambiguity required constant attention. It asked him to absorb questions rather than answer them, to hold space rather than define it.

But he sensed that something deeper was being protected. Belonging, he realised, was no longer a fixed location. It was a posture - one that could be adopted, tested, and sometimes set aside without shame.

As he sat alone one evening, notebook open, Caleb wrote slowly.

If belonging becomes conditional, grace shrinks.
If belonging becomes careless, love thins.
Somewhere between the two, faith learns to walk.

He closed the notebook and leaned back, aware that this chapter in Willowend's life was not one that could be managed to completion. The doors had stayed open. Now the harder work was learning how to live with what came through them - faithfully, attentively, and without fear.

And that work, he knew, would not end with answers.

It would continue in practice, one relationship at a time.

7. WHEN DISCERNMENT FINDS A VOICE

It began without announcement, without ceremony, and without anyone claiming to have noticed it first.

Discernment, when it came, did not arrive as a gift people spoke about. It arrived as a shift in how conversations unfolded - in what was named, and just as importantly, in what was allowed to remain unnamed.

Caleb became aware of it one Sunday morning during a conversation that unfolded after the service. A small group stood near the side of the hall, discussing a recent passage that had been read aloud. The exchange was very thoughtful but unremarkable, until one woman, usually quiet, spoke.

"I don't think this is something we need to *do* anything with yet," she said calmly. "It feels like something we're meant to sit with."

There was no defensiveness in her tone. No authority claimed. And yet the conversation slowed almost immediately.

Someone nodded. Another person murmured agreement. The group lingered for a few moments, then drifted apart without resolution - and without frustration.

Caleb noticed.

It was not the first time someone had suggested patience, but it was the first time such a suggestion had been received without resistance. No one challenged her. No one pushed back with urgency. The idea of waiting had been offered - and accepted - as wisdom rather than reluctance.

Later that week, Caleb encountered something similar in a different setting.

A gathering had formed organically, larger than expected but not chaotic. People sat in a loose circle, the conversation flowing easily. At one point, a suggestion was raised - well-intentioned, thoughtful - about taking a particular insight and exploring it more formally.

Before Caleb could respond, another voice spoke.

"I wonder," the man said slowly, "whether that's for us, or just for this moment."

The room quieted.

No one disagreed. No one defended the idea. Instead, people leaned back slightly, considering the question.

"It might be something that's meant to remain shared," someone offered. "Not carried forward."

Caleb felt a quiet recognition stir within him.

This was discernment - not expressed as certainty, but as restraint.

That evening, as Caleb walked home, he reflected on how easily discernment could be confused with caution. In other seasons, such comments might have been interpreted as resistance, or fear, or lack of faith. Here, they were received as care.

The difference, he realised, was not the words themselves, but the posture of the community receiving them.

Discernment required trust - not only in God, but in one another.

The following day, Caleb visited Graham, who had been unusually reflective of late. They sat on the veranda, the afternoon light stretching long across the paddocks.

"I've been thinking," Graham said after a while, "about how different this feels from other times when people talk about renewal."

Caleb nodded. "Different how?"

"There's less pressure to *prove* something," Graham replied. "Less urgency to show results."

Caleb smiled. "That's intentional."

Graham considered that. "It feels... safer."

"Yes," Caleb agreed. "And safer spaces often allow truer things to surface."

Graham nodded slowly. "I've noticed people saying no — gently."

Caleb looked at him. "To what?"

"To good ideas," Graham said. "Not because they're wrong. Just because they're not right *now*."

Caleb smiled again. "That's discernment."

Graham exhaled. "I didn't realise how rare that was."

Neither had Caleb, not until now.

Later that afternoon, Caleb received a message from someone who had attended only sporadically. They spoke of feeling unsettled, but not unwelcome. Of being challenged without being rushed. Of sensing that there was room to listen before responding.

It feels like people are paying attention to what's beneath the words, the message read.

Caleb folded the note and placed it beside his Bible.

Paying attention.

That, he thought, might very well be the simplest definition of discernment.

The following Sunday, the shift became more visible.

During a time of shared prayer, someone spoke a word that might once have prompted immediate response - an invitation to act, to move, to gather. Instead of rushing forward, the room remained still.

After a moment, Mary spoke quietly.

"Let's hold that."

No explanation followed. No instruction. The phrase itself seemed to carry enough weight.

The prayer time ended not with resolution, but with a shared sense of peace. People left thoughtful rather than energised, attentive rather than animated.

Afterward, a younger woman approached Caleb, her brow furrowed.

"Was that okay?" she asked.

"What do you mean?" Caleb replied.

"We didn't *do* anything with what was said."

Caleb smiled gently. "Sometimes receiving is the work."

She nodded slowly. "That's new for me."

"For many of us," Caleb said.

That evening, Ruth joined him on the veranda, her expression reflective.

"I've noticed something," she said.

Caleb waited.

"People are becoming more comfortable naming uncertainty," she continued. "And less comfortable naming conclusions."

Caleb smiled. "That's not accidental."

She glanced at him. "It must be tempting to steer things more clearly."

"It is," Caleb admitted. "But clarity imposed too early can close doors that discernment is still opening."

Ruth nodded. "At work, decisiveness is praised."

"And here?" Caleb asked.

"Here," she said thoughtfully, "it feels like listening is becoming the mark of leadership."

Caleb felt a quiet gratitude rise within him again.

This was the kind of leadership he had hoped would emerge - not charismatic, not directive, but attentive. Willing to pause. Willing to ask whether movement was required, or simply patience.

Discernment, he knew, would not announce itself with confidence.

It would speak softly, often through those least inclined to push. As the evening settled and the town quieted, Caleb reflected on the season unfolding around him. Renewal had begun with enthusiasm. It was now learning restraint.

That did not mean it was weakening.

It meant it was maturing.

And discernment, once given room to breathe, had begun to find its voice - not loud enough to dominate, but clear enough to guide.

The days ahead would test whether that voice would continue to be honoured.

But for now, Caleb allowed himself a quiet hope.

The church was learning not only how to speak - but how to listen.

The emergence of discernment did not make decisions easier.

If anything, it complicated them.

Where once a question might have been settled quickly - by consensus, habit, or deference to experience - now it lingered. People were less willing to rush to answers, more inclined to sit with tension. That patience carried a cost. It required people to tolerate uncertainty without immediately resolving it, to trust that clarity would come in time.

Caleb felt the weight of that shift most acutely in leadership conversations.

At a small meeting one evening, the discussion turned to a practical matter - whether to adjust the shape of a regular gathering to accommodate the growing number of people attending. The question was reasonable. The logistics mattered.

But the conversation did not move as Caleb expected.

Instead of proposals, people offered observations.

"It feels like the room changes depending on who's there," one person said.

"Yes," another added. "Some nights feel more reflective. Others feel more conversational."

A third nodded. "I'd hate to lock it into a format that only serves one of those."

Caleb listened, aware that the group was instinctively practising discernment rather than strategy. No one was avoiding responsibility. They were simply resisting premature certainty. Eventually, Howard spoke.

"I think we're trying to protect something," he said slowly. "Even if we can't yet say what it is."

The room went quiet.

Caleb felt grateful. That was the language of discernment - naming intention before outcome.

"But we still need to decide something," someone said, not impatiently, but honestly.

"Yes," Caleb replied. "We do. But perhaps the decision is not about structure yet."

They talked for another hour, circling the issue from different angles. When they finally agreed on a modest adjustment - provisional, able to be revisited - it felt less like a solution and more like a holding pattern.

No one left frustrated.

That, Caleb realised, was new.

In previous seasons, decisions had been expected to bring closure. Now, people seemed a lot more willing to live with incompleteness, trusting that discernment unfolded over time rather than at a single moment.

The shift was subtle, but it was reshaping expectations.

A few days later, Caleb encountered resistance - gentle, but real. It came from someone he respected deeply, a long-standing member who had seen many seasons pass through Willowend. They sat together in the quiet of the church office, afternoon light slanting across the floor.

"I don't want to sound critical," the man said. "But I'm finding this harder than I expected."

"In what way?" Caleb asked.

"It feels like we're hesitating," he replied. "As though we're afraid to move."

Caleb nodded. "I've heard that concern."

"I understand caution," the man continued. "I just don't want us to lose confidence."

Caleb considered his response carefully. "So, do you think that confidence only shows itself through action?"

The man paused. "Not only. But often."

"Yes," Caleb agreed. "And sometimes restraint is also confidence - confidence that we don't have to act immediately to remain faithful."

The man sighed softly. "That's not how I was taught."

"I know," Caleb said gently. "It wasn't how I was taught either." They sat in silence for a moment.

"I'm still learning," the man admitted. "I don't want to be left behind."

Caleb met his gaze. "You're not being left behind. You're being invited into something slower."

The man nodded, not fully convinced, but reassured enough to remain open.

That evening, Caleb spoke with Rachel about the conversation. "There's a grief beneath it," she said. "For the kind of leadership people understand."

"Yes," Caleb replied. "Certainty feels like care when you've relied on it for a long time."

Rachel nodded. "And discernment doesn't always feel caring in the moment. It feels… exposed."

"Yes," Caleb said. "Because it doesn't really protect us from uncertainty. It asks us to walk with it."

The following Sunday, the theme surfaced again during a shared reflection. Someone spoke about feeling pulled in two directions - eager to move forward, but hesitant to rush.

"I don't want to miss what God is doing," they said. "But I also don't want to run ahead of Him."

The honesty in the room was palpable.

Caleb did not respond immediately. He let the words settle.

Eventually, he said, "Discernment doesn't guarantee we won't make mistakes. It teaches us how to recognise them sooner."

That seemed to ease something in the room.

After the gathering, Ruth lingered, her expression thoughtful.

"I can see why this matters to you," she said as they walked home together.

Caleb smiled. "You mean discernment?"

"Yes," she replied. "It changes who gets to speak."

"How so?" he asked.

"At work," she said, "the loudest or quickest voice often sets direction. Here, it feels like attentiveness is becoming more influential than confidence."

Caleb nodded. "That's the hope."

She smiled faintly. "It's uncomfortable. But it's fair."

Later that week, a moment came that really tested whether this emerging discernment would hold.

During a gathering, someone offered a strong interpretation of a passage - articulate, passionate, persuasive. In another season, it might have carried the room. Instead, there was a pause.

Then a quieter voice spoke.

"I appreciate that," they said, "but something in me isn't settled yet."

The room remained still.

No one was challenging the statement. No one was demanding justification. The conversation just shifted, opening space for multiple readings, multiple resonances.

Caleb felt a quiet awe.

This was not confusion.

It was maturity.

Afterward, someone approached him, their expression mixed with wonder and unease.

"I've never been in a place where disagreement didn't feel like threat," they said.

Caleb smiled gently. "Neither have many of us."

That night, Caleb sat alone with his notebook, reflecting on the day. Then he found the right words and wrote:

Discernment does not silence conviction.
It teaches conviction how to listen.

He closed the notebook, aware that this season would continue to stretch everyone involved - himself included. Discernment demanded humility. It asked people to trust that truth was not diminished by patience.

As the house quieted and the town settled into darkness, Caleb felt both the weight and the gift of what was unfolding.

The church was learning to hear God's voice - not as a command shouted over the noise, but as a presence recognised in the pause. And if that voice continued to be honoured, it would shape not only what Willowend did next, but who they were becoming together.

Discernment, once welcomed, began to ask more of people than enthusiasm ever had. Enthusiasm had required energy - the willingness to show up, to speak, to act. Discernment required something quieter and more demanding: the willingness to remain present when clarity did not arrive on cue.

Caleb saw the cost of this most clearly in those who had once been quick to contribute. Some of them now sat longer in silence, not because they had nothing to say, but because they were learning to listen beneath their first impulse. Others spoke less frequently, weighing their words more carefully, uncertain whether what they sensed was meant to be shared or simply held.

Neither response was wrong. Both signalled growth.

Still, the adjustment was not easy.

One evening, after a gathering had ended and most people had drifted away, a woman remained seated, staring at the floor. Caleb approached her quietly and sat in the chair opposite.

"You seem troubled," he said gently.

She hesitated before speaking. "I'm not sure how to trust what I'm sensing anymore."

Caleb waited.

"I used to feel confident," she continued. "If something came to mind, I assumed it was meant to be shared. Now... I'm not so sure. I don't want to speak out of turn."

Caleb nodded. "What's changed?"

She thought for a moment. "I'm more aware that my perspective isn't the whole picture."

"That awareness," Caleb said, "is not a loss of confidence. It's the beginning of wisdom."

She frowned slightly. "It doesn't feel like it."

"No," Caleb agreed. "Wisdom rarely does at first."

They sat quietly for a moment.

"Discernment," he continued, "doesn't silence you. It teaches you to ask a different question."

"What question?" she asked.

"Not 'Is this true?' but 'Is this mine to speak — and is this the moment?'"

She exhaled slowly, as though releasing something she had been holding tightly. "That helps."

Caleb smiled. "Good. Because this is not about shrinking. It's about deepening."

As the weeks passed, the community began to internalise that distinction. People were learning that discernment did not eliminate conviction; it refined it. Statements were offered with less urgency, questions with more openness. The pace of gatherings slowed, not because there was less happening, but because more was being noticed.

That slowing created space - and within that space, differences became more visible.

Caleb became acutely aware that discernment did not flatten perspective. It actually highlighted it.

People began to name where their sense came from — from Scripture, from experience, from prayer, from something unresolved. These acknowledgements were not confessions of weakness, but acts of honesty. They allowed the community to hold insight without rushing to claim it as universal.

Not everyone found this easy.

One man approached Caleb at the end of a Sunday gathering, his expression troubled.

"I feel like I don't know how to participate anymore," he said. "I used to know what was expected."

"And now?" Caleb asked.

"And now," the man replied, "it feels like the expectations have disappeared."

Caleb considered his words. "They haven't disappeared," he said. "They've shifted."

"Shifted to what?" the man asked.

"To attentiveness," Caleb replied. "To humility. To presence."

The man nodded slowly. "That feels harder."

"Yes," Caleb said. "Because it asks more of who we are, not just what we do."

The conversation lingered with Caleb long after the man had gone. Discernment, he knew, was not neutral. It did not simply reveal wisdom; it exposed reliance - on certainty, on habit, on authority structures that relieved people of the burden of listening deeply for themselves.

That exposure could feel unsettling.

And yet, it was also freeing.

One evening, Caleb overheard a conversation between two people who had never spoken much before. They sat together, not animated, not intense, but engaged.

"I don't usually say much," one admitted. "I've always assumed others hear God more clearly than I do."

The other smiled. "I used to assume that too. Lately, I'm not so sure."

Once again, Caleb felt a quiet gratitude stir within him.

This was the fruit he had hoped for - not louder voices, but broader participation. Not dominance, but shared responsibility.

Later that night, Ruth raised the question from her own vantage point.

"I'm noticing something," she said as they sat together after dinner.

"What's that?" Caleb asked.

"People are becoming more honest about their limits," she replied. "They're not pretending to know things they don't."

Caleb nodded. "That's discernment at work."

She smiled faintly. "It would be valued in my world."

"In what way?" Caleb asked.

"It would slow things down," she said. "But it would save a lot of damage."

They sat quietly for a moment.

"You seem calmer lately," Ruth added.

Caleb smiled. "I feel steadier."

"Even though everything is less predictable?" she asked.

"Especially because of that," he replied. "Predictability can give the illusion of control. Discernment teaches trust."

The following week, a moment came that tested that trust. A proposal was raised - not unreasonable, not urgent - but it carried weight.

It would shape the direction of gatherings for months to come. The room listened carefully as it was explained. When the floor was opened for response, silence followed. Not awkward. Not resistant. Just attentive.

Caleb waited.

Eventually, someone spoke. "I think we need more time."

Another nodded. "I agree."

A third added, "Not because it's wrong. Just because it's significant."

The proposal was not dismissed. It was held - intentionally, collectively - without timetable.

As the gathering ended, Caleb felt both relief and responsibility. Discernment had found its voice.

Now the challenge would be to continue honouring it - not only when it felt comfortable, but when it delayed outcomes people were eager to see.

That night, Caleb wrote again in his notebook.

Discernment is not the absence of direction.
It is the courage to walk slowly enough to recognise it.

He closed the notebook and sat quietly, aware that the season unfolding in Willowend was shaping something deeper than practices or programs.

The community was learning how to listen together - not for certainty, not for speed, but for faithfulness.

And that learning, he knew, would continue to reshape everything that followed.

8. WHEN WISDOM OUTPACES CONFIDENCE

Wisdom rarely announced itself in Willowend.

It arrived instead as an afterthought, a pause between words, a decision not taken as quickly as it might once have been. Caleb noticed that confidence – which was once prized for its clarity - was beginning to be treated now with a gentle suspicion. Not dismissed, not silenced, but weighed.

And wisdom, when it came, often arrived later than expected.

The change was subtle enough that it could easily have been missed. No one spoke about it directly. But Caleb felt it in the way conversations lingered after gatherings, looping back to earlier comments, re-examining assumptions that once would have gone unchallenged.

He first named it to himself during a leadership conversation that stalled - not because of disagreement, but more because of restraint. The issue on the table was straightforward. A practical adjustment. The kind of matter that would once have been resolved quickly by those most accustomed to speaking. And indeed, the confident voices spoke first, offering clear opinions, reasonable solutions, well-articulated arguments.

Then the room quieted. Caleb waited.

Finally, someone spoke who had not said much at all over recent weeks.

"I think all of that makes sense," she said carefully. "I just don't feel at peace about deciding yet."

There was no apology in her voice. No need to justify the statement. It simply rested there, offered without pressure.

Caleb noticed the effect immediately.

No one contradicted her. No one rushed to fill the space. The confident arguments did not vanish, but they loosened their grip.

Howard nodded slowly. "I feel something similar," he said. "Not opposition. Just… a sense that we might be ahead of ourselves." The conversation did not collapse. It deepened.

People then began to speak differently - not about what they thought *should* happen, but about what they were noticing internally. Unease. Hesitation. A lack of clarity that no amount of discussion seemed able to resolve.

Afterward, as chairs were being stacked away, one of the more articulate contributors lingered near Caleb.

"I hope that didn't sound like I was pushing," he said.

Caleb shook his head. "You weren't."

"It's just…" The man hesitated. "I'm used to confidence being helpful."

"It often is," Caleb replied. "It just isn't always decisive."

The man smiled faintly. "That's new for me."

"For many of us," Caleb said.

Later that day, Caleb walked through town, his thoughts turning over what he had witnessed. Confidence had not disappeared from Willowend. People still spoke boldly, still named convictions, still offered insight with sincerity. But confidence was no longer enough on its own.

It was being asked to slow down.

Wisdom, he reflected, often outpaced confidence - not by being louder, but by arriving later and refusing to be rushed.

That evening, Ruth joined him as he sorted through notes at the kitchen table. She watched him for a moment before speaking.

"You're quieter than usual," she said.

"I'm listening," Caleb replied.

She smiled. "To what?"

"To the difference between clarity and certainty," he said. "They look similar at first."

Ruth leaned back in her chair. "At work, certainty is rewarded."

"Yes," Caleb said. "Even when it's premature."

She considered that. "And here?"

"Here," Caleb replied, "people are beginning to respect clarity that emerges slowly."

Ruth nodded. "That takes trust."

"Yes," Caleb agreed. "And patience."

The next Sunday, the theme surfaced again, this time in a way that surprised Caleb.

During a shared reflection, a man spoke confidently about a passage of Scripture, offering a strong interpretation. His words were thoughtful, carefully framed, and well received. In another season, they might have ended the conversation.

Instead, a woman spoke quietly after a pause.

"I hear what you're saying," she said. "But I'm wondering whether there's more than one way this speaks to us."

The room stilled.

The man did not bristle. He did not defend his position. He just nodded slowly.

"That's possible," he said. "I hadn't considered that."

The conversation reopened, unfolding gently, with multiple perspectives offered - none were dominant, none dismissed.

Caleb felt a quiet gratitude rise within him. This was wisdom at work - not contradicting confidence but expanding it.

After the service, a young couple approached Caleb outside, their expressions thoughtful.

"It feels like there's room to think here," one of them said.

"Yes," Caleb replied.

"And to change your mind," the other added.

"Yes," he said again.

They smiled, relieved.

Later that afternoon, Caleb met briefly with Mary, who had been observing the shifts with characteristic attentiveness.

"People are learning something important," she said.

"What's that?" Caleb asked.

"That being right isn't the same as being wise," she replied. Caleb smiled. "And wisdom often asks us to remain unfinished." Mary nodded. "That's uncomfortable for those who've built their identity on certainty."

"Yes," Caleb agreed. "But it's freeing for those who've never felt confident enough to speak."

Mary's eyes softened. "I'm seeing voices emerge that I've waited years to hear."

As the week unfolded, Caleb noticed how the culture continued to shift. People spoke with more care. Questions were valued as much as answers. Silence was no longer treated as absence, but as participation.

Confidence still had a place - but it no longer set the pace on its own.

That shift did not go unnoticed by everyone.

One afternoon, Caleb received a message that unsettled him. It was courteous, measured, but clear:

I'm grateful for the openness here. But I'm finding it harder to know what we stand for. Things feel... less defined.

Caleb read the message twice before replying:

We're still discovering what deserves definition. Some things reveal themselves only when we resist naming them too quickly.

He hesitated, then added:

Clarity is coming. We're just learning to wait for the kind that lasts.

That evening, Caleb sat alone for a while, reflecting on the cost of that waiting. Slowness required considerable courage. It invited misunderstanding. It asked leaders to absorb uncertainty without rushing to resolve it for others.

But it also protected something precious.

Wisdom, he was learning, did not compete with confidence.

It outlasted it.

And as Willowend continued to grow - not only in numbers, but in depth - Caleb sensed that the ability to distinguish between the two would matter more than any decision they made next. Confidence could initiate movement.

Wisdom would determine whether that movement endured. And the church, he realised, was slowly learning the difference. The discomfort around definition did not fade with time. It sharpened.

As wisdom began to outpace confidence, some people felt steadier, more grounded than they had in years. Others felt adrift, unsure how to measure faithfulness when certainty no longer anchored it. Caleb was keenly aware that both responses were sincere.

The tension surfaced most clearly in conversations that began with the phrase, *"I'm just trying to understand…"*

One such conversation unfolded late one afternoon when Caleb was locking up the church. A man who had been present since the early days of renewal lingered by the door, his expression thoughtful, almost troubled.

"I hope this doesn't sound negative," he said.

Caleb smiled gently. "Go on."

"I'm grateful for the depth," the man continued. "I really am. But I'm finding it harder to explain to others what's happening here."

Caleb nodded. "In what way?"

"Well," the man said slowly, "there used to be clearer markers. You knew what people believed. What the church stood for. Now… it feels more open. More patient. And I'm not sure how to describe that without it sounding vague."

Caleb considered his words carefully.

"Does it feel vague to you?" he asked.

The man hesitated. "No. It feels… careful."

Caleb smiled. "That's a helpful distinction."

"But careful doesn't always sound compelling," the man replied. "Especially to people who are looking for certainty."

"No," Caleb agreed. "It doesn't."

They stood in silence for a moment, the weight of the concern settling between them.

"I think what we're learning," Caleb said finally, "is that clarity and certainty aren't the same thing. We can be clear about our posture without being certain about every outcome."

The man nodded slowly. "That's harder to sell."

"Yes," Caleb said. "But it may be truer."

Similar conversations began to surface elsewhere.

A small group paused mid-discussion when someone asked, "Are we actually allowed to disagree here?" The question was asked without sarcasm, without challenge - genuinely uncertain.

"Yes," Caleb replied. "You are."

"And still belong?" the person asked.

"Yes," he said again.

The relief in the room was palpable.

Yet not everyone experienced that openness as relief.

At another gathering, a woman spoke with visible frustration. "I feel like we're circling everything," she said. "Like we keep naming how complex things are, but never landing anywhere."

Caleb nodded. "That can be tiring."

She exhaled sharply. "It is."

"What would landing look like for you?" he asked.

She paused. "Knowing where we stand."

Caleb considered that. "And what if where we stand is still in the process of unfolding?"

She frowned slightly. "Then how do we know we're not just avoiding hard decisions?"

The question hung in the air.

Caleb did not rush to answer.

"I think avoidance feels different," he said slowly. "Avoidance refuses to engage. What I'm seeing is people engaging deeply - just not quickly."

She absorbed that, not fully convinced, but less tense.

Later that night, Caleb and Rachel sat quietly after dinner, the windows open to the evening air.

"I'm sensing some fatigue," Rachel said.

"Yes," Caleb replied. "Discernment asks more endurance than enthusiasm."

"And more trust," she added.

"Yes."

Rachel leaned back. "I think people just want to know they're moving forward."

"And they are," Caleb said. "Just not in straight lines."

Rachel smiled faintly. "Straight lines are comforting."

"They're also rarely true," Caleb replied.

As the weeks unfolded, Caleb noticed something else emerging alongside the tension - a growing humility among those who had once relied heavily on confidence. Some of the strongest voices were now the most cautious, careful not to mistake clarity of speech for clarity of leading.

One evening, a man who had often spoken very decisively approached Caleb.

"I've been realising something," he said quietly. "I've always assumed that if I felt sure, I was meant to lead."

Caleb waited.

"I'm not sure that's true anymore," the man continued. "Feeling sure might just mean I'm comfortable."

Caleb smiled gently. "That's an important realisation."

"It's unsettling," the man admitted.

"Yes," Caleb said. "But it makes room for others."

And that room was being filled.

Caleb noticed newer voices emerging - people who had rarely spoken before now offering careful insights. Their contributions were not forceful, but they were thoughtful, often naming dimensions others had overlooked.

Wisdom, Caleb reflected, did not always belong to those most practiced at speaking. At the same time, some people began to drift. Not abruptly. Not angrily. They attended less often, spoke less freely. A few expressed quietly that the season no longer felt like home.

Caleb grieved those departures without resenting them. Not every pace suited every season. Not every person was meant to stay through every transition.

One such conversation stayed with him.

"I need something firmer right now," the person had said. "Something that tells me what to hold onto."

Caleb nodded. "I understand."

"I don't think what you're doing is wrong," they added. "It's just not what I can carry at the moment."

Caleb respected the honesty.

That evening, he wrote briefly in his notebook.

Wisdom asks us to live without guarantees.
Confidence offers them freely.

He closed the notebook and sat quietly, aware that the path Willowend was walking would continue to unsettle those who preferred certainty. But he also sensed that something essential was being protected - a depth that could not be rushed, a maturity that refused to perform.

As the town settled into night, Caleb felt again the familiar mixture of resolve and humility. He could not promise that everyone would stay. He could not ensure that discernment would always feel satisfying.

But he could remain faithful to the posture that was emerging. Wisdom, when it outpaced confidence, did not eliminate direction.

It clarified motive.

And that, he sensed, would matter deeply in the chapters still to come.

The question that lingered beneath everything was not whether Willowend was changing, but how much uncertainty people were willing to carry while it did.

Caleb felt that question pressing in on him one evening as he sat alone in the sanctuary. The building was quiet, the fans switched off, the air still warm but bearable. He had come in after dinner, not with an agenda, but with a need to listen - not for answers, but for steadiness.

He walked slowly down the centre aisle, past the familiar pews, the worn hymnbooks resting neatly in their racks. This space had held generations of conviction - firm, sincere, sometimes brittle. Now it was holding something else: a community learning to live without premature resolution.

He sat near the front and let the silence settle.

Wisdom, he reflected, was costly because it refused to reassure cheaply. It did not rush to fill the space where anxiety lived. It trusted that faith could endure questions without collapsing.

That trust, however, was unevenly shared.

The next day, Caleb encountered the tension again in a conversation that unfolded unexpectedly. He had stopped by the hardware store for a small repair when he ran into a man who had been attending sporadically. They exchanged greetings, then stood awkwardly for a moment among shelves of paint tins and garden tools.

"I've been meaning to ask you something," the man said finally.

"Go ahead," Caleb replied.

"Do you ever worry that all this... reflection... might dilute things?" he asked. "Like we'll end up believing everything and nothing at the same time?"

Caleb considered the question carefully. "What do you mean by dilute?"

"Well," the man said, "if everyone's perspective is held, how do we know which ones are true?"

Caleb nodded slowly. "Holding perspectives isn't the same as affirming them."

The man frowned slightly. "But it can feel like that."

"Yes," Caleb said. "Because discernment resists shortcuts. It doesn't declare truth by volume or speed."

"So how *does* it declare truth?" the man asked.

"Over time," Caleb replied. "By what endures. By what bears fruit. By what draws people toward love rather than fear."

The man nodded, thoughtful. "That takes patience."

"Yes," Caleb agreed. "And patience is not equally distributed."

The conversation ended without resolution, but not without respect. As Caleb walked back toward home, he was struck again by how often the work now lay not in explaining, but in accompanying - staying with people as they wrestled rather than guiding them quickly to conclusions.

That accompaniment was beginning to take a toll.

Not in the sense of burnout, but in the quiet accumulation of responsibility. Caleb felt it late at night, when questions replayed themselves without answers. He felt it when people looked to him for clarity he was deliberately withholding. He felt it when restraint was misread as hesitation.

And yet, beneath the weariness, there was also a deepening confidence - not the old kind, rooted in decisiveness, but a quieter one grounded in trust.

One afternoon, Mary came to see him. She moved slowly, her steps measured, her presence steady as ever. She sat across from him in the office, her hands folded loosely in her lap.

"You're carrying more than you let on," she said.

Caleb smiled faintly. "You always notice."

She returned the smile. "That's because you don't hide it. You just don't dramatise it."

He nodded.

"What you're doing," she continued, "won't satisfy everyone."

"I know," Caleb said.

"And some will say you've made things less certain," she added.

"Yes."

Mary leaned forward slightly. "But certainty was never the same as faith."

Caleb felt something ease in his chest at her words.

"Faith," she went on, "has always involved trusting God without knowing where the next step will land. We just became very good at pretending otherwise."

Caleb smiled. "You make it sound simple."

"It isn't," Mary said gently. "But it is honest."

As she stood to leave, she paused at the door. "The measure of wisdom," she said, "is not how clearly it speaks, but how faithfully it waits."

That phrase stayed with Caleb.

In the weeks that followed, the church continued to walk this slower path. Some conversations resolved themselves naturally. Others remained open-ended. People learned, slowly and imperfectly, how to live without forcing coherence where it had not yet formed.

Caleb noticed how often people now asked one another, *"What are you sensing?"* rather than *"What do you think?"* The shift was subtle, but meaningful. It invited attentiveness rather than opinion, humility rather than assertion.

Not everyone adapted easily.

A few people withdrew, uncomfortable with the lack of definition. Others stayed but grew quiet, watching, waiting. Caleb did not rush them. He trusted that presence itself was a form of participation.

One evening, after a particularly long day, Ruth sat with him on the veranda. The sky was darkening, the air cooling at last.

"You seem tired," she said.

"I am," Caleb replied honestly.

"But not discouraged," she observed.

"No," he said. "Not discouraged."

She nodded. "I've been thinking about what you said earlier. About wisdom arriving later."

"And?" he asked.

"At work," she said, "we reward whoever speaks first. Whoever sounds sure. But I'm starting to wonder how many mistakes we make because of that."

Caleb smiled. "More than we like to admit."

She looked at him thoughtfully. "This place… it is teaching people to live without immediate answers. That's rare."

"Yes," Caleb said. "And risky."

Ruth smiled faintly. "But maybe necessary."

He nodded. "I think so."

As the chapter of uncertainty continued to unfold, Caleb became increasingly convinced of one thing: wisdom could not be forced into prominence. It had to be given time, space, and permission to outlast confidence. And when it did, it reshaped everything - leadership, belonging, faith itself.

Late one night, Caleb returned to his notebook and wrote again, the words coming slowly.

Confidence moves quickly.
Wisdom waits to see what remains.

He closed the notebook, aware that the waiting itself had become the work.

The church of Willowend was learning not only how to speak carefully, but how to live faithfully in the absence of easy conclusions. And though that path felt fragile at times, Caleb sensed it was also deeply resilient.

Wisdom had outpaced confidence.

Now the question was whether they would continue to trust it - even when it asked them to move no faster than love would allow.

Attention had followed this renewal without most people even noticing. It had arrived quietly, carried on conversations that began with curiosity rather than concern.

People asked questions. They listened. They observed. For a time, that attention felt very affirming - a sign that what was unfolding in Willowend was now being recognised beyond its boundaries.

But attention, Caleb knew, rarely stayed neutral for long.

The first hint of scrutiny came not as criticism, but as interest shaped by expectation. An email arrived one morning from someone Caleb did not know personally, though the name was familiar enough. They wrote very warmly, appreciatively, commenting on things which they had heard about Willowend's "depth" and "maturity." They spoke of the rarity of such seasons, of how encouraging it was to see a church leaning into discernment rather than spectacle.

Then came the question.

How are you ensuring that what's emerging remains anchored and accountable?

Caleb read the message twice.

The question was not unreasonable. It was not hostile. And yet, it carried weight. It assumed that something potentially unstable was forming - something that required containment, oversight, definition.

Caleb set the email aside and did not respond immediately.

Later that day, he mentioned it to Rachel as they sat together at the kitchen table.

"That was bound to happen," she said calmly.

"Yes," Caleb agreed. "I just didn't expect it to come so gently." She smiled. "Gentle questions often reveal deeper concerns."

Over the following weeks, similar inquiries arrived - some direct, some more subtle, some framed as encouragement with the undercurrent of real caution. People wanted to know what Willowend Baptist Church stood for. What it believed. How it would prevent "drift." Whether the openness was intentional or simply unmanaged.

Caleb answered carefully, never defensively, never evasively. He spoke of posture rather than programs, of attentiveness rather than innovation. He resisted the temptation to reassure too quickly.

Not everyone was satisfied.

He noticed the shift first in tone rather than content. Conversations that had once been curious became evaluative. Observations carried a sharper edge. People listened not only to understand, but to assess.

Scrutiny had arrived.

The change became visible within Willowend itself one Sunday morning. A visiting couple attended the service, their presence noticeable without being disruptive. They listened intently, taking notes during the sermon, watching closely during the shared reflection.

After the service, they introduced themselves politely.

"We've heard a lot about what's happening here," one of them said.

Caleb nodded. "You're welcome."

They smiled. "It's... different."

"In what way?" Caleb asked.

The man hesitated. "There's less certainty than we expected."

Caleb smiled gently. "That's intentional."

The woman nodded. "We're just trying to understand."

"And you're free to," Caleb said.

The conversation remained cordial, but Caleb felt the familiar tightening in his chest - not anxiety, but awareness. They were not simply participating. They were evaluating.

That afternoon, Caleb took a walk through town, the sky wide above him, the familiar streets offering their quiet reassurance. He passed people who greeted him warmly, unaware of the growing attention focused on their small community.

He wondered briefly how much they sensed it - how the openness they were learning to inhabit was now being observed through more cautious eyes.

That evening, Howard called.

"I thought you should know," he said. "I've been asked a few questions."

Caleb nodded, though Howard could not see him. "What kind of questions?"

"About leadership," Howard replied. "About boundaries. About whether this season is being stewarded or simply allowed."

Caleb exhaled slowly. "And what did you say?"

"That we're learning as we go," Howard said. "Which didn't entirely reassure them."

Caleb smiled faintly. "No. It wouldn't."

"They're not accusing," Howard added quickly. "Just watching."

"Yes," Caleb said. "That's often how scrutiny begins."

The following week, Caleb sensed the impact of that watching within the church itself. People became more self-conscious in gatherings. Comments were offered more cautiously, sometimes withdrawn halfway through. A few people asked quietly whether certain things were "still appropriate" to share.

Caleb addressed it gently.

"We're not under examination," he said one evening. "But we are being seen. That doesn't require us to change who we are."

Someone asked, "But should we be more careful?"

Caleb considered the question. "Careful, yes. Afraid, no."

Still, he knew the presence of such scrutiny altered behaviour, whether acknowledged or not. It introduced a new pressure - the pressure to appear balanced, mature, orthodox enough to pass unseen tests.

That pressure unsettled him.

Late one night, Caleb sat with his notebook open, the words slow to come:

Scrutiny doesn't ask who we are.
It asks whether we are safe.

He paused, then added:

Faithfulness answers a different question.

The following Sunday, a moment occurred that crystallised the tension. During a time of shared prayer, someone spoke honestly about uncertainty - not doubt, but fatigue. The words were quiet, unguarded, offered without flourish. The room received them gently, as it had learned to do.

Afterward, a visitor approached Caleb.

"That was very open," they said.

"Yes," Caleb replied.

"Do you ever worry," they asked, "that such honesty might confuse people?"

Caleb met their gaze. "Only if that honesty is mistaken for instability."

The visitor nodded, though their expression remained uncertain. As they walked away, Caleb felt the familiar mix of resolve and vulnerability. This was the risk of openness - not that it would lead people astray, but that it would be misunderstood by those who equated safety with control.

That evening, Ruth joined him on the veranda, her expression thoughtful.

"You seem like you're carrying something," she said.

"I am," Caleb admitted. "Attention has shifted."

"To what?" she asked.

"To scrutiny," he replied.

Ruth nodded. "That happens when things stop being small."

"Yes," Caleb said. "And we're no longer as unseen as we were."

She considered that. "Does it change what you'll do?"

Caleb looked out across the darkened town, the lights soft against the night.

"It changes how carefully I listen," he said. "But not what I'm listening for."

Ruth smiled faintly. "That sounds exhausting."

Caleb smiled back. "It can be."

As the night deepened, Caleb felt the weight of the season pressing him now in new ways. The renewal had matured into discernment. Discernment had slowed the pace. Now scrutiny threatened to reintroduce pressure - not to move faster, but to appear settled.

The work ahead, he knew all too well, would not be to satisfy those watching. It would be to remain faithful to what had been entrusted even when that faithfulness invited a fair degree of misunderstanding.

Attention had turned to scrutiny.

And how Willowend responded would reveal whether wisdom truly had the final word.

Scrutiny altered the atmosphere long before it altered behaviour. Caleb sensed it most clearly in the way people began to look toward him at key moments - not for leadership as such, but for reassurance. A glance held a fraction longer than before. A question framed more carefully. A hesitation that carried the unspoken thought: *Is this all right to say?*

It troubled him.

Not because discernment had been abandoned, but because it was being quietly filtered through imagined eyes beyond the room. People were no longer only listening to God and one another; they were also listening for how things might sound if repeated elsewhere.

That double-listening was exhausting.

It surfaced one evening during a gathering that had once felt unguarded. Conversation flowed easily at first, but when someone spoke about a sense of grief they could not quite name - a heaviness that lingered even amid renewal - the room grew still in a different way than before.

Not attentive.

Cautious.

A pause stretched. Someone shifted in their chair. Another glanced toward Caleb.

The speaker faltered. "I'm not sure this is helpful," they said quickly. "Maybe I shouldn't have shared."

Caleb felt the shift immediately.

He leaned forward slightly. "It *is* helpful," he said gently. "And you're allowed to name what's true for you."

The person nodded, relief flickering across their face, but the moment had already been shaped by interruption. The openness that had once felt natural now required explicit permission.

After the gathering, Howard spoke quietly with Caleb near the door.

"I've noticed it too," he said. "People are editing themselves."

Caleb nodded. "They're imagining an audience that isn't here."

Howard sighed. "And trying to stay safe."

"Yes," Caleb said. "Which is understandable."

"But costly," Howard added.

"Yes," Caleb agreed again.

The cost became clearer as the week unfolded.

Caleb received another message - this one from someone he knew well, someone whose concern carried weight:

I'm supportive of what you're doing, but I'm hearing questions about accountability. About whether there are sufficient safeguards in place.

Caleb read the words carefully.

Safeguards.

The term was not wrong. But it framed the renewal as something potentially hazardous, something requiring containment. It shifted the narrative from formation to risk management.

He drafted a response, then deleted it. He tried again, slower this time:

We are accountable, but not in the sense of control. Accountability here looks like shared attentiveness, not oversight imposed from a distance.

He thought some more, then added:

I understand the concern. I just want to be careful not to sacrifice faithfulness to reassurance.

The reply came later that evening:

I appreciate your honesty. Just know that some will find that answer unsettling.

Caleb closed the message and leaned back in his chair.

Unsettling.

The word stayed with him.

Later that night, he spoke with Rachel about the growing pressure.

"They want you to define things more clearly," she said.

"Yes," Caleb replied. "And quickly."

"And you're resisting that," she observed.

"Yes."

She studied him for a moment. "Are you confident in that?"

Caleb did not answer immediately.

"I'm confident in what I'm protecting," he said slowly. "Less confident in how it will be perceived."

Rachel nodded. "Those are not the same thing."

"No," he agreed. "And I'm trying not to confuse them."

The next Sunday, Caleb addressed the undercurrent directly - not by naming scrutiny, but by speaking about faithfulness under observation.

"Sometimes," he said, "we become aware that others are watching how we live out our faith. That awareness can be helpful. It can also make us cautious in ways that close us in." The room was quiet, attentive.

"I want to say this clearly," he continued. "We are not performing our faith for approval. We are practising it for formation."

The words landed unevenly. Some nodded. Others looked thoughtful. A few appeared unsettled.

After the service, a man approached him, his tone respectful but firm.

"I agree with the principle," he said. "But surely there's wisdom in being careful about appearances."

"Yes," Caleb replied. "There is."

"So how do you know where the line is?" the man asked.

Caleb considered the question. "When care becomes fear, we've crossed it."

The man nodded slowly, though it was clear the answer did not fully satisfy him.

That afternoon, Caleb walked alone through the outskirts of town, the paddocks stretching wide beneath the sky. He felt the familiar ache of leadership - the loneliness that came not from lack of support, but from the responsibility of holding tension that could not be resolved for others.

He thought of the people who had found freedom in the slower pace, the deeper listening. He also thought of those who now felt unsettled, unsure whether openness might lead somewhere unsafe.

Both responses were valid. But they could not be resolved by compromise alone.

Later that week, a moment occurred that served to crystallise the challenge. During a gathering, someone asked a question that carried genuine weight. It touched on belief, on interpretation, on how Scripture was understood in light of experience. The room listened carefully.

Before the conversation could unfold, someone else spoke quickly.

"Maybe we shouldn't go there," they said. "I don't want us to get into trouble."

The words hung in the air.

Trouble.

Caleb felt a tightening in his chest - not anger, but grief.

He spoke calmly. "What kind of trouble are you worried about?"

The person hesitated. "Being misunderstood."

Caleb nodded. "That's a real concern."

He paused, then added, "But if fear of misunderstanding becomes our guide, we will probably stop asking the questions that form us."

The room remained quiet.

Eventually, the conversation resumed - cautiously, but honestly. The question was not resolved, but it was honoured. And something of the earlier openness returned, tentative but present.

Afterward, Ruth spoke to Caleb as they walked home.

"It's strange," she said. "Watching people negotiate being seen."

"Yes," Caleb replied. "Visibility changes everything."

"At work," she said, "we try to manage it with policies and messaging."

"And here?" Caleb asked.

"Here," she said thoughtfully, "you're asking people to manage it with integrity."

Caleb smiled faintly. "Which is much harder."

That night, Caleb returned again to his notebook:

Scrutiny does not test truth.
It tests courage.

He closed the book, aware that the season ahead would continue to sharpen that test. Willowend was no longer hidden. It was being observed, evaluated, quietly weighed.

The question was no longer whether renewal was genuine.

It was whether the community could remain faithful when faithfulness itself invited attention - and not all of it kind. And Caleb knew that the answer would not come through explanation. It would come through endurance, and Caleb was learning that endurance did not announce itself with resolve. It revealed itself in small, repeated choices - the decision not to react too quickly, the willingness to absorb misunderstanding without correcting it immediately, the discipline of returning again and again to what had first been entrusted.

Scrutiny did not relent. It simply changed shape.

It appeared in invitations that sounded flattering but carried expectation. In conversations that began warmly and ended with careful probing. In questions that were framed as curiosity but weighted with assessment.

One such invitation arrived late one afternoon. An email, polite and well-crafted, inviting Caleb to share about Willowend's journey with a wider group. The tone was very respectful, appreciative. The language was generous.

But the conditions were implicit.

They wanted clarity. A framework. Language that could be transferred, summarised, applied.

Caleb read the message slowly, then set it aside.

That evening, he spoke with Rachel about it.

"They want you to explain it," she said.

"Yes," Caleb replied. "And to tidy it."

She smiled faintly. "That would make it easier to receive."

"Yes," he agreed. "And less true."

Rachel nodded. "So what will you do?"

Caleb was quiet for a moment. "I don't know yet. But I know what I won't do."

"And that is?"

"I won't reduce this to something that sounds safer than it is."

Rachel reached across the table and squeezed his hand. "That clarity matters."

The next Sunday, a moment unfolded that tested that resolve. During a shared time of reflection, someone spoke carefully about a sense of unease they had been carrying - not about the direction of the church, but about their own capacity to stay open when scrutiny increased.

They named the pressure to self-monitor, to speak less freely, to wonder how their words might be interpreted beyond the room. The honesty in the confession was striking.

Caleb watched the room closely.

In another season, the response might have been reassurance, encouragement, a reminder not to worry. Instead, something else happened.

Mary spoke.

"What you're describing," she said gently, "is what happens when faith moves from being private to being visible."

The room stilled.

"It's not wrong," she continued. "But it is demanding. It asks us whether we are really willing to be misunderstood rather than misaligned."

The words landed deeply.

No one rushed to soften them.

After the gathering, Caleb noticed how people lingered longer than usual, conversations unfolding in low tones. There was less enthusiasm than there had once been, less animation - but more gravity. A shared awareness that something was being tested, not externally imposed, but internally revealed.

Later that afternoon, Caleb walked alone along the edge of town. The paddocks were dry, the horizon wide and unhurried. He felt the weight of leadership pressing in a new way - not as responsibility for outcomes, but as responsibility for posture. Scrutiny tempted him toward defensiveness.

Toward explanation.

Toward performance.

He recognised the pull easily. Years of ministry had trained him well in how to reassure others, how to articulate conviction clearly, how to pre-empt concern with well-formed answers.

What he was learning now was how to resist that impulse - not out of stubbornness, but out of faithfulness.

That evening, a message arrived from someone who had been observing Willowend from a distance:

I'm trying to understand what makes this season different. Is it the theology? The practices? The leadership style?

Caleb sat with the question for a long time before responding:

None of those on their own. What's different is the pace at which we're willing to name things. We're letting formation come before definition. That makes it difficult to package. But easier to inhabit.

The reply came the next day:

That may be where the concern lies. People don't know how to relate to something they can't categorise.

Caleb read the words and felt a quiet sadness.

That had always been the risk.

The more a community resisted being categorised, the more it invited suspicion from those who relied on categories for orientation and safety.

Yet he could not escape the sense that this was precisely the work they were being asked to do - to remain faithful even when faithfulness did not translate easily beyond its own context.

The following week, a subtle shift occurred within Willowend itself.

People became more deliberate in their care for one another. Less performative. Less eager to impress. Small acts of kindness multiplied quietly - meals shared, conversations held without agenda, prayers offered privately rather than publicly. It was as though scrutiny had stripped away any remaining appetite for display.

Caleb noticed that those who remained were not the most vocal or confident, but the most attentive. They stayed not because the season felt exciting, but because it felt true.

One evening, Ruth sat with him as the light faded.

"I've been thinking about something," she said.

Caleb looked at her. "What's that?"

"Visibility," she replied. "How it changes behaviour."

"Yes," Caleb said. "It does."

"At work," she continued, "we assume visibility improves accountability. But I'm seeing here that it also reveals motive." Caleb smiled. "That's well put."

She nodded. "Some people are energised by being seen. Others are formed by staying faithful even when being seen costs them."

Caleb felt a quiet gratitude rise within him. That distinction mattered. As the days passed, Caleb became increasingly aware that scrutiny was no longer the primary threat.

Fear was. The fear of being misunderstood. The fear of being misrepresented. The fear of being judged by standards that did not account for nuance or patience. And fear, he knew, could do more damage than criticism ever could.

One Sunday evening, after most people had left, Caleb remained seated in the quiet sanctuary. The building felt different now - not heavier, but more settled. Less eager to prove itself.

He opened his notebook and wrote slowly.

Scrutiny tests visibility.
Fear tests integrity.

Endurance, he realised, was not about withstanding pressure with clenched resolve. It was about continuing to choose faithfulness when fear offered easier alternatives.

As Willowend continued to be watched, evaluated, and quietly measured, the real question was not whether it would satisfy those looking on. It was whether it would remain aligned with what had first been given - the slower pace, the deeper listening, the courage to remain unfinished.

Caleb stood at last and turned off the lights, stepping out into the cool night air. The town lay quiet beneath the stars, unchanged in appearance, yet profoundly altered in spirit.

Attention had turned to scrutiny. Now the work was to remain - not reactive, not defensive - but grounded. Faithful. And willing to endure without needing to explain itself.

When Caleb arrived home, Ruth was waiting for him. She wanted to tell her dad that her long service leave was coming to an end, and the familiar pull of work and routine was beginning to assert itself again.

She spoke about meetings waiting, deadlines resuming, and a calendar that had quietly filled itself while she had been away. Yet there was no reluctance in her tone - only gratitude. "I didn't realise how much I needed this break," she said softly. "Or how much I needed to come back here for a while."

The next morning, after a quiet breakfast and a few lingering hugs, Caleb watched her car disappear down the road toward the highway.

The house felt suddenly still again, settling back into its usual rhythm. Later that day, Ruth messaged to say she had arrived safely and was already being pulled back into work:

I'll keep checking in, she wrote. And who knows - I might even pop back sometime to see how things are unfolding.

Caleb smiled as he put his phone away, sensing that while this chapter of her visit had closed, the story between them - and between Ruth and Willowend - was far from finished.

Decision-making had always existed at Willowend Baptist.

It had been quiet, largely unexamined, shaped by habit and trust rather than process. People knew who carried responsibility. They deferred easily. Decisions emerged without much friction, not because everyone agreed, but because disagreement rarely felt necessary.

That ease no longer existed.

It had not disappeared because of any conflict, but because attentiveness had changed the texture of leadership. People were listening more carefully now - not only to God, but to one another - and that listening made decisions slower, heavier, more visible.

Caleb felt the weight of it early one Monday morning as he sat at his desk, notes spread before him, the building quiet around him. A series of small decisions awaited his attention: scheduling, resourcing, responding to requests that had multiplied with the church's growth.

None of them felt urgent. All of them felt significant.

The question that pressed in on him was not *what* to decide, but *who* should decide it - and how.

That question surfaced explicitly later that day when Howard stopped by the office. He closed the door behind him, not with concern, but with intention.

"We need to talk about authority," Howard said.

Caleb nodded. "I agree."

They sat across from one another, the space between them marked by years of shared trust.

"I'm noticing something," Howard continued. "People are assuming that because more voices are being welcomed, fewer decisions are being made."

Caleb considered that. "And is that true?"

"Not exactly," Howard said. "But it *feels* that way to some."

"Yes," Caleb replied. "Because discernment takes time."

"And time feels like indecision," Howard added.

Caleb smiled faintly. "Especially to those who are used to clarity arriving quickly."

Howard leaned back. "I think the question people are asking - sometimes directly, sometimes not - is who ultimately holds the line."

Caleb did not answer immediately.

"I still do," he said eventually. "But not in the way some expect."

Howard nodded. "That's the tension."

Later that week, the issue emerged again during a conversation that unfolded after a midweek gathering. A few people lingered, talking quietly, their tone thoughtful rather than critical.

"I don't want to rush things," one person said. "But I'm also not sure how decisions are being made now."

Caleb joined the conversation, listening first.

"What's unclear?" he asked.

"Well," another replied, "it feels like everything is open to discussion. Which is good. But it also makes it hard to know when something is actually settled."

Caleb nodded. "That's a fair observation."

"So how do we know?" the first asked. "When something has moved from listening to deciding?"

Caleb paused, aware that the answer would matter. "Usually," he said slowly, "when continued discussion no longer deepens understanding, but begins to repeat itself."

They considered that.

"And who decides *that*?" someone asked.

Caleb smiled gently. "That's where leadership still matters."

The conversation did not resolve the tension entirely, but it named it - and naming it mattered.

That evening, Caleb walked home slowly, the streets quiet, the light fading. He reflected on how much leadership had shifted in recent months. Authority had not disappeared. But it had been reframed.

Where once authority had been exercised through decisiveness, it was now being expressed through restraint.

That change unsettled some.

It also empowered others.

The following Sunday, the tension became more visible.

A proposal had been circulating quietly - not formalised, not announced - but discussed enough that people had formed opinions. It concerned the shape of future gatherings, the balance between openness and structure.

Caleb chose not to introduce it publicly. Instead, he named the process.

"We're still listening," he said simply. "And that listening includes how decisions themselves are made."

The room was quiet, attentive.

"I want to say this clearly," he continued. "Openness does not mean leaderless. But leadership now looks less like direction and more like stewardship."

After the service, reactions were mixed.

Some expressed relief. Others frustration.

One man approached Caleb, his tone respectful but direct.

"I appreciate what you're doing," he said. "But I'm not sure how much longer we can stay in this middle space."

Caleb nodded. "What makes it difficult?"

"It feels like waiting without an end," the man replied. "Like we're hesitating to move forward."

Caleb met his gaze. "What would moving forward look like to you?"

The man hesitated. "Knowing what's decided."

Caleb smiled gently. "Sometimes what's decided is *how* we decide."

The man considered that, unconvinced but thoughtful.

Later that day, Rachel raised the issue from her own personal perspective.

"You're redefining leadership," she said as they sat together.

"Yes," Caleb replied. "At least in practice."

"All too often," she continued, "authority is often tied to speed. The faster you decide, the more competent you appear."

"So what is happening here?" Caleb asked.

"Here," she said, "you're teaching people that slowness can be a sign of care."

Caleb nodded. "That's the hope."

She smiled faintly. "Not everyone will appreciate it."

"No," he agreed. "But those who do will help carry it."

That night, Caleb returned again to his notebook, the page filling slowly.

Authority is not diminished when it listens. It is clarified.
The question is not who decides.
It is who bears the cost of deciding.

He closed the notebook, aware that the season ahead would continue to test that truth. Decisions would still need to be made. Lines would still need to be drawn. But the manner in which those decisions were held would matter as much as their outcome.

Who decides what comes next was not a problem to be solved once. It was a posture to be practised - carefully, courageously - in full view of those who were learning to trust a different kind of leadership. And Caleb knew that how he navigated this tension would shape not only the future of Willowend, but the integrity of the renewal itself.

The tension did not resolve itself with explanation.

If anything, naming it seemed to give it more substance.

Over the following days, Caleb noticed how conversations subtly changed. People spoke more carefully, choosing words that carried both conviction and caution. Questions lingered longer. Opinions were offered tentatively, then sometimes withdrawn altogether, as though people were testing not just what they believed, but whether it was safe to believe it out loud. Decision-making, once invisible, had become a shared concern.

Caleb felt it most strongly in meetings that used to be straightforward. A discussion about rosters stretched longer than expected. A conversation about teaching themes drifted into reflections on authority and responsibility. Even practical matters seemed to carry an added weight, as though everyone sensed that *how* decisions were made mattered more than the decisions themselves.

One evening, a small group gathered in the church hall to talk through the next season of gatherings. There was no agenda printed, no motion to pass - just chairs in a loose circle and a willingness to listen. Caleb deliberately took a seat among them rather than at the front.

For a little while, people spoke freely. Ideas surfaced. Hopes were named. Concerns were raised gently. Then, inevitably, the conversation stalled.

"I'm not sure where this is going," someone said finally. "Are we brainstorming, or are we actually deciding something tonight?"

The question hung in the air.

Caleb resisted the urge to answer immediately.

Another voice spoke up. "Maybe we don't need to decide yet."

"Yes," someone else replied, "but if we never decide, we just keep circling."

The room quietened, the energy shifting.

Caleb leaned forward slightly. "Can I name something?"

They nodded.

"We are learning a new rhythm," he said. "And new rhythms feel awkward before they feel natural. What we're doing tonight isn't indecision - it's formation. We're learning how to carry responsibility together without rushing to closure just to relieve discomfort."

A few people nodded. Others looked unconvinced.

"So when *will* decisions be made?" one asked.

"When they need to be," Caleb replied calmly. "And when they've been shaped by listening rather than pressure."

After the meeting ended, Howard walked with Caleb back toward the office.

"You're stretching people," Howard said. "Some of them don't like it."

"I know," Caleb replied. "I feel it too."

Howard stopped near the doorway. "Do you ever worry you're holding things open too long?"

Caleb considered the question carefully. "Yes," he said. "But I worry more about closing them too quickly."

Howard nodded slowly. "Fair."

The next day, Caleb received another email - this one from a regional leader he respected. It was supportive in tone, affirming the good work happening in Willowend. But it carried a familiar question:

At some point, clarity needs to be articulated. Otherwise, momentum dissipates.

Caleb reread the line several times.

Momentum.

The word lingered uncomfortably.

He understood the concern. Momentum was measurable. It reassured observers. It suggested progress.

But renewal, as he was learning, did not move in straight lines. It deepened before it advanced. It complicated before it clarified. He drafted a response, then deleted it.

That evening, he and Rachel sat together on the back verandah, the air cooling as the light faded.

"I feel like I'm disappointing people," Caleb admitted.

Rachel looked at him gently. "Which people?"

"The ones who want something clear they can point to," he said. "A statement. A direction. A plan."

"And what would you disappoint yourself by doing?" she asked.

Caleb smiled faintly. "Giving them that too quickly."

Rachel nodded. "Then you already know what matters more."

Later that week, a moment arose that clarified the issue in an unexpected way. During a shared gathering, a younger member spoke hesitantly about a sense they had been carrying - not a directive, not a solution, but a concern about pace.

"I don't feel rushed," they said quietly. "But I feel watched. And that makes me want to perform rather than listen."

The room grew still.

Several people nodded in recognition.

Caleb felt the weight of the words settle deeply.

"Thank you for naming that," he said. "It takes courage."

The honesty shifted the tone of the evening.

Others spoke more freely, admitting similar feelings - the subtle pressure to appear insightful, spiritually articulate, or aligned with what they assumed leadership wanted.

Caleb realised then that decision-making was no longer the primary issue.

Visibility was.

When people believed their words carried consequences beyond the room, they guarded themselves. They edited their responses. They offered what felt safe rather than what felt true.

And leadership, if not attentive, could unintentionally reinforce that fear.

After the gathering, Howard lingered.

"I think people are learning something important," she said.

"What's that?" Caleb asked.

"That authority doesn't disappear when it slows down," he replied. "But it does become harder to hide behind."

Caleb smiled. "Yes. It asks more of everyone."

Including him.

The following Sunday, Caleb addressed the issue directly - not as instruction, but as invitation.

"We're not trying to perfect our process," he said. "We're learning to trust each other with time. Decisions will come. But before they do, we're letting ourselves be shaped."

Some people looked relieved.

Others looked uncertain.

A few looked restless.

Caleb knew that not everyone would stay. Some would grow impatient. Others would feel exposed by the lack of clear boundaries.

That, too, was part of the cost.

That night, Caleb wrote again:

Leadership is not proved by speed.
It is revealed by what we refuse to rush.

He closed the notebook and sat quietly, realising that who decides what comes next was no longer just a structural question. It was a spiritual one.

And the answer would continue to unfold - not so much through announcements or resolutions, but through a community learning, imperfectly and courageously, how to trust the slow work of God together.

The days that followed carried a quieter tone, but not an easier one.

Caleb noticed how often people paused before speaking now, as though weighing not just their words, but the responsibility of offering them. There was less eagerness to be first, less desire to steer the room.

What emerged instead was a careful attentiveness - a sense that decisions were no longer transactions, but acts of trust.

That shift unsettled Caleb more than he expected.

Leadership, he was discovering, became lonelier when people stopped projecting certainty onto it. When no one demanded immediate answers, he could no longer hide behind urgency. He had to discern not just *what* to do, but *when* to speak and when to remain silent.

One afternoon, as he walked past the church, he saw two people sitting on the front steps, deep in conversation. They didn't look up when he passed. He felt no need to interrupt.

That alone would have been unthinkable a year earlier.

Inside the office, Caleb found a note left on his desk. It was brief, handwritten.

Thank you for not deciding too quickly.
It's helping me hear my own heart again.

He read it twice, then folded it carefully and placed it inside his notebook.

Later that week, a decision *did* need to be made.

A gathering had been proposed - not large, not formal - but intentional. A space for teaching and prayer, shaped carefully, without spectacle. Some felt it was time. Others worried it would draw attention too quickly.

The discussion circled for days, respectful but unresolved.

Eventually, Caleb called a small group together.

"We need to decide," he said plainly. "Not because the tension is uncomfortable, but because readiness is not infinite."

They sat quietly, absorbing the words.

"I'm going to make the call," Caleb continued. "But I want to tell you how I'm making it."

He spoke slowly, naming what he had heard, where the hesitations lay, what risks felt faithful and which felt premature. He did not present certainty. He presented alignment.

"I believe we should proceed," he said finally. "Not because we're confident, but because we're willing. And because the shape of this gathering matters more than its outcome."

No one argued.

Not because they all agreed, but because the decision felt *held*, not imposed.

Afterward, Howard walked with Caleb across the car park.

"That was different," Howard said.

"Yes," Caleb replied. "It felt exposed."

Howard smiled faintly. "It felt honest."

That evening, Caleb sat alone, the weight of the decision settling in. He did not feel relief - only responsibility. But it was a responsibility he recognised as familiar, even holy.

Authority, he realised, had not been diluted by listening.

It had been refined.

In the weeks that followed, the gathering unfolded quietly. No one advertised it widely. There were no expectations attached.

Those who came did so because they sensed invitation rather than obligation.

It was smaller than some hoped.

Larger than others feared.

But more importantly, it was *true*.

People spoke thoughtfully. Teaching was offered without flourish. Prayer was simple, attentive. No one tried to interpret the moment or frame it as evidence of anything.

Caleb watched from the side, resisting the urge to shepherd every movement. He noticed how others stepped forward naturally - not to lead, but to serve.

When it ended, there was no applause, no sense of completion. Just a gentle dispersing, conversations continuing quietly in pairs and small groups.

That night, Rachel joined Caleb for a walk.

"I think you're changing how people understand leadership," she said.

He smiled tiredly. "I hope I'm not confusing them."

"You probably are," she replied. "But in a good way."

He laughed softly. "How so?"

"At work," she said, "leaders are expected to have answers. Here, you're teaching people to carry questions without panic."

Caleb nodded. "Questions are often where formation begins."

They walked in silence for a while.

"Do you ever wish it were simpler?" Rachel asked.

"Yes," Caleb admitted. "But simpler usually means smaller."

She considered that. "Smaller can feel safer."

"Yes," he agreed. "But safety is not always what grows us."

As the weeks passed, Caleb noticed something unexpected.

People began making decisions *without* bringing everything to him.

Not impulsively. Not rebelliously.

But responsibly.

They checked in with one another. They asked questions before acting. They paused when uncertainty surfaced. Leadership was spreading - not as authority, but as attentiveness.

One evening, Caleb received another message from outside Willowend, asking for an update.

How are things progressing? it asked.

Caleb typed, then paused.

Progress no longer felt like the right measure.

Instead, he wrote:

We're learning to decide without fear.
That may not look like progress from the outside.
But it's changing everything from the inside.

He sent the message and closed his laptop.

Later, as he locked the church for the night, Caleb stood for a moment at the doorway, looking back into the darkened sanctuary. The room felt familiar, yet altered - no longer waiting for direction, but holding space for discernment.

Who decides what comes next?

The answer was no longer singular.

It was shared.

Not equally. Not carelessly.

But faithfully.

And Caleb knew that this shift - quiet, costly, and easily misunderstood - would shape Willowend Baptist long after the questions of structure and authority faded into the background. Because when a community learned how to decide together without fear, it discovered something more enduring than clarity.

It discovered trust.

And trust, once learned, had a way of leading people further than certainty ever could.

The change was not announced.

It arrived quietly, without naming itself, and for a while Caleb wondered whether he was imagining it - a subtle thickening of the air during conversations, a sense that words were landing with more weight than before.

It first became clear to him one Tuesday evening, not during a gathering, but afterward.

A small group had remained behind, cups of tea in hand, chairs loosely scattered. There had been no agenda beyond lingering. People spoke about ordinary things - work pressures, family strain, the fatigue that seemed to hum beneath modern life.

Then someone said something simple.

"I think we're being asked to slow down even more."

The room shifted.

It wasn't the statement itself - it was the way it was received. No one rushed to respond. No one challenged or affirmed it quickly. Instead, people sat with it, as though sensing there was more beneath the words than the speaker themselves realised.

Caleb felt it immediately - a gentle but unmistakable nudge, not toward explanation, but toward attention.

The speaker looked slightly startled by the silence.

"I don't know why I said that," they added quickly. "It just… felt right."

Caleb smiled gently. "Sometimes that's how wisdom arrives."

No one corrected him.

Later, as he walked home under a darkening sky, Caleb replayed the moment in his mind. He had felt something familiar - not dramatic, not intrusive - but recognisable. A kind of clarity that did not originate in reasoning alone.

He had felt it before, years earlier, in moments when words carried more than intent.

A gift.

The thought made him uneasy.

Not because he doubted the Spirit's work - but because he knew how quickly gifts could be misunderstood, mismanaged, or exaggerated.

Over the following weeks, similar moments surfaced.

A woman spoke with unusual insight into a situation she had no direct knowledge of, her words gentle but piercing. A young man offered a perspective during a discussion that brought unexpected coherence to what had felt scattered. Someone else named a tension that had been present for months but unspoken, and named it without accusation.

None of it was theatrical.

None of it drew attention to itself.

And yet, Caleb noticed how the room would still when these moments occurred - how people leaned in rather than pulled back.

Discernment, he realised, was beginning to operate corporately. That recognition carried responsibility.

One evening, Howard voiced what Caleb had been holding internally.

"Are you noticing what I'm noticing?" he asked as they stacked chairs.

"I think so," Caleb replied.

Howard hesitated. "People are speaking with... weight. Not confidence. Weight."

Caleb nodded. "Yes."

"And they're listening differently too," Howard continued. "As though they know something is being entrusted, not just shared."

"That's exactly it," Caleb said.

Howard exhaled slowly. "That can go very wrong if we're not careful."

"Yes," Caleb agreed. "And very quickly."

The challenge, Caleb knew, was not whether gifts were emerging - but how they would be held. In some contexts, such moments were elevated, labelled, platformed. In others, they were dismissed out of discomfort or fear.

Willowend stood at a delicate threshold.

If the gifts were named too quickly, they might be claimed.

If they were ignored, they might wither.

The following Sunday, Caleb addressed the issue - indirectly.

He spoke about attentiveness. About listening without rushing to interpret. About receiving insight as invitation rather than authority.

"We're learning," he said, "that God often speaks through people in ways that don't announce themselves. Our task isn't to amplify those moments - it's to honour them without owning them."

The room was quiet, receptive.

Afterward, Rachel raised an eyebrow at him.

"That was careful," she said.

"It needed to be," Caleb replied.

"You're trying not to create categories," she observed.

"Yes," he said. "Categories can become cages."

She considered that. "The world usually rewards clarity. Here, we are rewarding restraint."

Caleb smiled. "Restraint is harder to fake."

That same week, a moment unfolded that tested everything he had said.

During a midweek gathering, someone shared a strong impression - not a directive, but a sense that a particular person in the room was carrying an unseen burden. The words were spoken tentatively, without naming details.

The person named stiffened visibly.

The room held its breath.

Caleb felt the moment stretch dangerously thin.

Before he could speak, the person being referred to nodded slowly.

"That's true," they said quietly. "And thank you for saying it gently."

Relief washed through the room.

Caleb intervened carefully.

"I want to pause us here," he said. "Not to analyse what just happened - but to remind us of something important. Moments like this require trust, humility, and restraint. We don't build identity on insight. We build care."

Heads nodded.

The evening continued, grounded again, but something had shifted.

Later, as Caleb locked the church, his hands trembled slightly. He knew how close the moment had come to harm.

He also knew how close it had come to grace.

That night, he wrote in his notebook.

Gifts are not badges.
They are responsibilities.

The words stayed with him.

As the weeks passed, the emergence of gifts became more noticeable - not because they were named, but because they shaped the atmosphere.

Teaching became more layered. Discussions deepened. People grew more attentive to one another's stories, less eager to speak and more willing to listen.

What struck Caleb most was who *didn't* step forward.

Those who might once have been quick to assert insight now seemed quieter, as though sensing that this season required a different posture. Meanwhile, those who had rarely spoken found themselves offering words that carried surprising clarity.

It unsettled old assumptions.

Leadership was no longer aligned with visibility.

Giftedness was no longer confused with confidence.

One evening, Caleb and Rachel sat together, the house quiet around them.

"I'm noticing something," Rachel said.

"So am I," Caleb replied.

She smiled. "People are learning to trust what God gives without needing to possess it."

Caleb nodded. "That's the miracle."

She looked at him carefully. "You're carrying this cautiously."

"I have to," he said. "Because the danger isn't enthusiasm. It's misuse."

"And yet," she said gently, "you're not afraid of it."

Caleb thought for a moment. "No. I'm afraid of mishandling it. Not of God's generosity."

Rachel smiled. "That's a good fear."

As Caleb prepared for bed that night, he sensed again that quiet undercurrent - the sense that Willowend was being invited into deeper waters, not through intensity, but through trust.

Gifts were surfacing.

Not as spectacle.

Not as proof.

But as quiet expressions of care, discernment, and wisdom - entrusted to a community still learning how to receive without grasping. And Caleb knew that how they responded now would shape everything that followed. Because gifts, once awakened, could either deepen a community's humility - or fracture it.

The difference lay not in the gifts themselves, but in how they were held.

Caleb became increasingly aware that what was emerging in Willowend was not simply spiritual sensitivity, but a new kind of responsibility.

People were not just hearing more clearly - they were beginning to feel accountable for what they heard.

That distinction mattered.

In earlier seasons, insight had often been treated as something to be admired or shared. Now it carried weight. Words spoken carefully seemed to linger, shaping conversations long after they were said. Silence, too, had begun to speak.

Caleb noticed it one Thursday morning during a quiet meeting with a small group of teachers who regularly met to pray before the day began. The gathering had always been gentle, largely predictable - Scripture, brief prayer, quiet encouragement.

This time, the rhythm shifted.

As one woman read aloud a familiar passage, another quietly interrupted.

"Can I stop you for a moment?" she asked, her voice hesitant.

The reader looked up, surprised but open.

"I don't think we're meant to rush past that line," the woman continued. "It feels like it's for someone here."

The group fell silent.

No one asked who. No one demanded explanation.

They simply waited.

After a long pause, one of the teachers began to cry. Not loudly, not dramatically - just enough to reveal what had been carefully held together.

"I've been exhausted," she said. "Not physically. Spiritually. And I didn't know how to say it."

The moment passed quietly. Hands reached across the table.

Words were few.

When Caleb heard about it later, he felt both gratitude and concern.

The discernment had been gentle.

The outcome had been care.

But the potential for harm had been just as real.

That afternoon, Caleb met with Howard again.

"We need to talk about boundaries," Howard said, as though reading his thoughts.

"Yes," Caleb replied. "But not the kind people expect."

Howard raised an eyebrow.

"If we start policing language," Caleb continued, "we'll shut this down. But if we don't name limits, someone will overstep - not out of malice, but enthusiasm."

Howard nodded. "So how do we hold it?"

Caleb sighed. "By teaching posture, not permission."

They sat with that for a while.

"What does that look like?" Howard asked.

"It looks like reminding people that discernment is offered, not enforced," Caleb said. "That insight invites conversation, not compliance."

"And that no one owes obedience to someone else's sense of God," Howard added.

"Yes," Caleb said quietly. "Exactly."

The following Sunday, Caleb spoke again - briefly, intentionally. "We're noticing moments of insight among us," he said. "That's a gift. But I want to be clear about something. Insight does not override relationship. Discernment never bypasses consent. And no one here speaks *for* God to another person without humility and care."

The words were firm, but not heavy.

Afterward, several people thanked him - not because they felt corrected, but relieved.

That evening, Rachel raised the issue again.

"You're slowing things down just as they're picking up," she said, not critically, but curiously.

"Yes," Caleb replied. "Because acceleration without grounding creates damage."

Caleb paused.

"Faith has its own version of burnout."

Over the next weeks, a subtle pattern emerged.

Those who were genuinely attentive to others grew more confident in restraint. They checked impressions with humility. They asked permission before speaking. They withdrew words if they sensed resistance.

Meanwhile, a small number of people began to struggle.

One man, earnest and sincere, spoke frequently about what he felt God was showing him - not aggressively, but insistently. His language grew more declarative. Less invitational.

Caleb noticed how the room subtly withdrew when he spoke. After one gathering, Caleb asked if they could talk.

They sat together in the quiet of the office, the conversation careful but honest.

"I think you care deeply," Caleb said. "And I don't want to discourage that."

The man nodded. "I just don't want to miss what God's doing."

"Neither do I," Caleb replied. "But sometimes eagerness can outpace discernment."

The man looked puzzled.

"When insight becomes pressure," Caleb continued, "it stops being a gift."

There was a long pause.

"I don't want to hurt anyone," the man said quietly.

"I know," Caleb replied. "That's why we're talking."

The conversation did not resolve everything, but it softened something. The man spoke less frequently afterward — not withdrawn, but more attentive.

Caleb was grateful.

Not every moment ended that well.

In another gathering, someone shared a story that crossed a line - naming details that were not theirs to share. The harm was subtle, but real.

Caleb addressed it privately, then publicly, without naming names.

"We're learning," he said, "that spiritual insight does not grant relational permission."

The room received it soberly.

Later, Rachel reflected with him.

"This is the hardest part," she said. "Not the gifts. The maturity."

Caleb nodded. "Gifts appear before wisdom. Always."

"And wisdom," she added, "is learned through correction."

"Yes," he agreed. "And patience."

As the season continued, Caleb felt himself growing more watchful - not suspicious, but attentive. He listened not just to what was said, but to how it was received. He noticed who felt strengthened and who felt diminished.

The measure, he realised, was fruit.

Not intensity. Not frequency. Not certainty. But whether people felt more free or more constrained afterward.

One evening, as he sat alone, Caleb returned again to his notebook and wrote:

Discernment that does not lead to love is incomplete.
Insight that does not protect dignity is unfinished.

He closed the book, aware that the learning curve ahead would be steep.

Gifts had begun to surface. Now the deeper work was teaching a community how to carry them - without fear, without pride, and without harm.

The renewal was no longer just about attentiveness to God. It was about responsibility to one another. And Caleb knew that this chapter - perhaps more than any before - would determine whether what had been awakened would endure, or unravel.

The measure Caleb returned to again and again was not *accuracy*, but *impact*.

Not whether a word was insightful, but whether it left the room more open or more guarded. Not whether someone felt affirmed, but whether others felt diminished by comparison. He found himself listening less to content and more to atmosphere — the subtle aftertaste that remained once a moment had passed.

It was an unfamiliar way of discerning, and yet it felt right.

One evening, during a gathering that had unfolded gently and without incident, Caleb sensed a quiet heaviness settle in the room. Nothing had gone wrong. No boundaries had been crossed. And yet something felt unresolved.

As people began to leave, he noticed a woman sitting alone near the back, her posture withdrawn. He waited until the room had mostly cleared before approaching her.

"You all right?" he asked softly.

She hesitated. "Yes. I think so."

Caleb waited.

"I just feel… invisible," she said eventually. "Not because anyone's done anything. Just because there's so much focus on insight lately. I don't have words like that."

Caleb felt the weight of her honesty.

"Do you feel less seen because of it?" he asked.

She nodded. "A little."

Caleb sat beside her. "Then something's out of balance."

She looked surprised.

"I thought maybe it was just me," she said.

"No," Caleb replied gently. "When gifts surface, they can unintentionally shift attention. That's why care matters more than clarity."

The woman exhaled slowly, relief softening her shoulders.

"I don't want to stop what's happening," she said. "I just don't want to disappear."

"You won't," Caleb said firmly. "Not here."

That conversation stayed with him.

He realised that even well-held gifts could create unintended hierarchies if left unexamined - not hierarchies of authority, but of *visibility*. Those who spoke insightfully risked being seen as spiritually significant, while others quietly measured themselves against a standard they had never agreed to.

That danger, Caleb knew, was subtle - and therefore more corrosive.

The following Sunday, he addressed the issue carefully.

"I want to say something important," he began. "Not everyone hears God in the same way. And not everyone speaks what they hear. That does not make anyone more or less faithful."

The room was attentive.

"Some of the most faithful work done among us right now is happening quietly - through presence, hospitality, patience, prayer offered without words. If we begin to equate giftedness with audibility, we will miss half of what God is doing."

Several people nodded.

A few looked relieved.

After the service, Howard approached him.

"That needed to be said," he remarked.

"Yes," Caleb replied. "Before comparison takes root."

As the weeks continued, Caleb noticed a recalibration taking place.

Those who spoke less frequently were being drawn into deeper relationships. Acts of service multiplied quietly. Prayer became more mutual, less performative.

People asked one another how they were *actually* going, then stayed long enough to hear the answer.

The gifts did not diminish.

They settled.

One evening, as Rachel sat with Caleb at the kitchen table, papers spread between them, she said, "I've been thinking about how fragile this all is."

"Yes," Caleb replied. "It is."

"At work," she continued, "we talk about culture all the time. Everyone wants it, but few know how easily it can be distorted."

Caleb smiled faintly. "Spiritual culture is no different."

She nodded. "Except the stakes feel higher."

"They are," Caleb said. "Because they involve people's sense of worth."

That truth was tested not long after.

A disagreement surfaced - not explosive, but persistent. Two people held differing impressions about a direction the church might take. Both spoke respectfully. Both listened. And yet, tension lingered.

In another season, Caleb might have stepped in quickly to resolve it. This time, he waited before entering the conversation - not to arbitrate, but to reflect.

"What do you hear beneath the disagreement?" he asked.

They considered the question.

Eventually, one spoke. "Fear," they said quietly. "Mine."

The other nodded. "Mine too."

The admission changed everything.

They did not reach agreement that day.

But they left with mutual respect - and a deeper understanding of themselves.

Caleb watched them go, quietly grateful.

Discernment, he was learning, did not always produce alignment.

Sometimes it produced humility.

As the season matured, Caleb found that the language around gifts softened. People stopped naming them explicitly. They spoke instead of attentiveness, care, listening.

The Spirit's work had not receded. It had been integrated.

One night, as Caleb locked the church after a gathering, he stood for a moment in the quiet sanctuary. The room felt steady - not charged, not expectant in the earlier sense - but grounded.

He remembered the early days, the risk of enthusiasm tipping into excess, the careful corrections, the necessary restraint.

The danger had not passed.

But it had been faced.

He opened his notebook one last time that evening and wrote:

Gifts reveal capacity.
Character sustains it.
A community that learns the difference can be trusted with more.

He closed the book and turned out the lights.

Outside, the town lay quiet beneath a clear sky. No signs. No spectacle. Just a deepening sense that something real was taking root - not through display, but through faithfulness.

Gifts had surfaced.

Now they were being carried.

And Caleb knew that this was the moment that would define Willowend more than any visible expression ever could.

Because a community that learned how to hold what God entrusted without fear or pride was a community prepared not just for renewal - but for endurance.

12. WHEN GROWTH CHANGES THE ROOM

Growth announced itself in Willowend not with numbers, but with noise. Not loud noise - nothing that would have startled the town or drawn attention from the road but the gentle, cumulative sound of more voices occupying the same space.

Chairs scraped more often across the hall floor. Conversations overlapped. The kettle boiled twice as long on Sunday mornings. Someone started arriving early just to make sure there were enough mugs.

Caleb noticed it first in the way the room filled unevenly.

Not every gathering, not every week - but often enough that he began to feel it before he saw it. A sense of compression. Of bodies leaning closer. Of people adjusting instinctively to make space.

Growth, he knew, was not neutral.

It rearranged things.

One Sunday morning, as he stood near the back greeting people as they arrived, Caleb caught himself scanning the room - not anxiously, but attentively. He noticed who sat where. Who lingered on the edges. Who instinctively claimed familiar spaces without realising others were watching.

Nothing was wrong.

But something was changing.

After the service, Howard approached him quietly.

"We're starting to feel full," he said.

Caleb nodded. "Yes."

"Not just physically," Howard added. "Relationally."

Caleb understood immediately. "People are negotiating space."

Howard smiled faintly. "That's one way to put it."

Over the following weeks, the signs multiplied.

New faces appeared regularly - not crowds, not surges - but steady, consistent additions. Some arrived cautiously, sitting near the back, leaving quickly. Others stayed to talk, curious but reserved. A few returned again and again, gradually integrating into conversations that once felt closed.

Long-time members responded in different ways.

Some leaned in, welcoming newcomers with warmth and patience. Others retreated slightly, unsettled by the loss of familiarity. A few watched quietly, unsure whether this growth would last or fade like previous seasons of interest.

Caleb felt the tension keenly.

Growth, he knew, had a way of revealing unspoken assumptions - about belonging, ownership, and identity.

One evening, during a gathering that had grown noticeably larger, Caleb sensed a subtle shift in the atmosphere. People were engaged, attentive - but less relaxed. Conversations felt slightly more guarded. Laughter came, but it did not linger as long.

Afterward, a long-time member pulled him aside.

"I don't want to complain," they said carefully. "But it's starting to feel different."

"In what way?" Caleb asked gently.

"I used to feel like I belonged without trying," they replied. "Now I feel like I have to find my place again."

Caleb nodded slowly. "That makes sense."

The honesty mattered.

"So what happens now?" they asked.

Caleb did not answer immediately. "Now we learn how to make room without losing ourselves."

That conversation echoed in his mind for days.

Making room was not just logistical.

It was spiritual.

As numbers increased, so did complexity. Conversations that once happened easily now required intention. Decisions that once felt obvious now carried relational weight. Even shared language began to shift as newcomers brought different experiences and expectations.

Caleb resisted the urge to formalise things too quickly.

Growth often tempted leaders to stabilise prematurely - to create systems that preserved momentum at the cost of attentiveness. He had seen it before. Good intentions hardened into structures that protected comfort rather than community.

He was determined not to let that happen here.

Yet he also knew that refusing to adapt carried its own risks.

One evening, Rachel observed the shift from her own perspective. "It feels fuller," she said, sitting with Caleb after a midweek gathering. "But also less predictable."

Caleb smiled. "That's growth."

"At work," she continued, "we plan for it. Forecast it. Prepare systems."

"And here?" Caleb asked.

"Here," she said thoughtfully, "you're letting it change people before it changes structures."

Caleb nodded. "People are the structure."

That conviction was tested sooner than he expected.

A small disagreement surfaced over seating arrangements - nothing dramatic, but persistent. A group that had always gathered in a particular corner now found others occupying the space. No one said anything directly, but discomfort lingered.

Caleb noticed.

So did Mary.

She approached him one afternoon, her tone gentle but direct.

"This is where it gets tricky," she said.

"Yes," Caleb replied. "When growth touches habit."

Mary smiled. "Habits are where people feel safe."

"And safety," Caleb added, "is what people protect when they feel uncertain."

Mary nodded. "Then teach them how to feel safe again - not by preserving what was, but by trusting what's becoming."

That evening, Caleb addressed the issue obliquely.

"We're learning how to share space," he said. "Not just physical space - emotional space, spiritual space. That takes patience. And grace."

The room was quiet.

"No one here is losing their place," he continued. "But all of us are being invited to loosen our grip on how that place looks."

Some nodded.

Some looked uneasy.

Growth rarely moved at the pace of comfort.

As the weeks passed, Caleb noticed a shift in his own posture.

He found himself listening more carefully to undercurrents. Watching interactions rather than outcomes. Paying attention to who withdrew when energy rose, and who leaned in when things slowed.

Leadership, he realised, was no longer about guiding a small, familiar group. It was about shepherding a widening circle - one that included people at very different stages of trust.

One Sunday afternoon, as Caleb locked the church doors, he stood for a moment on the steps, looking back at the now-empty space.

The room had changed.

Not dramatically.

But unmistakably.

Growth had altered its shape.

The question now was not whether Willowend would continue to grow.

It was whether the community would grow *with* it - learning how to hold more people without hardening, how to welcome without losing depth, how to expand without drifting.

Caleb breathed deeply, aware that this season would require as much discernment as any that had come before.

Because growth, he was learning, did not simply add people to a room. It changed the room itself. And how Willowend responded would determine whether the renewal it carried would deepen - or fracture under its own weight.

The shift was subtle enough that some barely noticed it at first. It showed itself not in conflict, but in caution. People hesitated before speaking, gauging the room in ways they never had before. Conversations that once unfolded freely now carried an extra layer of awareness - Who else is listening? How will this sound? Is this still safe to say here?

Caleb felt it keenly during a midweek gathering that had grown steadily over the past month. The chairs had been set in a wider circle than usual, an unconscious adjustment to the number of people attending. The room felt full without feeling crowded, but something in the air had tightened.

The discussion that evening was thoughtful but restrained. People offered insights carefully, often qualifying their words before speaking them. Where once there had been ease, there was now politeness.

Afterward, Caleb lingered, sensing that the gathering had not fully resolved itself. A younger woman approached him as others drifted out.

"I hope this doesn't sound critical," she said, her tone tentative. "But it feels harder to know when to speak now."

Caleb nodded. "Harder than before?"

"Yes," she said. "Not because anyone's done anything wrong. Just... there are more people. And more expectations."

"What kind of expectations?" Caleb asked.

She hesitated. "To say something meaningful. Or spiritually perceptive. Or at least... appropriate."

Caleb felt a familiar weight settle in his chest.

"That's important," he said. "Thank you for naming it."

As she left, Caleb realised that growth had introduced a whole new dynamic - one that could quietly undermine the very attentiveness the renewal had cultivated. Where the early season had encouraged openness, the expanding community risked creating an unspoken performance pressure.

The next morning, Caleb sat with Howard over coffee, naming what he had observed.

"We're drifting toward self-consciousness," Caleb said. "People are editing themselves."

Howard nodded. "I've noticed it too. It's not fear exactly - more like uncertainty about belonging."

"Yes," Caleb replied. "And uncertainty breeds caution."

"So what do we do?" Howard asked.

Caleb sighed. "We slow the room down."

Howard smiled faintly. "That again."

"Yes," Caleb said. "Especially now."

Slowing the room, Caleb knew, did not mean fewer people or less energy. It meant intentionally creating spaces where voices were not measured by insight, eloquence, or perceived maturity.

That Sunday, Caleb made a small adjustment. Instead of inviting open sharing immediately, he allowed a longer silence at the beginning of the gathering. The pause felt uncomfortable at first. People shifted in their seats. A few glanced around uncertainly.

Then something softened.

When someone eventually spoke, their words were simple. Not profound. Not polished.

Others followed - not because they felt compelled, but because the pressure had eased.

Afterward, several people commented quietly.

"That felt different," one said.

"Yes," Caleb replied. "In a good way."

Still, not everyone responded positively.

A long-time member approached him later, their expression conflicted.

"I'm glad people are coming," they said. "Truly. But sometimes I miss how it was."

Caleb nodded. "What do you miss most?"

"Knowing everyone," they replied. "Knowing where I fit."

Caleb felt the honesty of the grief beneath the words.

"That makes sense," he said. "Loss often accompanies growth, even when the growth is good."

The person looked relieved - not because the loss was solved, but because it had been acknowledged.

That evening, Caleb and Rachel talked it through.

"People don't talk much about the grief of growth," Rachel said. "We celebrate expansion, but we rarely name what is left behind."

"Yes," Caleb agreed. "And if we don't name it, it can harden into resentment."

Rachel nodded. "So you keep naming it."

"That's is certainly the plan," Caleb said. "Before it becomes something else."

As the weeks unfolded, Caleb noticed another shift - newcomers began forming relationships with one another more quickly than they integrated with long-standing members. It wasn't intentional. It was instinctive. Shared unfamiliarity created its own bond.

Clusters formed.

Not factions - not yet - but affinities.

Caleb resisted the urge to intervene directly. Instead, he paid attention. He watched who gravitated where. Who felt confident. Who lingered on the edges.

One evening, during a shared meal, he deliberately changed his own habits. Rather than sitting with familiar faces, he moved between tables, listening more than speaking, introducing people gently where connections felt natural.

Leadership, he was learning, now required a different kind of visibility.

Not centrality.

Mobility.

Rachel noticed it.

"You don't stay in one place anymore," she observed afterward.

"No," Caleb replied. "If I do, the room settles around me."

"And you don't want that," she said.

"No," he agreed. "I want it to settle around trust."

That distinction mattered.

Later that week, a moment arose that tested everything Caleb was trying to hold together. During a gathering, a disagreement surfaced - mild, but public. Two people spoke from different perspectives about how open the church should be to change. The tone remained respectful, but tension flickered beneath the surface.

The room grew quiet.

Caleb felt the familiar urge to resolve it quickly - to smooth the edges, restore comfort. Instead, he waited.

He invited others to speak - not to take sides, but to reflect on what they were hearing. What emerged was not consensus, but understanding. People named fears of losing depth. Others named fears of exclusion. No one was rushed. No one was dismissed.

When the gathering ended, the tension had not disappeared - but it had been shared.

Afterward, a newer member approached Caleb. "I've never seen a disagreement handled like that," they said.

Caleb smiled. "We're learning."

"That makes me want to stay," they added.

Caleb felt a quiet gratitude rise within him.

Growth, he was realising, was not just about welcoming new people. It was about teaching everyone how to stay when things became unfamiliar.

That night, Caleb wrote again.

Growth tests hospitality.
Not the kind that welcomes strangers,
but the kind that makes room for difference.

He closed the notebook and sat quietly, aware that this season would stretch Willowend in ways that were not immediately visible.

Growth had changed the room.

Now the deeper question was whether the room would change the people - softening them, widening them, deepening them - or whether people would begin to protect themselves against it. Caleb knew the answer would not come quickly.

But he also knew that how he held this season - patiently, attentively, without rushing to control - would shape the church far more than any strategy ever could.

Because growth, left unattended, could fracture a community.

But growth, held with care, could teach a community how to love more honestly than ever before.

What surprised Caleb most was how growth began to reveal people's inner narratives. Not what they said out loud, but the stories they were telling themselves beneath the surface.

Some interpreted the fuller room as confirmation - that what was happening in Willowend was finally being recognised. Others experienced it as intrusion - a disruption of something fragile and personal. A few carried both responses at once, unsure whether to celebrate or brace themselves.

Caleb sensed that these unspoken narratives would shape the season more than any visible disagreement ever could.

One afternoon, he sat with a couple who had been part of the church for decades. Their voices were warm, but hesitant.

"We are glad people are coming," one of them said. "But sometimes it feels like the church isn't ours anymore."

Caleb nodded gently. "Can you tell me more about that?"

"It's not ownership," the other added quickly. "It's… familiarity. Knowing how things work. Knowing where we fit."

Caleb listened very carefully. "What you're describing isn't possession," he said. "It's belonging. And belonging feels threatened when the shape of community changes."

They sat quietly, absorbing that.

"So how do we hold on to belonging?" one asked.

"By sharing it," Caleb replied. "Not by guarding it."

They left thoughtful, not entirely reassured - but seen.

In contrast, a newer family expressed something different.

"We don't want to disrupt anything," they said apologetically. "We're just grateful to be here."

Caleb smiled. "You're not a disruption. You're a gift."

The words mattered more than he realised. The family relaxed visibly, their shoulders dropping as though permission had been granted.

Between these conversations, Caleb sensed the tension which Willowend was holding - the very delicate work of expanding identity without erasing memory.

Growth asked questions.

Who belongs?

Who decides?

Who gets to shape the culture?

And beneath those questions lay a deeper one:

Is there room for us all?

Caleb addressed this openly one Sunday.

"We're learning something important," he said. "Belonging doesn't shrink when shared. But it does require generosity - the willingness to let the room feel different than it used to."

He paused, letting the words settle.

"No one here is being replaced. But all of us are being invited to loosen our grip on familiarity."

The room was quiet.

Some nodded.

Some shifted uncomfortably.

But no one dismissed the truth of it.

As the weeks passed slowly, Caleb noticed small but significant changes.

People began to invite newcomers into long-standing rhythms - not formally, but relationally.

Meals were shared across unfamiliar lines. Conversations that once stayed surface-level deepened slowly, cautiously.

There were missteps. A joke that fell flat. An assumption that caused offence. A moment of awkward silence where no one quite knew what to say.

But there was also repair. Apologies offered. Clarifications made. Grace extended without fanfare.

Caleb learned to pay attention not to the mistakes, but to how quickly they were addressed.

That, he realised, was the true indicator of health.

One evening, Rachel reflected on this.

"In secular workplaces," she said, "growth usually means hierarchy. Here, it seems to be producing humility."

Caleb smiled. "Only if we keep choosing it."

She nodded. "That choice looks tiring."

"It is," he admitted. "But it's also where formation happens."

That formation was tested again when space itself became an issue.

The room was simply full.

Not uncomfortably so, but undeniably. Chairs were added. Corners used. Latecomers hesitated, scanning for somewhere to sit.

Caleb felt the familiar pressure rise - the temptation to solve the problem structurally. To expand, relocate, formalise.

He resisted.

Not because change was wrong, but because he sensed the timing really mattered.

Instead, he named the reality plainly.

"We're full," he said one morning. "And that's a gift. It's also an invitation - not to rush, but to listen carefully about what comes next."

Some people looked relieved.

Others looked anxious.

Growth had introduced possibility - and uncertainty.

That night, Caleb sat alone in the sanctuary after everyone had gone. The room felt fuller even in its emptiness, as though it held echoes of conversation and presence.

He thought of the early days, when the room had felt sparse but familiar.

He thought of now, when it felt alive but unsettled.

Neither was better.

Both required faith.

He opened his notebook and wrote:

Growth exposes what we cling to.
Formation teaches us what to release.

As he closed the book, Caleb felt a steady peace settle over him. The room had changed. It would continue to change.

But change, he was learning, was not the enemy of faithfulness.

Fear was.

And as long as Willowend continued to choose generosity over fear - patience over urgency, hospitality over control - the growth would not fracture them.

It would deepen them.

Not by preserving the room as it was, but by teaching everyone within it how to belong more fully - even when the room no longer looked the same.

Caution did not arrive as opposition.

It came disguised as care.

Caleb first sensed it not through criticism, but through concern - conversations that began with affirmation and ended with gentle hesitation. People spoke warmly about what was happening in Willowend, then leaned back slightly, as though testing the ground beneath their feet.

"I just want to make sure we're being wise," someone said after a gathering, their tone sincere.

"Of course," Caleb replied. "What does wisdom feel like to you right now?"

They hesitated. "Careful. Thoughtful. Not rushing."

Caleb nodded. "I agree."

But he noticed something beneath the agreement - a tightening, a subtle drawing in. Caution was no longer simply a posture. It was becoming a topic.

In earlier seasons, caution had existed quietly, absorbed into discernment. Now it was being voiced, examined, weighed. People were no longer just asking *what is God doing?* They were asking *how far should we let this go?*

That question carried weight.

Caleb felt it most strongly during a conversation with a group who had been faithfully present through every stage of the renewal. They gathered one evening after most others had left, chairs pulled into a close circle.

"We trust what's happening," one of them said. "Truly. But we're starting to wonder how we protect it."

Caleb leaned forward slightly. "Protect it from what?"

They exchanged glances.

"From excess," someone said. "From misunderstanding. From drifting into something we didn't intend."

Caleb listened carefully.

These were not fearful people. They were thoughtful. Invested. Loyal to the church and to one another. Their caution did not arise from suspicion, but from responsibility.

"I think that's an important question," Caleb said. "But I want to be careful how we answer it."

"How so?" another asked.

"If protection becomes our primary goal," Caleb replied, "we may end up guarding against the very thing God is inviting us into."

The room was quiet.

"So we do nothing?" someone asked.

"No," Caleb said gently. "We pay attention. And we stay honest."

As the conversation continued, Caleb sensed a shift. What people were really asking was not *how do we protect this?* but *who carries the responsibility if it goes wrong?*

That question lingered long after the evening ended.

Over the next weeks, Caleb noticed how caution threaded its way into different spaces.

A teaching moment that once might have been received openly was now followed by questions about balance. A story of discernment was quietly measured against past experiences — not in accusation, but in comparison.

"Does this remind you of…?" someone asked one afternoon, referencing a movement from years earlier that had ended poorly.

Caleb felt the weight of history pressing in.

He understood it well.

Every community carried their own memories - moments when enthusiasm had outpaced wisdom, when sincerity had not been enough to prevent harm. Those memories shaped caution, even when circumstances were different.

Caleb did not dismiss those concerns.

He named them.

"Yes," he said openly during one gathering. "Many of us have seen seasons that began well and ended painfully. That history matters. But we must be careful not to let past wounds become the lens through which we interpret present faithfulness."

Some nodded.

Others looked unconvinced.

Caution, he was learning, often felt safer than trust.

Later that week, Caleb met with Howard again, the familiar rhythm of their conversations grounding him.

"I'm sensing a subtle shift," Howard said, echoing Caleb's own thoughts.

"Yes," Caleb replied. "Caution is now becoming part of the conversation."

Howard nodded. "That's not necessarily bad."

"No," Caleb agreed. "But it can become paralysing if it's driven by fear rather than discernment."

"So how do we tell the difference?" Howard asked.

Caleb thought for a moment. "Fear wants control. Discernment wants alignment."

Howard smiled. "That's helpful."

The challenge, Caleb knew, was that fear rarely announced itself as fear. It usually spoke in the language of prudence, maturity, responsibility.

Caution could either deepen wisdom or suffocate growth.

Distinguishing between the two required patience - and courage. That distinction was tested during a gathering that unfolded quietly but carried unexpected weight.

Someone shared a reflection - careful, measured - about the importance of not over-interpreting spiritual impressions. It was well said, the tone respectful.

But as they spoke, Caleb sensed the room subtly constricting. Heads nodded, not in agreement so much as relief. The words gave voice to an anxiety many had been holding.

Afterward, Caleb sat alone, replaying the moment.

The reflection itself was not wrong.

But it had carried a subtext: *Let's pull back.*

Caleb knew he could not ignore that.

The following Sunday, he addressed it gently.

"Caution has a place," he said. "Wisdom includes restraint. But I want to say this clearly: retreating into safety is not the same as growing in maturity."

The room was quiet.

"Fear will often narrow our vision," he continued. "Discernment sharpens it. One pulls us inward. The other anchors us deeper so we can remain open."

He did not accuse.

He invited reflection.

After the service, reactions were mixed.

Some thanked him. Others avoided conversation altogether.

Caleb felt the familiar loneliness of leadership settle in - not dramatic, but real. He knew he was standing at an inflection point. How caution was held now would shape the months ahead.

That evening, Rachel made a perceptive observation.

"It feels like the room is holding its breath," she said.

"Yes," Caleb replied. "Waiting to see what happens next."

"And you?" she asked.

Caleb smiled faintly. "I'm trying not to exhale too quickly."

She considered that. "When things change, people either cling to process or step back and wait for direction."

"What's happening here?" Caleb asked.

"Here," she said thoughtfully, "you're asking people to stay present without certainty."

Caleb nodded. "That's the work."

As the week unfolded, Caleb noticed how caution revealed itself differently in different people.

Some became quieter.

Others more vocal.

A few withdrew slightly, attending less frequently, watching from a distance.

Caleb resisted the urge to chase reassurance.

Instead, he focused on posture - his own, and the community's.

He returned again to his notebook late one evening and wrote slowly, deliberately:

Caution rooted in fear seeks safety.
Caution rooted in wisdom seeks faithfulness.

He sat with the words for a long time.

Caution had entered the conversation.

That was inevitable.

The question now was not whether Willowend would become more careful.

It was whether caution would become a brake - or a guide.

And Caleb knew that how he responded in this season - not by silencing concern, but by naming its source - would determine whether the renewal continued to deepen, or quietly began to close in on itself.

Caution, once named, did not retreat.

It settled.

It took its place in conversations the way a chair is pulled closer to the table - not aggressively, not intrusively, but firmly enough that it could not be ignored.

Caleb began to notice how often people now prefaced their words.

"I don't want to sound negative, but…"

"I'm completely supportive - I just wonder if…"

"This may be my own history talking, but…"

The language was careful. Respectful. Earnest.

And yet, taken together, it formed a pattern.

People were no longer simply responding to what was happening; they were evaluating it. Measuring it against experiences, assumptions, and internal thresholds of comfort.

Caleb understood why.

Caution often emerged when responsibility increased.

What was happening in Willowend was no longer small enough to feel inconsequential. People sensed that what they were participating in mattered - and that if it went wrong, the cost would be personal.

That awareness sharpened everything.

One afternoon, Caleb met with a small group of long-standing leaders from neighbouring towns — not formally, just for conversation. Word of Willowend's renewal had spread quietly, and with it, curiosity.

The questions came gently at first.

"How are you holding things together?"

"What structures are you putting in place?"

"Who's overseeing discernment?"

Caleb answered honestly.

"We're paying close attention," he said. "But we're not formalising too quickly."

There was a pause.

"That's risky," someone said, not unkindly.

"Yes," Caleb replied. "It is."

The admission surprised them.

"But sometimes," he added, "structure introduced too early protects systems rather than people."

One of the leaders then leaned back, thoughtful. "We've seen movements burn out."

"So have I," Caleb said quietly. "That's why we're trying to build patience before momentum."

The conversation ended respectfully, but Caleb felt the tension linger.

Caution from outside the community carried a different weight. It arrived with authority, with experience, with the subtle implication that *this has been tried before.*

Caleb did not dismiss it.

But he also did not surrender to it.

Back in Willowend, the effect of caution was becoming more relational than theological.

People began checking in with one another more deliberately.

"Are you comfortable with this?"

"How did that land for you?"

"Does this feel safe?"

At first, Caleb was encouraged. Then he noticed something else. The constant checking began to produce hesitation. People deferred not out of humility, but uncertainty. Initiative slowed. Conversations circled.

Fear, he realised, did not always look like resistance. Sometimes it looked like excessive permission-seeking.

One evening, a younger man approached Caleb following a gathering.

"I keep waiting for someone else to speak," he admitted. "I don't want to say the wrong thing."

Caleb nodded. "What would 'wrong' mean to you?"

"That it disrupts something," the man replied. "That I overstep."

Caleb considered that carefully.

"Do you feel like you're trusted here?" he asked.

"Yes," the man said quickly. "I think so."

"Then the fear isn't about trust," Caleb said gently. "It's about consequence."

The man looked relieved, as though something had been named at last.

Caleb walked home that night with a growing clarity.

Caution had shifted the centre of gravity.

People were no longer asking, *What is God inviting us into?* They were now asking, *What could go wrong if we respond?*

Both were valid questions.

But the order mattered.

The next Sunday, Caleb addressed this directly.

"I want to acknowledge something," he said. "Many of us are holding caution right now. That's understandable. But I want to invite us to notice what our caution is responding to."

The room was attentive.

"If our caution comes from care - care for people, care for integrity - it will lead us deeper into listening. But if it comes from fear of consequence, it will quietly shrink our courage."

No one spoke.

"Caution that keeps us attentive is wise," Caleb continued. "Caution that keeps us silent is not."

The words hung in the air.

Afterward, reactions were mixed. Some thanked him for articulating what they had been feeling. Others grew quieter still, unsure how to respond.

Caleb felt the familiar tension again - the knowledge that leadership often clarified things before it comforted them.

Later that week, he sat with Mary, who had been watching the season unfold with her characteristic attentiveness.

"You're walking a narrow path," she said.

"Yes," Caleb replied. "And I can feel the edges."

Mary smiled. "That's where faith lives."

He looked at her. "Do you think I'm pushing too hard?"

She shook her head. "You're not pushing. You're holding. And holding is tiring."

That simple affirmation steadied him more than she realised.

As the days passed, Caleb began to notice how caution affected him personally.

He found himself rehearsing words before speaking them. Weighing tone. Anticipating reactions. Leadership was no longer just about discernment. It was about exposure.

Every decision, every word, every silence was now interpreted - not maliciously, but attentively. That attentiveness was a gift. It was also exhausting.

One night, Caleb sat with Rachel, naming the weight he was carrying.

"I don't want to become reactive," he said. "But I also don't want to become guarded."

Rachel listened quietly.

"You're allowed to feel the cost," she said. "That doesn't mean you're doing it wrong."

He smiled faintly. "It would be easier if caution had a clear voice."

Rachel nodded. "But it doesn't. It whispers."

Caleb laughed softly. "Yes. It does."

Over the following weeks, something unexpected happened.

Caution began to sort people.

Not dramatically. Not visibly. But perceptibly.

Those who were able to hold the tension without demanding resolution leaned in. They stayed curious. They asked questions without insisting on answers.

Those who needed certainty began to step back - not in anger, but in fatigue. Some attended less frequently. Others grew quiet, waiting for clarity that might not come.

Caleb felt the sadness of it.

But he also recognised the integrity.

Renewal, he was learning, did not simply attract.

It clarified.

Late one evening, Caleb returned to his notebook.

Caution is not the enemy.
Fear is not the enemy.
Avoidance is.

He read those words a number of times, reflecting on the reality which was unfolding in the church he loved.

Caution had entered the conversation. It was shaping the season now - not as resistance, but as refinement. The question was no longer whether Willowend would proceed carefully. It was whether they would allow caution to deepen faithfulness - or quietly replace it.

And Caleb knew that the next steps - how he named fear, how he honoured care, how he resisted paralysis without dismissing concern - would determine whether this season matured,
or slowly tightened around itself.

Caution had arrived.

Now it needed to be taught how to listen.

What Caleb found most unsettling was not the presence of caution itself, but how easily it began to feel *virtuous*. Caution sounded responsible. Mature. Faithful, even.

It spoke in the language of stewardship and care, of protecting people from harm and guarding what was precious. And because of that, it was difficult to question without sounding reckless.

Yet Caleb sensed something else slowly forming beneath it - a subtle reorientation of the community's imagination. Where once people had leaned forward, listening for invitation, they were now glancing sideways, checking for approval.

Where openness had been spacious, it was now becoming conditional.

Caution was quietly changing what people expected of one another.

One afternoon, Caleb sat with a small group who had asked for time to talk. Their tone was respectful, earnest, deeply invested. "We don't want to be reactionary," one of them said. "But we're feeling the need for clearer lines."

"Lines around what?" Caleb asked.

Around what's shared," another replied. "Around what's appropriate. Around what belongs in a communal space."

Caleb listened carefully.

"And what do you think happens when those lines are drawn?" he asked.

They hesitated.

"It creates safety," someone said.

"For whom?" Caleb asked gently.

The question unsettled the room.

"For everyone," one replied, though less confidently.

Caleb nodded. "Sometimes it does. And sometimes it creates safety for some by narrowing space for others."

Silence followed.

They were not arguing. They were thinking.

"That's not a criticism," Caleb continued. "It's an invitation to notice who benefits when caution becomes regulation."

The conversation ended without resolution, but with a shared awareness that something deeper was being asked of them.

As Caleb walked home later that evening, he reflected on how often faith communities mistook containment for care. Lines were easier to manage than relationships. Rules simpler than discernment. And yet, Willowend's renewal had been marked precisely by its resistance to premature closure.

The irony was not lost on him.

The very attentiveness that had allowed gifts to surface and trust to grow was now under threat from the desire to control its expression.

The following Sunday, a moment occurred that brought the tension into sharp focus.

A woman shared a reflection - brief, thoughtful, carefully worded. It was not confrontational. It did not overreach. But it carried an edge of vulnerability that made some uncomfortable.

When she finished, the room was quiet. Not the receptive quiet that had once felt familiar, but a hesitating one.

Caleb sensed the shift immediately.

Before anyone else could speak, someone offered a response - affirming, but gently redirecting, reframing the reflection in safer, more abstract terms. The effect was subtle, but unmistakable.

The vulnerability had been neutralised.

Caleb felt something tighten in his chest.

After the gathering, he spoke privately with the woman who had shared.

"I think I said too much," she said quickly. "I don't want to unsettle people."

Caleb shook his head. "No, you didn't say too much. You said something real."

She looked unconvinced. "It felt like the room pulled back."

"Yes," Caleb replied softly. "And that tells us something."

That moment stayed with him.

It revealed the quiet cost of caution - not that it prevented error, but that it subtly taught people what *not* to bring into the room.

That evening, Caleb spoke with Rachel about it.

"I'm worried," he admitted. "Not that people are being careless - but that they're learning to self-censor."

Rachel nodded. "Caution can often do that. It teaches people to manage perception rather than risk honesty."

"And once that happens," Caleb said, "we lose something essential."

Rachel looked at him thoughtfully. "Then you'll need to name it."

"Yes," Caleb replied. "And that will make some people even more uncomfortable."

"It already is," she said gently.

The next Sunday, Caleb did just that.

"I want to say something that may feel uncomfortable," he began. "Caution can serve us - but it can also teach us what not to say. And when that happens, we begin protecting the room instead of the people in it. Faithfulness is not measured by how safe our conversations feel, it's measured by whether people are becoming more honest, more humble, and more open to transformation." He paused. "So, if our caution begins to silence vulnerability, we need to pay attention."

No one spoke immediately.

The words landed slowly, heavily.

Afterward, reactions varied.

Some thanked him quietly, relief evident in their eyes. Others avoided conversation altogether. A few spoke with him later, expressing concern that the community might be drifting toward instability.

Caleb listened without defensiveness.

He knew that naming the tension did not resolve it.

But it prevented it from hiding.

In the days that followed, he noticed a subtle recalibration.

People did not suddenly become bold or unguarded. But there was a slight loosening - a willingness to risk being imperfect again. Conversations grew more honest, if not easier.

Caution did not disappear. It softened. Caleb began to see that caution itself needed formation. Not removal. Not suppression. But discipleship.

One evening, Rachel articulated it in her own way.

"It feels like the church is learning how to be brave again," she said. "But not loud-brave. Quiet-brave."

Caleb smiled. "That's exactly it."

She nodded. "in the world courage is rewarded when it produces results. Here, courage seems to be rewarded when it protects people."

"Yes," Caleb replied. "And that's harder to measure."

As the season continued, Caleb became more convinced that this moment mattered deeply. If caution was allowed to dominate, Willowend would grow careful, controlled, respectable - and closed.

If caution was held within discernment, it could become wisdom - a steadying force that deepened trust rather than shrinking it.

Late one night, Caleb returned again to his notebook, his writing slower now, more deliberate.

Caution must be invited into formation, not handed authority.

He closed the book and sat quietly reflecting on the fact that caution had entered the conversation. It was no longer something to resist or embrace outright.

It was something to shepherd.

And Caleb knew that this work - shaping how a community related to fear, responsibility, and risk - would not be quick or clean.

But if Willowend could learn to let caution serve faithfulness rather than replace it, then this season would not mark the beginning of retreat, but the deepening of courage.

Not the kind that charges ahead unthinkingly, but the kind that remains open, even when it would be easier to close.

14. WHEN TRUST IS TESTED QUIETLY

Trust is rarely tested by obvious threats.

More often it is tested by questions that sound reasonable, by concerns that arrive dressed as care, by glances that linger a moment too long on what used to feel uncomplicated. In Willowend, the renewal had not brought anything loud or spectacular, but it had brought change - and change has a way of drawing attention, even when nobody intends it.

Caleb noticed it in small ways at first.

A conversation that ended with a pause instead of a smile. A comment offered with a cautious tone rather than warmth. The way some people began to watch the room before they joined it, as though checking whether the atmosphere was still familiar enough to enter.

It was not hostility.

It was assessment.

One Tuesday morning, he stopped in at the hardware store for fencing staples, the kind of errand that belonged to ordinary pastoral life. Les was behind the counter, doing his usual slow inventory with a pencil and a battered notebook. He looked up and grinned.

"You lot are getting a bit famous, aren't you?"

Caleb gave a mild smile. "Famous is a strong word."

Les shrugged. "Maybe. But I had two blokes from out of town in here yesterday. Didn't buy much. Mostly just asked questions."

"About what?" Caleb asked, though he already suspected.

Les leaned forward, lowering his voice as if they were discussing something more scandalous than church. "About you. About what's happening down there. One of them asked if it's some kind of revival."

Caleb kept his expression even. "Did he now."

"Not nasty," Les added quickly. "Just curious. But it was odd. People don't usually ask me about church. They ask me about mower parts."

Caleb thanked him, paid for the staples, and stepped back into the heat. He walked to his ute slowly, letting the words settle.

Curiosity was not a problem in itself. But curiosity could become pressure if it carried the wrong expectations. And Caleb had lived long enough to know that attention had a strange way of reshaping things. Even good attention could bend a community toward performance, or trigger fear in those who preferred faith to stay quiet and contained.

That same day, Howard rang him.

"Got a minute?" Howard asked.

"Yes," Caleb replied. "What's going on?"

Howard exhaled. "I had a phone call from a mate over in Galloway. He asked me straight out if we've gone charismatic."

Caleb was quiet for a beat. "He used that word?"

"He did," Howard said, half amused, half irritated. "And he said it like it was a diagnosis."

Caleb leaned back in his chair. "What did you say?"

Howard's voice steadied. "I told him we've gone honest. And he didn't know what to do with that."

Caleb smiled despite himself. "That's a good answer."

"It's true," Howard replied. "But it won't satisfy everyone."

"No," Caleb agreed. "It won't."

Over the next two Sundays, Caleb noticed unfamiliar faces sitting near the back - people who did not carry the hesitant posture of locals searching for a home, but the measured watchfulness of visitors with questions.

They smiled politely. They thanked him for the sermon. They asked what time the midweek gathering ran. Then they left without lingering, without being drawn into conversation, without letting the place touch them in the way most newcomers eventually did.

Caleb greeted them as warmly as he greeted everyone. Still, he felt something tightening at the edges. Willowend was no longer simply being visited - it was being assessed.

It was strange to experience that in a town where everything usually moved at the pace of paddocks and post office queues. Here, people were used to noticing change slowly. But once the idea had taken hold that something was happening at the church, the town's quiet attentiveness became a kind of informal reporting system.

He felt it one afternoon when he walked into the bakery and Sheila gave him a look that was half proud and half wary.

"They're talking about you again," she said, sliding a loaf into a paper bag.

Caleb lifted an eyebrow. "In a good way or a bad way?"

She made a face. "In an interested way. Which can turn either direction, can't it."

Caleb nodded slowly. "Yes. It can."

She leaned closer. "They reckon you've got people coming from other towns. People who don't usually go to church."

Caleb smiled faintly. "Some are coming, yes."

She studied him. "That doesn't make you nervous?"

"It makes me careful," Caleb replied. "Not nervous."

She nodded, as though that distinction mattered. "Careful is good. Careful keeps you from getting silly."

Caleb chuckled. "I'll take that as pastoral advice."

Sheila grinned. "You can pay me later."

But as Caleb walked out with the bread tucked under his arm, he found his mind returning to the same thought.

Trust was being tested quietly.

Not only his trust in God's work, but the community's trust in itself. Could they remain grounded when eyes turned toward them? Could they stay gentle when attention tried to make them impressive? Could they keep their hands open when the temptation was to clench and defend?

That evening, Mary appeared at the church as Caleb was stacking chairs. He heard her walking stick before he saw her, the familiar tap on timber.

"You've noticed," she said, stepping into the hall.

It was not a question.

Caleb nodded. "Yes."

Mary looked around as though reading the room. "Scrutiny always comes eventually."

Caleb gave a small, humourless smile. "You make it sound inevitable."

"It is," Mary replied. "Not because God's work is wrong, but because people fear what they can't control."

Caleb rested both hands on the back of a chair. "What do we do?" Mary's eyes were steady. "We keep being who we are. We don't perform. We don't retreat. We don't start defending ourselves from shadows."

Caleb exhaled slowly. "That's harder than it sounds."

Mary's mouth softened. "Yes. That's why God gives grace one day at a time, not a year in advance."

Later, in the quiet of his office, Caleb opened his Bible, not to plan a sermon, but to steady himself. His mind landed in 1 Peter, and the words felt as though they had been waiting for him.

"Live such good lives among them that, though they accuse you of doing wrong, they may see your good deeds and glorify God on the day he visits."

Caleb closed the Bible gently, letting the page settle under his hand. The words lingered with him through the rest of the evening, not as a warning but as a kind of compass. Faithfulness, he was reminded, was not proven when everything felt affirmed. It was proven when motives were questioned and when restraint mattered more than explanation.

The following days confirmed that this would be a quieter kind of testing. It came through emails that asked some thoughtful questions but carried an undercurrent of concern. It came through phone calls from well-meaning colleagues who wanted reassurance that Willowend was "staying balanced." It came through denominational language that sounded supportive while gently signalling oversight.

None of it was overt.

That was what made it harder.

One message in particular stayed with Caleb. It came from a pastor he barely knew, someone serving in a larger regional centre.

"I've been hearing good things," the message read. "But also some confusion. Just wanted to check in and see how you're framing what's happening, especially around discernment and leadership."

Caleb read it twice.

There was no accusation in the words. No warning. Just a request for clarity. Still, he felt the familiar pressure rise - the urge to define, to categorise, to make what was happening sound neat and safe.

He didn't respond immediately.

Instead, he went for a walk.

The late afternoon sun sat low over the paddocks, turning the grass a muted gold. Willowend felt unchanged in its physical rhythms. A tractor moved slowly along the edge of town. A dog barked somewhere down the road. Children rode bikes in lazy circles.

It struck Caleb how disconnected these ordinary scenes were from the conversations happening beyond the valley.

Out there, people were trying to name what was happening.

Here, people were simply living it.

That evening, Rachel noticed the weight he carried.

"You're quieter than usual," she said as they prepared dinner.

Caleb smiled faintly. "Am I that obvious?"

"Only to someone who's known you a long time," she replied. He hesitated, then said, "People are starting to ask questions. Not the curious ones. The careful ones."

Rachel nodded slowly. "That was always going to happen."

"Yes," Caleb said. "But knowing it and feeling it are different things."

She handed him a plate. "Are the questions fair?"

"Mostly," he replied. "That's what makes them difficult."

Rachel leaned against the bench. "Then you don't need to answer them defensively."

Caleb looked at her. "You think silence is sometimes an answer."

"I think consistency is," she said. "You don't need to convince people. You just need to keep walking the same way."

He exhaled, grateful. Rachel had a way of naming what mattered without making it sound simplistic.

The next Sunday brought another small test.

During morning tea, a woman Caleb had not met before approached him. She introduced herself politely, then said, "I've been visiting churches in the area."

"That can be a long journey," Caleb replied gently.

She smiled. "I'm not looking for a home. I'm just… observing."

Caleb nodded. "And what are you observing?"

She hesitated. "A lot of warmth. A lot of openness. But also things that could be misunderstood if they're not handled carefully."

Caleb studied her face. There was no malice there. Only caution. "What do you think could be misunderstood?" he asked.

She gestured vaguely toward the room. "People speaking about sensing things. Responding to prayer in ways that are very… personal."

Caleb nodded slowly. "That's fair."

She looked surprised. "You're not offended?"

"No," he replied. "I think misunderstanding is always a possibility when people encounter God honestly."

She considered that. "So you're not trying to stop it?"

"I'm trying to shepherd it," Caleb said. "There's a difference."

She smiled faintly. "That's reassuring."

As she walked away, Caleb realised how important that distinction had become. He was not managing an experience. He was guiding people through formation. And formation could not be rushed, packaged, or defended into submission.

Later that afternoon, Howard joined Caleb on the veranda at the church. They sat side by side, cups of tea growing cold between them.

"You feel it too, don't you?" Howard said.

Caleb nodded. "Yes."

Howard chuckled quietly. "Funny thing is, I'm not worried about what's happening here. I'm worried about what people expect to happen next."

"That's exactly it," Caleb replied. "Expectation can be heavier than opposition."

Howard took a sip. "So what do we do?"

Caleb smiled faintly. "We keep refusing to give people a show."

Howard laughed. "That might disappoint some."

"Probably," Caleb said. "But it might save others."

That evening, Caleb finally replied to the message from the regional pastor. He kept it brief.

"What's happening here isn't a program or a movement," he wrote. "It's a community learning to listen more carefully to God and to one another. We're moving slowly on purpose. Not to avoid risk, but to allow formation to lead experience, not the other way around."

He read it once more, then sent it.

A few minutes later, he closed his laptop and sat quietly in the dim light of the office. He felt no triumph, no relief. Only a steady resolve.

Trust, he was learning, was not tested by storms alone.

It was tested by proximity.

By interest.

By the gentle pressure to become something more visible than faithful.

The renewal in Willowend was still fragile, not because it lacked depth, but because it was being noticed. And noticed things were always tempted to perform.

Caleb prayed simply that night.

Not for protection from scrutiny.

But for wisdom to remain unshaken by it.

Outside, the town settled into evening. Lights flickered on. Doors closed. Ordinary life continued.

And in the quiet between attention and anonymity, Willowend was being shaped again - not by fear, not by ambition, but by the slow, deliberate choice to trust God more than reputation.

That choice, Caleb knew, would be tested again.

And again.

Quietly.

The testing did not crescendo.

It simply stayed.

That, Caleb realised, was what made it formative rather than dramatic. There was no single confrontation to endure, no decisive meeting to navigate, no clear moment when he could say, *This is the challenge and now it is past.* Instead, trust was being tested in the long obedience of ordinary leadership - in restraint, consistency, and the refusal to become reactive.

One Wednesday evening, after the midweek gathering had finished, Caleb lingered in the hall as people drifted away. The conversations had been gentle, reflective. No one had dominated the space. A few people had shared insights that were thoughtful and measured, offered without urgency or performance.

Still, Caleb noticed the way a couple of newer faces watched carefully.

Not critically.

Carefully.

As the last chairs were stacked, one of them approached him. A man in his late forties, neatly dressed, his posture respectful.

"Thank you for tonight," he said. "I appreciate the pace you keep."

Caleb smiled. "I'm glad."

The man hesitated. "May I ask something?"

"You may," Caleb replied.

"How do you stop people from running ahead of themselves?"

"I don't always," he said honestly. "But I try to remind them that depth grows better when roots are allowed to form."

The man nodded slowly. "That's not always the answer people want."

"No," Caleb said. "But it's often the one they need."

The man thanked him and left, and Caleb felt again the quiet weight of leadership in a season where every word seemed to carry more consequence than before.

The following week, the State Baptist Association contacted him. The message was courteous, affirming, and carefully worded. They had received enquiries, they said. Nothing concerning. Simply interest. They wanted to check in, to stay connected, to ensure that Willowend felt supported.

Caleb read the message twice.

Support and scrutiny often shared the same language.

He responded with gratitude, affirming the relationship, offering transparency without defensiveness. He named what was happening plainly, without embellishment or minimisation.

When he finished, he sat back and felt the familiar mixture of relief and weariness. Leadership in quiet seasons demanded more discernment than leadership in crisis. There were no alarms to respond to, only signals to interpret.

Later that evening, Ruth arrived unexpectedly. She had not announced her visit in advance, and when Caleb opened the door and saw her standing there with a small overnight bag, he laughed in surprise.

"You could have warned us," he said, pulling her into a hug.

"I wanted it to be normal," she replied. "Is that still allowed?"

Rachel emerged from the kitchen, delighted, and soon the three of them were sitting around the table, catching up on the ordinary details of life.

Later, when Rachel excused herself to take a phone call, Ruth looked at her father thoughtfully.

"You're carrying something," she said.

Caleb smiled faintly. "You seem to have inherited your mother's perception."

Ruth shrugged. "I work with people for a living. It's hard not to notice."

He hesitated, then said, "Things are going well here. But they're also being watched more closely."

Ruth nodded. "That happens when something feels authentic. People want to know if it's real."

"Yes," Caleb said. "And they want to know whether it will stay real."

She leaned back in her chair. "That's a lot of pressure."

"It would be," he replied, "if we let ourselves become the proof." Ruth studied him. "What do you mean?"

"I mean," Caleb said slowly, "that the moment we start trying to demonstrate God's work rather than steward it, we've already lost our way."

Ruth was quiet for a moment. "I don't know much about church life," she said carefully. "But that sounds true in any organisation I've worked in. The healthiest cultures don't advertise themselves. They just keep showing up."

Caleb smiled. "That's wiser than you realise."

She smiled back. "I realise it enough."

After she went to bed, Caleb sat alone on the veranda, listening to the sounds of the town settling for the night. He thought about Ruth's words, about Mary's steady counsel, about Rachel's quiet grounding presence.

Trust was being tested.

Not only in the community, but in him.

Would he trust that faithfulness was enough when visibility increased? Would he resist the urge to clarify himself constantly, to manage perceptions, to guard the work too tightly?

He thought again of Peter's words - living such good lives that even accusations would be answered by visible goodness.

That kind of life could not be rushed.

It had to be lived.

The next Sunday, Caleb made a deliberate choice. He preached simply. No references to growth. No explanations of what was happening. Just the Word, faithfully handled, offered without commentary on the season itself.

The response was quiet.

And strong.

After the service, one of the long-standing members approached him, her eyes thoughtful.

"I've been nervous," she admitted. "About all the attention."

Caleb nodded. "So have I."

She smiled. "But today reminded me why I stayed all these years. It still feels like church."

Caleb felt something loosen in his chest. "I'm so glad."

As she walked away, he realised that trust was not being tested in the dramatic moments. It was being tested in whether people still recognised the place as home.

That afternoon, as the town moved through its unhurried rhythms, Caleb jotted down another observation in his notebook:

Trust is not proven by growth or criticism,
but by whether we remain ourselves when both arrive.

He closed the book gently.

The testing would continue. He knew that.

But so would the grace.

And for now, that was enough.

Caleb became aware of the tension not because something went wrong, but because nothing did.

The gatherings continued with the same quiet steadiness they had carried for weeks. Teaching remained thoughtful. Prayer remained grounded. People listened well to one another. There were no excesses to correct, no obvious errors to address. And yet beneath the calm, Caleb sensed a subtle tightening, as though the life of the church was beginning to lean slightly toward its edges.

It showed itself in enthusiasm.

Not the reckless kind, but the earnest kind - the kind that wants to be faithful and ends up impatient instead. People lingered longer after gatherings, replaying moments that had moved them. They spoke about what they sensed God might be doing next, sometimes with excitement, sometimes with concern. A few began to frame the renewal as something that needed protecting, as though it might be lost if not handled carefully enough.

Caleb listened.

He resisted the urge to intervene too quickly.

Holding the centre, he was learning, was not about constant correction. It was about modelling a posture that others could trust.

One Thursday morning, he met with a small group of leaders in the church hall. Nothing formal - just tea, notebooks, and the familiar creak of old chairs being pulled into a loose circle. Howard was there, along with two others who had quietly grown into roles of discernment and teaching over the past year. Caleb opened with prayer, then sat back and said, "I'd like to hear what you're noticing."

There was a pause before Anna spoke. She had always been thoughtful, choosing her words carefully.

"I think people are hungry," she said. "Not for something new exactly, but for something real. They're starting to recognise when something carries weight, and when it doesn't."

Howard nodded. "I agree. But hunger can turn into urgency if we're not careful."

Another leader, Mark, leaned forward. "That's what worries me. I'm hearing people ask, 'What's next?' as if we owe them an answer."

Caleb smiled faintly. "Do you think we do?"

Mark hesitated. "No. But they think we do."

Caleb let that sit.

"The danger," he said slowly, "is that the question shifts from 'What is God forming among us?' to 'How do we keep this going?' And those are not the same thing."

Anna nodded. "One trusts God. The other trusts momentum."

The group grew quiet.

Caleb felt grateful for the way the conversation unfolded - no alarm, no defensiveness. Just honesty. This was the centre he wanted to protect. A place where discernment was shared, not hoarded.

Later that day, Caleb walked through town, stopping to speak with people he passed. It grounded him in the ordinary rhythms that had always shaped Willowend. Growth had not changed the weather. It had not changed the pace of farming or the smell of bread from the bakery. It had not altered the way people greeted one another by name.

And yet, something beneath those rhythms was deepening.

At the post office, a woman he barely knew said quietly, "I've started praying again. I didn't tell anyone. I just wanted you to know."

Caleb thanked her, aware of how many stories like that were unfolding quietly, without announcement.

That evening, Ruth joined him on the veranda. She had been working remotely for a few days, her laptop often open on the dining table, her phone buzzing with the language of corporate urgency that felt slightly foreign in Willowend.

"I sat in on the midweek gathering," she said. "I didn't say anything."

Caleb smiled. "You didn't need to."

She watched the light fade over the paddocks. "It's interesting," she said. "At work, whenever something gains traction, the first thing people do is build systems around it. KPIs. Frameworks. Measures."

"And here?" Caleb asked.

"Here, you're doing the opposite," she replied. "You're slowing it down."

Caleb nodded. "Because the work isn't ours to scale."

Ruth turned to him. "That's counterintuitive."

"Yes," he said. "And costly."

She considered that. "Does it scare you?"

"Sometimes," Caleb admitted. "Not because I'm afraid of losing control, but because I know how easily people can confuse faithfulness with effectiveness."

Ruth smiled slightly. "You sound like someone who's had to unlearn a few things."

Caleb laughed quietly. "More than a few."

As the weeks unfolded, Caleb became increasingly aware that leadership in this season required a different kind of attentiveness. He was no longer simply responding to need. He was watching for imbalance. For moments when enthusiasm tipped toward pressure, or when discernment hardened into suspicion.

One Sunday, following the morning service, a well-meaning member approached Caleb.

"I think we need to teach more on the gifts," they said. "People are asking questions. We should give them answers."

Caleb nodded. "What kind of answers?"

"Clear ones," the person replied. "So people don't get confused."

Caleb smiled gently. "Sometimes clarity is a gift. Sometimes it's a shortcut."

The person frowned slightly. "What do you mean?"

"I mean," Caleb said, choosing his words carefully, "that formation doesn't always come through explanation. Sometimes it comes through patience."

They nodded, not entirely convinced, but willing to trust.

That was enough.

That night, Caleb sat alone in the sanctuary, the lights dimmed, the room quiet except for the faint hum of the fans. He thought of the phrase that had begun to shape his prayers in recent weeks.

Hold the centre.

Not hold control.

Not hold attention.

But hold the place where humility and courage met.

He opened his notebook and wrote:

The centre is not neutral.
It is active.
It resists drift by staying rooted.

He closed the book and sat quietly, aware that this season would not announce its challenges loudly. They would come softly, disguised as opportunity. And that, he knew, would require more discernment than any crisis ever had.

When he finally stood to leave, Caleb felt neither anxious nor triumphant. Only steady. The centre was holding. For now. And tomorrow, he would choose to hold it again.

The first real strain appeared not in conflict, but in expectation. Caleb felt it most clearly in the conversations that began with gratitude and ended with anticipation. People spoke warmly of what God was doing, then leaned forward slightly, as though waiting for him to outline the next step. It was subtle - a pause, a lifted eyebrow, a hopeful tone that carried the unspoken question.

What happens now?

Caleb did not resent the question. It came from a good place. People wanted to respond well. They wanted to be faithful. But he was increasingly convinced that the most faithful response in this season was not to answer too quickly.

One Monday afternoon, he met with a group who had begun gathering informally to pray before work. They were thoughtful people, earnest, and genuinely attentive to one another. After prayer, one of them spoke.

"We've been sensing that we should do more together," she said. "Maybe something regular. Something that helps people engage more deeply."

Caleb nodded. "Tell me what you mean by 'more.'"

She hesitated. "I'm not entirely sure. That's why we wanted to talk."

Another added, "It feels like there's momentum, and we don't want to waste it."

Caleb let the word settle.

Momentum.

He had heard it many times before, in other contexts, other seasons. Momentum was not wrong, but it was impatient. It assumed that movement must be sustained through effort rather than trust.

"What if," Caleb said gently, "the work right now is not to add more, but to deepen what's already forming?"

They looked uncertain.

"That feels risky," someone said.

"Yes," Caleb agreed. "But so does building too quickly."

They sat quietly, absorbing that.

"I'm not saying no," Caleb continued. "I'm saying not yet. And not because I want to slow things down artificially, but because I want to make sure whatever grows has room for roots."

They left thoughtful, not energised in the way they had perhaps hoped, but steadied. Caleb counted that as a quiet success.

Later that week, Howard stopped by the office.

"I think you're doing the right thing," he said without preamble. Caleb smiled. "That's reassuring."

Howard sat down heavily. "I've seen churches get addicted to momentum. It's like sugar. Feels good at first. Leaves you hollow later."

Caleb nodded. "People confuse activity with life."

"Yes," Howard said. "And leadership with control."

They shared a knowing look.

Still, holding the centre required more than discernment. It required visibility. Caleb knew that if he retreated too far into restraint, others would fill the gap with their own assumptions.

So he began to speak differently.

Not more often, but more intentionally.

When people asked what was happening, he named formation rather than growth. When they asked him where things were heading, he spoke about faithfulness rather than outcomes.

When they asked what they should do, he invited them to pay attention to what God was already stirring in their own lives.

Some found that liberating. Others found it frustrating.

One Sunday afternoon, Ruth raised the question from her own angle.

"You know," she said, "in my world, if something is working and the leadership doesn't capitalise on it, people will assume incompetence."

Caleb laughed softly. "That's encouraging."

She smiled. "I don't mean you. I mean the mindset."

"Yes," he replied. "And churches can fall into the same trap, just with different language."

Ruth considered that. "How do you stop people from projecting expectations onto you?"

Caleb thought for a moment. "I don't think you stop it," he said. "You absorb it without letting it shape you."

She nodded slowly. "That sounds exhausting."

"It can be," he admitted. "But it's also clarifying. It forces you to ask who you're actually accountable to."

The pressure intensified slightly when a regional gathering was announced. Nothing alarming - just an invitation for pastors to share what was happening in their contexts.

Caleb felt the weight of it immediately.

Share.

Explain.

Frame.

Rachel noticed his hesitation and said, "You don't owe anyone a performance," she said.

"I know," Caleb replied. "But I also don't want to be dismissive."

She nodded. "Then be honest. And restrained."

At the next regional Pastors gathering, Caleb spoke briefly. He described a church learning to listen, to wait, to respond gently to God and to one another. He avoided dramatic language. He did not offer strategies or models.

The response was mixed.

A few thanked him warmly. Others asked practical questions he did not answer fully. One pastor looked faintly disappointed.

Afterwards, a colleague approached him quietly.

"You're making people uncomfortable," he said, not unkindly.

Caleb smiled. "That's not my intention."

"I know," the man replied. "But people want something they can replicate."

Caleb nodded. "That's exactly the problem."

Back in Willowend, the effects of that wider attention filtered slowly through the community. Nothing overt. Just a slight shift in tone. A few people asked whether they were doing enough. Others wondered aloud if they were missing something.

Caleb addressed it one evening during a small gathering.

"Faithfulness isn't measured by intensity," he said. "And it isn't measured by visibility. It's measured by love, patience, and obedience over time."

Someone asked, "But how do we know we are not just being complacent?"

Caleb smiled gently. "Complacency avoids cost. What we're doing is costly. It asks us to stay attentive without being driven." That seemed to settle the room.

As the season progressed, Caleb found himself returning again and again to the same internal prayer.

Keep us centred. Not successful. Not impressive. Centred.

He understood now that holding the centre was not passive. It required constant recalibration. A willingness to disappoint some expectations in order to remain faithful to the deeper work unfolding.

One evening, sitting alone with his notebook, Caleb wrote:

The centre is where trust replaces urgency.

He closed the book and felt a quiet resolve settle in him. The pressure would not disappear. If anything, it would increase. But so would the grace to meet it. And tomorrow, once again, he would choose to hold the centre - not tightly, but faithfully.

The moment Caleb realised how fragile the centre could be, came during a conversation that seemed, at first, entirely ordinary. He was standing outside the church after a Sunday service, the late-morning sun warming the steps, when a man he respected deeply approached him. The man had been part of Willowend for years, steady and faithful, not given to drama or strong opinions.

"I wanted to say thank you," he began. "The church feels alive again."

Caleb smiled. "I'm glad."

The man hesitated, then continued. "But I've been wondering… how long can we keep it like this?"

Caleb tilted his head slightly. "What do you mean?"

"Like this," the man said, gesturing vaguely toward the building. "Unplanned. Open-ended. Surely at some point we'll need to formalise things a bit more."

Caleb nodded slowly. "Perhaps."

The man looked relieved. "Good. I just didn't want us to drift."

After he walked away, Caleb remained on the steps longer than usual, the question lingering.

How long can we keep it like this?

It was not an unreasonable question. In fact, it was a responsible one. But Caleb sensed how easily responsibility could tip into control, and how quickly the centre could be crowded out by well-intentioned certainty.

That afternoon, he walked home with Rachel, neither of them speaking much at first. Eventually she said, "You're turning something over."

"Yes," Caleb replied. "People are starting to feel the tension between freedom and structure."

She nodded. "That's inevitable."

"I know," he said. "But I don't want the answer to come from anxiety."

Rachel smiled gently. "Then it will need to come from trust."

That evening, Caleb sat with his Bible open but unread, his thoughts moving slowly. He realised that holding the centre was not only about resisting pressure from outside. It was also about recognising the subtle pressures that rose from within the community itself.

People wanted to belong.

People wanted to understand.

People wanted reassurance that they were doing this right.

And beneath all of that lay the deeper longing to be safe.

Caleb understood that longing well. He felt it too.

The following week, he met with a small group that had begun to take on informal leadership responsibilities. They gathered around a table scattered with notebooks and half-drunk mugs of tea.

"I want to talk about balance," Caleb said. "Not as a strategy, but as a posture."

They listened attentively.

"We're learning to listen to God together," he continued. "That's a gift. But listening doesn't mean we rush to interpret everything. Sometimes it means we let things remain unresolved for a while."

One of them spoke up. "That makes people uneasy."

"Yes," Caleb said. "Because uncertainty exposes what we rely on."

Another added, "Some people are just worried we might lose momentum."

Caleb nodded. "Momentum isn't really something we need to preserve. Faithfulness is."

They sat with that.

"I'm not against structure," Caleb went on. "But structure should serve formation, not replace it. When we build too quickly, we risk protecting ourselves from the very work God is doing."

There was a quiet agreement in the room, not enthusiastic but sincere. These were people willing to hold tension without forcing resolution.

That gave Caleb hope.

Still, the strain of the season began to show in small ways. He noticed it in himself when he felt the urge to pre-empt questions in his preaching, to clarify too much, to explain away ambiguity before it had time to do its work.

Each time, he pulled back.

He reminded himself that leadership was not about managing perception.

It was about stewarding presence.

One evening, Ruth joined him in the kitchen while Rachel was out. She leaned against the bench, watching him absently.

"You seem tired," she said.

Caleb smiled. "Perceptive as always."

"Is it the workload?" she asked.

"Not exactly," he replied. "It's the attentiveness. Staying present to what's happening without trying to control it."

Ruth nodded. "That's hard in any environment. Especially when people start projecting expectations."

"Yes," Caleb said. "And churches are particularly good at projecting spiritual expectations."

She smiled faintly. "Do you ever wish it would all settle down again?"

Caleb considered the question carefully. "Sometimes," he admitted. "But then I remember that settling isn't the same as being grounded."

Ruth looked thoughtful. "I see that at work too. The healthiest teams aren't always the calmest ones. They're the ones that can sit with tension without panicking."

Caleb smiled. "You're teaching me now."

She laughed softly. "Don't tell anyone."

As the season continued, Caleb became increasingly aware that holding the centre required courage as much as restraint. It meant saying no to some good ideas. It meant disappointing people who wanted clarity now. It meant trusting that God was not in a hurry, even when others were.

One Sunday morning, as he stood at the front of the sanctuary before the service began, Caleb looked out over the gathered community. The room was fuller than it had been a year earlier.

Faces were more varied. Stories more layered.

Yet beneath the diversity, there was a shared stillness.

Not silence.

Stillness.

It struck Caleb that the centre was not a place of neutrality. It was a place of active attentiveness. A place where humility, patience, and courage met.

During the service, nothing remarkable happened. No striking insight. No emotional swell. Just Scripture read faithfully, prayer offered simply, people listening well.

And somehow, that felt like the point.

After the service, as Caleb walked through the town later that day, he felt a quiet confidence settle in him. Not confidence in outcomes or growth, but confidence in the posture they were cultivating.

The centre was holding.

Not because it was being guarded aggressively, but because it was being inhabited faithfully.

That night, Caleb returned to his notebook and wrote:

The centre is not preserved by caution alone,
but by courage that refuses to rush.

He closed the book and sat quietly, aware that the season ahead would continue to test that courage.

But for now, Willowend was learning something rare.

How to grow without grasping.

How to change without losing itself.

How to hold the centre - not perfectly, but faithfully.

And tomorrow, once again, Caleb would choose that work anew.

16. WHERE GROWTH TOUCHES ORDINARY LIVES

The first sign that the renewal was reaching far deeper into Willowend did not come from a meeting or a gathering.

It came from the servo.

Caleb stopped there late one afternoon, more out of habit than need. The day had been warm without being oppressive, the kind of heat that settled into the town quietly rather than announcing itself. The forecourt was empty except for a ute parked crookedly near the air pump.

Amelia stood behind the counter, sleeves rolled up, hair pulled back in a way that suggested she had stopped thinking about how she looked sometime before lunch.

She smiled when she saw him, but it was different from the cautious smiles of earlier months. This one carried ease.

"Afternoon, Pastor," she said. "You look like you have been walking again."

Caleb smiled. "Is it that obvious?"

"You only come in this late when you've been thinking," she replied. "Fuel, or just an excuse?"

"Probably both," he said.

She rang it up without rushing. As he reached for his wallet, she hesitated.

"Can I ask you something?" she said.

"Of course."

She leaned slightly on the counter. "Do you ever feel like God asks you to pay attention to things you'd rather ignore?"

Caleb considered the question carefully. "Quite often," he said. "Why do you ask?"

Amelia glanced toward the window, as though checking that no one else was listening. "I've been noticing people lately. Really noticing them. Not just what they say, but what they don't."

Caleb nodded slowly. "And how does that feel?"

She exhaled. "Uncomfortable … and… necessary."

He smiled gently. "That sounds like discernment beginning to stretch its legs."

She blinked. "You don't think I'm just overthinking?"

"No," Caleb said. "Overthinking usually leads inward. What you're describing sounds outward."

She absorbed that quietly.

"I don't want to become strange," she said after a moment. "I just keep sensing when someone may be carrying more than they're saying. And sometimes I don't know whether to speak or stay quiet."

Caleb nodded. "That tension is part of learning to listen well. Discernment isn't about always having something to say. Often it's about knowing when silence is the gift."

Amelia smiled faintly. "That's a relief."

As Caleb walked back out to his ute, he felt a familiar warmth settle in him. Amelia's faith had not grown loud. It had grown attentive. That mattered more than enthusiasm ever could.

Later that evening, Caleb noticed Daniel sitting on the edge of the church steps, headphones around his neck, phone in his hand but unused. He looked up when Caleb approached, startled, as though he had not expected to be seen.

"Hey," Daniel said.

"Hey yourself," Caleb replied. "You waiting for someone?"

Daniel shrugged. "Not really. Just needed some quiet."

Caleb sat beside him, the timber still warm from the day. "Quiet can be good."

Daniel nodded. "Sometimes. Other times it just makes your thoughts louder."

Caleb smiled. "That's true."

They sat in silence for a while, watching the last of the light slip behind the buildings across the road. Daniel broke it eventually. "I've been thinking about helping out more," he said. "Not on the platform or anything. Just… practical stuff."

"That's good," Caleb replied. "What kind of things?"

Daniel shrugged again. "Whatever needs doing. Chairs. Sound. Helping people get home if they need it."

Caleb nodded. "Those things matter."

Daniel hesitated. "I just don't want people to think I'm trying to be someone I'm not."

Caleb turned to him. "Who do you think they'd think you're trying to be?"

Daniel frowned. "More spiritual than I actually am."

Caleb smiled gently. "Serving doesn't make you more spiritual. It makes you available."

Daniel let that settle. "That sounds less scary."

"Good," Caleb said. "Because fear is usually a clear sign we are imagining expectations that no one has actually placed on us."

Daniel laughed quietly. "I do that a lot."

"Most people do," Caleb replied.

As they stood to leave, Daniel said, "I might come by tomorrow and see what needs doing."

"I'll be here," Caleb said. "But don't feel obliged."

Daniel nodded. "I know."

Walking home, Caleb felt the weight of something shifting. Not dramatically. Not quickly. But steadily. The renewal was no longer only shaping how people gathered. It was shaping how they noticed one another.

The following Sunday, the effect became clearer.

During morning tea, Amelia found herself in a long conversation with a woman she barely knew, listening more than she spoke. Daniel helped stack chairs without being asked, slipping in and out of conversations quietly. Neither of them drew attention to themselves. And yet both carried a presence that was different from before.

Caleb watched from a distance, resisting the urge to intervene or interpret. He had learned that naming things too quickly could flatten them.

Instead, he prayed.

Keep this gentle, he thought. Keep it human.

After the service, Mary approached Caleb, her walking stick tapping lightly on the concrete.

"They're growing," she said simply.

Caleb smiled. "Yes."

"Not fast," Mary added. "But true."

"That's the hope," Caleb replied.

Mary's eyes were sharp and kind. "You'll need to protect that."

Caleb nodded. "I know."

"Not from danger," she continued. "From haste."

As the week unfolded, Caleb found himself more aware o4f how growth showed itself in ordinary decisions. A willingness to wait. A readiness to serve without recognition. A growing sensitivity to one another's burdens.

None of it would impress anyone looking for signs of revival. But it was precisely the kind of growth that endured.

One evening, as Caleb locked up the church, he noticed Daniel had left his headphones on a chair. He picked them up and smiled to himself. Small things. Ordinary things. Signs of someone beginning to belong.

Across town, Amelia closed the servo later than usual, pausing before turning off the lights to pray quietly for a customer who had left with tears in her eyes.

Neither moment would be recorded.

Neither would be celebrated.

And yet Caleb sensed that these were the places where the renewal was truly taking root.

Not in what was said aloud.

But in how people began to live differently when no one was watching.

He walked home under a sky already deepening toward night, aware that Willowend was entering a new phase. One where growth would be measured not by numbers or attention.

But by the quiet courage of ordinary lives being gently reshaped. If the renewal was shaping people quietly, it was also beginning to expose places of hesitation that had long gone unexamined.

Caleb became aware of this one morning when he received an email from a long-standing member of the church. The message was warm, affirming, and carefully worded. It expressed gratitude for the season Willowend was in, then gently raised a concern.

"I'm grateful for what God is doing," the message read. "But I'm also wondering how we make sure people don't start assuming things that haven't been taught."

Caleb read it twice.

There was no accusation in the words. No resistance. Just a question shaped by caution. He recognised it immediately as the voice of someone who cared deeply about the church, and who was feeling the subtle unease that comes when familiar patterns begin to shift.

He did not reply straight away. Instead, he went for a walk.

The road out past the silos was quiet at that hour, the air already warming, the smell of dust and grass hanging low. As he walked, Caleb reflected on how often fear entered through concern that sounded reasonable. People were not afraid of God's work. They were afraid of misunderstanding it, of losing clarity, of being caught off-balance.

That fear deserved patience, not correction.

That afternoon, Caleb met Daniel at the church. True to his word, the young man had turned up quietly, asking what needed doing. Caleb handed him a small list - nothing significant. Chairs to straighten. Cables to coil. A cupboard to tidy that no one had opened in months.

Daniel worked without comment, occasionally humming to himself, occasionally stopping to ask a question that revealed his careful attention.

"You want these stacked the same way as before?" he asked.

"Yes," Caleb replied. "Familiarity helps people feel at ease."

Daniel nodded. "I've noticed that."

Caleb smiled. "You notice a lot."

Daniel shrugged. "I think I always did. I just didn't know what to do with it."

They worked in companionable silence for a while before Daniel spoke again.

"I don't always know where I fit," he said quietly.

Caleb paused. "What makes you say that?"

Daniel leaned against the wall, thinking. "Everyone seems… confident. Or at least settled. I feel like I'm still figuring out what I even believe half the time."

Caleb met his gaze. "That doesn't disqualify you."

Daniel frowned. "It doesn't?"

"No," Caleb said. "It makes you honest."

Daniel let out a breath he hadn't realised he was holding. "That's good to hear."

Later that day, Caleb found himself back at the servo. Not for fuel this time, but because Amelia had left a message asking if he could stop by when he had a moment. She met him outside, wiping her hands on a cloth.

"I didn't want to say this in front of anyone," she said, leading him to a quieter corner near the cool room. "But something happened this morning."

Caleb nodded. "Tell me."

She hesitated, then said, "A man came in - someone passing through. He was angry. Not at me exactly, just… carrying something. And as he spoke, I kept feeling like his anger wasn't the real issue."

Caleb listened carefully.

"I didn't say anything about it," she continued. "I just listened. And then I asked him how long it had been since he'd slept properly. He just stared at me. Then he sat down and started crying."

Caleb was quiet for a moment. "What did you do?"

"I made him a coffee," Amelia said. "And I listened some more."

Caleb smiled. "That was enough."

She looked uncertain. "It felt like more than coincidence."

"It probably was," Caleb replied. "But notice what you didn't do."

Amelia frowned slightly. "What?"

"You didn't try to fix him. You didn't label what you sensed. You didn't turn it into a moment."

She nodded slowly. "I just… stayed present."

"Yes," Caleb said. "That's discernment maturing."

She exhaled, relief evident on her face. "I was worried I was imagining it."

Caleb shook his head. "Imagining tends to centre on ourselves. What you described centred on him."

As he left the servo, Caleb felt again the quiet joy of watching faith grow into attentiveness rather than confidence. Amelia was not becoming bolder in the way some people expected. She was becoming kinder, more patient, more aware.

That evening, Caleb gathered a small group of leaders for a conversation he had been sensing was necessary. Not a meeting, exactly. More a space to listen together.

They sat in a loose circle, the room warm, windows open to catch the breeze.

"I want to talk about how growth feels," Caleb began. "Not what we think about it, but how it lands in us."

There was a pause before one of them spoke.

"I feel grateful," she said. "And unsettled."

Another nodded. "I'm excited. But I am also afraid of doing something wrong."

Howard spoke last. "I feel protective. And I don't like that about myself."

Caleb nodded. "Those are honest responses."

He leaned forward slightly. "What we're experiencing isn't just renewal. It's exposure. Growth reveals where we rely on certainty instead of trust."

They sat quietly, letting that sink in.

"We don't need to resolve these feelings," Caleb continued. "We just need to name them. And then choose how we respond."

"And how do we respond?" someone asked.

"With patience," Caleb replied. "With listening. With restraint when we're tempted to rush."

Howard smiled faintly. "You're saying the work isn't to get it right, but to stay present."

"Yes," Caleb said. "Exactly that."

After the group dispersed, Caleb remained in the hall, stacking chairs slowly. He felt tired but not depleted. The tiredness came from attentiveness, not anxiety.

As he locked the doors, he thought again of Daniel quietly serving without needing to be noticed, of Amelia listening without needing to interpret, of leaders willing to admit their unease rather than hide it behind certainty.

This was how growth touched ordinary lives.

Not by elevating them.

But by deepening them.

Walking home under the fading light, Caleb felt a quiet, deep confidence settle in him. The renewal was no longer something he worried might drift or fracture. It was becoming woven into the fabric of daily life.

Not perfectly.

But faithfully.

And that, he knew, was how it would endure.

By the end of the week, Caleb had stopped trying to track where the renewal was most visible. It was everywhere and nowhere at once.

It showed up in conversations that ended differently than they once had. In pauses where people chose not to fill the silence. In small acts of care that were offered without being announced or organised. The work was no longer confined to gatherings or conversations about discernment. It was moving outward, settling into the ordinary patterns of Willowend.

Caleb noticed it one evening as he locked up the church and found Daniel waiting nearby, hands shoved into his pockets, kicking lightly at the gravel.

"You heading home?" Caleb asked.

Daniel nodded. "Yeah. Just thought I'd walk instead of riding tonight."

Caleb smiled. "Mind some company?"

Daniel shook his head. "Not at all."

They walked together along the quiet street, the town settling into its usual rhythm. A few houses glowed warmly behind curtains. Somewhere a radio played softly.

After a few minutes, Daniel spoke. "I helped Mrs Carter this afternoon."

Caleb glanced at him. "Did you?"

"She was trying to move some stuff in her shed. I was just passing and asked if she wanted a hand." He shrugged. "It wasn't much."

Caleb nodded. "It rarely is."

Daniel hesitated. "She started talking. About her husband. About how lonely it gets sometimes."

Caleb listened.

"I didn't know what to say," Daniel continued. "So, I just kept lifting boxes and let her talk."

Caleb smiled gently. "That sounds like exactly the right thing."

Daniel looked relieved. "I thought maybe I should have prayed with her or something."

"You might one day," Caleb said. "But today, you listened. That matters."

They walked a little further before Daniel said, "I don't feel like I'm doing anything spiritual."

Caleb stopped and turned to him. "Let me tell you something," he said quietly. "Most of the most spiritual things I've ever seen didn't look spiritual at the time."

Daniel absorbed that.

As they parted ways, Caleb watched Daniel head down the street, shoulders relaxed, steps unhurried. There was no sense of achievement in him. Only a growing ease, as though he was learning how to inhabit his own faith without forcing it.

The next morning, Amelia appeared at the church unexpectedly. "I had a day off," she said, holding a takeaway coffee. "Thought I'd see if you were around."

Caleb smiled. "Come in."

They sat in the small office, the sunlight was filtering through the window.

"I'm realising something," Amelia said after a moment. "This faith thing - it's not adding things to my life. It's changing how I pay attention."

Caleb nodded. "That's a good way of putting it."

She leaned back. "I used to rush people. Not deliberately. Just... because that's what you do in a servo. Keep things moving. Now I find myself slowing down without thinking about it."

He smiled. "That kind of change usually sticks."

She hesitated. "But it's tiring."

"Yes," Caleb agreed. "Love often is."

She laughed quietly. "No one told me that part."

Caleb smiled. "They should."

After she left, Caleb sat quietly, reflecting on how differently the two journeys were unfolding. Amelia's faith was becoming gentler, more grounded. Daniel's was tentative but sincere, finding expression in service rather than certainty.

Neither path was impressive.

Both were real.

That Sunday, Caleb chose not to reference growth or renewal at all. He preached from a simple passage about faithfulness in small things, about seeds growing unseen. He watched as people listened, some nodding, others simply sitting with the words.

After the service, a woman approached him whom he had not spoken with much before.

"I think I understand now," she said. "Why you keep saying we don't need to rush."

Caleb smiled. "What do you understand?"

"That God seems to be doing His work in the margins," she replied. "Not in the spotlight."

Caleb nodded. "That's often where it lasts."

Later that afternoon, Mary stopped him as he was leaving the church.

"They're settling," she said.

Caleb smiled. "I think so."

She tapped her walking stick lightly on the ground. "That's when you need to be most attentive."

"Yes," Caleb said. "Because it's too easy to mistake settling for completion."

Mary's eyes twinkled. "You're learning."

"I am," Caleb replied.

That evening, Caleb sat on the veranda at home, watching the last light drain from the sky. Rachel sat beside him, neither of them speaking for a while.

"Something feels different," she said eventually.

"It does," Caleb replied. "Less fragile. More woven in."

She nodded. "That's what I hoped for."

He smiled. "Me too."

As darkness settled over Willowend, Caleb felt a quiet gratitude rise in him. The renewal had not turned the town upside down. It had turned people toward one another. Toward patience. Toward presence.

This was not the kind of story that would travel far or impress many.

But it was the kind that endured.

And as Caleb rose to go inside, he knew the work ahead would not be about protecting something extraordinary.

It would be about continuing to notice the ordinary places where God was already at work - and choosing, again and again, not to rush past them.

That, he was learning, was where faith grew best.

17. WHEN GROWTH CREATES FRICTION

The first disagreement arrived quietly.

So quietly, in fact, that Caleb almost missed it.

It surfaced not as conflict, but as contrast - two conversations, held only a day apart, that pulled in subtly different directions. Each was sincere. Each was grounded in care for the church. And yet, when Caleb held them side by side, he could feel the faint tension beginning to form.

The first came from a woman who had been part of Willowend for years. She spoke with affection, her voice warm.

"I love what's happening," she said. "But I'm finding it harder to know where I fit. Things feel… different. Less predictable."

Caleb nodded, listening carefully.

"It's not bad," she added quickly. "Just unfamiliar."

The second conversation came from someone newer. Younger. Less cautious.

"I feel like we're holding back," he said. "Like we're afraid to step into what God might be doing."

Caleb heard the echo between the two voices - one wary of losing familiarity, the other eager to move forward. Neither was wrong. Both were responding honestly to change.

That was when Caleb realised the renewal had reached a new stage.

It was no longer only forming individuals.

It was beginning to test relationships.

Later that week, Howard raised the issue more directly.

"I think we're starting to feel the stretch," he said as they sat together in the church office. "Nothing sharp yet. But people are noticing differences in expectations."

Caleb nodded. "I've sensed that too."

Howard leaned back. "This is where churches often stumble. Not because of doctrine or behaviour, but because people start assuming the other side doesn't care as much as they do."

"Yes," Caleb said. "When in fact they often care just as deeply - just differently."

That distinction mattered. Caleb knew from experience just how quickly misinterpretation could turn into distance if it is left unattended.

He began to watch more closely.

Not for arguments, but for moments of misunderstanding. A comment that landed awkwardly. A suggestion that was received defensively. A silence that lingered a little too long.

One such moment occurred during a small group gathering midweek.

The group had been discussing a passage about unity, the conversation flowing easily until someone said, "I think God is inviting us to take more risks together."

Another responded almost immediately, "I think God is asking us to be careful."

The room fell quiet. Both statements were true. But they were heard as opposites.

Caleb watched as people shifted in their seats, unsure how to hold the tension. He resisted the urge to smooth it over too quickly.

Instead, he asked a question.

"What kind of risks do you think God invites us into?" he said gently.

The first person spoke about vulnerability, about speaking honestly, about stepping beyond comfort.

"And what kind of care do you think God is asking of us?" Caleb asked.

The second spoke about discernment, about not rushing, about protecting those who were still finding their footing.

As the conversation unfolded, the tension softened. People began to see that the difference was not between faith and fear, but between different expressions of care.

Afterwards, Daniel approached Caleb quietly.

"That was uncomfortable," he said.

"Yes," Caleb replied. "But useful."

Daniel nodded. "I used to think disagreement meant something was wrong."

Caleb smiled. "Sometimes it means something is growing."

That insight stayed with Daniel.

Later that day, Caleb encountered Amelia again at the servo. She looked more tired than usual, her smile a little thinner.

"You all right?" Caleb asked.

She shrugged. "Just thinking."

"That can do it," he replied lightly.

She leaned against the counter. "Two people told me completely different things today. Both wanted advice. Both were convinced they were right."

Caleb smiled. "Welcome to discernment in community."

She frowned. "Is it supposed to feel this complicated?"

"Yes," Caleb said. "Because God works with people, not principles."

She sighed. "I wish that made it easier."

Caleb chuckled. "It makes it truer."

Amelia hesitated, then said, "I didn't tell either of them what to do. I just listened. But I worried that I should have been clearer."

"You honoured them by listening," Caleb replied. "Clarity often comes after people feel heard."

She nodded slowly. "That helps."

As the days passed, Caleb noticed more moments like these. Small points of friction where growth rubbed against habit. Where enthusiasm met caution. Where new voices unsettled old rhythms.

None of it escalated.

But all of it mattered.

One evening, Caleb sat with his notebook open, reflecting on what he was seeing.

Friction isn't failure, he wrote. *It's evidence of movement.*

He paused, then added another line.

The danger is not disagreement, but withdrawal.

That was what he wanted to guard against - people retreating into camps, into assumptions, into quiet resentment.

The following Sunday, Caleb addressed the issue gently, without naming it directly.

"Growth doesn't always feel harmonious," he said. "Sometimes it feels awkward. Sometimes it stretches our patience. That doesn't mean something has gone wrong. It means we're being asked to learn how to love across difference."

He watched the room as the words settled.

Some nodded.

Some looked thoughtful.

Some looked relieved.

After the service, a long-time member approached him. "I didn't realise I was feeling defensive until you said that," she admitted. "I don't want to be."

Caleb smiled. "Awareness is a good place to start."

That afternoon, as Caleb walked through town, he felt the weight of leadership shift again. The work ahead was no longer only about holding the centre. It was about helping people stay connected when the centre began to feel contested.

Not loudly.

But quietly.

That evening, as he locked the church doors, Caleb prayed simply.

"Teach us how to disagree without dividing, teach us how to grow without turning on one another."

The renewal was deepening.

And with depth came complexity.

Caleb knew this was a necessary stage.

The question was not whether friction would appear.

It already had.

The question was whether Willowend would learn to hold it with grace - or allow it to harden into distance.

As he walked home under a sky thick with stars, Caleb sensed that the next season would require a new kind of courage.

Not the courage to act.

But the courage to stay present when things felt uncomfortable. That, he suspected, would shape the story of Willowend as much as anything that had come before.

The friction did not settle evenly.

Some people carried it lightly, curious rather than threatened. Others felt it more deeply, as though the ground beneath familiar certainties had begun to tilt. Caleb became increasingly aware that the same moments were being interpreted in different ways, not because people were listening poorly, but because they were listening through different histories.

One afternoon, he sat with a couple who had been part of Willowend for decades. Their faith had been steady, faithful, shaped by routine and perseverance rather than intensity. They spoke kindly, but with an edge of uncertainty.

"It's not that we don't trust what's happening," one of them said. "We just don't recognise the church the way we used to."

Caleb nodded. "What feels unfamiliar?"

"It used to be simpler," the other replied. "We knew what to expect when we came through the doors."

Caleb let that sit. "Simplicity can be a gift," he said. "But sometimes it's also a season rather than a permanent state."

They exchanged a glance.

"We're not asking for things to go back," one added quickly. "We just don't want to feel left behind."

Caleb felt the weight of that sentence.

"Being left behind isn't the same as being stretched," he said gently. "But they can feel similar when change comes quietly."

They left without full resolution, but with something important named. Caleb knew that naming mattered. Unspoken fears had a way of growing sharper in the dark.

Later that week, Daniel experienced friction from the other side. He was helping set up chairs before a gathering when another young man, newer to the church, leaned over and said, "Don't you think we could do more? It feels like we're playing it safe."

Daniel paused, chair half-lifted. "I don't know," he said honestly. "I think we're learning."

The man frowned. "Learning what?"

"How to just be together," Daniel replied. "Before we try to be impressive."

The man looked unconvinced. "That sounds like hesitation."

Daniel felt his chest tighten. For a moment, he wondered if the other was right. He finished stacking the chairs in silence, unsure whether he had defended something true or simply avoided conflict.

That evening, Daniel found Caleb and updated him about the exchange.

"I didn't know what to say," he admitted. "I didn't want to argue. But I also didn't want to pretend."

Caleb nodded. "What you did was honest."

"It didn't feel strong," Daniel said.

"Strength isn't always loud," Caleb replied. "Sometimes it's choosing not to push when pushing would divide."

Daniel considered that. "So friction doesn't mean I failed?"

"No," Caleb said. "It means you're paying attention."

Amelia, too, felt the strain in her own way. A regular customer at the servo, someone she had known casually for years, leaned across the counter one morning and said, "I hear you've gone all churchy lately."

Amelia laughed awkwardly. "I still sell fuel."

The woman smiled, but there was a hint of distance in her eyes. "Just be careful you don't start seeing everything as spiritual. Some things are just life."

Amelia felt the comment more than she expected. It stayed with her long after the customer drove away. That afternoon, she found herself replaying the words, wondering if she had changed too much, too quickly.

She mentioned it to Caleb when he stopped by later that day.

"But I also don't want to pretend nothing's different."

Caleb nodded. "Both of those desires are understandable."

"So what do I do?" she asked.

"Stay yourself," Caleb replied. "Not the version you were, and not the version you think you should become. Just the person you are now."

She exhaled slowly. "That's harder than it sounds."

"Yes," he agreed. "Because it means letting people adjust at their own pace."

As these small points of friction accumulated, Caleb began to address them more intentionally, not by resolving each one, but by shaping the culture around them.

In one gathering, he said, "We're going to misunderstand one another sometimes. That doesn't mean we've failed. It means we're human."

In another, he reminded them, "Discomfort is not the same as danger. And caution is not the same as fear."

People listened.

Some relaxed.

Some remained guarded.

But fewer withdrew.

Caleb noticed that the most significant shifts were happening in conversations that followed these moments, not during them. People began to ask one another questions instead of making assumptions. They paused before responding. They checked their interpretations.

It wasn't smooth.

But it was real.

One evening, Howard joined Caleb for a walk through town. The air was cool, the streets quiet.

"You're doing well," Howard said suddenly.

Caleb smiled faintly. "That sounds like encouragement with an asterisk."

Howard chuckled. "Maybe. I just want you to know that not everyone will say it out loud."

Caleb nodded. "I know."

Howard grew serious. "This is the part where leaders sometimes panic. They see friction and try to eliminate it."

"Yes," Caleb said. "Or they choose sides."

Howard glanced at him. "You're not doing either."

"I'm trying not to," Caleb replied. "Because I don't think the answer is found in being right. I think it's found in staying connected."

Howard smiled. "That's a rare instinct."

As they walked along, Caleb felt again the quiet weight of responsibility. Growth had brought energy, attentiveness, and depth. It had also brought difference, discomfort, and the risk of misunderstanding.

This was not a setback.

It was a threshold.

That night, Caleb wrote in his notebook:

Friction reveals where we're still learning to love.

He closed the book and sat quietly, aware that the season ahead would continue to test patience and humility.

But he also sensed something else beneath the strain.

A growing resilience. Not the kind that avoided tension.

But the kind that learned how to live with it without breaking. And that, he believed, was one of the truest signs that Willowend was growing well.

By the end of the week, Caleb had come to recognise a pattern. The friction did not erupt where he expected it to. It didn't arise from the loud or the opinionated, nor from those who openly resisted change. Instead, it surfaced quietly, in people who cared deeply and feared losing something precious without knowing how to name that fear.

On Friday morning, he received a call from Margaret Ellis.

She rarely phoned anyone, and when she did, it was usually brief and practical. This time, her voice held a hesitancy he hadn't heard before.

"Pastor," she said, "I wondered if you might come by for a cuppa this afternoon. If you're free."

"I'd be glad to," Caleb replied.

Her small home sat at the edge of town, shaded by an old jacaranda that had begun to drop purple blossoms onto the path. Inside, everything was neat, deliberate, and unchanged - a place where order had long been a form of comfort.

They sat at the kitchen table with mugs of tea cooling between them.

"I've been thinking," Margaret began. "About the church."

Caleb waited.

"I'm grateful for what's happening," she said carefully. "Truly. But I don't always know where I fit anymore."

Caleb nodded slowly. "What makes you feel that way?"

She folded her hands together. "People talk more now. They share things. Feelings. Experiences. I'm not used to that."

He smiled gently. "You've always shown your faith through faithfulness rather than words."

She met his eyes. "Yes. And I don't want that to be less valued."

"It isn't," Caleb said without hesitation. "It's essential."

She relaxed slightly. "I was hoping you'd say that."

They talked for some time after that, not resolving everything, but easing the weight of what had been pressing on her. When Caleb left, she walked him to the door and said quietly, "Thank you for not assuming that growth means noise."

That sentence stayed with him.

The following Sunday, the service unfolded simply.

There were no unusual moments, no unexpected contributions. The music was familiar, the prayers unhurried. And yet, Caleb sensed a deeper attentiveness than before. People listened not just to him, but to one another. They lingered after the final song, conversations were stretching naturally rather than dispersing quickly.

Daniel stood near the back, talking with two others his age. Their voices were low, earnest. Caleb noticed how Daniel listened more than he spoke, nodding thoughtfully before offering a word.

It struck him that leadership was beginning to surface in Daniel not as confidence, but as presence.

Amelia, meanwhile, moved between people quietly, refilling mugs, asking gentle questions, noticing when someone stood alone. She didn't lead from the front, but the room seemed to settle wherever she paused.

Caleb didn't comment on either of these things. He had learned that naming growth too quickly could harden it into performance. Some things needed space to remain organic.

That afternoon, he sat alone in the sanctuary for a while after everyone had gone. Sunlight filtered through the windows, dust motes drifting slowly in the air. He thought about the week - the conversations, the tensions, the moments of reassurance and uncertainty.

Growth, he was learning again, was rarely dramatic. It was cumulative. Subtle. Often invisible until reflected back through relationships.

He thought of the words he had written earlier in the week about friction revealing where love was still being learned. That learning, he now realised, required time - not just patience, but permission.

Permission to hesitate.

Permission to ask.

Permission to remain present even when unsure.

That evening, as he and Rachel sat together after dinner, she asked, "How are you holding all of this?"

He smiled. "Some days better than others."

She nodded. "You're carrying a lot of stories right now."

"Yes," he said. "And they don't all want the same ending."

She leaned back, thoughtful. "They don't need the same ending. They just need space to keep being told."

Caleb considered that. "That might be the truest thing you've said all week."

She smiled. "I'll take that as a compliment."

Later, before bed, Caleb opened his notebook again. He didn't write much. Just one line:

Growth that lasts is patient with those who grow at different speeds.

He closed the book and turned out the light.

Outside, Willowend rested quietly. There was no sense of urgency in the town that night. No pressure to resolve every tension or define every change. Just the steady work of people learning to walk together in unfamiliar territory.

Caleb knew the coming weeks would bring more questions, more moments of friction, and more misunderstanding. But he also sensed something strengthening beneath it all - a shared willingness to remain engaged rather than retreat.

Not everyone would move forward at the same pace.

Not everyone would agree on the shape of what was emerging.

But fewer people were walking away.

And that, Caleb believed, mattered more than clarity.

As he drifted toward sleep, one thought settled gently in his mind:

This was what it looked like when a community learned not just how to grow - but how to stay.

And in that quiet learning, Willowend was becoming something deeper than it had ever been before.

The shift did not announce itself.

There was no defining moment when Caleb could say, *This is when it began*. Instead, it revealed itself gradually, like a change in posture rather than direction. People were not simply more open or more expressive; they were more attentive. They listened differently. They paused more often before speaking. And increasingly, they asked questions that carried weight rather than urgency.

Caleb noticed it first in meetings.

What had once been predictable rhythms - updates, decisions, prayer, closure - began to slow down. Not inefficiently, but deliberately. Silence was no longer something to be filled as quickly as possible. It became a space people were willing to sit in, even if it felt unfamiliar.

At one gathering, a discussion about a minor practical matter stalled unexpectedly. No one argued. No one rushed to resolve it. They simply stopped talking.

Caleb waited.

After a long moment, one of the older men cleared his throat. "I don't think we're stuck," he said slowly. "I think we're just not ready to decide yet."

There were nods around the room.

Caleb felt a quiet recognition rise in him. This wasn't indecision. It was discernment beginning to take shape.

Afterward, he walked home through the cooling air, thinking about how different this felt from other seasons of change he had known. In the past, growth had often demanded momentum. This time, it seemed to require restraint.

At the servo the next morning, Amelia was wiping down the counter when Caleb came in. The place was quiet, the early rush already passed.

"You look thoughtful," she said.

"Do I?" Caleb smiled. "I was hoping it didn't show."

She leaned against the counter. "It's a familiar look lately."

He nodded. "I think we're learning something new as a church."

"About what?" she asked.

"About listening," he said. "Not just to God, but to one another. And to what's underneath the words."

She considered that. "I've noticed something like that too."

"Tell me."

She hesitated, then said, "People don't come in asking for answers anymore. Not like they used to. They talk. Then they stop. Then they talk again."

Caleb smiled. "That sounds about right."

"It's strange," she added. "But it feels… safer."

That word stayed with him as he drove back toward the church. Safer.

Later that week, Daniel came by in the late afternoon. He lingered in the doorway longer than usual, shifting his weight from one foot to the other.

"Got a minute?" he asked.

"Of course," Caleb said, closing his notebook.

Daniel sat, then stood again, then finally settled into the chair opposite Caleb's desk.

"I think I might be noticing things," he said.

Caleb raised an eyebrow slightly. "Noticing what?"

"People," Daniel replied. "When they're saying one thing but carrying something else."

Caleb nodded slowly. "That's not uncommon when people feel seen."

Daniel frowned. "Is that… normal?"

"It can be," Caleb said. "What are you noticing?"

Daniel rubbed his hands together. "Sometimes I feel like I know when someone needs space. Or when they're not ready to talk, even if they're asking questions."

"That's a good instinct," Caleb said.

"But what do I do with it?" Daniel asked. "I don't want to assume things. Or get it wrong."

Caleb leaned back. "Discernment isn't about certainty," he said. "It's about attentiveness. You don't act on it by declaring what you see. You act on it by responding gently."

Daniel absorbed that. "So I don't need to name it."

"No," Caleb said. "Not most of the time. You just let it shape how you listen."

Daniel exhaled, visibly relieved. "That feels manageable."

Caleb smiled. "It should. Gifts that overwhelm us tend to be misused."

Daniel nodded, thoughtful. "I'm glad you said that."

After Daniel left, Caleb sat quietly for a while. He was becoming increasingly aware that what was emerging in Willowend wasn't a sudden surge of ability or confidence, but a deepening sensitivity. People were becoming more aware of one another's inner lives, and more cautious about handling them.

This was not flashy.

But it was profound.

On Sunday morning, Caleb addressed it very briefly, without labelling it specifically.

"We don't need to rush what God is shaping among us," he said. "Some things grow best when we give them room to breathe."

He watched as people listened. Not all with agreement, but with interest.

After the service, Margaret Ellis approached him. She moved slowly, as always, but her eyes were bright.

"I wanted to tell you," she said, "I prayed with someone this week."

Caleb smiled. "That's wonderful."

"It wasn't out loud," she added quickly. "We just sat together. But I knew when to be quiet."

Caleb nodded. "That's a rare wisdom."

She smiled faintly. "It felt right."

As she walked away, Caleb felt a deep sense of gratitude. The gifts emerging in Willowend were not drawing attention to themselves. They were drawing people closer together.

That evening, Caleb wrote again in his notebook:

Discernment doesn't announce itself. It reveals itself in how carefully we handle one another.

He closed the book and sat back, aware that this season would require more trust than instruction. More patience than clarity.

But he also sensed that the church was being shaped in ways that would sustain it through challenges yet unseen.

Not because they were becoming stronger individually.

But because they were learning how to listen - together.

The following weeks confirmed what Caleb had begun to sense - discernment, once awakened, changed the pace of everything. Decisions took a little longer, but they now landed more gently. Conversations lingered without drifting.

People began to trust pauses instead of fearing them. Caleb found himself speaking less in meetings, not out of strategy, but because there was less need to fill the space.

One evening, the leadership group gathered in the small meeting room behind the sanctuary. The agenda was ordinary enough - schedules, resources, a question about how to respond to a recent increase in attendance. But the tone felt different from the outset.

They opened in prayer, then sat quietly.

Seconds passed.

No one rushed to speak.

Caleb watched the room carefully, not to control it, but to learn from it. Faces were thoughtful, attentive. No one looked uncomfortable with the silence. It was as if they were waiting for something to settle before moving forward.

Eventually, Margaret spoke.

"I think we're being invited to notice something," she said.

The others turned toward her, unhurried.

"I don't know exactly what yet," she continued, "but it feels like this isn't just about logistics. It's about care."

Caleb felt a quiet affirmation rise in him. "Tell us more."

She paused, choosing her words. "People are coming because they feel safe here. Not because we've promised anything. Just because they can breathe."

There were nods around the table.

Howard leaned forward slightly. "If that's true," he said, "then our question isn't how to manage growth. It's how to protect that safety."

Someone else added, "And how not to rush people through it." The conversation unfolded slowly from there. No single person dominated it.

Ideas emerged freely, were tested, then set aside without any defensiveness. When they finished, there was no sense of triumph, but there was clarity.

Afterward, as Caleb locked up the church, he realised something had shifted again. The group had not just discussed discernment - they had practised it.

The next day, Amelia noticed it in a different setting.

A young woman she barely knew stood at the counter longer than necessary, fingers tapping lightly against the edge.

"Is something wrong?" Amelia asked gently.

The woman shook her head. "No. I just… didn't want to leave yet."

Amelia nodded. "You don't have to."

They stood in silence for a moment, the hum of the refrigerator filling the space. Eventually, the woman said, "I don't go to church. But I know people who do. And they don't talk like you." Amelia smiled. "How do they talk?"

"Like they already know what's wrong with me."

Amelia felt a quiet sadness at that. "I don't know what's wrong with you," she said honestly. "I just know you're here."

The woman exhaled slowly. "That helps."

After she left, Amelia rested her hands on the counter and stayed still for a while. She hadn't offered advice. She hadn't shared her own story. She hadn't prayed aloud.

And yet something had shifted.

She mentioned it to Caleb later that week.

"I didn't do anything," she said.

Caleb smiled. "You did exactly enough."

Daniel, meanwhile, was discovering that discernment also carried cost. He had begun to notice when people subtly avoided certain topics, when laughter covered discomfort, when enthusiasm masked uncertainty. Sometimes he wanted to step in, to help, to say something that might ease the tension. Other times, he sensed that silence was the kinder response.

It wasn't always clear which was which.

One afternoon, he sat alone on the steps behind the church, wrestling with the weight of it. Caleb joined him quietly and sat beside him.

"You're carrying something," Caleb said.

Daniel nodded. "I feel like I'm seeing more than I used to. And I don't always know what to do with it."

Caleb leaned back against the wall. "Seeing more doesn't mean acting more."

Daniel frowned. "It feels like responsibility."

"It can," Caleb said. "But responsibility without wisdom becomes control."

Daniel absorbed that. "So how do I know when to speak?"

Caleb considered for a moment. "Often, the question isn't 'Should I speak?' but 'Who is this for?'"

Daniel looked at him. "What do you mean?"

"If speaking will relieve your discomfort more than it will help the other person," Caleb said, "it might be better to wait."

Daniel nodded slowly. "That makes sense."

"And sometimes," Caleb added, "discernment is simply the invitation to pray quietly and trust that God is already at work."

Daniel smiled faintly. "I can do that."

As these small lessons accumulated, Caleb became increasingly aware that Willowend was being shaped from the inside out.

The gifts emerging were not spectacular. They were relational. They made people slower to judge and quicker to listen. Not everyone was comfortable with that.

A few people drifted toward other congregations where things felt more familiar or more defined. They left kindly, without accusation. Caleb let them go with blessing, resisting the urge to interpret every departure as failure.

Growth, he was learning again, always clarified calling.

One Sunday afternoon, after the building had emptied, Caleb sat in the sanctuary alone. The quiet felt full rather than empty now. He thought about the people whose lives were intersecting in new ways, often without realising it.

He thought about Amelia's gentle presence. Daniel's careful attentiveness. Margaret's steady wisdom. The whole leadership group's willingness to slow down. This was discernment taking shape - not as a skill, but as a posture.

Before leaving, Caleb stood at the front of the sanctuary and looked out over the rows of pews. He didn't pray for direction. He prayed for faithfulness.

Faithfulness to keep listening.

Faithfulness to resist urgency.

Faithfulness to trust that what God was forming here would unfold in its own time.

As he turned off the lights and stepped outside, the evening air felt cool and steady. Willowend rested quietly, unaware of the subtle work being done within it.

But Caleb knew.

Something was being shaped here.

Not loudly.

Not quickly.

But carefully.

And he sensed that the shape it was taking would matter more than anyone yet understood.

As the month unfolded, Caleb became increasingly aware of how discernment, once welcomed, began to ripple outward into places no one had planned for. It showed up in very ordinary encounters. In small choices. In the way people spoke about one another when the person wasn't present. Willowend had not become perfect, but it had become more careful with itself.

One morning, Caleb received an email from a neighbouring minister asking if they might meet for coffee. The tone was polite, curious, and a little guarded.

They met halfway between towns at a small roadside cafe. The minister, older than Caleb by a few years, stirred his coffee slowly before speaking.

"I've heard things are changing in Willowend," he said.

Caleb nodded. "Some things are. Some aren't."

The man smiled faintly. "That's usually how it goes."

There was a pause, then he added, "People talk. Some are encouraged. Some are wary."

Caleb waited.

"I wanted to ask," the man continued, "how you're keeping things grounded."

Caleb considered his words carefully. "By listening longer than we used to," he said. "And by not rushing people toward any conclusions."

The man thought for a while. "That sounds simple."

"It isn't," Caleb replied. "But it's honest."

They spoke for some time after that, not debating methods, but sharing concerns. When they parted, the conversation felt unfinished in a good way, like a door left ajar rather than shut.

Back in Willowend, discernment was quietly shaping pastoral care as well. Caleb visited a couple who had begun attending sporadically. They were polite, attentive, but hesitant. During the visit, the wife spoke openly while the husband remained silent, his gaze fixed on the floor.

At one point, Caleb felt the familiar urge to draw him out, to ask a question that might invite engagement. But something held him back. Instead, he allowed the silence to remain.

After a while, the man looked up and said, "I'm not ready to talk yet."

Caleb nodded. "That's all right."

The relief in the man's shoulders was immediate.

Later, as Caleb walked back to his car, he realised how different this would have been in another season. Once, he might have mistaken silence for resistance. Now, he recognised it as honesty.

Amelia experienced a similar moment one afternoon at the servo. A regular named Bill, known for his bluntness, stood at the counter longer than usual. He cleared his throat.

"You've changed," he said.

Amelia smiled cautiously. "Have I?"

"Not in a bad way," he added quickly. "Just... slower."

She laughed softly. "I've always been slow."

He shook his head. "Not like this. It's like you're listening before people finish talking."

Amelia considered that deeply. "Maybe people are finishing differently."

He nodded once. "That could be."

Then, unexpectedly, he said, "My wife's not well."

Amelia didn't rush to respond. She didn't offer words she wasn't sure he wanted. She simply said, "I'm sorry."

They stood there for a moment, the hum of the fridges filling the space.

"Thanks," he said quietly, then paid and left.

That night, Amelia found herself praying for Bill's wife without knowing her name. She didn't feel compelled to do more. The prayer felt complete as it was.

Daniel, meanwhile, was beginning to feel the tension between discernment and action more sharply.

He had been invited to help with a small discussion group, nothing formal, just a few people gathering midweek. During one session, a conversation veered toward frustration about how slow everything felt.

"I thought renewal would feel more… obvious," someone said. "Like we'd know what to do."

Daniel felt the pull to respond, to offer reassurance or direction. But he remembered Caleb's words. Instead, he asked, "What would obvious look like to you?"

The group went quiet.

Eventually, someone said, "Less uncertainty."

Another added, "More confidence."

Daniel nodded. "What if uncertainty is part of the work?"

No one answered immediately, but the tone shifted. The conversation deepened rather than scattered. When the group ended, a woman lingered behind.

"I'm glad you didn't try to fix that," she said.

Daniel smiled. "I wasn't sure what to fix."

"That's what helped," she replied.

As these moments accumulated, Caleb became increasingly aware that discernment was reshaping leadership. Authority was no longer asserted. It was recognised. People trusted those who listened well, not those who spoke most clearly.

One evening, Caleb sat alone on the back steps of the church, watching the sky fade toward dusk. He thought about how easily this season could be misunderstood. From the outside, it might look like hesitation. From within, it felt like faith taking a deeper root.

Rachel joined him quietly, sitting beside him.

"You've been quieter lately," she observed.

"Have I?" he asked.

"Yes," she said. "But not withdrawn."

He smiled. "I think I'm learning to let things breathe."

She nodded. "That suits you."

They sat in silence for a while, the sounds of the town settling around them.

"I don't know where this leads," Caleb said finally.

Rachel leaned her head against his shoulder. "You don't have to."

He considered that, feeling the truth of it settle.

Later that night, Caleb wrote again in his notebook:

Discernment doesn't give answers.
It teaches us how to wait without fear.

He closed the book, sensing that Willowend was being prepared not for a single challenge, but for a way of walking that would serve it long after this season passed.

The town slept quietly. No declarations were being made. No lines drawn. Just people learning, slowly and imperfectly, how to hold one another with care.

And Caleb knew, with a calm certainty, that this quiet shaping would sustain them far more deeply than clarity ever could.

19. WHEN ATTENTION BRINGS SCRUTINY

Caleb noticed the scrutiny before he heard it.

It arrived quietly, not as accusation or confrontation, but as a change in tone. Conversations that once felt open began to carry a careful edge. Questions were now phrased more precisely. Compliments arrived with qualifiers. Even encouragement, when it came, sometimes felt measured.

It wasn't hostile. But it was observant.

He became aware of it one Sunday morning as he stood near the door after the service. People lingered as they always did, but their conversations bent inward rather than outward. A few unfamiliar faces hovered at the edges of the room, watching more than engaging. They were polite, attentive, and curious in a way that suggested they were taking notes, even if only mentally.

Caleb greeted them warmly, but he felt the shift.

This was no longer just Willowend paying attention to itself. Others were watching too.

Later that afternoon, Howard stopped by the manse. He didn't sit down immediately. Instead, he stood near the window, hands clasped loosely behind his back.

"You've probably noticed it already," he said.

Caleb smiled faintly. "That depends what you mean."

Howard turned. "People are asking questions. Not just here."

Caleb nodded. "I suspected as much."

Howard exhaled. "Nothing alarming. Just interest. Curiosity. A few raised eyebrows."

"And some concern," Caleb added.

Howard smiled wryly. "That too."

They sat at the table with cups of tea between them.

"Renewal always attracts attention," Howard said. "Even quiet renewal."

Caleb nodded. "Especially quiet renewal."

Howard tilted his head. "Why do you say that?"

"Because it doesn't fit all the usual categories," Caleb replied. "People don't know what to call it. And when they can't name something, they start examining it more closely."

Howard considered that. "You think this will become an issue?" "I think it will become a conversation first," Caleb said. "And conversations carry expectations."

Howard asked, "You're not worried?"

Caleb paused. "I'm aware."

That evening, Caleb received an email from a denominational contact he hadn't heard from in some time. The message was cordial, affirming, and gently inquisitive. It asked about the attendance patterns, leadership structures, and how Willowend was navigating what it described as 'a season of attentiveness'.

Caleb read it twice.

There was nothing wrong with any of the questions. They were reasonable. Responsible, even. But he sensed what lay beneath them - a need to understand, to categorise, to ensure that what was happening could be explained within familiar frameworks.

He drafted a reply slowly, choosing clarity over enthusiasm, honesty over reassurance.

He did not embellish.

He did not minimise.

He described what he could, and left space where certainty did not yet exist.

When he sent it, he felt neither relief nor anxiety. Just readiness.

The scrutiny arrived closer to home as well.

At the servo, Amelia noticed that some customers were asking more pointed questions about the church.

"Is it growing?" one asked.

"A bit," she replied.

"What kind of growing?" another pressed.

Amelia smiled politely. "The kind that takes time."

That answer seemed to satisfy some and frustrate others.

One afternoon, a man she didn't recognise leaned against the counter and said, "So what's the angle?"

Amelia raised an eyebrow. "Angle?"

"You know," he said. "What you're aiming for. Big vision. Bigger crowd."

Amelia shook her head. "I don't think we're really aiming for anything."

The man frowned. "Everything aims somewhere."

She met his gaze calmly. "Sometimes it just grows where it's planted."

He studied her for a moment, then nodded slowly and said, "Fair enough."

After he left, Amelia stood quietly, aware that not everyone would find that answer sufficient.

Daniel encountered scrutiny differently.

A friend from outside Willowend asked him bluntly, "So are you joining some movement now?"

Daniel laughed. "No."

"Then what's going on?"

Daniel hesitated. "I think people are just listening more."

His friend snorted. "That's vague."

Daniel smiled. "That's honest."

The conversation ended awkwardly, and Daniel felt the familiar pull of doubt. Was he being unclear? Or was clarity being demanded too quickly?

He mentioned it to Caleb later.

"I don't really know how to explain what's happening," Daniel admitted. "It sounds weak when I try."

Caleb shook his head. "It sounds incomplete. That's different."

"So what do I say?" Daniel asked.

"You say what you know," Caleb replied. "And you leave room for what you don't."

Daniel considered that. "People don't like room."

"No," Caleb agreed. "But faith often lives there."

As scrutiny increased, Caleb became more intentional about how he spoke publicly. He resisted the temptation to define the season too clearly. He avoided language that promised outcomes or implied momentum.

Instead, he spoke about posture.

About attentiveness.

About patience.

Some appreciated that.

Others wanted more.

One Sunday evening, after a particularly full day, Caleb sat alone in the sanctuary again. The quiet felt different now. Not just restful, but watchful. He thought about the way attention had shifted.

What had once been unseen was now observed.

What had grown unnoticed was now examined.

This was not unexpected. But it was significant.

He realised that the next season would test not just the church's openness, but its integrity. How would they respond when unseen faithfulness became visible? When quiet obedience drew commentary?

Caleb bowed his head, not in worry, but in resolve.

He did not pray for protection from scrutiny.

He prayed for humility within it.

Outside, Willowend carried on as it always had. The streets were quiet. The lights came on at dusk. Life moved at its familiar pace.

But something had changed.

The town was no longer simply listening to itself.

Others were listening too.

And Caleb knew that how they responded now would shape not just what people saw - but what they trusted.

The scrutiny did not arrive with a single face or voice. It came layered, indirect, and cumulative, like pressure building slowly rather than striking suddenly.

Caleb began to feel it most clearly in conversations that sounded supportive but carried an unspoken assessment beneath them.

"How are you managing it all?" someone would ask.

"Are you finding the changes sustainable?"

"What safeguards do you have in place?"

None of the questions were hostile. In fact, they were often framed as concern. But Caleb recognised the shift. People were no longer simply curious about what they noticed happening in Willowend. They were measuring it.

One afternoon, he received a call from a regional coordinator he respected. The tone was warm, affirming, and cautious in equal measure.

"We've been hearing encouraging things," the man said. "And we just wanted to check in. Make sure you're feeling supported."

"I am," Caleb replied honestly.

"That's good," the man said. "Sometimes seasons like this can move faster than leaders realise."

Caleb smiled faintly. "This one isn't moving fast."

There was a pause on the line.

"Yes," the man agreed. "That's… part of what people are trying to understand."

After the call ended, Caleb sat quietly for a while. He felt no resentment toward the questions. Oversight always mattered. Accountability mattered. But he was becoming aware of a subtle tension between what could be explained and what could only be witnessed over time.

Not everything that was forming in Willowend lent itself to neat reporting.

At the next leadership gathering, the atmosphere reflected that same tension.

Howard opened with prayer, then looked around the room. "I want us to talk openly tonight," he said. "Not about what's happening here, but about how it's being perceived."

A murmur of agreement moved through the group.

Margaret spoke first. "I've had three people ask me if we're changing direction."

"Are we?" someone asked.

Margaret smiled. "I don't think so. I think we are actually just changing depth."

There were nods, but also hesitation.

"One of my friends warned me to be careful," another person said. "She said movements like this can drift."

Caleb listened carefully. "What did she mean by drift?"

"She couldn't really say," the person replied. "Just that when things become less predictable, they can become unsafe."

The room grew quiet.

Caleb spoke slowly. "Unpredictability and unsafety are not the same thing. But I understand why people confuse them."

Howard leaned forward. "So what do we do?"

Caleb didn't answer immediately. He looked around the table, meeting each face in turn. "We stay honest," he said. "We don't exaggerate what's happening, and we don't defend it either. We keep inviting conversation rather than closing it."

"And if people keep pressing?" someone asked.

"Then we keep listening," Caleb replied. "Not because we owe explanations for everything, but because listening is part of who we're becoming."

The discussion moved on, but the weight remained. Leadership now required not just discernment, but endurance.

That week, Amelia encountered scrutiny that felt closer to home. A long-time acquaintance stopped her near the pumps and said quietly, "I've heard you've been saying some pretty spiritual things lately."

Amelia blinked. "Have I?"

The woman smiled tightly. "Just… be careful. People might get the wrong idea."

Amelia felt the familiar mix of doubt and resolve rise within her.

"What wrong idea?"

"That you think you've got answers for everyone."

Amelia shook her head. "I don't."

The woman studied her for a moment. "Then make sure people know that."

After she left, Amelia stood still, feeling the old urge to shrink back, to become less visible. Instead, she breathed slowly and reminded herself of Caleb's words.

Stay yourself.

That evening, she wrote a note in her phone, something she'd begun doing recently when thoughts felt crowded:

If being myself makes others uneasy, I can still be kind.

Daniel faced scrutiny in a more internal way.

He had been invited to attend a small gathering in a nearby town, a mix of young adults from different churches.

During the conversation, someone asked him where he was from.

"Willowend," he said.

"Oh," the person replied, eyebrows lifting slightly. "I've heard about that place."

Daniel waited.

"They say things are getting… intense there."

Daniel laughed softly. "Not really."

"Then what's happening?"

Daniel searched for words that wouldn't distort the truth. "People are learning how to listen."

The person frowned. "That's it?"

Daniel nodded. "That's a lot."

After the conversation had moved on, Daniel felt the familiar uncertainty linger. He wondered if what he was experiencing made sense only from the inside. Whether it would ever sound convincing to those who weren't living it.

Later, he mentioned it to Caleb.

"I feel like I can't explain what is happening without it sounding underwhelming," Daniel said.

Caleb smiled. "Underwhelming isn't always a flaw."

Daniel tilted his head. "How so?"

"Because what's genuine doesn't need to impress," Caleb replied. "It just needs to endure."

That word stayed with Daniel.

As the weeks progressed, Caleb became aware that scrutiny had a clarifying effect. Some people leaned in further, drawn by the integrity they sensed. Others stepped back, uncomfortable with the lack of definition.

Neither response surprised him.

What mattered was how Willowend held itself in the midst of it.

One Sunday, Caleb addressed the congregation briefly at the close of the service.

"We may not always be able to explain what God is doing among us," he said. "But we can choose how we carry it. With humility. With patience. And with care for one another."

He did not mention scrutiny. He did not name critics. He simply spoke of posture.

Afterward, as people filtered out into the afternoon light, Caleb felt a quiet steadiness settle within him. Attention had brought scrutiny, yes. But it had also revealed something else.

A deeper resolve. Not to protect a movement. But to protect the way people were learning to walk together.

And Caleb sensed that if they could remain faithful there, the questions - however persistent - would never become the thing that defined them.

As scrutiny settled in, Caleb became aware of a subtle temptation creeping in alongside it - the urge to manage perception.

It wasn't loud or obvious. It surfaced quietly, in moments when he caught himself wondering how something might sound if repeated elsewhere. When he considered whether a conversation should be framed differently, or whether a moment of honesty might be misunderstood if it travelled beyond the room it occurred in.

He recognised the danger immediately.

Managing perception was not the same as shepherding people. One sought control. The other required trust.

On a quiet Tuesday afternoon, Caleb sat with his notebook open but untouched, watching the light shift across the floor of his office. He thought about the questions coming from outside Willowend and the expectations beginning to press in.

There was a growing sense that people wanted reassurance, not just that something good was happening, but that it would remain contained, predictable, and safe by all familiar standards.

But safety, he was learning, was not the same as control.

That evening, he met with Howard again, this time walking slowly along the edge of town as the sun dipped low.

"People are starting to ask what comes next," Howard said.

Caleb nodded. "That's usually when trouble starts."

Howard smiled. "You're not wrong."

"They're not asking out of bad intent," Caleb added. "They just want to know where to place this."

"And can you tell them?" Howard asked.

Caleb considered the question carefully. "I can tell them where we are," he said. "But not where we're going."

Howard stopped walking. "Does that worry you?"

"No," Caleb replied. "It worries me when people pretend they know."

Howard studied him for a moment. "You're comfortable with uncertainty."

Caleb shook his head. "No. I'm learning not to fear it."
That distinction mattered.

Back in Willowend, the effect of scrutiny was beginning to show in small, revealing ways.

A few people became quieter in the gatherings, weighing their words far more carefully than before. Others became more articulate, trying to ensure their experiences were expressed in ways that sounded grounded and responsible. A handful withdrew slightly, unsure whether what they had been experiencing belonged in a space that now felt observed.

Caleb watched these responses closely.

None of them were wrong.

But all of them required care.

One Sunday afternoon, Amelia found herself unexpectedly frustrated. A customer who had previously been warm and very curious now seemed guarded, offering polite conversation but little else.

"It's like they're watching me," she said later to Caleb. "Waiting to see if I'll say something strange."

Caleb nodded. "That can make people self-conscious."

"I don't want to start filtering everything," she said. "But I don't want to push people away either."

Caleb smiled gently. "You don't need to perform authenticity," he said. "You just need to live it."

She exhaled. "That sounds freeing."

"It is," he replied. "And sometimes costly."

Daniel encountered a different cost.

He found himself becoming more aware of how quickly words could be labelled. A comment that might once have been received as thoughtful was now interpreted as indicative. A question could be heard as a position. A pause could be read as uncertainty.

One evening, after a small group meeting, he stayed behind, restless.

"It feels like everything means more now," he said to Caleb.

Caleb nodded. "It does."

"I'm afraid of saying the wrong thing."

"That's understandable," Caleb replied. "But don't let fear teach you silence."

Daniel frowned. "How do I know the difference?"

Caleb thought for a moment. "Fear silences you to protect yourself. Wisdom quiets you to protect others."

Daniel nodded slowly. "I think I can feel that difference."

"That's discernment doing its work," Caleb said.

As the scrutiny continued, Caleb became increasingly intentional about modelling restraint without retreat. He spoke plainly when needed. He declined invitations to defend or promote what was happening. He refused to frame Willowend as an example or a solution.

When asked directly whether the church was experiencing renewal, he answered simply, "We're learning how to listen and love more faithfully. If that's renewal, it's not ours to manage."

Some found that answer refreshing.

Others found it evasive.

Caleb let both responses stand.

Late one night, unable to sleep, he stepped outside and stood beneath the wide country sky. The town was very quiet, lights dimmed, the air was cool and still.

He thought about how far Willowend had come, and how little of it could be explained without flattening it.

Scrutiny, he realised, was not the enemy.

Fear was.

Fear of being misunderstood.

Fear of being judged.

Fear of losing something fragile by mishandling it.

But fear did not belong in this season.

Faith did.

The faith to remain unhurried.

The faith to resist self-protection.

The faith to trust that what was being shaped here did not need defending to survive.

The next morning, Caleb opened his notebook and wrote:

When attention increases, integrity must deepen.

He closed the book, feeling the weight of the words settle within him. Willowend was being seen now, not just by those who lived its rhythms, but by those who observed from a distance.

That visibility would continue.

Questions would persist.

Expectations would grow.

But Caleb sensed a quiet resolve taking root, not just in himself, but in the community around him.

A shared understanding that what mattered most was not how they were perceived, but how they remained faithful to the slow, careful work unfolding among them.

Scrutiny might test them.

But it would not define them.

Only their posture would.

And in that posture - patient, attentive, unassuming - Willowend was discovering a strength that did not announce itself, but endured.

20. THE COST OF STAYING GENTLE

The cost did not arrive all at once.

It revealed itself slowly, in the accumulation of small decisions that required restraint rather than action. Caleb had learned to recognise that seasons of attentiveness carried their own fatigue - not the exhaustion of busyness, but the weariness that came from holding tension without resolving it prematurely.

Gentleness, he was discovering, demanded stamina.

One morning, as he walked through the church grounds before anyone else arrived, Caleb paused near the old gum tree at the edge of the property. Its branches stretched wide, uneven, shaped by decades of wind rather than careful pruning. He had always liked that tree. It had grown without symmetry, but with strength.

He wondered, not for the first time, whether the church was beginning to resemble it.

Inside, the sanctuary was quiet. The stillness no longer felt empty to him. It felt inhabited, as though the space itself remembered the prayers spoken within it. Caleb sat in the front pew and allowed his thoughts to settle.

There were days now when leadership felt less like direction and more like containment. He wasn't pushing forward or pulling back. He was holding space - for questions, for hesitations, for differences that could not yet be reconciled.

That work was invisible.

And it was tiring.

Later that morning, he met with a small group of leaders who had asked for clarity about where things were heading. They were respectful, engaged, and clearly committed. But their questions pressed against the edges of what Caleb could offer.

"We just want to know how to support you," one of them said.

"It feels like we're walking carefully all the time."

Caleb nodded. "You are."

"Is that sustainable?" another asked.

Caleb considered the question honestly. "It depends on what we think sustainability looks like."

They waited.

"If sustainability means efficiency or predictability," he continued, "then no. This season will feel slow and uncertain.

But if it means forming people who can listen well, disagree kindly, and remain faithful under pressure, then yes. It will be sustainable. It's just costly."

One of them frowned slightly. "Costly how?"

"In patience," Caleb replied. "In ego. In the temptation to prove that what's happening here is legitimate."

The room grew quiet.

Afterward, Caleb wondered whether he had said too much or too little. He had learned that gentleness did not always feel reassuring. Sometimes it felt like absence, even when it was not. At the servo, Amelia was feeling the cost in a different way.

The novelty had now worn off. People no longer asked curious questions as often. Instead, they watched. Conversations felt more measured. There were fewer spontaneous openings, fewer moments of unexpected vulnerability.

She found herself missing them.

One afternoon, after a particularly quiet shift, she sat alone in the small staff room and stared at the wall. The sense of usefulness she had felt earlier in the season had faded into something less defined.

When Caleb came in later, she said simply, "I think I'm tired."

He nodded. "What kind of tired?"

"The kind where you don't know what you're for anymore," she replied.

Caleb considered that. "That's not exhaustion," he said gently. "That's transition."

She sighed. "I liked it when things felt clearer."

"So did everyone," Caleb said. "Clarity feels kind. But depth often feels confusing while it's forming."

She smiled faintly. "You always say that."

"And I always forget how hard it is," he replied.

Daniel was encountering the cost more internally.

He had become quieter again, not withdrawn, but reflective. The attentiveness he had learned was now turned inward as well as outward. He noticed his own motives more closely. He questioned impulses that once felt straightforward.

One evening, he confessed to Caleb, "Sometimes I wish someone would just tell me what to do."

Caleb smiled. "So do I."

Daniel laughed. "That doesn't help."

"It might," Caleb said. "Because it reminds us that certainty isn't a reward for maturity. It's often something we let go of as we grow."

Daniel frowned. "That seems unfair."

Caleb nodded. "It is. But it's also freeing."

Daniel leaned back, staring at the ceiling. "I don't feel very free."

"Not yet," Caleb replied. "Freedom usually follows trust."

As the weeks passed, Caleb became increasingly aware that gentleness was not being celebrated the way enthusiasm often was. It didn't generate stories that travelled well. It didn't offer metrics or milestones. It required explanation without defence, and confidence without assertion.

And it asked something difficult of everyone involved.

To remain present without demanding resolution.

One Sunday morning, after a service that felt unremarkable by any outward measure, a man approached Caleb quietly.

"I don't know why," he said, "but I keep coming back."

Caleb smiled. "You don't need to know why."

The man nodded. "I think that's what helps."

That afternoon, Caleb walked home alone. Rachel was visiting someone, and the house would be quiet when he arrived. The town moved around him at its usual pace, unhurried and familiar.

He felt the weight of the season then, more clearly than he had allowed himself to earlier.

Not burden.

Responsibility.

The responsibility to resist becoming harder in response to pressure.

The responsibility to protect a way of being rather than a set of outcomes.

The responsibility to stay gentle when firmness might feel easier. As he unlocked the front door, Caleb paused for a moment, hand resting on the handle.

He realised that the cost of gentleness was not something to be avoided.

It was something to be chosen.

Again.

And again.

And again.

This, he understood now, was the quiet labour of leadership in a season like this. Not to accelerate what was growing, and not to retreat when it became demanding.

But to stay.

To stay soft.

To stay faithful.

And to trust that what was being shaped through patience would, in time, reveal its strength.

The pressure to harden did not come only from outside voices. Caleb became aware of it rising within himself, subtle but persistent. It surfaced in moments when he felt misunderstood, when careful leadership was mistaken for hesitation, when restraint was read as a lack of conviction. There were days when decisiveness would have been easier than discernment, when drawing a line would have felt cleaner than holding a tension.

Those were the days gentleness cost him the most.

One afternoon, after a long morning of conversations that circled rather than settled, Caleb drove out beyond town without quite deciding to. The road narrowed, bitumen giving way to gravel, paddocks stretching wide and quiet on either side.

He pulled over near a fence line and turned off the engine.

The silence was immediate.

He rested his hands on the steering wheel and stared out across the land. Willowend felt distant out here, not geographically but emotionally, as though the expectations pressing in on him had loosened their grip.

He prayed quietly, not asking for direction so much as honesty.

"I don't want to become sharp," he said. "Even if it makes things simpler."

The words surprised him with their clarity.

He knew the temptation well. To become efficient. To move people along. To define the season with confidence rather than humility. None of those things were wrong in themselves. But they were not what was being asked of him now.

When he returned to town, the weight had not lifted entirely, but it had settled into something more manageable.

That evening, the leadership group met again. The conversation was thoughtful but strained. Questions about sustainability returned, this time with more urgency.

"We can't keep absorbing this indefinitely," someone said. "People want direction."

Caleb nodded. "They do."

"So what are we waiting for?" another asked.

Caleb chose his words very carefully. "We're not waiting for permission. We're waiting for alignment."

A few exchanged glances.

"Alignment with what?" someone pressed.

"With what God is forming among us," Caleb replied. "Not just what we're capable of organising."

There was a pause.

Margaret spoke quietly. "Gentleness is doing something to us. I don't think it's finished yet."

The room grew still.

Caleb felt both gratitude and vulnerability in that moment. Gratitude that someone had named it. Vulnerability because naming it did not make it easier.

After the meeting, Howard walked with Caleb out into the cool night air.

"You're carrying this carefully," Howard said.

"Am I?" Caleb asked.

Howard nodded. "Carefully enough that it costs you."

Caleb smiled faintly. "That doesn't sound reassuring."

"It is," Howard replied. "It means you haven't turned it into something manageable yet."

At the servo, Amelia was navigating a similar tension.

A regular customer complained openly one morning about how things felt different in town.

"Everything's so quiet now," he said. "Like people are thinking too much."

Amelia smiled politely. "Maybe people are noticing more."
He shook his head. "Feels like hesitation to me."

She felt the familiar urge to defend what she had come to value, but she resisted it. "Sometimes hesitation is how people learn where they stand," she said.

He grunted, unconvinced.

After he left, Amelia felt the sting of the exchange more sharply than she expected. She wondered whether gentleness was making her vulnerable in ways she wasn't prepared for. Whether staying open would eventually wear her down.

Later that day, she mentioned it to Rachel.

"I don't want to become guarded," Amelia said. "But I don't want to feel exposed either."

Rachel nodded. "Gentleness isn't the absence of boundaries," she said. "It's choosing not to weaponise them."

Amelia considered that. "That sounds exhausting."

Rachel smiled. "It can be. But it's also freeing."

Daniel felt the cost differently again.

He had begun to notice when he was tempted to perform maturity rather than live it. To say the right thing instead of the true thing. To appear settled when he was still wrestling.

One evening, after a small group meeting, he stayed back alone, stacking chairs with more force than necessary. Caleb noticed and joined him.

"You're carrying something," Caleb said.

Daniel nodded. "I'm tired of being careful."

Caleb smiled gently. "Carefulness isn't the same as caution."

Daniel paused, hands resting on the back of a chair. "It feels like I'm always weighing my words."

"That's because you're learning responsibility," Caleb said. "But responsibility doesn't mean silence. It means choosing honesty without urgency."

Daniel sighed. "I don't know how to do that yet."

Caleb nodded. "No one does at first."

As the season continued, Caleb became increasingly aware that gentleness did not prevent conflict. It simply changed the way conflict was held. Disagreements still emerged. Frustrations still surfaced. But fewer people were storming out or shutting down. That mattered.

One Sunday afternoon, a woman approached Caleb quietly after the service.

"I don't always agree with where things are going," she said. "But I feel safe saying that here."

Caleb smiled. "That means more than agreement."

She nodded. "I thought so."

That night, Caleb sat at the kitchen table long after dinner, notebook open in front of him. He wrote slowly, carefully.

Gentleness is not weakness.
It is the discipline of refusing to trade depth for control.

He closed the book and leaned back, feeling the weight of the words settle.

The cost of staying gentle was real.

It demanded patience when impatience would have been most justified.

It demanded trust when certainty would have been comforting.

It demanded presence when withdrawal would have protected him.

But as Caleb looked back over the weeks, he realised something else. Gentleness was not draining the life from Willowend.

It was anchoring it.

And though the cost was ongoing, it was forming something resilient beneath the surface. Something that would not fracture easily when pressure increased.

The season ahead would test that resilience further.

Caleb did not doubt it.

But for now, he remained committed to the slow, careful work he had been given.

To stay.

To listen.

To lead without hardening.

And to trust that what was being shaped through gentleness would endure far longer than anything built through force.

The true cost revealed itself not in moments of confrontation, but in the long stretches between them.

Caleb discovered that gentleness required a particular kind of vigilance. Not alertness that waited for trouble, but attentiveness that resisted becoming numb. It was easier, some days, to withdraw slightly - to conserve energy by narrowing his focus, to respond efficiently rather than carefully. The temptation wasn't to abandon gentleness altogether, but to ration it.

He knew that temptation well.

One afternoon, after a series of pastoral conversations that left him quietly depleted, Caleb sat alone in the sanctuary with the lights off. The room was dim, shadows stretching across the pews, the faint hum of the ceiling fans the only sound. He rested his elbows on his knees and lowered his head.

"I don't want to lose the tenderness," he prayed. "Even if it costs more than I expect."

The prayer surprised him with its honesty. He had prayed for wisdom, for endurance, for clarity. But tenderness felt more fragile. More easily lost.

As he sat there, he became aware of how often leaders hardened not out of malice, but out of fatigue. How sharpness could feel like relief. How decisiveness could masquerade as faithfulness when it was really self-protection.

Caleb rose slowly and turned on a single light near the front of the sanctuary. The space felt smaller then, more intimate. He took that as a quiet reminder: gentleness thrived in proximity, not distance.

Later that week, a meeting did not go well.

It wasn't that dramatic. No voices were raised. No ultimatums issued. But there was a sense of strain that lingered long after it ended. Several people wanted clearer boundaries around what Willowend was becoming. Others resisted any language that sounded like definition at all.

Caleb listened carefully, but by the time the room emptied, his chest felt tight.

Howard remained behind.

"You all right?" he asked.

Caleb nodded, though he wasn't entirely sure it was true. "I think so."

Howard leaned against the table. "You're absorbing a lot."

"That's part of the role," Caleb replied.

Howard studied him. "Absorbing isn't the same as carrying alone."

Caleb smiled faintly. "I know."

"Then let some of it rest," Howard said. "Even if only for one night."

That evening, Caleb took Howard's advice. He did not open his notebook. He did not replay conversations in his mind. He sat with Rachel on the back veranda as the light faded, neither of them speaking much.

After a while, Rachel said, "You're tired in a very different way lately."

Caleb nodded. "It feels like everything requires discernment now. Even rest."

She smiled gently. "Then rest without trying to make sense of it."

He laughed softly. "That sounds like wisdom."

She shrugged. "It's survival."

Daniel encountered the cost in his own growing awareness.

He had begun to notice how easily he mirrored the tone of the room he was in. Around those who were cautious, he became reserved. Around those who were enthusiastic, he felt pressure to sound confident.

Gentleness required him to remain himself in both spaces, and that was harder than adapting.

One night, after a gathering, he admitted to Caleb, "I don't know who I am in this yet."

Caleb nodded. "That's because you're still becoming."

Daniel frowned. "That answer feels incomplete."

"It is," Caleb replied. "But it's also honest."

Daniel sighed. "I wish there were markers. Some way to know I'm doing this right."

Caleb smiled. "If you're still listening, you probably are."

Amelia felt the cost acutely when gentleness went unnoticed.

There were days when her quiet presence seemed to make no difference at all. When conversations stayed shallow. When people brushed past her without pause. She wondered whether her attentiveness mattered if no one acknowledged it.

One afternoon, as she closed up the servo, she found a small note tucked beneath the register.

Thank you for listening the other day.
I didn't say much, but it helped.

There was no name.

Amelia stood still for a moment, the weight she hadn't realised she was carrying easing slightly. Gentleness, she realised again, often worked in secret.

As the season progressed, Caleb noticed something subtle but significant.

Those who remained were becoming steadier.

They were not louder or more confident, but more rooted. Less reactive. More willing to stay in conversation when discomfort arose. Gentleness, costly as it was, was doing its quiet work.

One Sunday evening, Caleb addressed the congregation briefly at the end of the service.

"We won't always feel certain," he said. "But we can choose how we respond to that uncertainty. With fear. Or with faithfulness." He did not elaborate. He didn't need to.

That night, Caleb walked through town alone. The air was cool, the streets familiar. Lights glowed softly behind curtains. Life continued, ordinary and unremarkable.

And yet, beneath that ordinariness, something durable was being formed.

Not through bold initiatives. Not through decisive statements. But through the daily, deliberate choice to remain gentle when pressure invited hardness.

Caleb paused outside the church, looking up at the modest sign, its paint weathered by years of sun and wind. He thought about the cost of staying gentle and the ease with which it could be abandoned.

Then he thought about the alternative. Gentleness, he knew now, was not a personality trait. It was a discipline. A discipline that required courage. A discipline that demanded trust. A discipline that shaped people who could endure scrutiny, tension, and fatigue without losing their humanity.

As he unlocked the door and stepped inside, Caleb felt the familiar mixture of weariness and resolve settle within him.

The cost would continue.

The pressure would not disappear.

But neither would the grace that met him there, steady and sufficient, inviting him once again to choose the slower, harder, and ultimately truer way.

To stay gentle.

Even when it cost him.

Especially then.

Caleb first noticed it in the gaps. Not in what was added, but in what no longer required his presence to hold together.

Conversations continued after he stepped away.

Small gatherings formed and dissolved without needing permission. People began checking in on one another without looping him in, not out of secrecy, but out of confidence.

It was subtle, almost easy to miss.

One Tuesday morning, he arrived at the church earlier than usual, expecting the building to be empty. Instead, he heard voices drifting from the hall. Not loud. Not organised. Just a low murmur of conversation.

He paused at the doorway.

Inside, four people sat around a table with mugs of tea. Margaret was there, her hands folded loosely. Amelia sat beside her, listening. Two others leaned in, attentive rather than animated. No one was leading. No one was teaching. They were simply present with one another.

Caleb waited, not wanting to intrude.

After a few moments, Amelia looked up and noticed him. She smiled, but didn't stand.

"Morning," she said quietly.

"Morning," Caleb replied. "I didn't realise anyone was meeting."

Margaret smiled. "We weren't planning to. It just… happened."

Caleb nodded. "That seems to be happening more often."

"Yes," Margaret said. "And it doesn't feel rushed."

Caleb felt a familiar mix of gratitude and caution. Multiplication, he knew, could be a gift or a strain, depending on how it was handled.

Growth that spread too quickly could lose its grounding. But growth that was ignored could wither.

This felt neither frantic nor fragile.

It felt natural.

Later that morning, Caleb received a call that shifted his attention briefly but meaningfully.

"Dad?"

Ruth's voice carried warmth, with just enough brightness to suggest she was calling between commitments.

"Ruth," he said, smiling. "How are you?"

"Busy," she replied. "But good. I've been thinking about you."

"That's rarely a neutral statement," Caleb said lightly.

She laughed. "Fair. Mum mentioned things have been… full lately."

"They have," Caleb said. "In a quiet way."

There was a pause on the line.

"I just wanted to say," Ruth continued, "I'm proud of you. Of both of you. I don't always understand what you're navigating, but I can hear it in your voice when you talk. You sound steady." Caleb felt the words settle more deeply than he expected.

"Thank you," he said. "That means a lot."

"I know I'm not there," she added. "And I know my life looks different. But I'm cheering you on. Even from a distance."

Caleb smiled. "We feel that."

They spoke for a few more minutes about ordinary things - her work, an upcoming trip, the weather. When the call ended, Caleb sat quietly for a moment, aware of how the encouragement had arrived without demand or expectation.

It was enough.

That afternoon, Daniel stopped by the church unexpectedly. He didn't stay long, but he lingered just enough to suggest he had something on his mind.

"I think something's changing," he said.

Caleb raised an eyebrow. "Tell me what you're seeing."

Daniel shifted his weight. "People don't ask me what they should do anymore. They ask what I think."

Caleb smiled. "How does that feel?"

"Strange," Daniel admitted. "I don't feel qualified."

Caleb nodded. "Neither did most people who took time to grow into responsibility."

Daniel frowned slightly. "What if I say the wrong thing?"

"You will," Caleb replied calmly. "And you'll learn from it."

Daniel considered that. "That doesn't sound very reassuring."

"It's realistic," Caleb said. "And it keeps you humble."

Daniel laughed softly. "I suppose that's something."

At the servo later that day, Caleb noticed a similar pattern.

Amelia was speaking with a woman he didn't recognise. The conversation looked unremarkable from a distance, but there was a quality to it that drew his attention.

Amelia wasn't animated. She wasn't explaining or persuading. She was simply listening, nodding occasionally, offering a word here and there.

When the woman left, she did so slowly, as though reluctant to return to the pace of the day.

"I think you've become a gathering place," Caleb said as he approached.

Amelia looked surprised. "I've just been doing my job."

Caleb smiled. "Exactly."

She leaned against the counter. "I think people are trusting one another more. Not just me."

"That's what happens when care begins to multiply," Caleb said. "It stops being centralised."

She considered that. "Is that good?"

"Yes," Caleb replied. "As long as it stays grounded."

That evening, Caleb walked home through town, noticing how often people stopped to greet one another now. Not out of obligation, but recognition.

Conversations didn't stretch longer than they needed to, but they felt more present.

At home, Rachel noticed his quiet attentiveness.

"You're watching something," she said.

"Yes," Caleb replied. "I think the care is starting to multiply."

She nodded. "That's when it becomes harder to control."

"And easier to trust," Caleb added.

She smiled. "Only if you're willing to let go."

Later, as Caleb sat at his desk, he reflected on the day. The unplanned gathering. Daniel's uncertainty. Amelia's quiet influence. Ruth's phone call.

None of it dramatic.

All of it connected.

He opened his notebook and wrote:

What multiplies gently often lasts longer than what expands quickly.

As he closed the book, Caleb felt a quiet confidence take shape. The renewal in Willowend was no longer dependent on his presence in every space. It was being carried by people who were learning, imperfectly but sincerely, how to hold one another with care.

This was not an ending.

It was a beginning that no longer required constant supervision. And Caleb sensed that as this multiplication continued, it would bring new challenges, new tensions, and new responsibilities.

But it would also bring resilience.

The kind that grew slowly.

The kind that endured.

The kind that, once rooted, could not easily be undone.

Multiplication, Caleb was learning, carried with it a subtle shift in responsibility.

It no longer asked him to initiate everything. Instead, it asked him to notice, to bless, and sometimes to step back. That was not always comfortable. Years of ministry had trained him to be alert to gaps, to step into silence quickly, to ensure no one felt unattended.

Now, he was discovering that attentiveness sometimes meant trusting what he did not directly oversee.

The change was quiet, but it was unmistakable.

One Wednesday evening, Caleb arrived at the church to prepare for a small gathering and found the chairs already arranged. Not in the usual way, but thoughtfully. A loose circle rather than rows. A small table in the centre with a candle and a Bible resting beside it.

Daniel stood nearby, looking slightly unsure of himself.

"I hope that's all right," he said quickly. "I didn't want to make it formal. It just felt like… this might help."

Caleb looked around the room, then back at Daniel. "Tell me why you chose this."

Daniel shrugged. "People talk differently when they can see each other."

Caleb nodded slowly. "That's a good instinct."

Daniel hesitated. "I wasn't trying to lead."

"I know," Caleb said. "You were paying attention."

As people arrived, the atmosphere settled naturally. No one commented on the arrangement. They simply took their seats, some glancing at one another with curiosity, others with relief. The conversation unfolded without prompting. There was no teaching, no agenda. Just stories, pauses, and moments where words were offered carefully rather than confidently.

Caleb spoke very little.

As he watched, he became aware of something that both encouraged and unsettled him. The group did not need him in the way it once would have. His presence mattered, but it was no longer central.

That night, as he locked up the building, he felt the familiar mix of gratitude and vulnerability surface again.

Letting go was never neutral.

At the servo the next day, Amelia experienced the same shift from a different angle.

A small group of women had begun stopping by together after school drop-off. They didn't say they were meeting. They didn't name what they were doing. They just lingered, coffees in hand, conversations weaving in and out of ordinary topics.

One of them laughed and said, "This place feels different lately."

Amelia smiled. "Different how?"

"Quieter," the woman replied. "But in a good way."

Another added, "Like no one's rushing you."

Amelia nodded. "That's Willowend."

But she knew it wasn't just the town.

Later, when the group left, Amelia stood behind the counter and felt a strange sense of responsibility settle on her. Not to guide or correct, but to remain attentive. To resist the temptation to shape the conversations or direct their meaning.

Care that multiplied could also be mishandled.

That afternoon, Caleb stopped by briefly. Amelia told him about the women.

"I don't know what to do with it," she admitted. "I don't want to turn it into something."

Caleb smiled. "Then don't."

She looked relieved. "Really?"

"Yes," he said. "Not everything that gathers needs to be organised."

She considered that. "That's harder than it sounds."

"It usually is," Caleb replied.

Daniel, meanwhile, was beginning to feel the weight of being trusted.

A few people had started seeking him out, not for answers exactly, but for perspective. He found himself listening more carefully than ever, aware that his responses carried more influence than before.

One evening, after a conversation that left him unsettled, he sought out Caleb.

"I think people are expecting more from me," Daniel said.

Caleb nodded. "They probably are."

"I don't feel ready."

Caleb smiled. "Readiness rarely arrives before responsibility."

Daniel frowned. "That doesn't seem fair."

Caleb laughed softly. "Leadership often isn't."

Daniel sighed. "I don't want to mess this up."

"You will," Caleb said calmly. "But you'll also learn when you do."

Daniel looked at him, uncertain. "How do you live with that?"

Caleb thought for a moment. "By staying accountable. By staying teachable. And by remembering that what's multiplying here doesn't depend on perfection."

Daniel nodded slowly. "I can try that."

As these little moments accumulated, Caleb began to notice something else. The stories people told were changing. They spoke less about what was happening to them and more about what they were noticing in others. Less about experiences and more about relationships. The language of ownership was giving way to the language of participation.

It wasn't dramatic.

But it was formative.

One Sunday afternoon, Caleb sat with Margaret after most people had gone home. She sipped her tea slowly, watching the light through the hall windows.

"It feels like things are spreading," she said. "Not outward. Inward."

Caleb smiled. "That's a good way of putting it."

She nodded. "It also means we can't keep track of everything."

"No," Caleb agreed. "And that's part of the trust."

Margaret looked at him thoughtfully. "You're doing something difficult, Pastor."

"What's that?" he asked.

"You're letting people grow without hovering."

Caleb smiled faintly. "It doesn't always feel like success."

"It rarely does," she said. "But it feels faithful."

That evening, at home, Caleb told Rachel about the chairs, the conversations, the quiet gatherings forming without instruction. She listened, then said, "You sound both encouraged and unsettled."

"That's accurate," Caleb replied.

She smiled. "That usually means you're in the right place."

Later, as the house grew quiet, Caleb opened his notebook once more.

Multiplication does not ask to be managed.
It asks to be trusted.

He closed the book and sat back, aware that Willowend was entering a new phase. One where care, attentiveness, and responsibility were no longer held centrally, but shared.

That sharing would bring risk.

It would also bring life.

And Caleb sensed that the church was learning, slowly and imperfectly, how to carry that life together.

Not by controlling what multiplied.

But by remaining faithful to the posture that allowed it to grow.

By the end of the month, Caleb could feel the shift settling into something more stable. Not fixed. Not finished. But established enough that it no longer depended on novelty or momentum.

What was multiplying across Willowend was not activity, but confidence - a quiet confidence that people could respond to God and to one another without waiting for instruction at every turn. That confidence brought with it a new set of questions.

One morning, Caleb received a message from a couple who had recently begun attending more regularly. They weren't asking for a meeting or guidance. They simply wrote to say they had checked on a neighbour who had been unwell and wondered if the church had a system for that sort of thing.

Caleb read the message twice.

They were not seeking permission.

They were seeking connection.

He replied simply, thanking them and letting them know they had done well. There was no mention of any structure or coordination. He trusted that if something more was needed, it would become clear in time.

Later that day, he ran into Howard outside the post office.

"You're getting quieter," Howard observed.

Caleb smiled. "So I'm told."

Howard studied him. "That can make people nervous."

"Yes," Caleb agreed. "Especially those who expect leadership to be visible."

"And does that concern you?"

Caleb considered the question. "It would, if people were becoming less engaged. But they're not. They're just engaging with one another."

Howard nodded slowly. "That takes courage."

"It takes restraint," Caleb replied. "Courage comes later."

At the servo, Amelia was discovering that multiplication did not always feel affirming.

The small groups of women continued to gather sporadically, but the conversations were not always gentle or hopeful. Sometimes they carried frustration. Sometimes it was weariness. Sometimes disappointment with the church itself.

Amelia listened carefully, resisting the urge to correct or explain. She reminded herself that attentiveness did not require agreement.

One afternoon, after a particularly heavy conversation, she found herself sitting alone, wondering whether she should have said more.

When Caleb came in later, she said quietly, "I don't know if I'm helping."

Caleb looked at her. "What makes you think that?"

"I didn't make anything better," she replied.

Caleb smiled gently. "You made it safe. That's not nothing."

She exhaled slowly. "It just doesn't feel very productive."

"Multiplication rarely does," Caleb said. "Until you look back."

Daniel was experiencing something similar.

He had begun meeting informally with a few others his age. They didn't call it a group. They didn't meet regularly. Sometimes they talked about faith. Sometimes they didn't. What mattered was that they kept coming back.

One evening, after one of these gatherings, Daniel sat with Caleb on the steps behind the church.

"I think they expect me to lead," Daniel said.

Caleb nodded. "Do you want to?"

Daniel shook his head. "I want to walk with them. Not get ahead."

Caleb smiled. "Then you're already leading."

Daniel frowned. "That doesn't feel like leadership."

"It rarely does from the inside," Caleb replied. "Especially when it's shared."

As these threads wove together, Caleb began to see a broader pattern forming. The renewal in Willowend was no longer something that could be described easily. It was no longer located in services or gatherings. It was taking place in conversations, in decisions made without fanfare, in the courage to act without certainty.

That made it harder to explain.

It also made it harder to disrupt.

One evening, Caleb received another message from outside the town. A polite inquiry. A request for an update. He read it, then set it aside for the night. Some things, he was learning, did not need immediate articulation.

Later, as he sat with Rachel after dinner, he said, "It's spreading faster than I can follow."

She smiled. "That's usually a good sign."

"It's also unsettling," he admitted.

She nodded. "Because it means it's no longer centred on you."

"Yes," Caleb said quietly.

They sat in silence for a while, both aware of the truth of that. Before bed, Caleb opened his notebook once more and wrote:

What multiplies beyond our control invites us to trust more deeply than we ever planned.

He closed the book and turned out the light.

Outside, Willowend rested under a wide, quiet sky.

No announcements marked the shift that had taken place.

No declarations signalled the change.

But something had moved.

Care had become shared.

Responsibility had become mutual.

Faith had become lived rather than managed.

And Caleb knew that from this point forward, the story would not belong to any one person or voice. It would unfold through the choices people made when no one was watching.

That knowledge did not lessen his role.

It changed it.

From guide to witness.

From organiser to steward.

From centre to participant.

And as that understanding settled within him, Caleb felt a strange, steady peace.

What had begun was no longer dependent on him.

And that, he realised, was exactly as it should be.

The questions did not arrive dramatically.

They surfaced in ordinary places, at ordinary times, when people thought they were simply making conversation.

Caleb noticed them first in the way sentences trailed off rather than concluded. In the pauses that followed statements once delivered with certainty.

In the gentle rise of *I'm not sure* … where … *this is how it is* … had once stood.

It wasn't doubt in the sense he had known before. It was not disbelief, nor was it rebellion. It was something more unsettled and more honest.

People were no longer satisfied with borrowed language.

One Wednesday morning, Caleb stopped at the bakery on his way back from a hospital visit. Sheila greeted him as usual, but instead of chatting about the weather or the price of flour, she hesitated.

"Can I ask you something?" she said.

"Of course," Caleb replied.

She wiped her hands on her apron, eyes thoughtful. "I've been thinking a lot lately. About prayer. About whether I actually believe what I say I believe."

Caleb nodded. "That sounds important."

She looked relieved at his response. "It feels important. But also uncomfortable. I don't want to sound ungrateful or negative."

"You don't," Caleb said gently. "You sound awake."

She smiled faintly. "Is that allowed?"

Caleb smiled back. "It's often the beginning."

As he left the bakery, Caleb felt once again that familiar tension between reassurance and permission. There had been seasons in his ministry where questions were treated as problems to be solved. This season was different. Questions were not obstacles. They were signs of engagement.

At the servo later, Amelia encountered something similar. A man she recognised but barely knew leaned on the counter and said abruptly, "Do you ever wonder if we've just been going along with things because it's easier than thinking?"

Amelia blinked. "Sometimes," she said honestly.

He nodded, as if that was all he needed. "Me too."

He paid and left without another word.

Amelia stood quietly for a moment, struck by how little had been said and how much had been shared. The questions people carried were no longer looking for answers as much as they were looking for permission to exist.

Daniel felt that shift keenly.

He had begun to notice that conversations with friends often circled around uncertainty. Not just about faith, but about life direction, relationships, and purpose.

The old confidence of youth had softened into something more reflective.

One evening, sitting with a small group behind the church, someone said, "I feel like I don't know what I believe anymore. Or maybe I'm just not sure how to say it."

Daniel felt the familiar urge to respond with something helpful, something clarifying. Instead, he waited.

After a moment, he said, "I think I'm learning that not knowing isn't the same as losing faith."

The group grew quiet.

"That helps," someone murmured.

Daniel felt a mixture of relief and uncertainty. He wasn't sure whether what he had said was wise or simply true to where he was. But no one pushed back. The conversation deepened rather than scattered.

Caleb watched these developments with both gratitude and care. Questions, he knew, could deepen faith. They could also destabilise it if handled poorly. The difference lay not in the questions themselves, but in how they were held.

At the next leadership gathering, the theme emerged again.

"I've noticed people asking harder questions lately," someone said. "About Scripture. About church. About God."

Howard nodded. "That's true."

Another added, "Some of them feel uncomfortable. Almost like they're doubting."

Caleb spoke slowly. "Doubt isn't always the opposite of faith. Sometimes it's the refining of it."

The room grew still.

Margaret spoke next. "When people stop asking questions, that's when I worry."

There were murmurs of agreement.

Caleb felt encouraged. This was not panic. It was awareness. Still, he knew the terrain ahead would be delicate. Questions had a way of spreading, not because people wanted to disrupt, but because they wanted to belong honestly.

That evening, as he walked home, Caleb was thinking about the difference between certainty and trust. Certainty usually closed conversation. Trust kept it open.

At home, Rachel noticed his quiet preoccupation.

"You're carrying something again," she said.

"Yes," Caleb replied. "People are asking more questions."

She smiled. "That sounds like growth."

"It is," he said. "But it also asks more of us."

She nodded. "Listening usually does."

Later, as Caleb sat at his desk, he opened his notebook and wrote:

Questions that refuse to stay quiet are often
asking for space, not answers.

He closed the book, aware that the next season in Willowend would require courage of a different kind. Not the courage to proclaim or defend, but the courage to remain present when clarity did not arrive quickly.

Outside, the town settled into evening. Lights flickered on. Conversations drifted through open windows. Life continued in its familiar rhythms.

But beneath that familiarity, something was stirring again.

Not certainty.

Not rebellion.

But a deeper honesty.

And Caleb sensed that if Willowend could learn to hold its questions with patience and care, they would discover a faith that did not depend on having everything resolved.

A faith strong enough to live with mystery.

A faith willing to stay.

As the questions multiplied, Caleb became increasingly aware that they were not all of the same kind. Some were theological, pressing gently against long-held interpretations. Others were deeply personal, rooted in grief, disappointment, or unfulfilled longing. Still others were practical, asking what faith looked like when life refused to follow familiar patterns. Treating them all the same would have been easier, but it would not have been faithful.

One afternoon, Caleb met with a man who had been part of Willowend on and off for years. They sat across from one another in the small meeting room, sunlight falling unevenly across the table.

"I don't know if I believe the same things anymore," the man said abruptly.

Caleb nodded. "Tell me what's changed."

The man rubbed his hands together slowly. "I don't know that anything's changed. That's the problem. I've just realised I don't know why I believe what I believe."

Caleb listened without interruption.

"I've been repeating many words for years," the man continued. "Creeds, prayers, songs. And now I'm not sure which of them are mine."

Caleb leaned forward. "That doesn't sound like disbelief," he said. "It sounds like ownership beginning."

The man frowned. "It feels like loss."

Caleb nodded. "It often does. Especially when borrowed faith starts to loosen."

They sat in silence for a moment.

"So what do I do?" the man asked quietly.

"You stay," Caleb replied. "You ask. You don't rush to replace what's loosening with something else."

The man exhaled slowly. "I was afraid you'd say that."

Caleb smiled faintly. "I know."

At the servo, Amelia noticed a similar pattern emerging.

People no longer spoke in generalities as much. Their comments were more specific, more tentative.

"I don't know how to pray anymore," one woman admitted one morning. "It feels like I'm talking to the ceiling."

Amelia nodded. "Sometimes prayer feels like waiting rather than speaking."

The woman looked relieved. "So it's not just me?"

"No," Amelia said. "It's a lot of us."

That simple exchange stayed with Amelia throughout the day. She realised that people weren't asking for techniques or explanations. They were asking whether uncertainty disqualified them from belonging.

That night, she wrote another note to herself:

If doubt feels lonely, presence matters more than answers.

Daniel was experiencing the questions in a more internal way.

He had grown up assuming faith would eventually feel settled, that maturity would bring clarity. Instead, he felt as though each step forward revealed new layers of uncertainty.

One evening, after a long conversation with friends, he found himself walking alone through town, unsettled.

When he saw the light on in Caleb's office, he stopped by.

"I thought faith was meant to simplify things," Daniel said once they were seated.

Caleb smiled. "Many people think that."

"But it feels like it's doing the opposite," Daniel continued. "The more I engage, the more complicated it becomes."

Caleb nodded. "That's often a sign that you're no longer dealing in abstractions."

Daniel frowned. "Is that good?"

"It's real," Caleb replied. "And real things are rarely simple."

Daniel leaned back. "I don't know if I like that."

Caleb smiled gently. "You don't have to like it. You just have to stay with it."

As these conversations accumulated, Caleb became aware that the church's role was shifting yet again. It was no longer simply a place of comfort or renewal. It was becoming a space where unresolved questions could be held without embarrassment.

That was both gift and risk.

Not everyone appreciated it.

One Sunday morning, a long-time member approached Caleb with a concerned expression.

"I'm worried," she said. "Things feel less certain lately."

Caleb nodded. "They do."

"Isn't church meant to provide answers?" she asked.

"Sometimes," Caleb replied. "But it's also meant to teach us how to live with questions."

She frowned. "That feels dangerous."

Caleb smiled. "Only if we believe faith depends on certainty."

She walked away unconvinced, and Caleb let her go with quiet prayer. Not every concern needed immediate resolution.

At the next leadership gathering, the tension surfaced again.

"How do we stop people from drifting?" someone asked.

Caleb considered the question carefully. "We don't stop them from drifting," he said. "We walk with them while they're drifting."

Howard nodded slowly. "That takes patience."

"Yes," Caleb agreed. "And trust."

Margaret spoke next. "People drift when they feel alone. Not when they feel heard."

The group fell quiet, absorbing the truth of it.

Later that night, Caleb sat alone at home, the house unusually still. Rachel had gone to bed early, and the silence felt heavier than usual.

He thought about the expectations people placed on church - to resolve, to clarify, to reassure. And he thought about the quieter calling he felt settling in this season.

To host questions rather than answer them.

To create safety rather than certainty.

To trust that God was not threatened by honest uncertainty.

Before turning in for the night, Caleb wrote in his notebook:

Faith deepens not when questions disappear,
but when they are allowed to stay.

He closed the book and sat quietly for a while, aware that the weeks ahead would require discernment of a different kind.

Not the discernment to guide action, but the discernment to recognise when restraint was the truest form of leadership.

Outside, Willowend rested as it always had. The same streets.

The same houses. The same quiet pace.

But beneath the surface, something was shifting again.

Questions were no longer whispering.

They were speaking aloud.

And Caleb sensed that if Willowend could learn to listen without fear, those questions would not weaken faith - they would deepen it.

By the middle of the week, Caleb began to feel the cumulative weight of the conversations he had been having.

None of them were confrontational. None were hostile. Yet together they formed a steady pressure, like water against a bank - not threatening to burst through, but reshaping the edges all the same.

On Thursday morning he arrived at the church earlier than usual. The building was quiet, the sanctuary still dim, the air cool before the day gathered its heat. He sat in the front pew rather than his office, letting the silence settle around him.

For years, his instinct as a pastor had been to move toward resolution. To guide people toward clarity. To help them name what they believed and why it mattered. That instinct had not disappeared, but it was being re-trained. What Willowend needed now was not resolution, but room.

Room for questions that did not yet know how to become prayers.

Room for faith that was loosening its grip on borrowed certainty.

Room for people who were discovering that doubt was not the opposite of belief, but often its companion.

As he sat there, he remembered something Mary had once said to him years earlier, long before the fire, long before the renewal. "God doesn't rush the soil," she had said. "He waits for it to soften."

At the time, Caleb had just nodded politely without fully understanding. Now the words felt like instruction.

Later that morning, Amelia stopped by the church with a bag of sandwiches. She had begun doing this, unannounced, as though testing whether small acts of generosity could be expressions of faith rather than obligations.

"I figured you'd forget to eat," she said, setting the bag down.

Caleb smiled. "You're probably right. Thank you."

She lingered near the doorway instead of leaving straight away. "I've been thinking," she said slowly. "About all the questions people are asking."

"Yes?" Caleb replied.

"I don't think they're asking because they want answers," she said. "I think they're asking because they're afraid of asking them alone."

Caleb nodded. "I think you're right."

She hesitated. "Does that mean we're doing something wrong? Letting things feel so… unfinished?"

Caleb considered the question carefully. "I think we're doing something harder," he said. "We're resisting the urge to tidy things up too quickly."

Amelia smiled faintly. "That sounds like something Rachel would say."

Caleb laughed softly. "She's taught me a lot."

After Amelia left, Caleb received a call from Ruth. It caught him by surprise - she rarely rang during the week.

"Hi, Dad," she said brightly. "Have you got a minute?"

"For you? Always."

"I was just calling because I've been thinking about Willowend," she said. "And about what you're doing there."

Caleb leaned back in his chair. "That's dangerous."

She laughed. "I know. But listen… I had coffee with a colleague this morning. She's not religious at all. And she asked me what kind of church you lead."

Caleb waited.

"I didn't know how to explain it properly," Ruth continued. "So I just said, 'It's a place where people are allowed to be honest.'"

Caleb felt a quiet tightening in his chest. "That sounds accurate."

She paused. "I hope that's okay."

"It's more than okay," he said gently.

"Well," she replied, "whatever you're doing, keep doing it. It sounds like something people need."

After the call ended, Caleb sat quietly for a moment. Ruth's words stayed with him longer than he expected. Not because they affirmed his work, but because they named it simply.

A place where people are allowed to be honest.

That afternoon, Daniel arrived at the church looking unsettled. "I think I upset someone," he said as soon as he sat down.

Caleb raised an eyebrow. "That happens."

Daniel ran a hand through his hair. "I told them I wasn't sure what I believed about something. And they looked at me like I'd said I was leaving the faith altogether."

Caleb nodded. "Uncertainty can feel threatening to people who rely on certainty for safety."

"So what do I do?" Daniel asked. "Stop talking?"

"No," Caleb replied firmly. "You speak carefully, not silently." Daniel frowned. "What's the difference?"

"Silence hides questions," Caleb said. "Careful speech honours them without weaponising them."

Daniel absorbed that.

"I don't want to break anything," he said quietly.

Caleb smiled. "You won't. This community is learning how to bend without breaking."

As the week drew toward Sunday, Caleb sensed that something important was taking shape beneath the surface. Not an initiative. Not a program. A posture.

The church was becoming a place where certainty was no longer the currency of belonging.

That did not sit easily with everyone.

On Saturday evening, a small group gathered for prayer. The tone was quieter than it had been in previous weeks. No one rushed to fill the silence.

When people spoke, their words were simple.

"Teach us to listen," one woman prayed.

"Give us patience," another said.

Caleb did not lead the prayer time. He did not need to.

As he drove home later that night, he realised that leadership in this season was not about direction, but about containment. Holding the space steady enough that people could remain present without collapsing into fear or defensiveness.

It was exhausting work in a way he had not anticipated.

But it was also deeply hopeful.

On Sunday morning, the sanctuary filled slowly. There was no sense of urgency, no anxious energy. People greeted one another warmly, but without chatter.

When Caleb stood to speak, he did not preach a sermon designed to resolve tension. Instead, he spoke about God's patience. About Jesus' willingness to sit with questions. About faith as a journey that included seasons of clarity and seasons of unknowing.

He did not tell people what to think.

He invited them to stay.

After the service, no one rushed out.

Conversations unfolded in small clusters.

Some were light. Others were serious. All felt unhurried.

As Caleb watched the room, he understood something that had been forming quietly all week.

Renewal did not always arrive with fire or fervour.

Sometimes it arrived as permission.

Permission to ask.

Permission to wait.

Permission to trust that God was not finished simply because answers had not yet arrived.

Willowend was learning how to live with open hands.

And Caleb sensed that this, too, was holy ground.

By the time Caleb realised that Willowend had changed again, the change was already visible.

It showed itself not in numbers first, but in movement. People lingered longer after services. They arrived earlier for gatherings that once required reminders.

Conversations began before chairs were set out and continued after lights were dimmed. There was a sense that people were no longer attending church as an event, but inhabiting it as a place.

Caleb noticed it on a Tuesday morning when he arrived to find three cars already parked outside the church. He paused for a moment before getting out, mildly surprised. There was nothing scheduled. No meeting, no working bee, no prayer gathering.

Inside, he found Margaret Ellis sitting with Amelia at one of the long tables, mugs of tea between them. Daniel was nearby, leaning against the wall, listening more than speaking.

"We didn't mean to interrupt," Amelia said quickly when she saw him. "We were just talking."

"You're not interrupting," Caleb replied. "You're early."

Margaret smiled. "We thought we'd use the space."

That phrase stayed with him - *use the space.*

It was not possessive. It was not presumptive. It was simply honest. The building no longer felt like something people borrowed. It felt like something they belonged to.

As the morning unfolded, more people came and went. No one asked permission. No one waited for instruction. They greeted one another, shared updates, then drifted apart again.

By midday, Caleb had answered fewer emails than usual. Instead, he had listened. A lot. One man spoke about feeling called to start visiting an elderly neighbour.

A woman admitted she had been reading Scripture again for the first time in years, slowly, without agenda. Another quietly confessed that she was learning how to pray without apologising for her doubts.

None of them asked, "Is this allowed?"

They were no longer looking for permission.

That afternoon, Caleb took a walk through town, needing air more than answers. At the servo, Amelia waved him over.

"Busy today?" she asked.

"Unexpectedly," he replied.

She grinned. "Good busy?"

"Yes," he said after a moment. "Good busy."

She hesitated, then said, "Some people asked if we're starting something new."

Caleb raised an eyebrow. "And what did you tell them?"

"That nothing's been announced," she said. "But something's happening anyway."

He smiled. "That sounds about right."

As he continued walking, Caleb became aware of another shift. People were beginning to talk about the church again - not defensively, not apologetically, but naturally.

The questions were changing too.

Not *What does your church believe?*

But *What's going on there?*

That evening, Caleb met with Howard and a small group of leaders. The atmosphere was thoughtful rather than urgent.

"I think we need to talk about visibility," Howard said.

Caleb nodded. "I've been thinking the same thing."

"It's not that we're trying to attract attention," Margaret added. "It's that attention is coming anyway."

"And not all of it will be friendly," someone else said.

Caleb reassured them, "Growth always brings scrutiny. Especially when it's quiet and unstructured."

"So what do we do?" Howard asked.

"We stay the same," Caleb replied. "We don't perform. We don't explain more than is necessary. We let fruit speak for itself."

There was a pause.

"That takes nerve," Howard said.

"Yes," Caleb agreed. "And trust."

Later that night, Caleb sat at home, the day replaying itself in fragments. He was not anxious, but he was alert. Growth was no longer theoretical. It was embodied, relational, visible.

And visibility always carried consequence.

Rachel noticed his restlessness as he moved around the kitchen.

"You're thinking again," she said gently.

"I am," he admitted. "Things are changing."

"They always do," she replied. "The question is whether we panic when they do."

He smiled faintly. "I don't feel panicked. Just aware."

She nodded. "That's different."

He paused, then said, "People are starting to take ownership. Real ownership."

Rachel smiled. "That's what you've been praying for."

"Yes," he said. "And now that it's here, it feels... weighty."

She reached across the table and took his hand. "Growth always asks more of us than we expect. Not more activity. More wisdom."

He squeezed her hand lightly. "I don't want to over-direct."

"Then don't," she said simply. "Trust what God is already doing."

Later, as Caleb prepared for bed, he checked his phone and saw a message from Daniel.

Just wanted to say thanks for earlier. I think I'm starting to understand what faith looks like when it's lived, not explained.

Caleb stared at the screen for a long moment before replying.

That's a good thing to understand early.

He set the phone aside and sat quietly, the house settling around him. Willowend was not what it had been a year ago. It was not even what it had been a month ago.

The renewal was no longer something that could be contained within private conversations and small gatherings. It was beginning to leave traces.

And Caleb sensed that the season ahead would require discernment of a sharper kind.

Not to generate movement.

But to guard it.

Because when growth becomes visible, it also becomes vulnerable.

And how Willowend navigated that truth would matter more than anyone yet realised.

By midweek, the visibility Caleb had sensed earlier began to show itself in subtler, more complicated ways. It arrived first as curiosity. A phone call from a pastor in a neighbouring town, asking casually how things were going.

An email from someone connected loosely to the State Baptist Association, congratulating Willowend on "the recent momentum." A comment from a local councillor, made half in jest, that the church seemed to be "busy these days."

None of it was hostile. None of it was overtly supportive either. It was simply attention.

Caleb found himself weighing his responses carefully. Not because he wanted to control the narrative, but because he did not want to distort it.

There was a temptation, subtle but persistent, to frame what was happening in ways others would understand more easily. To name it. To summarise it. To package it.

He resisted that impulse.

What was happening in Willowend was not a strategy. It was not even a clearly defined movement. It was the slow accumulation of faith expressed honestly, imperfectly, and without spectacle. Any attempt to explain it too neatly would reduce it.

On Wednesday afternoon, he met with Amelia and Daniel at the church. They had not asked for the meeting. They had simply stayed after a casual conversation until it became clear they were all circling the same unease.

"It feels like people are looking to us now," Amelia said, voicing what all three of them were sensing.

Caleb nodded. "They are."

"That scares me a bit," Daniel admitted. "I don't feel equipped for that."

"You're not meant to," Caleb replied. "That's not a failure. It's a safeguard."

Amelia frowned slightly. "But if people are watching, shouldn't we be more... intentional?"

Caleb considered the word. "Intentional about what?"

She hesitated. "About not messing it up."

Caleb smiled gently. "You will mess it up. We all will. The question is whether we do it honestly or defensively."

Daniel leaned forward. "So what does leadership look like in this season?"

Caleb paused before answering. "It looks like resisting the urge to become impressive."

They both absorbed that.

"People are drawn to authenticity right now," he continued. "Not confidence. Not certainty. Authenticity. The moment we start performing faith, we lose the very thing people are responding to."

Amelia nodded slowly. "So we keep doing what we're doing."

"Yes," Caleb said. "And we let responsibility grow organically, not hierarchically."

Daniel exhaled. "That feels risky."

"It is," Caleb agreed. "But it's also faithful."

That evening, Caleb attended a gathering of local ministers. It was informal, held in the back room of a pub, and the tone was friendly but cautious.

"So," one pastor said lightly, "what's the secret over there at Willowend?"

Caleb smiled. "There isn't one."

Another chuckled. "Come on. Churches don't just grow quietly."

Caleb met his gaze calmly. "Sometimes they do."

The conversation moved on, but Caleb felt the undercurrent remain. He knew that some would interpret Willowend's renewal through their own frameworks. Others would feel threatened. A few might feel inspired. He could not control that. What he could control was his own posture.

Driving home that night, he reflected on something Rachel had once said to him a few years earlier, during a season of real discouragement.

"Faithfulness doesn't need defending," she had said. "It needs tending."

That phrase returned to him now, not so much as comfort, but as instruction.

On Thursday morning, he received another unexpected visitor. A woman he recognised vaguely from town but had never spoken with before stood hesitantly at the church door.

"I hope I'm not intruding," she said.

"You're not," Caleb replied. "Come in."

She sat awkwardly, hands folded tightly in her lap.

"I've been watching," she said, then flushed. "That sounds a little strange."

Caleb waited.

"My husband says the church has changed," she continued. "That it feels… different. Kinder."

Caleb nodded. "I hope so."

She swallowed. "I haven't been to church in years. But I was wondering … would it be all right if I came and just sat?"

"Yes," Caleb said immediately. "It would."

She looked relieved, almost startled by the simplicity of the answer.

"I thought there might be expectations," she admitted.

"There are," Caleb said gently. "But they're not about behaviour. They're about honesty."

She smiled faintly. "I think I can manage that."

After she left, Caleb sat for a long time, reflecting on how many people were approaching the church not because they were ready to commit, but because they were ready to risk being seen.

That, he realised, was the cost of visibility. People brought not only hope, but history. Not only openness, but wounds.

The church would need to learn how to carry both.

That night, at home, he spoke quietly with Rachel about the week.

"It feels heavier," he admitted. "Not burdensome. Just... significant."

She nodded. "Growth always adds weight."

"I'm concerned about burnout," he said. "Not just mine, but everyone's."

Rachel smiled. "Then pace matters. And permission to rest."

He looked at her. "I don't want us to become the centre of everything."

She met his gaze. "Then keep pointing away from yourselves."

Later, lying awake, Caleb thought about the word *responsibility*. It had always carried a sense of duty for him. Obligation. Expectation.

But now it felt different.

Responsibility was not about control.

It was about care.

Care for people discovering faith anew.

Care for those carrying doubts they had never named.

Care for leaders emerging without scripts or certainty.

And care for a community learning how to be seen without becoming self-conscious.

As sleep finally came, Caleb sensed that Willowend was entering a season where growth would test not its capacity, but its character.

Not whether it could expand.

But whether it could remain gentle.

Because carrying what God gives requires more wisdom than asking for more. And the weeks ahead would reveal whether Willowend was ready for that weight.

By the end of the week, Caleb was beginning to recognise a new kind of fatigue settling into his body. It was not the exhaustion that came from overwork or crisis, but the slower weariness that accompanied attentiveness. The kind that came from listening carefully, weighing words, and holding space without rushing to fill it.

On Friday morning, he took his Bible and notebook down to the river track on the edge of town. It was a path he had walked many times before, often when sermons felt heavy or decisions unclear. The river itself was low this time of year, moving slowly between exposed stones, but it still carried a steady sound - a reminder that movement did not require urgency.

He sat on a fallen log and read without agenda. Not searching for a passage to preach. Not looking for confirmation. Simply reading.

The words that stayed with him were ordinary ones. Jesus withdrawing from the crowds. Pausing before responding. Refusing to perform when pressed for signs.

Caleb closed the Bible and let the stillness do its work.

Visibility had arrived in Willowend. He could no longer pretend otherwise. People were watching, not in a voyeuristic way, but with expectation. And expectation, even when gentle, had the power to shape behaviour if left unchecked.

What concerned him was not opposition. It was imitation.

Already, he had noticed small shifts in language. People repeating phrases they had heard him use. Others deferring decisions to those who seemed more confident. A subtle drift toward hierarchy, not imposed, but assumed.

That was how movements hardened. Not through malice, but through habit.

Later that day, Caleb met briefly with Howard and Margaret. The conversation was unplanned, but it moved quickly to what was weighing on all of them.

"We need to protect the centre," Margaret said quietly.

Howard nodded. "Whatever that centre is."

Caleb considered the words. "The centre isn't a doctrine or a leader," he said. "It's actually a posture. Openness. Humility. A willingness to listen."

Howard sighed. "Those are hard to institutionalise."

"Yes," Caleb replied. "Which is why we must resist trying."

Margaret leaned forward. "So how do we guard something we can't structure?"

Caleb paused. "By naming it. And by modelling it consistently."

That evening, Caleb received another call from a pastor he barely knew. The tone was friendly enough, but the question was direct. "Are you planning to formalise what's happening?"

Caleb chose his words carefully. "No," he said. "We're trying to stay responsive rather than strategic."

There was a pause on the line.

"That sounds… vague," the pastor replied.

Caleb smiled. "It probably is."

After the call ended, Caleb sat quietly for a while. He understood the discomfort.

Many leaders felt safer when renewal could be defined, categorised, and replicated. What was happening in Willowend resisted all three.

On Saturday afternoon, Daniel stopped by unexpectedly. He looked thoughtful rather than troubled.

"I've been asked to lead something," he said.

Caleb raised an eyebrow. "Have you?"

"Yes," Daniel replied. "A few people want to meet and talk about Scripture. Not a study exactly. More like… shared reading."

Caleb nodded. "And what do you think?"

"I'm not sure," Daniel admitted. "I don't want to become someone people rely on too much."

"That's wise," Caleb said. "But don't confuse humility with avoidance."

Daniel frowned. "How do I tell the difference?"

"You ask whether you're willing to stay honest," Caleb replied. "And whether you're willing to let others lead alongside you."

Daniel smiled faintly. "That feels doable."

"Then say yes," Caleb said. "And keep it simple."

On Sunday morning, the service unfolded quietly. No sense of urgency. No overt emotion. Just steady presence. When Caleb spoke, he addressed the growing awareness directly.

"Growth can make us nervous," he said. "Especially when it doesn't come with instructions. But the work God does among us is not fragile. It doesn't need managing. It needs attending."

People listened closely.

"We are not here to build something impressive," he continued. "We are here to remain faithful. And sometimes faithfulness looks like restraint."

After the service, Caleb noticed something that reassured him. People did not cluster around him. They spoke with one another. Listened to one another. Prayed quietly in pairs and small groups.

Leadership was dispersing, not consolidating.

That afternoon, as the town settled into its usual rhythm, Caleb walked home with Rachel. The air was warm, the pace unhurried.

"You seem lighter," she said.

"I am," he admitted. "I think I was afraid we'd lose our way once things became visible."

"And now?"

"And now I think the centre is holding."

She smiled. "Because it was never about you."

He laughed softly. "That helps."

As evening fell, Caleb sat on the veranda and watched the last light fade from the paddocks. Willowend looked as it always had. Quiet. Unassuming. Easy to overlook.

But beneath that surface, something steady was forming. Not a movement that demanded attention, but a community learning how to remain open without becoming unguarded.

The renewal had moved beyond novelty. Beyond excitement. It was entering a stage that required maturity.

And Caleb knew that the true test of what God was doing would not be how quickly it spread, but how gently it was held.

The quiet centre mattered.

If Willowend could guard that, everything else would find its place.

Caleb noticed the shift not because something new appeared, but because something familiar began to feel heavier.

It happened on a Monday morning, quietly, as so many things did in Willowend. He arrived at the church just after eight, expecting the usual stillness, only to find two cars already parked outside. That alone was not unusual anymore. What unsettled him was the way both drivers remained seated, hands on steering wheels, as though waiting for something unspoken to happen.

He unlocked the front door and stepped inside. The sanctuary smelled faintly of polish and dust, warmed by the early sun pressing through the windows. He set his bag down, flicked on the lights, and waited.

A few minutes later, the door creaked open and one of the drivers entered - a woman Caleb recognised but did not know well. She hesitated, then smiled apologetically.

"I wasn't sure if this was a good time," she said.

"It's fine," Caleb replied. "Come in."

She sat near the back, posture careful, as though unsure how much space she was allowed to occupy.

"I've been thinking a lot," she began, then stopped. "Everyone seems to be thinking a lot lately."

Caleb nodded. "That's true."

She took a breath. "I don't want to be a burden."

"You're not," he said gently.

Her shoulders relaxed a fraction. "I just… people keep telling me to come and talk to you. Like you'll know what to say."

Caleb smiled faintly. "That's optimistic of them."

She laughed softly, then grew serious again. "What if you don't?"

"Then we'll sit with that together," he replied.

She looked relieved, and they talked quietly for a while. Nothing dramatic. No revelation. Just words laid carefully on the table between them.

When she left, the second car was gone. Whoever had been waiting had changed their mind.

Caleb stood for a moment in the empty sanctuary, aware that something subtle was unfolding. People were no longer merely curious about the church. They were turning inward, bringing questions that had nowhere else to land.

By mid-morning, Amelia dropped by with her usual easy confidence, but Caleb noticed the slight tension beneath it.

"Busy already?" she asked.

"Yes," he said. "And not in the usual ways."

She nodded. "People are asking things at the servo too. Not about fuel or prices. About meaning. About whether what's happening here is real."

"And what do you tell them?"

"I tell them it feels real," she said. "But that it doesn't come with a manual."

Caleb smiled. "That's honest."

She hesitated. "Some of them want reassurance. They want to know they won't lose themselves if they lean in."

Caleb considered that. "Sometimes people are afraid that faith will take more than it gives."

Amelia nodded. "I think that's exactly it."

As she left, Caleb felt the weight settle more clearly.

The renewal had reached a stage where enthusiasm was giving way to discernment. People were no longer asking whether something was happening. They were asking what it would cost them if it did.

That afternoon, Daniel arrived, quieter than usual.

"I think I messed up," he said, once they were seated.

Caleb raised an eyebrow. "Tell me."

"I tried to explain what faith looks like for me now," Daniel said.

"And someone told me I sounded uncertain."

"And were you?"

"Yes," Daniel admitted. "But not lost."

Caleb smiled. "That's an important distinction."

"They didn't see it that way," Daniel said. "They said faith should sound more confident."

Caleb leaned forward slightly. "Confidence can be comforting. But it's not the same as depth."

Daniel frowned. "So what do I do?"

"You stay truthful," Caleb replied. "And you accept that not everyone will be comfortable with that."

Daniel sat back, absorbing the words. "It feels like the closer people get, the more afraid they become."

"Yes," Caleb said quietly. "Because proximity removes illusion."

That evening, Caleb and Rachel sat together on the veranda as the day cooled. The sky was streaked with pale orange, the paddocks still and quiet.

"You're carrying a lot," Rachel said gently.

"I feel it," he admitted. "People are no longer asking whether God is near. They're asking what that nearness demands."

Rachel nodded. "That's the very moment when faith becomes personal."

"And costly," Caleb added.

"Yes," she agreed. "But also honest."

He looked out across the town, lights beginning to flicker on one by one. Willowend appeared unchanged, yet beneath that familiar calm, something was pressing inward.

"I'm worried about dependency," he said after a while. "That people will start leaning too heavily on a few voices."

Rachel turned to him. "Then keep widening the circle."

"I'm trying," he said. "But it's much harder when people want certainty."

She smiled faintly. "Certainty is easier to borrow than courage."

Later that night, Caleb sat alone with his notebook. He did not write much, just a single line that felt important enough to hold onto.

When attention turns inward,
leadership must become quieter, not louder.

He closed the book and sat in the stillness, aware that Willowend was entering another delicate season. Not one defined by growth or visibility, but by depth.

People were no longer standing at the edges, observing.

They were stepping closer, asking what it meant to remain.

And Caleb knew that how the church responded now would shape not just what Willowend became, but how safely people could bring their whole selves into that becoming.

The work ahead would require restraint, patience, and courage of a different kind. And he sensed that this season, more than any before it, would test not the strength of Willowend's faith - but its gentleness.

Caleb became more aware of the inward turn as the days unfolded, not because people spoke more loudly about it, but because they spoke more carefully. Words were chosen with greater hesitation. Pauses lingered a little longer than before. Conversations that once circled around church life now turned toward interior landscapes - fears, hopes, quiet resistances that had gone unnamed for years.

On Wednesday morning, he met with a small group that had begun gathering informally after the midweek service. There was no agenda. No leader assigned. Chairs were arranged in a loose circle, close enough to feel personal, far enough apart to allow breathing room.

They sat for a few moments before anyone spoke.

"I'm realising I don't know how to listen," one woman said finally. "Not properly. I'm used to fixing."

Several people nodded.

"I thought faith would make me more certain," another admitted. "But it's made me more aware of how much I don't know."

Caleb listened, resisting the familiar urge to summarise or to respond. He sensed that what mattered was not his contribution, but his restraint.

Afterward, as people drifted away, one man lingered.

"I hope this isn't selfish," he said quietly. "But everything feels closer lately. God. People. Even myself. And it's uncomfortable."

Caleb nodded. "Depth often is."

The man frowned. "Does it get easier?"

Caleb considered the question honestly. "It gets truer," he said. "Which sometimes feels harder before it feels lighter."

The man smiled faintly, as though relieved not to be reassured too quickly.

Over at the servo, Amelia noticed a similar pattern. Customers lingered longer at the counter. Questions that once ended with jokes now trailed off into silence.

One afternoon, a regular leaned against the counter and said, "I keep thinking about my father. Things I never said."

Amelia nodded. "That's been happening to a lot of people."

"Is that normal?" he asked.

"I think it's human," she replied. "Faith just gives it somewhere to land."

Later, she wrote another note to herself, the habit now firmly established.

If faith draws us inward, it's not to trap us there,
but to make us honest before we step outward again.

Daniel found the inward turn more unsettling.

He had always been comfortable with action. Doing something felt safer than sitting with questions. Now he found himself caught between a desire to help and an awareness that not everything needed his input.

One evening, he met with a few people who had asked him to read Scripture with them. The gathering was small, quiet, almost tentative. When the passage ended, no one spoke.

Daniel waited.

After a while, someone said, "I don't know what to say."

Daniel nodded. "That's okay."

Another added, "I thought I'd feel something."

Daniel hesitated, then replied, "Sometimes what we feel comes later."

They sat in silence for several more minutes before someone finally stood and said, "Thank you," and left.

Daniel drove home unsettled but strangely calm. He realised that leadership in this season was not about providing insight, but about being willing to remain present when insight refused to arrive on schedule.

That awareness stayed with him.

At home, Caleb and Rachel talked quietly late into the night.

"I'm seeing a lot more tenderness," Rachel said. "But also more vulnerability."

"Yes," Caleb replied. "People are no longer hiding behind activity."

"That's good," she said.

"It is," he agreed. "But it also means old wounds are closer to the surface."

Rachel nodded. "Then care matters more than momentum."

Caleb smiled faintly. "I think that's the lesson of this season."

The following Sunday, Caleb chose his words carefully. He did not speak about growth or renewal. He spoke about listening. About Jesus withdrawing when crowds pressed in. About the difference between urgency and faithfulness.

After the service, a woman approached him with tears in her eyes.

"I've been holding my breath for years," she said. "I didn't know it until now."

Caleb listened as she spoke of expectations she had never questioned, roles she had accepted without reflection, faith she had inherited but never examined.

"I don't know who I am without all that," she said quietly.

Caleb nodded. "Sometimes faith leads us through unknowing before it gives us clarity."

She exhaled slowly, as though releasing something she had been carrying alone.

That afternoon, Caleb took a walk through the town. The streets were quiet, the pace unhurried. He passed familiar houses, gardens tended with care, verandas worn smooth by years of use.

Willowend looked the same.

Yet he knew it was not.

The renewal had moved beneath the surface now, shaping interior spaces rather than public ones. This was not a season that would attract attention or applause. It was a season that would test patience, discernment, and trust.

As he walked, his phone buzzed. A brief message from Ruth.

Thinking of you today. I hope you're not carrying it all alone.

Caleb smiled and typed a simple reply.

I'm not. And I'm learning not to.

That evening, he sat with his notebook again, the words coming slowly.

When faith turns inward, leadership must resist urgency.
Depth cannot be rushed without being damaged.

He closed the notebook, aware that Willowend was entering a quieter, deeper stretch of the journey. Not one marked by visible change, but by interior realignment.

People were learning to sit with themselves. To listen without needing immediate answers. To trust that God was present even in the absence of clarity.

And Caleb sensed that if Willowend could learn to honour this inward season, it would emerge steadier, humbler, and more resilient than before.

The work was slower now. But it was no less holy.

By the end of the week, Caleb could feel the inward turn settling more firmly into the life of the church. It no longer surprised him.

What surprised him was how unevenly people carried it.

Some seemed to find relief in the slower pace, as though they had been waiting years for permission to stop striving. Others appeared unsettled, unsure what to do without clear markers of progress. The same quiet that brought peace to one person felt like absence to another.

On Friday afternoon, Caleb found himself sitting with Howard in the shade beside the church, both men watching the light shift across the gravel car park.

"I've had three conversations this week that left me uneasy," Howard said at last.

Caleb waited.

"Not because of what people said," Howard continued, "but because of what they expected me to do with it."

Caleb nodded. "Fix it?"

Howard smiled wryly. "Or at least name it. Wrap it up."

"Yes," Caleb said quietly. "That pressure is growing."

Howard sighed. "I'm not sure everyone realises how much restraint this season is asking of us."

"I think it is asking us to trust that God works without our commentary," Caleb replied.

Howard laughed softly. "That's harder than it sounds."

Later that day, Amelia came by with a bag of groceries she had picked up for Margaret Ellis. She set them down in the kitchen and lingered.

"People keep asking me how long this phase will last," she said. Caleb raised an eyebrow. "And what do you tell them?"

"I tell them I don't think it's a phase," Amelia replied. "I think it's a layer."

Caleb smiled. "That's well put."

She hesitated. "But sometimes I wonder if people are hoping it ends soon. Like they're waiting for the next clear direction."

"Yes," Caleb said. "Some people feel safest when faith gives instructions."

"What if that never comes?"

Caleb considered the question carefully. "Then we'll learn to live faithfully without it."

That evening, Daniel knocked on the door at home. He looked thoughtful, his energy quieter than usual.

"I'm not sure I'm helping," he said once they were seated.

Caleb met his gaze. "What makes you say that?"

"I don't have answers," Daniel said. "And sometimes I feel like that disappoints people."

Caleb nodded. "It might. But disappointment does not always mean failure."

Daniel frowned. "How do you know when it is?"

"When people leave because you won't give them certainty," Caleb replied, "or when they stay because you won't pretend."

Daniel absorbed that in silence.

"I'm staying," he said finally. "Even if I don't know where this leads."

Caleb smiled gently. "That's enough."

On Saturday morning, Caleb took a long walk through town. He passed the servo, the bakery, the school grounds. Familiar places, unchanged on the surface. Yet beneath that familiarity, he sensed a collective interior shift - people thinking, remembering, reconsidering.

Faith was no longer something external that people approached. It was something they were encountering within themselves, sometimes awkwardly, sometimes painfully.

As he walked, Caleb realised that the greatest temptation of this season was not fear, but impatience. The desire to move forward simply to escape the discomfort of waiting.

That night, the church hosted a quiet prayer gathering. No music. No structure. People arrived and left without ceremony. Some prayed aloud. Others sat silently. No one seemed in a hurry.

Caleb watched from the back, resisting the urge to shape the moment. This was not his to lead.

As the gathering ended, a woman approached him quietly.

"I don't feel any clearer," she said. "But I feel less alone."

Caleb nodded. "That matters."

She smiled faintly. "More than I expected."

On Sunday afternoon, Caleb and Rachel sat together on the veranda, the air warm and still.

"I think this season will cost some people," Caleb said softly.

Rachel nodded. "Yes. But it will deepen others."

"And some will leave," he added.

She met his gaze. "They might. But they won't leave because they weren't welcome."

Caleb exhaled slowly. "I want us to remain gentle."

Rachel smiled. "Then keep choosing listening over control."

As dusk settled, Caleb reflected on the subtle shift Willowend was undergoing. The renewal had moved beyond excitement, beyond visibility, beyond even growth.

It had entered a season of interior work.

Questions were being faced rather than answered. Silence was being honoured rather than filled. Faith was being disentangled from performance and expectation.

This was not a season that would impress anyone looking in from the outside.

But Caleb sensed, with quiet conviction, that it was the season that would determine whether Willowend's renewal had depth enough to last.

Because faith that cannot endure inward work will not withstand outward pressure.

And if Willowend could learn to remain faithful here - unhurried, attentive, and gentle - it would be ready for whatever lay ahead.

Not because it had clarity.

But because it had learned to listen.

The first sign that not everyone was experiencing the renewal in the same way came not through argument, but through distance.

Caleb noticed it on a Sunday morning when he scanned the sanctuary and realised a few familiar faces were missing. Not absent entirely - just intermittent. People who had once arrived early and stayed late now slipped in quietly or left without lingering. Others who had once spoken freely seemed more guarded, careful about what they shared and with whom.

At first, he assumed it was fatigue. Seasons shifted. Lives grew busy. Willowend had always ebbed and flowed. But as the weeks unfolded, the pattern became harder to ignore.

One afternoon, Howard asked if they could talk.

They sat in the small room off the sanctuary, the same place where many quiet conversations had unfolded over the years. Howard leaned back in his chair, arms folded loosely.

"I think we need to name something," he said.

Caleb nodded. "Go on."

"Not everyone is comfortable anymore," Howard continued. "Some people feel unsettled. And they don't quite know why."

Caleb listened.

"They're not angry," Howard added. "At least not openly. But they're uneasy. Like the ground beneath them has shifted just enough to make them unsure of their footing."

Caleb nodded slowly. "I've sensed that too."

Howard sighed. "They keep asking when things will settle."

"And what do you tell them?" Caleb asked.

"That I'm not sure they will," Howard replied. "Not in the way they mean."

Later that week, Caleb had a similar conversation with a woman who had been part of Willowend for decades. She sat across from him, hands folded carefully in her lap.

"I don't feel at home the way I used to," she said quietly.

Caleb did not rush to respond.

"It's not that anyone's done anything wrong," she continued. "It's just… everything feels less certain."

Caleb nodded. "That's true."

She looked up sharply. "You agree?"

"Yes," he said gently. "Things are less certain."

She frowned. "Isn't that a problem?"

Caleb considered his words carefully. "It can be. Or it can be an invitation."

She looked unconvinced. "An invitation to what?"

"To deeper trust," he replied. "Not in methods or patterns. In God."

She sat in silence for a long moment.

"I liked knowing what to expect," she said finally.

Caleb nodded. "Most of us do."

As she left, Caleb felt the familiar tension settle again. Renewal always revealed differences. Not in belief, but in temperament. Some people leaned naturally toward openness and process. Others found safety in structure and clarity. Neither was wrong. But they did not always move at the same pace.

At the servo, Amelia noticed it too.

A regular customer leaned on the counter one morning and said,

"Things feel a bit loose at the church."

Amelia raised an eyebrow. "Loose how?"

"Less defined," he replied. "Like nobody's quite steering."

Amelia smiled faintly. "Maybe the steering wheel is now being shared."

He laughed, but his expression remained thoughtful. "I'm not sure everyone likes that."

"No," Amelia agreed. "They don't."

Daniel encountered the differences more personally.

After one of the Scripture gatherings, someone pulled him aside.

"I don't think this is helping," the man said.

Daniel frowned. "What do you mean?"

"It feels vague," the man replied. "We read. We talk. But there's no conclusion."

Daniel nodded. "That's true."

"So what's the point?" the man asked.

Daniel hesitated, then answered honestly. "To listen together. To let Scripture speak before we decide what it says."

The man shook his head. "I prefer teaching."

Daniel smiled gently. "That's fair."

The man didn't return the following week.

That night, Daniel sat with Caleb, unsettled.

"I feel like I'm driving people away," he said.

Caleb shook his head. "Not at all - you're revealing preferences, not creating problems."

Daniel frowned. "Is that better?"

"It's certainly truer," Caleb replied. "And truth always brings differentiation."

As the differences surfaced, Caleb became increasingly aware of the temptation to smooth them over. To reassure everyone that nothing essential was changing. To restore a sense of uniform comfort. He resisted it. Uniformity had never been the goal.

One Sunday morning, he addressed the tension directly.

"We won't all experience this season the same way," he said calmly. "Some of us will feel quite energised. Others will feel unsettled. That doesn't mean something has gone wrong. It means we're being invited to walk together without insisting on identical experiences."

The room was quiet as he spoke.

"There is space here for those who need structure," he continued. "And space for those who need room. We don't have to resolve that tension. We have to honour it."

After the service, reactions were mixed. Some thanked him. Others avoided eye contact. A few left early.

That afternoon, Caleb walked home with Rachel in thoughtful silence.

"I feel like we're losing some people," he said eventually.

Rachel nodded. "Possibly."

"I don't want to," he added.

She met his gaze. "You are not pushing them away. You are just refusing to pretend."

He sighed. "That feels like a thin comfort."

"It's not comfort," she said gently. "It's integrity."

Later that night, Caleb sat alone with his notebook again.

Difference is not division,
but unmanaged fear can turn it into one.
The work of this season is not agreement, but grace.

Outside, Willowend rested quietly. No arguments. No drama. Just the subtle realignment of a community learning that faithfulness did not require sameness.

The differences were now visible.

What mattered was how they would be held.

As the differences became more visible, Caleb found that the conversations themselves were changing shape.

Earlier in the renewal, people had spoken tentatively, unsure whether their questions were welcome. Now the uncertainty lay elsewhere. People were no longer asking if they could speak honestly, but whether honesty would still be safe if it led them in different directions.

On Tuesday morning, Caleb met with a couple who had been part of Willowend for years. They sat close together, hands clasped, their posture both united and tense.

"We're not on the same page anymore," the woman said quietly. Caleb waited.

"At least not about church," her husband added. "She feels like this season has given her room to breathe. I feel like the ground keeps shifting under me."

Caleb nodded. "That's a hard place to be."

"It feels unfair," the man continued. "I haven't changed what I believe. But suddenly that feels like a problem."

Caleb leaned forward slightly. "Has anyone told you it is?"

"No," he admitted. "But I feel it."

The woman looked at her husband with tired affection. "I'm not trying to leave anything behind," she said. "I'm just trying to understand what I actually believe."

They sat in silence for a moment, the weight of it settling.

Caleb said gently, "You don't all have to arrive at the same conclusions at the same time, faithfulness does not require synchronisation."

The man exhaled slowly. "That sounds good. But living it feels harder."

"Yes," Caleb agreed. "It usually is."

After they left, Caleb remained seated for a long time. These were not conflicts that could be resolved with clarity or compromise. They required patience of a deeper kind - the patience to remain connected when shared certainty loosened.

At the servo, Amelia encountered the differences more bluntly. One afternoon, a customer shook his head as he paid for fuel. "Church feels strange these days."

Amelia smiled politely. "Strange how?"

"Too open," he replied. "I liked it better when things were clearer."

She nodded. "Clearer for whom?"

He hesitated, then shrugged. "For everyone."

Amelia didn't argue. "Sometimes clarity depends on whose questions are being asked."

He frowned, but said nothing more.

Later, another customer approached her quietly.

"I've never felt more welcome," the woman said. "And I don't understand why some people are uncomfortable with that."

Amelia smiled gently. "Sometimes comfort and welcome aren't the same thing."

She began to realise that the renewal was not dividing people into believers and non-believers, but into those who valued certainty and those who valued honesty. Most people carried both desires, but not always in equal measure.

Daniel felt the tension keenly.

One evening, after a Scripture gathering, two people stayed behind. One looked energised. The other looked frustrated.

"This isn't teaching," the frustrated one said. "It feels like drifting."

Daniel nodded. "It might feel that way."

"I don't want feelings," the man replied. "I want truth."

Daniel met his gaze calmly. "So do I. I just think truth sometimes takes longer to surface."

The man shook his head. "I don't have time for this."

After he left, the other person spoke quietly. "I'm grateful you didn't rush."

Daniel sat back, the contrast sharp.

Later, he spoke with Caleb about it.

"I feel like I'm always disappointing someone," Daniel said.

Caleb smiled faintly. "That's often a sign you're not catering to a single preference."

"I don't want to fracture things," Daniel added.

Caleb nodded. "Neither do I. But difference isn't fracture unless we refuse to stay in relationship."

Midweek, Caleb met again with the leadership group. The tone was sober but not anxious.

"We need to talk about expectations," Margaret said. "Some people want us to draw clearer lines."

Howard nodded. "Others are relieved we haven't."

Caleb leaned forward. "If we rush to resolve this tension, we'll do it at the expense of someone's faith."

"So what's the alternative?" someone asked.

"We keep naming the tension," Caleb replied. "And we keep making room for it."

Howard frowned slightly. "That won't satisfy everyone."

"No," Caleb said. "But it will keep us honest."

That night, Caleb and Rachel talked quietly after dinner.

"I'm worried we'll lose people who have been here a long time," Caleb admitted.

Rachel nodded. "We might."

"I don't want them to feel displaced," he said.

"They're not being displaced," she replied gently. "They're being asked to share space."

He was quiet for a moment. "That feels like a fine distinction."

"It is," she agreed. "But it matters."

As the days passed, Caleb became aware of how easily difference could slide into defensiveness if left unattended. A passing comment here. A quiet withdrawal there. A number of small misunderstandings accumulating without being named.

On Sunday morning, he chose to speak plainly again.

"Unity doesn't mean sameness," he said calmly. "And difference doesn't mean disloyalty. We are learning how to remain connected even when our experiences of this season are not identical."

The room was still.

"If you feel unsettled," he continued, "you belong here. If you feel energised, you belong here. If you feel unsure where you fit, you belong here."

After the service, responses were again mixed. Some thanked him warmly. Others nodded politely and left.

That afternoon, Caleb walked alone through town, the tension sitting with him more heavily than before. Not because it felt unmanageable, but because it felt consequential.

Difference was no longer theoretical.

It was relational.

And how Willowend learned to carry it would determine whether the renewal deepened into maturity or fractured into camps.

As he turned toward home, Caleb knew that the work ahead would not be about choosing sides.

It would be about teaching the community how to remain present to one another when comfort was no longer shared. Grace would need to become more than a word.

It would need to become a practice.

By the end of the week, Caleb sensed that the differences within Willowend had moved from the background to the centre of the community's awareness.

Not in an explosive way. There were no confrontations. No dramatic departures. Just a growing recognition that the same season was being experienced very differently by different people.

And that recognition brought discomfort.

On Friday afternoon, Caleb sat alone in the sanctuary, the late light stretching across the pews in long, uneven bands. He had not come to pray in any structured way. He had come because the building itself felt like a place where the tension could be held without needing to be resolved.

He thought about the people who felt energised by the openness, who were discovering freedom in naming questions they had carried quietly for years. He thought about those who felt unsettled, who missed the predictability of clearer teaching and firmer direction.

He thought about the quieter group in between, unsure what they felt but aware that something had shifted beneath their feet.

None of them were wrong.

That, Caleb realised, was the hardest truth to hold.

The following morning, Howard rang him early.

"I had a conversation last night that didn't sit well," Howard said.

Caleb listened.

"Someone asked me whether we were still a Baptist church," Howard continued. "Not angrily. Just… uncertain."

Caleb sighed quietly. "What did you say?"

"I said yes," Howard replied. "But I'm not sure that answered what they were really asking."

"No," Caleb said. "They're asking whether the familiar markers still hold."

Howard was quiet for a moment. "And do they?"

"Yes," Caleb said firmly. "But they're no longer being used as fences."

Howard exhaled. "That's what I thought."

After the call, Caleb sat with the implications. People were not questioning doctrine so much as security. For some, faith had always been intertwined with clarity, predictability, and shared language. The loosening of those elements felt like loss, even if nothing essential had been taken away.

That afternoon, Amelia stopped by unexpectedly. She did not sit down. She paced slightly, her energy restless.

"I think people are choosing sides," she said.

Caleb frowned. "Are they?"

"Not openly," she replied. "But I hear it. The way they talk. Who they mention. Who they don't."

Caleb nodded. "That's how it begins."

"I don't like it," Amelia said. "This wasn't meant to divide anyone."

"No," Caleb agreed. "But difference always reveals where fear is hiding."

She stopped pacing and looked at him. "So what do we do?" Caleb paused. "We refuse to let fear set the terms."

Later that evening, Daniel arrived looking tired.

"I'm thinking about stepping back," he said quietly.

Caleb looked up sharply. "Why?"

"I don't want to be part of something that creates tension," Daniel replied. "I didn't sign up for that."

Caleb nodded slowly. "No one ever does."

Daniel rubbed his hands together. "I feel like every conversation now carries weight. Like there's something at stake."

"There is," Caleb said gently. "But not what you think."

Daniel frowned. "What then?"

"Whether we learn to stay," Caleb replied. "Not because it's easy, but because it's honest."

Daniel was quiet for a long moment.

"I don't want to hurt anyone," he said finally.

"You won't," Caleb said. "But you may unsettle them. And that's not the same thing."

Daniel sighed. "I need to think."

"Yes," Caleb said. "Take all the time you need. But don't just disappear."

On Sunday morning, the atmosphere in the sanctuary was subdued. Not tense, but cautious. People greeted one another warmly, yet there was a restraint in the room, as though everyone was aware of something unspoken moving among them.

When Caleb stood to speak, he did not try to smooth over the differences. He named them.

"We are not all experiencing this season the same way," he said calmly. "And that can be unsettling. But difference does not mean disloyalty. And discomfort does not mean something has gone wrong."

He paused, letting the words settle.

"Faith that cannot sit with difference becomes brittle. Faith that learns to remain present becomes resilient." He did not offer solutions. He did not give instructions. He invited reflection.

After the service, people lingered, but conversations were quieter than usual. Some nodded at him with gratitude. Others avoided his gaze. A few left quickly.

That afternoon, Caleb walked alone through town, the weight of the week sitting heavily in his chest. He passed the servo, the bakery, the familiar streets that had shaped so much of his life.

Willowend still looked peaceful. Still looked unchanged. But inside the community, something important was being tested.

Not belief.

Belonging.

At home, Rachel listened as he spoke, her attention steady.

"I don't want us to fracture," he said quietly.

She nodded. "You're not creating the fracture. You're revealing the fault lines."

"That doesn't feel like comfort," he replied.

"No," she said gently. "But it is truth."

He leaned back, weary. "I don't know how to hold everyone."

"You can't," she said. "You can only keep the space open."

He looked at her. "What if some people choose to leave?"

She met his gaze. "Then they leave knowing they were not being pushed."

That night, Caleb returned to his notebook and wrote,

Difference reveals what we trust to keep us together

He closed the book and sat in the quiet, aware that the renewal had reached another threshold. One that would not be crossed with enthusiasm or strategy, but with patience and grace.

Willowend was being asked to grow up.

Not by choosing sides.

But by learning how to remain a community when sameness was no longer guaranteed.

And Caleb sensed that the way they answered that invitation would shape not only the future of the church, but the kind of people they would become together.

Caleb had learned over his many years in pastoral ministry to recognise the difference between absence and departure. Absence was usually temporary. Illness. Travel. Fatigue. The quiet ebb and flow of rural life. Departure carried a different weight. It announced itself slowly, often long before anyone said the words aloud. Conversations shortened. Eye contact softened. Familiar rhythms loosened at the edges.

It was that loosening Caleb felt now.

He noticed it first in the small things. A chair left empty week after week. A greeting offered politely but without warmth. People leaving just a little earlier than they used to, as though reluctant to linger in a space that no longer felt certain.

On Tuesday morning, he sat in his office reading emails when one message stopped him.

It was brief. Respectful. Careful.

We've been grateful for our time at Willowend. But we think it's time for us to move on. This season has been meaningful for many, but we're finding we need something different right now.

Caleb closed the laptop and sat back in his chair.

The words were measured. There was no accusation. No anger. That almost made it harder. It was the kind of message that asked for understanding rather than permission.

Later that day, Howard stopped by, his expression sober.

"I just heard from the Thompsons," he said quietly. "They are leaving."

Caleb nodded. "I know."

Howard exhaled. "I thought they were settling."

"So did I," Caleb replied. "But settling looks different when the ground keeps shifting."

They sat in silence for a moment.

"I keep wondering whether we should have slowed things down," Howard said. "Held things more tightly."

Caleb shook his head gently. "Holding tightly doesn't prevent loss. It just changes who feels it first."

Howard gave a faint smile. "You always have a way of making it sound less personal."

Caleb met his gaze. "It is personal. That's why it hurts."

That afternoon, Amelia mentioned it without naming names.

"People are talking," she said, leaning against the counter at the servo. "Not gossiping. Just noticing."

Caleb nodded. "That was always going to happen."

"They're asking whether this is the beginning of something breaking," she added.

"And what do you think?" Caleb asked.

Amelia considered the question carefully. "I think it's just the beginning of people choosing honestly. And that's not the same thing."

Caleb smiled faintly. "I agree."

Daniel felt the tension in a more immediate way. One evening, after a Scripture gathering, he noticed that only half the usual group had arrived. The conversation was still thoughtful, still open, but the absences sat heavily in the room.

Afterward, one of the remaining participants spoke quietly.

"I hope we're not doing harm."

Daniel hesitated. "I don't think harm always looks like loss."

"But people are leaving," the person replied.

"Yes," Daniel said. "But others are staying because they finally feel they can."

The person nodded slowly. "That feels like a hard trade."

Daniel smiled gently. "Most honest ones are."

At home, Caleb spoke quietly with Rachel about the week. "I knew this would happen," he said. "But knowing doesn't soften it."

Rachel nodded. "No. It just prepares you to face it without panic."

"I really don't want Willowend to become a place people drift through," he added. "I want it to be a place people belong."

Rachel met his gaze. "Belonging that demands sameness isn't belonging. It's compliance."

He sighed. "That's true. But it doesn't make the goodbye easier." "No," she said softly. "It makes it cleaner."

As the week unfolded, Caleb became aware of another subtle shift. Those who remained were beginning to ask some different questions.

Not: *Why are people leaving?*

But: *What does it mean to stay?*

One man stopped him after a service.

"I've been thinking about going elsewhere," he said honestly. "Not because I'm unhappy. Because I'm unsure."

Caleb nodded. "And what keeps you here?"

The man hesitated. "The freedom. And the cost of it."

Caleb smiled. "That's a faithful answer."

By Friday afternoon, Caleb found himself back in the sanctuary, sitting in the same pew where he had spent so many quiet hours. The building felt unchanged. The same creaks. The same light filtering through old glass. Yet the community it held was no longer static.

Leaving had become possible.

And that, Caleb realised, was both risk and gift.

A community that does not allow people to leave honestly will eventually teach them to stay dishonestly. Willowend was learning something harder - how to bless departure without collapsing under it.

That night, Caleb opened his notebook and wrote slowly.

Faithfulness is not measured by how many stay,
but by how truthfully people choose.

He closed the book, aware that more departures might come. And that each one would test his resolve in new ways.

But he also sensed that the remaining community was being refined. Not by agreement, but by courage.

Willowend was learning how to hold open hands.

And Caleb knew that what emerged from this season would not be defined by loss alone, but by the depth of trust that remained. As leaving became more visible, staying took on a different quality.

Those who remained were no longer doing so by habit or inertia. They were staying with intention, sometimes with cost. Caleb noticed it in the way people spoke - more deliberately, and less casually.

Attendance no longer carried the same easy assumptions. Each presence felt chosen.

On Wednesday morning, Caleb met with a man who had been part of Willowend for decades. They sat opposite one another, the space between them filled with years of shared history.

"I'm not leaving," the man said quietly. "But I need you to know I've thought about it."

Caleb nodded. "Thank you for telling me."

"I don't agree with everything that's happening," he continued. "Some of it makes me uncomfortable."

Caleb waited.

"But I also don't want comfort to be my compass anymore," the man said. "I've had enough of faith that never asks anything of me."

Caleb felt the words settle deeply. "That's not an easy decision."

"No," the man agreed. "But it feels honest."

After he left, Caleb sat for a long time, aware that honesty was now shaping the community in ways that could not be reversed. Once people had tasted the freedom to choose, there was no returning to unconscious belonging.

At the servo, Amelia felt the shift too.

One afternoon, a woman she hadn't seen in weeks came in for fuel. Their conversation was polite but careful.

"I heard some people left," the woman said.

"Yes," Amelia replied simply.

The woman hesitated. "Does that worry you?"

Amelia thought for a moment. "It saddens me. But it doesn't frighten me."

The woman nodded slowly. "I'm still deciding."

Amelia smiled gently. "That's allowed."

Later, Amelia reflected on how different that response would have been just months earlier. Once, uncertainty would have been met with reassurance or persuasion. Now it was met with permission.

Daniel experienced the weight of staying most sharply. The Scripture gatherings had grown smaller, but also deeper. The conversations were slower. Silences longer. People spoke less often, but more honestly.

One evening, after most had left, Daniel sat alone, the room quiet around him. He wondered whether the smaller numbers meant failure.

When Caleb stopped by, Daniel voiced the thought aloud.

"It feels like we're shrinking," he said.

Caleb sat beside him. "In some ways, we are."

"That doesn't sound hopeful," Daniel replied.

Caleb smiled faintly. "Pruning rarely does."

Daniel frowned. "I thought pruning was something God did."

Caleb nodded. "Sometimes God prunes by allowing people to choose where they belong."

Daniel sat with that.

"So this isn't something to fix?" he asked.

"No," Caleb said gently. "It's something to walk through."

As the week unfolded, the emotional tone of Willowend shifted again. There was grief, quiet and restrained. But there was also a surprising sense of steadiness.

People who had once deferred to others now spoke more freely. Decisions were made collaboratively. Leadership was less visible, but more distributed.

Caleb noticed how often the conversations now ended not with conclusions, but with commitments.

"I'll stay with this a while longer."

"I'm not ready to leave."

"I don't know what's next, but I'm here."

These were not declarations of certainty. They were declarations of presence. On Friday evening, Caleb and Rachel sat together after dinner, the house unusually still.

"I feel like we're watching something mature," Rachel said softly.

"Yes," Caleb replied. "But maturation always involves loss." Rachel nodded. "And trust."

"I don't want to romanticise it," Caleb added. "Some of these goodbyes hurt more than I expected."

She met his gaze. "That means you're not numb."

He smiled faintly. "That's good to know."

Later that night, Caleb received a brief phone call from Ruth.

"I heard from Mum that things are shifting again," she said.

"They are," he replied.

She paused. "I want you to know I'm proud of you. Not because things are going well. But because you're letting people choose honestly."

Caleb felt something loosen in his chest. "That means a lot."

"I've been thinking," Ruth continued. "About what kind of church I'd want to belong to if I ever went back. And I think this is closer than I realised."

Caleb smiled, though she couldn't see it. "You're always welcome."

"I know," she said quietly. "That's the point."

After the call ended, Caleb sat for a long time, reflecting on how leaving and staying were now shaping Willowend in equal measure. The renewal had moved beyond momentum and into discernment.

The easy days were behind them. What lay ahead would require courage, humility, and patience.

On Sunday morning, the sanctuary felt quieter. Not emptier, but calmer. People greeted one another with warmth, aware of the cost of presence.

When Caleb spoke, he did not mention those who had left. He spoke instead about commitment as something freely given, not enforced.

"Staying matters," he said. "But only when it's chosen."

After the service, no one rushed to leave. Conversations were slower, more attentive. People listened more than they spoke. As Caleb watched them, he sensed that Willowend was becoming something leaner, but also more resilient. A community no longer defined by numbers or familiarity, but by the courage to remain honest together.

Leaving had become possible.

And in that possibility, staying was becoming more meaningful.

The work ahead would not be easier.

But it would be truer.

And Caleb knew that truth, even when costly, was the soil in which lasting faith took root.

By the time the following Sunday arrived, Caleb was no longer surprised by the quieter feel of the sanctuary. What struck him instead was the quality of attention in the room. People were present in a way that felt deliberate. Not eager. Not anxious. Simply present.

He stood at the back for a moment before the service began, watching people take their seats. Some sat alone where they once would have clustered. Others leaned in close to one another, voices low, conversations brief but intent. There was less chatter, but more eye contact.

Staying had begun to carry weight.

After the service, Caleb found himself speaking with a woman who had rarely spoken up in the past. She waited until others had moved away, then stepped closer.

"I nearly left," she said quietly.

Caleb nodded. "I'm glad you told me."

"I wasn't angry," she continued. "Just tired. I didn't know if I had the energy for another season of uncertainty."

"And now?" Caleb asked.

She smiled faintly. "I still don't know. But I realised I didn't want to leave because I was afraid. That felt worse."

Caleb let the words settle. "That's a brave realisation."

She shrugged. "It doesn't feel brave. Just honest."

Later that afternoon, Howard rang again.

"I think we've passed a threshold," he said.

Caleb waited.

"People aren't asking whether this will settle anymore," Howard continued. "They're asking whether they're willing to stay unsettled."

Caleb smiled faintly. "That's a different kind of question."

"Yes," Howard said. "And not everyone likes the answer."

"No," Caleb agreed. "But it's the right one."

At the servo, Amelia noticed the change too. Fewer people lingered aimlessly. When they stayed, it was purposeful. Conversations moved quickly to what mattered, without the need for small talk to soften the edges.

One afternoon, a regular leaned against the counter and said, "I thought church was meant to make life simpler."

Amelia smiled gently. "Sometimes it makes life truer."

He considered that, then nodded. "That's harder."

"Yes," she replied. "But it lasts longer."

Daniel felt the shift most acutely in himself.

He no longer wondered whether he was equipped or not. He wondered now whether he was willing. The Scripture gatherings continued, smaller than before, but steadier.

People arrived knowing there would be no conclusions waiting for them, only presence.

One evening, as the last person left, Daniel sat quietly and realised something had changed.

He no longer felt responsible for outcomes.

That felt like freedom.

When he told Caleb later that week, Caleb nodded. "That's when leadership becomes sustainable."

At home, Caleb and Rachel sat together in the quiet of the evening. The house felt settled, as though it too had adjusted to the new rhythm.

"I keep thinking about those who left," Caleb said softly. "Whether they feel pushed."

Rachel shook her head. "They were given honesty. What they did with it was theirs."

He sighed. "I wish it didn't hurt."

"It should," she replied gently. "If it didn't, we'd be guarding ourselves instead of people."

As the days passed, Caleb became aware that Willowend was no longer defined by what it was becoming, but by what it was willing to release.

Expectations.

Familiar comforts.

Unquestioned patterns.

Leaving had stripped the community of illusion.

Staying was stripping it of pretence.

On Friday afternoon, Caleb returned once more to the sanctuary alone. He sat in the middle pew, the room quiet around him. He thought about the early days of the renewal - the energy, the hope, the sense of possibility. He had not lost that hope. But it had changed shape.

It was quieter now.

More grounded.

Less interested in growth for its own sake.

More committed to truth.

He opened his notebook and wrote slowly.

Faith that survives choice is faith
that can survive pressure.

He closed the book and sat in the stillness, aware that Willowend was no longer asking to be protected from loss. It was learning how to live faithfully in its presence.

The renewal had not failed.

It had matured.

And Caleb sensed that what lay ahead would require even greater courage. Not the courage to begin something new, but the courage to remain steady when enthusiasm faded and conviction was tested.

Willowend was becoming a community which was shaped not by momentum, but by resolve.

And that, Caleb knew, would matter far more in the long run.

The attention did not arrive with confrontation. It arrived quietly, in the form of interest that lingered just a little too long.

Caleb noticed it first through questions that sounded supportive but carried an edge of evaluation. A phone call from a regional leader asking how Willowend was "managing the changes." An email enquiring about safeguarding, governance, and teaching clarity, framed as concern rather than critique. Conversations that circled carefully around what was happening without quite naming it.

None of it was hostile. That was what made it more difficult to navigate.

Scrutiny rarely announced itself as opposition. More often, it dressed itself as responsibility.

On a Tuesday morning, Caleb sat with Howard in the church office, both men aware that something had shifted.

"We're being watched now," Howard said plainly.

Caleb nodded. "Yes."

"Not like before," Howard continued. "This isn't curiosity. It's assessment."

Caleb leaned back slightly. "That was inevitable."

Howard frowned. "Does it concern you?"

"It alerts me," Caleb replied. "Concern would imply surprise."

Howard smiled faintly. "You always sound calmer than I feel."

"That's because I get to sit with it longer," Caleb said gently.

The scrutiny did not come only from outside.

Within Willowend, people were also paying closer attention. Words spoken publicly were replayed privately. Decisions were weighed. Silences were interpreted.

Caleb became more careful, not because he feared saying the wrong thing, but because he wanted to avoid shaping the community through reaction rather than discernment.

One afternoon, Daniel stopped by looking unsettled.

"I think I said too much," he admitted.

Caleb raised an eyebrow. "About?"

"About how I don't always know what I believe," Daniel replied.

"Someone asked whether that was appropriate for a leader."

Caleb smiled slightly. "And what did you say?"

"That I wasn't sure leadership required certainty," Daniel said. "Now I'm wondering whether that was naive."

Caleb considered the question carefully. "It wasn't naive," he said. "But it does make people uncomfortable."

Daniel sighed. "I don't want to make things harder."

Caleb nodded. "Scrutiny makes everything feel harder. That doesn't mean we retreat."

At the servo, Amelia noticed the shift in tone as well. People still spoke openly, but there was a new self-consciousness creeping into conversations. A sense that words might travel further than intended.

One afternoon, a customer lowered her voice and said, "I heard someone say the church has gone soft."

Amelia met her gaze calmly. "Soft doesn't mean shallow."

The woman hesitated. "Some people think it does."

Amelia nodded. "Some people always will."

That night, Caleb and Rachel spoke quietly after dinner.

"I don't like the feeling of being evaluated," Caleb admitted. "Even when it's subtle."

Rachel nodded. "No one does."

"I don't want us to ever become defensive," he added. "Or performative."

Rachel smiled faintly. "Then don't let scrutiny define the work."

"That's easier said than done."

"Yes," she agreed. "But it's necessary."

As the week unfolded, Caleb became increasingly aware of how scrutiny shaped behaviour if left unchecked. It tempted leaders to clarify prematurely, to tighten language, to restore familiar markers of orthodoxy simply to reassure observers.

He resisted those impulses.

Clarity was not the problem. Fear was.

On Thursday afternoon, Caleb received a call from someone he respected deeply. The tone was measured, careful.

"I've been hearing things about Willowend," the voice said.

Caleb waited.

"Nothing alarming," the person continued. "But some people are wondering whether you've lost your theological centre."

Caleb exhaled slowly. "And what do you think?"

There was a pause. "I think you're asking people to grow up," the person replied. "And not everyone appreciates that."

Caleb smiled faintly. "That's generous."

"It's honest," the voice said. "But honesty invites scrutiny."

After the call ended, Caleb sat quietly for a long time. He was not shaken by the concern itself. He was shaken by how easily scrutiny could pull a community off course if it was allowed to set the agenda.

Scrutiny sharpened things.

Sometimes it sharpened clarity.

Other times, it sharpened fear.

On Sunday morning, the sanctuary felt different again. Not tense, but alert. People listened closely. Watched one another. Not suspiciously, but with awareness.

When Caleb spoke, he chose his words carefully.

"We're not here to impress anyone," he said calmly. "And we're not here to defend ourselves. We're here to remain faithful. That may not always look tidy."

There was no reaction in the room. No murmurs. Just quiet attention.

After the service, conversations were subdued but thoughtful. People spoke less about what others might be saying and more about what they themselves were wrestling with.

That afternoon, Caleb walked home alone, the weight of the week settling in his body. Scrutiny had arrived, not as a threat, but as a test.

Not of doctrine.

But of posture.

Would Willowend tighten under pressure?

Or would it remain open, grounded, and gentle even when being watched? Caleb sensed that the answer to that question would shape the next season more than any program or plan ever could. Scrutiny was sharpening the edges. What mattered now was what the community allowed itself to become under that pressure.

As scrutiny sharpened, Caleb became increasingly aware of how easily a community could begin to perform for its observers without realising it. It rarely happened deliberately. No one suggested adjusting language or softening emphasis to appear more acceptable.

Instead, it crept in quietly. A pause before answering a question. A hesitation before naming uncertainty. A subtle instinct to reassure before listening fully.

On Wednesday morning, Caleb met with the leadership group again. The tone was thoughtful, but there was a new restraint in the room.

"We need to be careful," someone said. "People are listening more closely now."

Caleb nodded. "They always have been. We're just noticing it more."

"But words can be taken the wrong way," another added. "Especially if they're repeated out of context."

"Yes," Caleb agreed. "Which is why our posture matters more than our phrasing."

There was a pause.

"So do we say less?" Howard asked.

Caleb considered the question. "We say what's true," he replied. "And we say it without anxiety."

"That's not always easy," Margaret said.

"No," Caleb said. "But anxiety distorts clarity faster than honesty ever will."

As the meeting ended, Caleb sensed a collective tension still hanging in the air. Everyone felt the pressure. No one quite knew how best to respond to it.

Later that day, Amelia stopped by the church, her expression thoughtful.

"I think people are starting to self-edit," she said.

Caleb raised an eyebrow. "How so?"

"They speak, then stop," she replied. "Or they change direction mid-sentence. Like they're worried about sounding wrong."

Caleb nodded. "That's the cost of scrutiny if it goes unchecked."

"It worries me," Amelia added. "This place felt safe because people could be honest. I don't want us to lose that."

"Neither do I," Caleb said. "Which means we have to model honesty even when it feels risky."

Daniel experienced the same pressure in sharper ways. At one of the Scripture gatherings, a new attendee spoke confidently, offering clear conclusions and strong interpretations. The tone was not aggressive, but it shifted the atmosphere. Others grew quieter.

Afterward, Daniel sat with the discomfort.

"I think certainty just walked into the room," he said to Caleb later.

Caleb smiled faintly. "Certainty often arrives that way."

"It wasn't wrong," Daniel said. "But it changed everything."

"Yes," Caleb said. "Certainty has weight. It can settle a room or silence it."

"So what do we do?" Daniel asked. "Challenge it?"

Caleb shook his head. "We don't challenge confidence. We make room for other voices."

The following evening, Daniel tried that approach. When the confident voice spoke again, Daniel responded gently.

"That's one way of seeing it," he said. "Does anyone see it differently?"

The room stayed quiet for a moment, then someone spoke hesitantly. Another followed. The certainty did not disappear, but it no longer dominated. Later, Daniel reflected on how fragile openness could be. Not because of hostility, but because of imbalance.

At home, Caleb spoke with Rachel as the week pressed on.

"I'm noticing how easily fear disguises itself as responsibility," he said.

Rachel nodded. "Fear often dresses well."

"I don't want to overreact," Caleb added. "But I don't want to ignore it either."

"That's discernment," she said. "Not control."

On Friday afternoon, Caleb received another call from outside Willowend. This one was more direct.

"There's concern," the voice said carefully. "About how loosely things are being held."

Caleb listened.

"Some feel there's a noticeable lack of clear leadership," the voice continued.

Caleb responded calmly. "There's a difference between absence and restraint."

The person hesitated. "Restraint can look like indecision."

"Yes," Caleb replied. "Especially to those who prefer direction over discernment."

After the call ended, Caleb felt the familiar tension return. Scrutiny had a way of framing everything as deficiency. Not enough clarity. Not enough structure. Not enough reassurance. Yet he knew that rushing to provide those things could cost Willowend what it had gained.

That night, he sat alone with his notebook, words slow to come.

*Scrutiny tempts leaders to exchange faithfulness
for credibility. But credibility without courage
leads nowhere worth following.*

On Sunday morning, the atmosphere in the sanctuary felt alert again. People listened closely, not with suspicion, but with awareness.

When Caleb spoke, he addressed the moment without naming it directly. "There are times," he said, "when faith is tested not by opposition, but by observation. When being watched makes us wonder whether we should become something else."

He paused.

"The temptation in those moments is to tighten. To explain ourselves. To prove something. But faithfulness doesn't require performance."

The room was quiet.

"We don't need to impress," he continued. "We need to remain honest."

After the service, conversations unfolded slowly. Some people thanked him. Others said little. A few seemed relieved. A few seemed unsettled.

That afternoon, Caleb walked alone again, the town familiar beneath his feet. Scrutiny had not diminished. If anything, it had become more focused.

But Caleb sensed something steady beneath it.

The community had not closed ranks.

It had not retreated.

It was learning how to remain open under pressure.

And that, he knew, was no small thing.

Scrutiny could harden a church or refine it. It could push people toward performance or draw them deeper into truth.

What Willowend became would depend not on how loudly it defended itself, but on how quietly it remained faithful.

The edge was sharpening.

The question now was whether the centre would hold.

By the end of the week, Caleb sensed that scrutiny had moved from something external to something internal. It was no longer only about what others might say or think. It was about how easily those imagined voices could begin to shape decisions from the inside. He felt it in his own hesitation, the momentary urge to qualify a statement before making it, the temptation to explain more than was necessary.

Scrutiny had a way of creeping inward like that.

On Friday afternoon, Caleb sat alone in the church office, the late light slanting through the window. He had been rereading notes from the past few weeks, trying to trace where the tone had shifted. Not dramatically. Just enough to be felt.

He closed the notebook and leaned back, aware that this season required a different kind of vigilance. Not against error, but against fear.

Later that day, Howard came by unannounced. He didn't sit straight away. He stood near the door, hands in his pockets.

"I almost said something this morning," Howard admitted.

Caleb raised an eyebrow. "Almost?"

"I was talking with someone who was concerned," Howard continued. "They wanted reassurance. Clear lines. Definitions."

"And you didn't give them?" Caleb asked.

Howard shook his head. "I wanted to. But I realised I was more concerned about calming them than listening to them."

Caleb smiled faintly. "That's not an easy thing to notice."

Howard sighed. "No. But once I did, I couldn't ignore it."

They sat in silence for a moment, the weight of the awareness settling between them.

"This scrutiny," Howard said, "it's making us choose."

"Yes," Caleb replied. "And not always in obvious ways."

At the servo, Amelia experienced the same internal pressure. One afternoon, a customer leaned across the counter and said quietly, "I hope you're not losing your way."

Amelia smiled politely. "What makes you think that?"

"Things feel different," the customer replied. "Less clear."

Amelia nodded. "Different doesn't always mean lost."

The woman hesitated, then said, "I suppose not."

After she left, Amelia felt the familiar tug to explain more, to justify the changes she herself barely understood. She resisted it. Later, she wrote another line in her notebook.

When people ask for certainty, they are often asking for safety.

Daniel felt the pressure personally. He noticed how often he replayed conversations in his head after they ended, wondering how his words might be interpreted. Whether he had said too much. Or not enough.

One evening, after a gathering, he stayed behind alone, sitting in the quiet room. He realised he had begun to censor his own questions.

That unsettled him more than any external scrutiny.

When he spoke with Caleb about it later, his voice was low.

"I think I'm starting to shrink," he admitted.

Caleb met his gaze. "Then it's time to push back."

Daniel frowned. "How?"

"By telling the truth again," Caleb said. "Even when it feels risky."

Daniel nodded slowly. "I don't want to become careful instead of honest."

Caleb smiled gently. "That's the right fear to have."

As the weekend approached, Caleb sensed a subtle resolve forming within the leadership. Not defiance. Not anxiety. A quiet determination to remain themselves even when being watched.

On Sunday morning, the sanctuary felt attentive, but not tense. People listened closely, not out of suspicion, but out of care. When Caleb spoke, his words were simple.

"We don't measure faithfulness by how well we are perceived," he said calmly. "We measure it by whether we remain truthful when perception pressures us to adjust."

He did not elaborate.

He did not explain.

He let the words stand.

After the service, a man approached him hesitantly.

"I don't always understand what's happening here," the man said. "But I don't feel manipulated. And that matters to me."

Caleb nodded. "It matters to us too."

That afternoon, Caleb walked home slowly, the town quiet around him. The scrutiny had not disappeared. It likely wouldn't. But it no longer felt like a threat.

It felt like a mirror.

A mirror revealing where fear could still find a foothold.

A mirror showing where courage was beginning to take root.

Scrutiny had sharpened the edges of Willowend. It had exposed habits, assumptions, and vulnerabilities that might otherwise have remained hidden.

But it had also clarified something essential.

The renewal was not about freedom from being watched. It was about faithfulness when being watched.

And as Caleb sat that evening on the veranda, the light fading gently across the paddocks, he felt a quiet confidence settle within him.

Not confidence in outcomes.

Not confidence in approval.

Confidence that Willowend, for all its fragility, was learning how to remain itself under pressure.

The centre was holding.

And that, he knew, would matter more than anything the scrutiny might yet bring.

Caleb noticed the change first in the way people began to speak after the service. It was not louder, nor more restrained. It was quieter, but with a steadiness that had not been there before.

Conversations no longer circled anxiously around what others might think. They moved instead toward what people were learning to trust.

On Monday morning, Caleb unlocked the church early, the building cool and still from the night air. The sanctuary carried that familiar scent of timber and dust, sunlight just beginning to edge its way through the windows. He stood for a moment near the door, not in prayer exactly, but in attentiveness.

Confidence, he had learned, rarely arrived with force. It came more often as permission.

He made tea and sat at his desk, reviewing notes from the past few weeks. There were no dramatic breakthroughs recorded, no moments he could point to and say, *this is where it turned.* Yet something had turned all the same.

People were beginning to act without waiting to be told.

Margaret arrived mid-morning carrying a folder of handwritten pages. "I hope this isn't presumptuous," she said, hovering slightly in the doorway.

Caleb smiled. "It rarely is."

She sat and opened the folder. "I've been meeting with three women from different parts of town. No agenda. We just read a psalm and talk. It's been… grounding."

Caleb listened as she described the conversations. Nothing remarkable on the surface. No urgency. No solutions offered. Just listening, prayer, and honesty. "I didn't ask permission," she added quickly. "I just felt it was right."

Caleb nodded. "That sounds exactly right."

Margaret exhaled, relieved. "I was afraid you might say we needed to formalise it."

He smiled. "Not everything that's healthy needs a structure."

Later that day, Daniel stopped by, his energy quieter than usual but more settled.

"I've been thinking," he said, sitting across from Caleb. "About confidence."

Caleb raised an eyebrow. "In what sense?"

Daniel leaned forward. "I always thought confidence meant certainty. Answers. Being sure. But lately, it feels more like courage to stay open."

Caleb smiled. "That's a good insight."

Daniel hesitated. "I'm starting to notice when people confuse confidence with control."

"Yes," Caleb said. "Control is loud. Confidence doesn't need to be."

Daniel nodded. "I think I want to help protect that difference."

"How?" Caleb asked.

"By not rushing people," Daniel said. "By not filling silence. By letting questions stay questions."

Caleb felt a quiet gratitude rise within him. Daniel's faith had grown not into assertiveness, but into discernment.

At the servo, Amelia experienced a similar shift. A regular customer lingered longer than usual, leaning against the counter.

"I don't know much about church," he said awkwardly. "But something feels steady about that place lately."

Amelia smiled. "Steady is a good word."

"It doesn't feel like anyone's trying to sell anything," he added.

"No," she said. "We're just trying to stay honest."

He nodded, thoughtful. "That makes it easier to listen."

That afternoon, Caleb walked through town, stopping where he was invited, listening where people wanted to talk.

He noticed how often people were no longer asking him what they should do. Instead, they were telling him what they had begun to do already. Checking on neighbours.

Offering rides.

Sitting with grief without needing to fix it.

None of it was dramatic.

All of it was confident.

That evening, Caleb sat with Rachel at the kitchen table, mugs between them, the light softening outside.

"I'm noticing something," Rachel said quietly.

"Tell me," Caleb replied.

"People aren't leaning on us the same way," she said. "Not because they don't need us. But because they're finding their footing."

Caleb nodded. "I see it too."

Rachel smiled. "It's good. But it also means letting go."

"Yes," he said. "And trusting that what's growing doesn't depend on us holding it together."

She reached across the table and squeezed his hand. "That's a different kind of confidence."

Later that night, Caleb wrote again in his notebook.

Confidence grows when fear loses its grip,
not when certainty takes its place.

The following Sunday, Caleb spoke briefly, intentionally leaving space.

"There are seasons when confidence looks like strength," he said. "And seasons when it looks like patience. Both matter."

He paused.

"But when confidence becomes quiet, it often means it has stopped needing to prove itself."

After the service, an older man approached him, eyes thoughtful.

"I used to think faith meant being sure," he said. "Now I think it means being willing."

Caleb nodded. "Willingness often outlasts certainty."

That afternoon, Caleb sat alone on the veranda, watching the shadows lengthen across Willowend. Confidence was taking shape in the town, not as boldness, but as calm. Not as answers, but as steadiness.

It was not confidence that demanded attention.

It was confidence that made room.

And as the evening settled gently around him, Caleb sensed that this quieter strength might carry Willowend further than any display ever could.

This was not a season of proving.

It was a season of becoming.

By midweek, Caleb could feel the subtle weight of expectation beginning to shift again - not away from him, but around him.

It showed up in small moments. A question that lingered longer before being answered. A pause that was no longer awkward, but deliberate.

People were learning not to rush toward resolution, and that restraint carried its own quiet authority.

On Wednesday afternoon, Caleb met with a small group who had asked for time together. They gathered in the back room of the church, chairs loosely arranged, no table between them. No one had prepared notes. No one had nominated a leader.

They waited.

Eventually, Margaret spoke. "I don't really know why we're here," she said gently. "Except that I felt we should be."

No one laughed. No one tried to clarify.

"That feels enough," Howard replied after a moment.

Caleb watched them carefully, resisting the familiar urge to frame the moment, to offer reassurance that this was how things were meant to work. Instead, he remained still.

After a few minutes, someone read a short passage of Scripture. No commentary followed. Another person prayed - briefly, honestly, without polish. The prayer did not aim to explain anything. It simply named gratitude and uncertainty in equal measure. When the gathering ended, no one asked what should happen next. They stood, exchanged quiet smiles, and left.

Later, as Caleb locked up, he realised how little had been required of him. He had not guided, interpreted, or concluded anything. And yet, something meaningful had occurred.

Confidence, he reflected, did not always need articulation.

The following morning, Daniel stopped by the church before work. He looked tired, but thoughtful.

"I think I made a mistake yesterday," he said.

Caleb gestured for him to sit. "Tell me about it."

Daniel leaned forward, elbows on his knees. "Someone shared something personal at the gathering. I jumped in too quickly. Tried to respond, to help."

"And?" Caleb asked.

"And afterward, I realised I'd filled a space that didn't need filling."

Caleb nodded slowly. "That awareness matters."

Daniel sighed. "I didn't mean to shut anything down."

"No," Caleb said gently. "But learning when not to speak is part of learning to lead."

Daniel looked up. "That still feels strange to hear."

"It should," Caleb replied. "We're used to thinking leadership means direction. Sometimes it means restraint."

Daniel sat with that for a moment. "I'm not sure people expect that from me."

Caleb smiled. "They don't need to expect it. They'll notice it."

At the servo, Amelia was having similar conversations, though she did not name them that way. A regular came in late one afternoon, shoulders slumped.

"Feels like everyone's got opinions lately," he muttered as she rang up his purchase.

Amelia nodded. "Opinions are easier than listening."

He gave a small laugh. "You've noticed that too?"

She smiled. "I work a counter. I notice a lot."

He hesitated, then said, "I don't mind people having strong beliefs. I just don't like being told what mine should be."

Amelia met his gaze. "Neither does God."

The man blinked, then smiled. "That's oddly comforting."

After he left, Amelia wrote another short line in her notebook.

Confidence doesn't instruct. It invites.

That evening, Caleb received a call from Ruth. Her voice was warm, familiar, but distant in the way that came from living elsewhere.

"I just wanted to check in," she said. "You sounded… settled the last time we spoke."

Caleb smiled. "That's a good word for it."

"I keep thinking about Willowend," Ruth continued. "About how small things there seem to matter more."

"They always have," Caleb replied. "We're just noticing them now."

She paused. "I don't know if I'd know how to live that way."

Caleb considered his answer carefully. "Most people don't at first. It grows on you."

Ruth laughed softly. "That sounds like a warning."

"Maybe an invitation," he said.

After the call ended, Caleb felt a quiet gratitude for her honesty. Ruth was not resistant. She was attentive. And that mattered more than readiness.

On Friday afternoon, Caleb walked the long way home, passing familiar houses, familiar faces. He noticed how often people greeted him now with a nod rather than a question. A sign, perhaps, that reassurance was no longer being sought from him alone.

At home, Rachel was sitting on the veranda, sorting through a small pile of notes from people who had written quietly over the past week. Not requests. Not complaints. Reflections.

"They're naming what they're learning," she said, handing one to Caleb.

He read it slowly.

I don't feel like I need to be certain anymore. I just need to stay open.

Caleb handed it back. "That's confidence."

Rachel smiled. "It doesn't look like what I expected."

"No," he agreed. "But it feels truer."

That Sunday, Caleb spoke again only briefly. He chose his words carefully, not to manage perception, but to honour what was emerging.

"There's a kind of confidence that doesn't rush to speak," he said. "It listens first. It trusts that God is already at work in places we haven't reached yet."

He paused.

"When that confidence grows, leadership becomes shared, not assigned."

The room was still.

After the service, no one crowded him. Conversations unfolded naturally, overlapping, unhurried. People lingered, not waiting for direction, but enjoying one another's presence.

As the afternoon light softened, Caleb sat alone in the sanctuary for a few moments before locking up. The space felt full, even in its quiet.

Confidence was settling into Willowend, not as certainty, not as control, but as trust.

Trust in God's patience.

Trust in one another.

Trust that growth did not need to be hurried to be real.

And Caleb knew that this kind of confidence would be tested in time. But for now, it was being learned gently.

Which made it strong.

Very strong indeed.

By the weekend, Caleb became aware of how quietly confidence was reshaping the way people related to one another.

It was most visible not in gatherings, but in what happened between them. People lingered after conversations instead of rushing away. They asked important follow-up questions. They remembered details and returned to them days later, as though what had been shared mattered enough to carry forward.

On Saturday morning, Caleb was walking past the oval when he noticed a small group gathered under one of the gum trees. No chairs, no structure. Just people standing, talking. One of them saw him and waved, but no one beckoned him over.

He kept walking.

Later, Howard mentioned it casually. "That group's been meeting for a couple of weeks now."

Caleb raised an eyebrow. "I didn't know that."

Howard smiled. "That's the point."

They both laughed softly, but Caleb felt a deeper satisfaction underneath it. This was what he had hoped for, even if he had never quite known how to describe it. Initiative that did not require endorsement. Faith that did not wait for permission.

That afternoon, Daniel stopped by again, his energy thoughtful rather than restless.

"I think something's changing in me," he said.

Caleb gestured for him to sit. "Go on."

"I'm not looking to be noticed as much," Daniel admitted. "Not because I'm withdrawing, but because I'm less anxious about being useful."

Caleb nodded. "That's a significant shift."

Daniel hesitated. "Is it wrong to want to be useful?"

"No," Caleb said. "But usefulness driven by anxiety will always exhaust you."

Daniel smiled faintly. "I think I've been living there for a while."

"You're not alone," Caleb replied.

Daniel leaned back. "It feels like confidence is giving me permission to be unfinished."

Caleb considered that. "That might be its greatest gift."

At the servo, Amelia experienced the same permission in unexpected ways. A woman she barely knew lingered after paying, then said quietly, "I don't know if I believe what you believe."

Amelia smiled gently. "That's all right."

The woman looked surprised. "You're not going to argue?"

"No," Amelia said. "I'm more interested in knowing what you've lived."

They talked for several minutes, not about doctrine, but about loneliness, grief, and the strange courage it took to start again later in life.

When the woman left, she said, "That was easier than I expected."

Amelia nodded. "It often is, once no one's trying to win."

That evening, Caleb and Rachel sat together as dusk settled over Willowend. The air was cooler now, the long days beginning to shorten.

"I'm noticing something," Rachel said. "People are less reactive." Caleb smiled. "That's a good sign."

"They're not rushing to defend themselves," she continued. "Or to justify what they're doing."

"Yes," he said. "They're learning to stand without bracing."

Rachel leaned back, thoughtful. "That kind of confidence isn't flashy."

"No," Caleb agreed. "But it lasts."

The following Sunday, the sanctuary felt settled in a way that was difficult to name. Not subdued. Not energised. Just present. When Caleb spoke, he chose not to expand on confidence or leadership or growth. Instead, he told a brief story about a farmer who learned to trust the soil more than the weather forecast.

"Some seasons," he said, "we do less because we trust more."

He let the words rest.

After the service, a woman approached him quietly. "I used to think faith meant having answers," she said. "Now I think it means staying open when answers don't come quickly."

Caleb nodded. "That's often where growth begins."

That afternoon, Caleb took a longer walk than usual, circling the edges of town. The paddocks stretched out, familiar and steady. He thought about how easily confidence could still slip into control if it was not watched carefully. How quickly reassurance could turn into performance.

But for now, Willowend was holding its centre.

Not because everyone agreed.

Not because nothing was questioned.

But because people were learning to trust God's pace more than their own.

As evening approached, Caleb sat on the veranda once more, notebook resting on his knee. He wrote slowly, choosing his words with care.

Confidence matures when fear loosens
its grip and trust takes its place.

He closed the notebook and set it aside.

This season would not remain untouched.

There would be misunderstandings. Tensions. Moments when confidence would be tested and misunderstood as weakness.

But the foundation was forming quietly now.

Confidence that listened.

Confidence that waited.

Confidence that did not need to announce itself to be real.

And as the last light faded across Willowend, Caleb felt certain of this much - not with certainty born of answers, but with confidence shaped by trust.

What was growing here did not need to hurry.

It knew where it was going.

And it would take the time it needed to get there.

29. WHEN INFLUENCE SPREADS

Caleb first became aware of it not through invitation, but through conversation. It was a passing remark made after a midweek gathering, spoken lightly and without any agenda. Someone mentioned a friend from a neighbouring town who had asked questions. Not urgent ones. Curious ones. The kind that lingered.

"They wanted to know what we're doing differently," the person said, almost apologetically. "I didn't really know how to answer."

Caleb smiled. "What did you say?"

"I told them we weren't doing anything different. That we were just listening more carefully."

Caleb nodded. "That was probably the best answer."

Over the next few days, similar comments surfaced. A visiting relative. A phone call from someone who had heard a story second-hand. A quiet email that began with, *I don't quite know why I'm writing this…*

None of it felt strategic. None of it carried expectation. But taken together, it formed a pattern that Caleb recognised.

Influence was extending, not because Willowend was trying to be seen, but because something was being noticed.

On Thursday morning, Caleb met with Howard and Margaret for coffee at the small cafe near the post office. The place was half full, the hum of conversation steady but unobtrusive.

"I've had two people ask me this week if they can come and sit in," Margaret said, stirring her cup. "Not to join anything. Just to observe."

Howard frowned slightly. "That makes me uneasy."

Caleb looked at him. "Why?"

"Because observation can often turn into expectation," Howard replied. "And expectation can turn into pressure."

"Yes," Caleb said. "But curiosity doesn't always want to control. Sometimes it just wants to learn."

Margaret nodded. "That's how it felt to me. Not evaluative. Just attentive."

Howard considered that. "Still, it changes the dynamic."

"It does," Caleb agreed. "Which means we need to be careful not to change ourselves in response."

The conversation lingered there, unresolved but honest.

Later that afternoon, Caleb received a call from a pastor he barely knew. They had met once years ago at a regional gathering. Their conversation then had been polite and brief.

"I'm ringing because your name came up," the man said. "Not in a formal way. More in passing."

Caleb listened quietly.

"There's a sense," the pastor continued, "that something healthy is happening in Willowend. I'm not asking you to explain it. I just wondered if you'd be willing to talk sometime."

Caleb paused before responding. "I can do that," he said. "As long as you're not looking for a model."

There was a small laugh on the other end. "No. I'm mostly looking for permission to breathe."

After the call ended, Caleb sat for a moment, the weight of that phrase settling on him. *Permission to breathe.*

That evening, he mentioned the call to Rachel as they prepared dinner.

"It's beginning," she said quietly.

"Yes," Caleb replied. "But not in the way I expected."

Rachel smiled. "It rarely does."

"What concerns me," Caleb continued, "is how easily this could shift from influence to expectation. From invitation to demand."

Rachel nodded. "Which means the boundaries will matter."

"Yes," he said. "And the pace."

Over the next week, Caleb noticed how quickly stories travelled. A conversation overheard. A moment shared casually. Someone retelling an experience without embellishment, but with clarity.

Willowend was not becoming famous.

It was becoming referenced.

Daniel noticed it too. "I had someone ask me if we're starting something new," he said one afternoon.

"And what did you say?" Caleb asked.

"I said no," Daniel replied. "That we're just paying attention to what's already here."

Caleb smiled. "That answer is becoming familiar."

"It's also becoming harder to say," Daniel added. "People seem to want more."

"Yes," Caleb said. "They often do."

At the servo, Amelia found herself fielding some questions that surprised her. "Is it true your church doesn't rush people?" someone asked.

Amelia smiled. "We rush sometimes. We're just learning not to."

Another person asked, "Do you have special meetings?"

"No," she replied. "Just ordinary ones."

The person looked puzzled. "Then why are people talking about it?"

Amelia shrugged lightly. "Maybe ordinary done honestly stands out more than we realise."

That Saturday, Caleb walked the outskirts of town, thinking carefully about what lay ahead. Influence carried responsibility, whether sought or not. And the temptation would be to manage it. To explain. To define.

But defining something too early could close it down just as easily as neglect.

On Sunday morning, Caleb chose his words carefully.

"There are times," he said, "when God works quietly in a place, and others notice before we do. The danger in those moments is not being seen. It's forgetting who we are in response to being seen."

He paused.

"We don't owe anyone a performance. We don't owe anyone certainty. We owe one another faithfulness."

After the service, a visiting couple approached him. They had driven from an hour away.

"We didn't come to evaluate," the woman said quickly. "We just wanted to sit and listen."

Caleb nodded. "You're welcome to do that."

They stayed only briefly afterward, offering thanks without any questions.

That afternoon, Caleb felt both the weight and the gift of what was unfolding. Influence was no longer theoretical. It was relational. It moved at the speed of trust, not planning.

As evening settled, Caleb sat again with his notebook.

Influence is not something to be protected or pursued.
It is something to be stewarded gently,
lest it demand more than it gives.

He closed the notebook, aware that this chapter of Willowend's story was expanding beyond the town's borders.

Not with noise.

Not with urgency.

But with a widening circle of attention that would require wisdom, patience, and courage in equal measure.

The walls had not moved.

But the horizon had.

As the days passed, Caleb began to sense how subtly influence altered the way people listened.

It was not that conversations became guarded. If anything, they grew more open. But there was an added attentiveness now, a sense that words might travel further than the room in which they were spoken.

Not immediately.

Not dramatically. Just further.

Caleb noticed it in himself first.

He found that he paused more often before answering questions, not out of fear, but out of care. He wanted his words to remain true to what was unfolding in Willowend, not to what others hoped it might become.

One afternoon, he received an email from a church council in a regional centre two hours away. The tone was respectful, even hesitant.

We have been hearing about the way things are being held in your community. Would you be willing to visit and simply talk with us? Not to teach. Not to advise. Just to share what you are noticing.

Caleb read the message twice, then closed his laptop without replying. Not because he was unwilling, but because he wanted to consider the invitation slowly.

That evening, he mentioned it to Rachel as they walked along the quiet road behind their home.

"They're not asking for answers," she said thoughtfully. "I think they're asking for witness."

"Yes," Caleb replied. "And that feels heavier."

"Only if you try to carry it," she said gently.

He smiled. "You always say things like that."

"And you always need reminding," she replied.

They walked in silence for a while, the paddocks stretching out on either side, familiar and steady.

"What worries me," Caleb said eventually, "is how easily people start looking to you once you're perceived as helpful."

Rachel nodded. "Helpfulness can turn into expectation."

"And expectation can quietly become authority," he added.

"Yes," she agreed. "Especially if you don't notice it happening."

The following morning, Caleb met with Howard and two others from the leadership group. They sat around the small table in the meeting room, mugs in hand, no agenda laid out.

"I think we need to talk about boundaries," Howard said.

Caleb nodded. "I've been thinking the same thing."

One of the others leaned forward. "People are starting to refer to Willowend as though it's a destination."

"That language makes me uneasy," Howard admitted.

"Me too," Caleb said. "Destinations always imply arrival. What's happening here isn't something you arrive at."

"So what do we do?" Margaret asked. "Ignore it?"

"No," Caleb replied. "But we also don't lean into it."

Howard frowned slightly. "That sounds vague."

"It is," Caleb said calmly. "Because clarity too soon might shut down something that needs space."

They sat with that for a moment.

"Then perhaps our task," Margaret said slowly, "is to keep naming what this is not."

Caleb smiled. "That might be wise."

"What it is not," Howard repeated.

"It's not a movement," Margaret continued. "Not a method. Not a program."

"And not an answer to anyone else's frustration," Caleb added. The conversation settled there, not resolved, but steadied.

Later that week, Daniel encountered the widening influence in a more personal way.

A friend from his workplace approached him quietly during a break. "You've changed," the man said.

Daniel looked surprised. "How so?"

"You listen more," the man replied. "You don't rush to fix things."

Daniel smiled faintly. "I'm learning."

The man hesitated, then said, "Would it be strange if I came along one Sunday? Not to commit. Just to see."

Daniel shook his head. "It wouldn't be strange at all."

Afterward, Daniel sat alone for a while, aware of how easily such invitations could accumulate. He felt the pull to prepare, to anticipate, to manage what someone else might experience.

Instead, he let it go.

At the servo, Amelia noticed a different shift. People were no longer just asking about the church. They were asking about her.

"How did you get involved?" someone asked.

"What changed for you?" another wondered.

Amelia answered honestly, but briefly. She did not tell a dramatic story. She did not offer conclusions.

"I just started listening," she said more than once. "And then something met me there."

That seemed to be enough.

One evening, Caleb received a call from Ruth again. This time her voice carried a hint of hesitation.

"I had coffee with someone today," she said. "They mentioned Willowend."

Caleb smiled. "It's travelling."

"They asked what was happening there," Ruth continued. "I didn't really know what to say."

"What did you say?" Caleb asked.

"I said it wasn't about events," she replied. "That it was more about how people were changing."

Caleb felt a quiet warmth. "That sounds right."

Ruth paused. "It made me realise something. People aren't looking for new churches. They're looking for permission to be honest."

"Yes," Caleb said softly. "That's what we're discovering too."

After the call ended, Caleb sat with the weight of that observation. Honesty, once tasted, was difficult to forget. And influence that pointed people toward honesty would inevitably draw attention.

The challenge was not whether that attention would come. It already had. The challenge was whether Willowend could now continue to hold its centre while the circle widened.

On Sunday morning, Caleb addressed the congregation gently, without urgency.

"There's a quiet temptation," he said, "when others begin to notice what's happening among us. The temptation is to become what we think they need."

He paused.

"But we don't belong to anyone else's expectations. We belong to God, and to one another."

The room was still, attentive.

"If others find help here," he continued, "that's a gift. But we don't reshape ourselves to be useful. We remain faithful, and trust God with the reach of it."

After the service, conversations unfolded as they always did. Unhurried. Unforced. But Caleb noticed how often people spoke about what they were resisting, not just what they were embracing.

Resisting pressure.

Resisting performance.

Resisting the need to explain themselves.

That afternoon, Caleb returned to his notebook.

Influence widens the path,
but faithfulness keeps the footing sure.

He closed it, aware that the next season would test that footing in new ways.

The walls of Willowend were still where they had always been. But the questions arriving at them were coming from further away.

And how those questions were received would matter just as much as how they were answered.

By the time the week turned, Caleb could feel the weight of widening attention pressing gently but persistently against the life of the church.

It did not arrive as urgency. No one demanded explanations. No one issued warnings. But the sense of being quietly observed had settled into the background of daily life, like a change in weather that altered how people dressed without anyone naming it directly.

Caleb noticed it on Monday morning when he received three separate messages, each from a different place, each carrying the same tone.

Not, *what should we do?*

But, *how are you holding this?*

He sat with that question for a long time before responding to any of them.

Holding something implied care rather than control. It suggested attentiveness rather than authority. And that clear distinction mattered more now than ever.

He replied briefly, choosing his words carefully. He spoke of patience. Of listening. Of resisting the urge to rush meaning into what was still forming. He offered no steps, no frameworks, no language that could be replicated easily.

When he finished, he felt the familiar unease of knowing that restraint could be misunderstood as evasion. But he trusted it anyway.

Later that morning, Howard joined him for a walk through town. They moved slowly, stopping occasionally as people greeted them. The rhythm felt unforced, familiar.

"I've been thinking," Howard said eventually, "about how quickly people want to turn attention into affirmation."

Caleb nodded. "Yes. As though being noticed means being validated."

"And as though being validated means being right," Howard added.

"That's the dangerous leap," Caleb replied.

They walked on in silence for a while.

"What worries me," Howard continued, "is that if we are not able to explain ourselves, others will explain us."

"Yes," Caleb said. "That's always the risk."

Howard glanced at him. "And you are still choosing not to explain."

"I am," Caleb replied. "Because once we start managing the perception, we stop tending reality."

Howard smiled faintly. "You've always had a way of saying things like that."

Caleb returned the smile. "It's easier to say than to live."

At the servo, Amelia found herself facing the same tension from a different angle. A customer leaned on the counter longer than usual and said, "People say something special's happening here."

Amelia met his gaze. "People say lots of things."

He laughed softly. "That's true. But they seem calmer when they say this."

Amelia thought for a moment. "Maybe that's because nothing's being pushed."

The man nodded. "I like that."

After he left, Amelia felt the familiar tug to say more, to clarify, to shape the narrative. Instead, she let the moment stand as it was.

Later, she wrote another line in her notebook.

Not every story needs a narrator.

Daniel encountered the widening reach more sharply than he expected.

A group he had once been part of invited him back, curious about what he had been involved in lately. They asked questions carefully, not sceptically, but with interest.

"So what's different about Willowend?" one of them asked.

Daniel hesitated. He felt the urge to summarise, to present something coherent and convincing. Instead, he spoke slowly.

"It's not different in the way people expect," he said. "There's no shift in style or theology. It's more about how people are being allowed to take responsibility for their own faith."

There was a pause.

"That sounds harder," someone said.

Daniel nodded. "It is."

The conversation moved on, but Daniel carried the weight of that exchange with him. Harder did not always mean less attractive.

Sometimes it meant more honest.

That evening, Caleb and Rachel sat together after dinner, the house quiet around them.

"Do you feel the pull?" Rachel asked.

"Yes," Caleb replied. "Not to change what we're doing, but to account for it."

"That's understandable," she said. "People want to know what to make of it."

"I know," he said. "But the moment we define it too tightly, it stops breathing."

Rachel nodded. "So we keep making room."

"Yes," Caleb said. "Even when the room feels exposed."

On Thursday afternoon, Caleb finally responded to the email from the regional church council. His reply was brief.

I'm happy to come and listen, but I don't bring answers.
Only observations, and questions I'm still living with.

The response came quickly.

That's exactly what we hoped you'd say.

Caleb closed the laptop, aware that the path ahead would require more discernment than direction. Influence would continue to widen. That was no longer in question.

The question was whether Willowend could continue to resist becoming a reference point instead of a living community.

On Sunday morning, Caleb addressed the congregation again, this time with a clarity that felt steady rather than emphatic.

"There are moments," he said, "when God entrusts a community with more attention than it asked for. The temptation then is to become a signpost instead of a home."

He paused.

"But homes don't exist to be examined. They exist to be lived in."

The room was still, attentive.

"If others come and find rest here," he continued, "we receive them. But we do not turn our life together into a demonstration."

After the service, a visitor approached him quietly.

"I didn't come to see anything special," she said. "I came because someone told me this place felt honest."

Caleb nodded. "That's something we're trying to protect."

She smiled. "Then I hope you succeed."

That afternoon, Caleb walked the edge of town again, the paddocks stretching outward, the horizon wide and unhurried.

He felt the tension of responsibility settle into something steadier. Influence would continue to extend beyond the walls of Willowend.

That could not be controlled.

But how it was held could be tended with care.

Back at home, Caleb opened his notebook one last time that day.

*When influence grows, the task is not to expand
the voice, but to guard the heart.*

He closed the book.

The circle had widened.

Now the work was to remain rooted at the centre.

Not by resisting attention.

But by refusing to let attention define them.

And in that quiet resolve, Caleb sensed that Willowend was learning something few communities ever do - how to remain faithful not only when unseen, but when noticed.

Caleb had learned that not every significant season announced itself.

Some arrived with urgency - fire on the ridge, fear in the air, people gathering because they had nowhere else to go. Others arrived almost unnoticed, marked not by intensity but by a gentle settling. This felt like the latter.

On Tuesday morning, he unlocked the church earlier than usual, more out of habit than necessity. The building was cool and dim, the air holding the faint scent of old timber and dust. He paused just inside the door, listening to the familiar stillness, aware of how much had changed and how much had not.

The pews were the same.

The cross at the front wall had not moved.

The ceiling fans still turned with the same patient rhythm.

And yet the space felt different. Not charged. Not expectant in the way it had been before. Just... inhabited. As though the prayers spoken here recently had settled into the walls and decided to stay.

Caleb moved slowly down the aisle, running his hand along the end of a pew as he passed. He was not preparing a sermon. Not planning a meeting. He was simply present, letting himself notice what had become familiar again after months of change.

Faithfulness often felt like this, he reflected. Unremarkable. Quiet. Easy to overlook if one was waiting for momentum.

Later that morning, he met Daniel outside the church. Daniel had arrived early too, holding a takeaway coffee and wearing an expression that was thoughtful rather than tired.

"I didn't realise how much I'd miss the intensity," Daniel said as they stood together on the steps.

Caleb smiled. "Miss it already?"

"A little," Daniel admitted. "Everything felt sharper for a while. More urgent."

"Yes," Caleb said. "Urgency has its own clarity."

"And now?" Daniel asked.

"Now comes endurance," Caleb replied. "Which is less dramatic, but more demanding."

Daniel nodded slowly. "I'm noticing that."

They walked together toward the side of the building where the small garden bed sat, recently tidied by someone Caleb had never seen working there.

"I keep wondering," Daniel said, "how do you know when something is still happening if it no longer feels new."

Caleb considered the question. "Usually by whether people keep choosing it."

Daniel frowned slightly. "Choosing what?"

"Showing up. Listening. Staying open. Forgiving one another when things rub the wrong way," Caleb said. "Those choices are quieter than excitement, but they last longer."

Daniel took that in, eyes following a bird as it lifted from the grass and disappeared over the fence.

"I don't want to mistake calm for stagnation," he said.

"Nor should you," Caleb replied. "But calm can also mean something has taken root."

At the servo later that day, Amelia experienced the same quiet shift from a different angle.

The conversations were still there. People still lingered, still shared fragments of their lives across the counter. But the urgency had softened. There was less explaining, less searching for reassurance. One man paid for his fuel and said, almost casually, "I went back last Sunday."

Amelia smiled. "How was it?"

"Ordinary," he said. Then he paused. "In a good way."

She nodded. "I know what you mean."

As he left, Amelia felt the familiar gratitude rise again. Not for growth, or change, or visibility - but for steadiness. For the way faith had slipped into the shape of daily life without demanding attention.

That afternoon, Caleb sat with Howard and Margaret under the large gum tree behind the church. The shade was generous, the air warm but manageable.

"I've been thinking," Margaret said, "about how much less I feel the need to say something profound."

Howard laughed quietly. "That's not a bad thing."

"No," she agreed. "But it surprised me. I used to think faith was about having words ready."

"And now?" Caleb asked.

"And now it feels more about knowing when to be silent," she said.

Howard nodded. "Silence is harder to misquote."

They sat with that for a while, the breeze stirring the leaves above them.

"What concerns me," Howard said eventually, "is whether people will think something has faded."

Caleb considered that carefully. "Some will."

"And if they do?" Margaret asked.

"Then we will trust that faithfulness doesn't require constant visibility," Caleb replied.

Later that evening, Caleb walked home alone, the town quiet around him. Lights glowed softly in windows. Someone laughed in the distance. A dog barked once, then settled.

He thought about how easily churches measured themselves by movement. By evidence of progress. By stories that could be told clearly and convincingly.

But what if the truest work of God was not always legible in that way? What if faithfulness was meant to be lived rather than narrated?

At home, Rachel was reading at the kitchen table when he arrived. She looked up and smiled.

"You seem thoughtful, again" she said.

"I think we're entering a season where nothing much appears to be happening," he replied.

She closed her book gently. "And how does that feel?"

He considered it honestly. "Both relieving and unsettling."

Rachel nodded. "That sounds about right."

They sat together in the quiet for a while, no need to fill the space. "I think this might be the real test," Caleb said eventually. "Not whether we can respond when something happens, but whether we can remain faithful when it doesn't."

Rachel smiled softly. "That's where most pastors live, whether anyone notices or not."

Later, as the night settled, Caleb opened his notebook again. He did not write much.

Just one line.

Faithfulness is often measured in days that feel unremarkable.

He closed the book and set it aside.

Outside, Willowend rested. No urgency. No anticipation. Just the steady continuation of life lived attentively.

And Caleb sensed, with a quiet certainty that did not need reinforcement, that this was not a pause before something more important. This was the work itself.

By the middle of the week, Caleb began to notice how easily quiet faithfulness could be misunderstood. Not by those who lived it, but by those who watched from a distance.

He heard it in the phrasing of a phone call from a colleague he had not spoken to in months. The voice was friendly, well-meaning, but edged with assumption.

"So things have settled down there now?" the man asked.

Caleb paused. "In what sense?"

"Well," the man continued, "the intensity. The attention. I suppose it's moved on."

Caleb considered his reply carefully. "Some things have moved on," he said. "Others have gone deeper."

There was a brief silence. "Ah," the man said, as though unsure what to do with that answer.

After the call ended, Caleb sat for a while with the unease it left behind. Settled down was a phrase that often carried judgment disguised as relief. As though the absence of visible momentum meant the absence of meaning.

Later that afternoon, Daniel raised a similar concern from a different angle.

"I had someone say to me," he said, "that it all feels quieter now. Like maybe the moment has passed."

Caleb nodded. "And what did you think?"

Daniel frowned slightly. "I wasn't sure how to answer. Because it is quieter. But it doesn't feel empty."

"No," Caleb said. "It feels inhabited."

Daniel smiled faintly. "That's the word I was looking for."

They walked together for a while along the side of the church, gravel crunching softly underfoot.

"I think I'm learning," Daniel said slowly, "that faithfulness doesn't feel rewarding in the way excitement does."

"That's true," Caleb replied. "Excitement feeds on response. Faithfulness feeds on conviction."

"And conviction doesn't always feel dramatic," Daniel added.

"No," Caleb agreed. "Often it feels repetitive."

At the servo, Amelia noticed the same shift in tone from customers who had once been eager to talk. Some still lingered. Some still shared. But a few seemed almost disappointed that nothing new was happening.

"It was exciting for a while there," one woman said, not unkindly. "Felt like something big."

Amelia smiled gently. "Big things don't always stay loud."

The woman nodded, though she did not look convinced.

After she left, Amelia felt a flicker of doubt rise. Not about what had happened, but about how it might be perceived now. She resisted the urge to explain, to justify the quieter season as somehow equally valid.

Later, she wrote in her notebook.

If faith needs to be defended constantly,
it has already shifted its centre.

That evening, Caleb met with a small group who had asked for time together. Not for guidance. Just space.

They gathered without agenda. No one introduced the time. No one concluded it formally. People spoke when they felt ready. Silence was allowed to linger without apology.

One person shared a frustration that had not resolved. Another admitted disappointment that certain hopes had not materialised. No one rushed to correct or reframe what was said. Caleb listened, aware of how easily such honesty could be interpreted as failure by those who equated faith with constant uplift.

Yet there was no despair in the room. Only realism.

When the gathering ended, one of them said quietly, "I don't feel fixed. But I feel held."

Caleb smiled. "That matters."

Walking home afterward, Caleb reflected on how often churches were tempted to narrate their lives in terms of seasons of growth and decline. As though the only alternatives were expansion or loss.

But perhaps there was another category altogether. A season of depth. Of consolidation. Of faith becoming less visible because it was no longer searching for expression.

At home, Rachel was sorting through papers at the table when he arrived.

"You look tired," she said.

"I think I'm realising how tiring it is to resist expectations," Caleb replied.

"Whose expectations?" she asked.

"Everyone's," he said. "Including my own."

Rachel nodded. "That's often the hardest part."

They sat together quietly for a moment.

"Do you ever worry," Caleb asked, "that people will think we've stalled?"

Rachel smiled gently. "Some probably will."

"And that doesn't trouble you?" he asked.

She shook her head. "Not if what's happening is honest."

Caleb said. "But honesty doesn't always look that impressive."

"No," Rachel said. "But it lasts."

The following morning, Caleb returned to the church early again. He sat in one of the back pews, not preparing anything, just being present.

The stillness felt familiar now, it was no longer charged with expectation. It reminded him of early mornings in ministry years ago, before experience had taught him how quickly momentum could become a substitute for faith.

He thought about the pastors who might read about Willowend one day. The ones serving faithfully in places where nothing dramatic happened, where Sundays blended into one another, where progress was measured in quiet perseverance rather than visible change.

He hoped they would recognise this season.

Not as failure.

Not as decline.

But as the long obedience of faith lived without applause.

Later that day, Caleb received a short message from Ruth.

Work's busy. Life's good. I was thinking about Willowend today. It sounds like things are… steady.

Caleb smiled at the word.

He replied simply.

They are. And that's enough.

As the week drew on, the quiet continued. No new visitors. No crises. No breakthroughs.

And yet, beneath the surface, something firm was forming.

Faithfulness that did not depend on being noticed.

Faith that did not require novelty to stay alive.

A community learning how to remain present in the absence of drama.

That evening, Caleb returned again to his notebook.

Quiet seasons reveal whether faith was built on movement or on trust.

He closed the book, feeling the truth of it settle.

This was not the chapter people would retell with enthusiasm. But it might be the chapter that kept everything else from unravelling.

And that, Caleb knew, was no small gift.

By the weekend, Caleb felt the quiet season pressing most firmly not on the church, but on himself.

There were fewer decisions to make now, fewer moments that demanded discernment in real time. The days felt deceptively manageable. And yet, he sensed that this was where the deeper work was happening - the kind that did not reward attentiveness with immediate confirmation.

On Saturday morning, Caleb walked through town earlier than usual. The air was cool, the streets mostly empty. He passed the bakery just as Sheila was opening up, waved to a farmer unloading supplies at the hardware store, and nodded to a young couple walking their dog. Ordinary scenes, unchanged by anything that had happened in recent months.

That, he realised, was both comforting and unsettling.

It would have been easier if the town itself looked different. If something visible had marked the season they had been through. But Willowend looked much as it always had. The same streets. The same buildings. The same quiet resilience.

Only the people were changing, and even that was subtle.

At the oval, Caleb stopped for a moment and sat on one of the low benches near the fence. He watched a small group of teenagers kicking a football back and forth, laughing easily.

None of them had been part of the church conversations. None of them had been drawn into the renewal in any obvious way. And yet, Caleb found himself praying quietly for them. Not with urgency, but with trust. The kind of prayer that assumed God was already at work long before any words were spoken.

Later that morning, Daniel joined him at the church to help prepare for Sunday. They moved around one another easily, setting out chairs, checking the sound, tidying the front space. No one spoke much.

After a while, Daniel broke the silence.

"Do you ever feel," he said carefully, "like you're supposed to want more than this?"

Caleb paused, his hands resting on the back of a chair. "More in what sense?"

"More visibility. More momentum. More confirmation that it's working," Daniel replied.

"Yes," Caleb said simply. "I've felt that."

"And?" Daniel asked.

"And I've learned that wanting more isn't always wrong," Caleb said. "But chasing more often is."

Daniel nodded. "I think I'm afraid that if nothing happens, it means we've missed something."

Caleb smiled. "Or it might mean we've arrived somewhere we don't know how to recognise yet."

Daniel considered that, then laughed softly. "That sounds like something you'd say."

Caleb chuckled. "Years of practice."

At the servo that afternoon, Amelia experienced a similar moment of unease. A customer she knew well said, "It all feels quieter lately."

Amelia nodded. "It does."

"Is that okay?" the man asked.

She thought for a moment. "I think it depends on what we think faith is for."

He frowned slightly. "What do you mean?"

"If faith is meant to excite us," Amelia said, "then quiet feels like loss. But if it's meant to steady us, then quiet might be a gift."

The man smiled slowly. "That's not how I've usually thought about it."

"Me neither," Amelia replied. "Until recently."

That evening, Caleb and Rachel sat together on the veranda, the sky deepening into dusk. A breeze moved through the trees, carrying the smell of dry grass and distant wood smoke.

"I've been thinking," Rachel said, "about how many pastors feel like something's wrong when nothing dramatic is happening."

Caleb nodded. "As though faith needs to justify its existence."

"Yes," she said. "As though staying isn't enough."

They sat quietly for a while, watching the light fade.

"I wonder," Caleb said eventually, "how many churches quietly unravel because people mistake stillness for stagnation."

Rachel leaned back in her chair. "Probably a lot more than we realise."

"And how many pastors end up leaving because the work becomes invisible," he added.

Rachel looked at him thoughtfully. "And how many stay, quietly faithful, without ever knowing how much it mattered."

The thought lingered between them.

On Sunday morning, the service unfolded without incident. No unusual moments. No particularly striking words. The hymns were sung steadily, the prayers spoken simply.

Caleb preached briefly, not because he had less to say, but because he sensed that the congregation did not need more explanation.

"Faith doesn't always feel alive," he said. "Sometimes it feels steady. Sometimes it feels repetitive. But endurance is not the absence of faith - it is often its most honest form."

The congregation listened quietly. No one rushed forward afterward. No one lingered anxiously. People talked as they always did, exchanged greetings, made plans for the week ahead.

That afternoon, Caleb returned alone to the sanctuary. He sat again in the back pew, the room still and familiar.

He thought about the pastors in towns smaller than Willowend. The ones unlocking buildings early, flicking on fans that stirred warm air, preaching to people they had known for decades. The ones wondering whether what they were doing still mattered.

He hoped they would recognise this season.

Not as the end of something.

But as the proof that something had endured.

As he stood to leave, Caleb felt no surge of certainty, no reassurance that everything would unfold neatly from here. But he did feel grounded.

Faithfulness was not meant to be impressive.

It was meant to be lived.

And as he turned off the lights and closed the door behind him, Caleb knew that this quiet chapter - easily overlooked, rarely celebrated - was as much a work of God as any moment of urgency that had come before it.

Perhaps more so.

Because it asked less for attention.

And required more trust.

Caleb recognised the weariness before he felt it.

It showed up not as exhaustion, but as a dulling of edges. A slight heaviness behind the eyes. A reluctance to begin things that once felt straightforward. He still woke early. He still unlocked the church. He still listened carefully. But the effort it took had increased, quietly, almost imperceptibly.

He noticed it one morning as he stood at the sink, rinsing his mug before leaving the house. The simple task felt slower than usual. Not difficult - just weighted.

Weariness, he had learned, did not announce itself loudly. It slipped in disguised as responsibility faithfully carried too long without rest.

On his walk into town that day, Caleb passed familiar faces and exchanged familiar greetings. Nothing seemed amiss. The church was steady. The community was settled. If anything, things were healthier now than they had been months earlier.

And yet, he felt thin.

At the church office, he sat longer than usual before opening his notebook. The words did not come readily. He stared instead at the window, watching dust drift in the light.

Later that morning, Daniel stopped by unexpectedly. He looked concerned before he even spoke.

"You're quieter than usual," he said.

Caleb smiled faintly. "Am I?"

"Yes," Daniel replied. "Not absent. Just... muted."

Caleb considered that. "That might be accurate."

Daniel hesitated. "Is everything all right?"

"Yes," Caleb said honestly. "Everything is fine."

Daniel frowned slightly. "That doesn't sound reassuring."

Caleb chuckled. "It shouldn't. Fine is very often where weariness hides."

They sat together in silence for a moment.

"I don't feel burnt out," Caleb continued. "I just feel… spent."

Daniel nodded. "I've heard that from some others lately. Not complaints. Just tiredness."

"Yes," Caleb said. "Faithfulness accumulates."

Daniel leaned forward. "What do you do when you notice that?"

Caleb paused. "You resist the urge to push through it as though it were a failure."

Daniel smiled slightly. "That sounds harder than pushing through."

"It is," Caleb agreed.

That afternoon, Caleb visited Graham on his farm. They walked slowly along the fence line, the air warm and dry, cicadas buzzing in the trees.

"You look worn," Graham said bluntly.

Caleb laughed. "I thought pastors were meant to hide that better."

Graham shook his head. "Farmers don't trust people who pretend they're never tired."

Caleb smiled. "That's fair."

They walked in companionable silence for a while before Graham spoke again.

"You've carried a lot," he said. "Quietly."

Caleb nodded. "So have others."

"Yes," Graham replied. "But you've been carrying the weight of everyone else's carrying."

The words landed gently, but firmly.

"I think," Graham continued, "that the season is now asking something different of you."

Caleb looked at him. "What do you think it's asking?"

"Rest," Graham said simply. "Not retreat. Just rest."

Caleb considered that. "Rest feels undeserved when there's still work to be done."

Graham smiled. "That's how you know you need it."

Back in town later that day, Caleb stopped briefly at the servo. Amelia looked at him carefully before speaking.

"You okay?" she asked.

"Yes," Caleb replied automatically.

She raised an eyebrow. "That wasn't convincing."

Caleb smiled, conceding the point. "I'm just a little tired."

Amelia nodded. "That's allowed, you know."

"I know," he said. "Remembering it is harder."

She leaned on the counter. "People think strength means always being available. But the strongest seasons I've seen here were held by people who knew when to pause."

Caleb met her gaze. "You've learned that quickly."

She smiled. "Because I watched you learn it slowly."

That evening, Caleb sat with Rachel at the table, the house quiet around them.

"You've been carrying a lot," she said gently.

He nodded. "I didn't notice until recently."

"That's usually how it works," she replied.

"I don't feel dramatic about it," he said. "Just… tired in a way that doesn't lift overnight."

Rachel reached across the table and took his hand. "Then this isn't something to solve. It's something to tend."

He looked at her, grateful. "I don't want to withdraw."

"I know," she said. "And you don't need to. But you might need to let others carry more visibly."

Caleb considered that. "That feels like loss."

"It's not," Rachel said softly. "It's trust."

The following morning, Caleb returned to the church early again. He sat in the sanctuary, not preparing anything, just breathing.

He thought about the pastors who read quietly at night, wondering why the work felt heavier even when nothing was wrong. The ones who felt guilty for being tired in healthy churches.

He hoped they would hear this truth clearly:

Weariness is not failure.

It is often the sign of faithfulness sustained over time.

Later that day, Caleb made a small decision. Not a public one. Not a formal one. He cancelled two meetings that did not need to happen immediately. He delegated one responsibility he had been holding unnecessarily.

Nothing dramatic changed.

And yet, something eased.

That evening, as the sun dropped low over Willowend, Caleb walked slowly through town once more. He felt no rush to arrive anywhere. Grace, he was learning, did not always appear as strength renewed.

Sometimes it appeared as permission to stop pretending you were not tired. And as he turned toward home, Caleb felt the first stirrings of that grace settling in.

Not as relief.

But as kindness.

The kind that allows a faithful servant to remain faithful without carrying more than was ever asked of him.

As the week unfolded, Caleb began to notice how weariness altered not only his energy, but his attention.

He still listened carefully, still noticed details, still carried the quiet awareness that had marked his ministry for years. But there was a new slowness in him now, a slight delay between what he heard and how quickly he responded. Not indifference. Discernment shaped by fatigue.

He noticed it during a conversation with Howard late one afternoon. They sat beneath the shade of the gum tree again, the same place where so many unplanned conversations had settled naturally.

"I've been thinking," Howard said, "about how much we rely on you without realising it."

Caleb smiled faintly. "That sounds like a confession."

Howard nodded. "It is. Not an accusation. Just an observation."

Caleb let that sit for a moment. "Reliance isn't always wrong," he said. "But it becomes dangerous when it goes unnoticed."

Howard leaned back. "I think some of us assumed you'd always be the one holding the threads together."

"Yes," Caleb replied quietly. "I've probably reinforced that without meaning to."

Howard looked thoughtful. "You don't need to stop leading."

"No," Caleb said. "But I might need to lead differently."

They sat in silence for a while, the breeze moving gently through the leaves above them.

"What would that look like?" Howard asked eventually.

Caleb considered the question. "Less immediacy. More patience. Allowing things to remain unresolved a little longer."

Howard smiled. "I am sure that might make some people uncomfortable."

"Yes," Caleb agreed. "Including me."

That evening, Daniel experienced his own version of this discomfort. He had been asked to facilitate a small gathering, nothing formal, just a few people who wanted space to talk and pray. Normally, Caleb would have been present, listening quietly in the background. This time, he was not.

Daniel felt the absence keenly.

At first, the conversation stalled. People looked around as though waiting for someone else to speak. Daniel resisted the urge to fill the space.

Eventually, one person spoke hesitantly. Then another. The conversation unfolded slowly, unevenly, but honestly.

Later, Daniel reflected on how much confidence he had drawn simply from knowing Caleb was nearby. Without that assurance, he had felt exposed.

But something else had happened too.

He had listened more carefully.

He had spoken less.

And the gathering had not faltered.

At the servo, Amelia noticed a similar shift in the rhythms of responsibility. Caleb still stopped by, still asked how things were going. But he lingered less. He listened, then trusted her to hold what was shared without his presence reinforcing it.

At first, she missed the reassurance. Then she realised what it offered her. Space.

One afternoon, she caught herself offering quiet counsel to someone who had come in burdened. Not advice. Just presence. After the person left, Amelia felt a flicker of surprise.

She had not waited for permission.

That night, Caleb and Rachel walked together after dinner, the road quiet, the sky wide above them.

"I feel strangely unanchored," Caleb admitted.

Rachel glanced at him. "Because you're not holding everything as tightly?"

"Yes," he said. "And because I'm not sure how much is enough now."

Rachel nodded. "That question only appears when we stop over functioning."

He smiled wryly. "You make it sound so clinical."

"I've had years of practice watching pastors," she replied gently. They walked on in silence.

"I'm afraid," Caleb said eventually, "that if I pull back too much, things will unravel."

Rachel stopped and turned to face him. "And I'm afraid that if you don't pull back at all, you will."

The truth of it settled between them.

Back at home later, Caleb sat alone at the table, notebook open but untouched. He thought about the seasons of his ministry when his strength had seemed endless. When he could carry more than was reasonable and still feel alive.

Those seasons had not lasted.

Nor were they meant to.

He wrote slowly.

Weariness exposes where faith has quietly become effort.

The next morning, Caleb received a message from a pastor he had met recently, someone serving in a small town even quieter than Willowend.

*I don't know why I'm writing, I just wanted to say
it helps to know others get tired too.*

Caleb read it twice.

He replied simply.

We all do. The mistake is pretending otherwise.

Later that day, Caleb declined an invitation he would once have accepted without hesitation. It was not urgent. It was not necessary. And saying no felt both uncomfortable and oddly freeing.

He noticed the resistance rise immediately. The familiar voice whispering that availability equalled faithfulness. That saying no meant failing someone.

He resisted that voice gently, deliberately.

On Sunday morning, Caleb spoke briefly again. Not about weariness directly, but about grace.

"There are times," he said, "when the most faithful thing we can do is acknowledge our limits. Not as weakness, but as truth."

He paused.

"Grace is not given because we are strong. It is given because we are not."

The congregation listened quietly. No one responded audibly. But Caleb sensed something loosen.

After the service, an older woman approached him, her eyes kind.

"I've been tired for years," she said quietly. "I thought it meant I wasn't doing enough."

Caleb smiled gently. "It might just mean you've been doing something faithfully for a long time."

She nodded, tears welling briefly. "That helps."

That afternoon, Caleb sat again on the veranda, watching the light move slowly across the paddocks. He felt no sudden renewal. No surge of strength.

But he felt held.

Held by grace that did not demand more.

Held by a community learning to carry one another.

Held by the quiet truth that weariness, when met with honesty, did not diminish faith.

It refined it.

And in that refinement, Caleb sensed the beginning of something gentler than endurance.

He sensed kindness taking root.

The kind that allows a pastor to remain present not by striving harder, but by trusting deeper. And that, he knew, would carry him further than strength ever could.

By the time the week turned again, Caleb had finally stopped measuring his days by how much he completed.

It was not a conscious decision at first. More an erosion of an old habit. The quiet release of an internal ledger he had carried for years, tallying conversations, visits, meetings, responsibilities.

Somewhere in the midst of weariness, the numbers had lost their authority.

He noticed it one morning as he locked the church door after a brief, unplanned prayer gathering.

Only a handful of people had come. No structure. No agenda. Just a shared stillness and a few honest words offered without flourish.

As he turned the key, he felt no disappointment at the smallness of it. No sense that something more should have happened. It had been enough.

Later that day, he met with Mary Kline, who had asked him to come by. She was seated near the window when he arrived, sunlight warming her thin hands resting in her lap.

"You look different," she said without preamble.

Caleb smiled. "That could mean many things."

She waved a dismissive hand. "Less burdened. Not less serious. Just… lighter."

He considered that. "I've been learning to carry less."

Mary nodded approvingly. "Good. God has never needed us to carry everything. Only to stay attentive."

They sat together quietly for a moment.

"I've watched pastors," Mary continued, "mistake exhaustion for holiness. They think depletion is the cost of faithfulness."

Caleb nodded. "I've thought that too."

She looked at him keenly. "And now?"

"Now I think grace is the greater teacher," he replied.

Mary smiled. "It always has been."

As he left her home, Caleb felt a deep gratitude for the voices that had shaped him quietly over time. Not loud mentors. Not influential names. But steady witnesses who had walked long enough to recognise the difference between sacrifice and erosion.

That afternoon, Caleb received a brief phone call from Ruth. She sounded tired, but bright.

"I just wanted to check in," she said. "Mum said you've been slowing down."

Caleb chuckled. "That sounds like her."

"I mean it as a good thing," Ruth added quickly. "You've always been… full-on. In a gentle way. But still."

He smiled. "I suppose I have."

There was a pause.

"I'm really proud of you," Ruth said quietly. "Both of you. What you've built there. It matters more than you probably realise."

Caleb felt the words settle deeply. "That means a lot."

"I don't know where I fit in all of it yet," she continued. "But I like knowing it's there."

"You always fit," Caleb said. "There's no hurry."

After they ended the call, Caleb sat for a long while, thinking about the different ways faith unfolded across a lifetime. How some stayed close, others circled from a distance. How God never seemed anxious about timing.

As evening came, Caleb walked through town again, slower than usual, greeting people without lingering. He noticed how many conversations now carried their own momentum. How people spoke to one another without looking to him for affirmation.

This, he realised, was fruit.

Not dependence.

But maturity.

At the servo, Amelia was deep in conversation with someone he did not recognise. She noticed Caleb but did not break off immediately. When she did, it was with ease.

"Everything okay?" she asked.

"Yes," Caleb said. "I was just passing through."

She nodded, understanding something unspoken. "Good."

As he walked on, Caleb felt no sense of being replaced. Only relief.

That night, sitting with Rachel, he spoke more openly than he had in weeks.

"I think I'm finally learning how to stop before exhaustion becomes damage," he said.

Rachel smiled. "That's not something you learn quickly."

"No," he agreed. "Or alone."

She reached for his hand. "You've given people permission to grow. Now you're giving yourself permission to rest."

He nodded. "It feels unfamiliar."

"Most healthy things do at first," she replied.

The following Sunday, Caleb preached briefly again. No outline that demanded precision. No urgency in his tone. Just a quiet invitation.

"We often assume," he said, "that faithfulness means doing more. But sometimes it means listening more carefully to what God is no longer asking of us."

He paused.

"Grace does not only sustain us when we are strong. It also releases us when we are tired."

As the service ended, there was no rush to leave. People lingered, talking softly. Not because they needed direction, but because they were comfortable staying.

Caleb stood near the door, greeting people simply.

One man paused as he shook Caleb's hand. "Thanks for not trying to fix everything," he said.

Caleb smiled. "You're welcome."

Later, as the church emptied, Caleb returned briefly to the sanctuary. He stood in the centre aisle again, as he had so many times before.

But something had changed.

The space no longer felt like something he was responsible to fill.

It felt shared.

He breathed deeply.

Weariness had not vanished. But it no longer frightened him. It had become a signal rather than a threat. An invitation rather than a warning.

As he turned off the lights and stepped outside, the air was cool, the sky soft with late afternoon colour.

Caleb walked home unhurried.

Grace, he realised, was not asking him to be more resilient.

It was teaching him how to be human.

And in that humanity, he found himself steadier than he had been in a long time.

Not because the weight had disappeared.

But because he was no longer carrying it alone.

Caleb had not planned to notice it, but once he did, he could not ignore it.

Decisions were being made without him.

Not the large ones. Not the obvious ones. But the small, ordinary choices that shaped the life of the church week by week. Someone rearranged the chairs without asking. A visit was made quietly, without his prompting. A conversation was followed up days later by someone other than him.

At first, it unsettled him more than he expected. Not because he wanted control, but because for so long, attentiveness had flowed through him by default.

He had been the one who remembered, who noticed, who held the threads together. Now those threads were being picked up elsewhere.

And the fabric was holding.

On Monday morning, Caleb arrived at the church to find a note on his desk.

Dropped meals around to the Harrisons yesterday. Didn't want to bother you. Just thought you'd like to know.

There was no name attached.

He smiled.

Later that day, he met with Daniel, who seemed both energised and uncertain.

"I think I might have overstepped," Daniel said.

Caleb raised an eyebrow. "Tell me."

"I spoke with someone after the service. They were struggling. I didn't ask you first."

Caleb waited.

"I listened," Daniel continued. "I didn't try to fix anything. But afterward, I wondered if I should have checked with you."

Caleb shook his head gently. "Why?"

Daniel hesitated. "Because that's how we used to do things."

"Yes," Caleb said. "And this?"

"This felt... different," Daniel replied. "Right, but unfamiliar."

Caleb smiled. "That's what shared trust feels like at first."

Daniel leaned back, exhaling. "So I didn't cross a line?"

"No," Caleb said. "You honoured one."

That afternoon, Caleb walked through town again, slower now, not out of fatigue but intention. He stopped at the bakery, where Sheila greeted him warmly, then moved on without lingering. At the post office, he nodded to a couple deep in conversation and kept walking.

He was learning not to insert himself where he was no longer needed.

At the servo, Amelia waved him over briefly.

"Just so you know," she said, "a few of us are meeting on Thursday mornings. No structure. Just checking in with each other."

Caleb smiled. "That sounds good."

"You don't need to come," she added quickly.

"I know," he said. "And I'm glad."

She studied his face. "You really mean that."

"I do," Caleb replied. "It tells me something important."

"What?" she asked.

"That the work doesn't collapse when I'm not in the room."

Amelia smiled. "It never did. We just didn't realise it."

That evening, Caleb and Rachel sat together after dinner, the house quiet around them.

"I think something's shifted," Caleb said.

Rachel looked up from her book. "How so?"

"I don't feel like the centre anymore," he said.

She smiled gently. "That's not a loss."

"No," he agreed. "It feels more like alignment."

Rachel considered that. "You've been praying for maturity for a long time."

"Yes," Caleb said. "I just didn't expect it to include my own decentring."

Rachel laughed softly. "God has a way of answering prayers thoroughly."

The next morning, Caleb received a message from Howard.

We covered the pastoral visit roster for the next few weeks. You're not on it.

Caleb stared at the screen for a moment.

Then he typed back.

Thank you.

He meant it.

Later that day, he met with Mary Kline again. She listened as he spoke about the changes he was noticing.

"You're watching trust redistribute," she said.

"That's a good way to put it," Caleb replied.

Mary nodded. "When trust stays centralised, people remain dependent. When it's shared, people grow."

Caleb smiled. "And leaders?"

Mary met his gaze. "They learn whether they believe what they've been teaching."

The words lingered.

That afternoon, Caleb sat alone in the sanctuary again, not out of habit now, but reflection. He noticed how the space felt less like something he was stewarding alone and more like something held collectively.

He thought about how many pastors struggled to let go of roles they had inhabited faithfully for years. Not because they were proud, but because stepping back felt like abandonment.

Yet here, in Willowend, something gentler was happening.

Trust was being shared, not seized.

Responsibility was being carried, not delegated downward.

And the church was not fragmenting.

It was maturing.

On Sunday morning, Caleb spoke only briefly. "There comes a moment," he said, "when faith moves from being something we receive to something we carry for one another."

He paused.

"That moment is rarely announced. But when it comes, it changes everything."

After the service, Caleb stayed back while others stacked chairs and tidied quietly. No one asked him what to do. No one looked to him for approval.

And he felt no need to offer it.

That afternoon, he walked home with Rachel, the late light soft around them.

"You seem lighter," she said.

"I think I am," he said. "Not because there's less responsibility. But because it's no longer all mine."

Rachel nodded. "That's how trust works."

That evening, Caleb opened his notebook again.

Shared trust does not diminish leadership,
it fulfils it.

He closed the book and set it aside.

There would still be moments when he would need to step forward. Times when clarity and courage would be required of him in visible ways. He was not disappearing.

But the centre was no longer his to guard alone.

And as Willowend settled into another ordinary evening, Caleb felt a deep assurance.

This was not an ending.

This was the work continuing in the hands of many.

Quietly.

Faithfully.

Together.

As the week continued, Caleb began to feel the difference between absence and availability.

He was still present. Still attentive. Still listening. But he was no longer the first point of contact for every concern, nor the final authority on every decision. People checked in with him, not out of dependence, but out of relationship. The distinction mattered more than he had expected.

He noticed it one morning when he arrived at the church to find a small group already gathered near the front, chairs drawn into a loose circle. No one had asked permission. No one looked surprised when he entered. They simply nodded, smiled, and continued.

Caleb took a seat at the back, content to listen.

The conversation was unpolished. People spoke hesitantly at first, then more freely. There were no conclusions reached, no summaries offered. But something solid was happening. People were listening to one another with care, and no one seemed to be waiting for him to intervene.

Afterward, as they stood to leave, one of them turned to Caleb and said, "Thanks for giving us space."

Caleb smiled. "You're doing well with it."

The person looked surprised, then thoughtful. "I suppose we are."

Later that day, Daniel came by, his expression carrying a mix of confidence and uncertainty.

"I said yes to something," he said.

Caleb raised an eyebrow. "Tell me."

"A couple asked if I'd meet with them regularly for a while," Daniel explained. "Not counselling exactly. Just conversation. They didn't ask you first."

"And how did that feel?" Caleb asked.

Daniel hesitated. "Right. But also… weighty."

Caleb nodded. "That's the cost of shared trust."

"I'm not sure I know what I'm doing," Daniel admitted.

Caleb smiled gently. "None of us ever really does. We just learn how to listen well."

Daniel exhaled. "I was hoping you'd say that."

At the servo, Amelia felt the same weight settling in. A woman she had been talking with for weeks finally said, "I don't know why I keep telling you these things."

Amelia smiled. "You don't have to know."

"But you don't try to fix anything," the woman said. "You just… stay."

Amelia felt the deep significance of the words settle on her. "Sometimes staying is enough."

That evening, Amelia mentioned the conversation to Caleb in passing. "I don't feel equipped," she said honestly.

Caleb nodded. "That's usually a sign you're doing something real."

"I'm afraid of saying the wrong thing," she added.

"So am I," Caleb replied. "Often."

She laughed softly. "That helps."

As the days went on, Caleb noticed how often his instinct to step in was being gently tested. A question arose in a meeting and someone else answered it thoughtfully. A concern was raised and resolved without his involvement. A disagreement surfaced and was navigated patiently by others.

Each time, Caleb felt a flicker of tension, then relief.

Trust, he was learning, did not arrive as certainty. It arrived as risk shared wisely.

One afternoon, Howard stopped by with a small stack of papers. "We've been thinking about the next few months," he said. "Nothing formal. Just planning."

Caleb nodded. "And?"

"And we realised you don't need to be in every conversation," Howard continued. "So we've taken a few things off your plate."

Caleb looked at the papers, then back at Howard. "Thank you."

Howard smiled. "It feels strange, you know."

"Yes," Caleb said. "But it feels right too."

Howard hesitated. "We're not trying to push you out."

"I know," Caleb replied. "You're inviting others in."

That distinction mattered deeply.

At home that evening, Caleb spoke quietly with Rachel.

"I feel exposed," he admitted. "Not in a bad way. Just... visible in a different sense."

Rachel nodded. "You're allowing people to see you as a fellow member, not just a shepherd."

He smiled faintly. "That's unsettling."

"And freeing," she added.

"Yes," he agreed. "Both."

The following Sunday, the service unfolded with a different rhythm. Others read Scripture. Others prayed. Others lingered afterward to talk and listen.

Caleb found himself standing to the side more often than at the centre. He did not feel diminished by it.

He felt trusted.

After the service, an older man approached him slowly.

"I've been coming here for years," the man said. "This is the first time I've felt like the church belonged to all of us."

Caleb nodded. "That's something we're learning together."

The man smiled. "It's about time."

That afternoon, Caleb took a longer walk than usual, letting his thoughts settle. He reflected on how easily leadership could become centralised under the banner of care. How quickly responsibility could slip into control if not watched carefully.

But here, in Willowend, something gentler was taking shape.

Leadership was not disappearing. It was diffusing.

That evening, Caleb returned to his notebook and wrote slowly.

Trust shared becomes strength multiplied.

He closed the book, feeling the truth of it settle.

This season would require vigilance. Shared trust could falter if clarity faded or courage waned. But it also carried promise. A community that no longer depended on one voice was a community capable of enduring change.

As the sun dipped below the horizon and Willowend settled into another quiet night, Caleb felt no urge to reclaim the centre.

He felt grateful to stand alongside.

And in that posture, he sensed the work continuing - not less faithfully, but more fully shared than ever before.

As the month drew on, Caleb began to sense that shared trust did not only change structures - it changed posture.

People stood differently now. Not physically, but inwardly. Conversations carried less urgency, less checking for approval. There was a steadiness to the way people spoke, as though they had begun to believe that what they offered mattered, even if it was incomplete.

Caleb noticed it during one quiet moment following a midweek gathering. Chairs were being stacked without direction. Two people lingered near the doorway, talking softly. Someone else wiped down a table without being asked. None of it was remarkable. And yet, taken together, it felt like something had settled.

This was not enthusiasm. It was ownership.

Later that evening, Caleb sat alone in the sanctuary again, not to prepare, not to reflect deeply, but simply to be present. He listened to the creak of the building as it cooled, the distant sound of a car passing through town, the faint hum of electricity in the lights overhead.

For years, this space had felt like a responsibility he carried. Now it felt like a place he shared. He thought about the subtle fear many pastors carried - the fear that if they loosened their grip, everything would unravel. That people would drift. That standards would slip. That care would be diluted.

And yet, here in Willowend, the opposite was unfolding.

Care was widening.

Responsibility was spreading.

Faith was deepening.

Not because anyone had planned it that way, but because trust had been allowed to move.

The following morning, Caleb received a short message from Amelia.

Just wanted you to know - a few of us met this morning.
We prayed for you too.

Caleb read it twice.

He had prayed for people quietly for decades. Rarely had he imagined being named so simply in the prayers of others.

He did not feel embarrassed.

He felt seen.

That afternoon, he met briefly with Daniel again. They walked together along the edge of town, the paddocks stretching wide and open beside them.

"I'm starting to understand something," Daniel said.

Caleb waited.

"I thought leadership meant being ready with answers," Daniel continued. "But lately it feels more like being willing to stay when things aren't clear."

Caleb smiled. "That's a very good observation."

Daniel nodded. "It's harder than I expected."

"Yes," Caleb said. "Because it asks us to trust God's work in others, not just through ourselves."

They walked on in silence for a while.

"I used to think," Daniel said quietly, "that you were holding everything together."

Caleb glanced at him. "And now?"

"Now I think you were helping us learn how to hold things together too."

The words stayed with Caleb long after they parted.

That evening, as the sun dropped low, Caleb and Rachel sat on the veranda, the air cooling gently around them.

"You seem settled," Rachel said.

"I think I am," Caleb replied. "Not because things are finished. But because they're not dependent on me anymore."

Rachel nodded. "That's always been your hope, hasn't it?"

"Yes," he said. "I just didn't realise how much letting go it would require."

She smiled. "Growth often costs what we're most used to offering."

Later that night, Caleb opened his notebook again.

Shared trust reveals where control was never meant to live.

He closed it and set it aside.

There would still be moments of tension. Times when decisions would be difficult, when clarity would be needed, when leadership would need to step forward again.

Shared trust did not remove the need for guidance. It simply changed its shape.

The following Sunday, Caleb noticed something small but telling. As the service ended, no one looked to him to signal what came next. People moved naturally into conversation, into prayer, into quiet presence with one another.

Caleb stood near the doorway, greeting people as he always had. But now, his role felt less like holding space and more like witnessing it. An older woman paused beside him.

"I used to think church was something we came to," she said quietly. "Now it feels like something we are."

Caleb smiled. "That's a perfect way to put it."

As the building slowly emptied, Caleb remained behind for a moment. He walked once more down the centre aisle, then stopped halfway, just as he had so many times before.

But the feeling was different now. He no longer stood there as the centre of attention, nor as the one responsible for what happened next. He stood there as one among many. And that, he realised, was not a loss of calling. It was its fulfilment.

As he turned off the lights and stepped outside, the evening had settled into stillness. Willowend lay quiet around him, steady and unremarkable, faithful in its own unassuming way.

Caleb breathed deeply.

Shared trust had not weakened the church.

It had strengthened it in ways no single leader ever could.

And as he walked home, unhurried and at peace, he knew this season was teaching him something essential: That the work of God endures not because it is carefully held by one, but because it is faithfully carried by many.

Quietly.

Together.

And for the long journey ahead.

33. WHEN DISCERNMENT DEEPENS

Caleb noticed it first not in words, but in tone. Conversations carried more weight now. Not heavier, but steadier. People spoke with less hurry, less need to fill space. Questions lingered longer before answers emerged. There was a growing patience in the life of the church - a willingness to sit with uncertainty rather than rush past it.

He sensed it during a midweek gathering that unfolded without agenda. Chairs had been arranged in a loose circle, not because anyone planned it that way, but because it seemed natural. People arrived quietly, greeting one another softly, settling without instruction.

Caleb sat among them, not at the centre, not on the edge. Just present.

A silence stretched at the beginning. No one hurried to break it. Eventually, Mary spoke. Her voice was gentle, but clear. "I think God is asking us to listen more carefully to one another."

No one responded immediately. Not because they disagreed, but because the words felt complete. Daniel nodded slowly. Amelia leaned forward slightly, thoughtful. Others held the silence.

Caleb felt a familiar impulse rise - the urge to affirm, to explain, to guide the moment forward. He let it pass. Listening, he was learning, was now the work.

After a time, someone else spoke. "I've noticed that too," they said. "It's like the noise inside me has quietened enough for something else to come through."

Again, no rush.

The conversation unfolded gently, shaped by attentiveness rather than urgency. No one tried to steer it. No one claimed authority. Insights surfaced, not as declarations, but as offerings. Caleb felt a quiet awe settle in him.

This was discernment.

Not dramatic revelation. Not certainty delivered whole. But a shared attentiveness to what was forming beneath the surface.

Later, as people stood to leave, Amelia caught Caleb's eye.

"That felt different," she said quietly.

"Yes," Caleb replied. "It did."

"I wasn't sure what to say," she continued. "So I didn't."

Caleb smiled. "That was wisdom."

She looked surprised. "Really?"

"Yes," he said. "Sometimes discernment sounds like restraint."

That evening, Caleb walked home alone, letting the cool air settle around him. He thought about how easily spiritual maturity could be mistaken for confidence. How often discernment was confused with decisiveness.

But what he had witnessed tonight was something else entirely.

Patience.

Humility.

A shared willingness to wait.

At home, Rachel noticed the quiet in him.

"You're thoughtful," she said.

"Yes," Caleb replied. "In a good way."

They sat together at the table, the house still.

"It feels like people are beginning to trust the process," he said. "Not just the outcome."

Rachel nodded. "That's a sign of depth."

"Yes," Caleb agreed. "And also vulnerability."

The next morning, Caleb received a message from a woman he did not know well.

I don't know how to explain this, it read. *But I feel like God has been giving me clarity about some things I've been avoiding. Not answers exactly. Just... direction.*

Caleb read it carefully.

He replied slowly.

That sounds like discernment. It often arrives quietly.

She responded a few minutes later.

That's reassuring. I was worried it wasn't real enough.

Caleb smiled.

Later that day, he met with Howard again. They sat outside, the familiar gum tree casting long shadows across the ground.

"I think we're entering a delicate season," Howard said.

Caleb nodded. "I agree."

Howard frowned slightly. "Not because anything's wrong. But because things are opening."

"Yes," Caleb said. "And open things require care."

Howard leaned back. "People are starting to speak with more confidence about what they sense God doing. That's good. But it could also get messy."

Caleb smiled faintly. "Discernment always does."

Howard raised an eyebrow. "You don't sound concerned."

"I'm attentive," Caleb replied. "Concerned would imply fear. I don't feel that."

Howard nodded slowly. "So what do we do?"

Caleb considered the question before responding.

"We keep modelling patience. We keep reminding people that wisdom grows best in community, not in isolation."

Howard smiled. "That sounds very… you."

Caleb laughed softly. "I suppose it is."

That afternoon, Caleb stopped briefly at the servo. Amelia was deep in conversation with Daniel. They both looked up as he approached.

"We were just talking," Daniel said, "about how different things feel lately."

Caleb nodded. "Different how?"

"Slower," Amelia said. "But not stalled."

"More intentional," Daniel added. "Like we're paying attention to the right things."

Caleb smiled. "That's discernment at work."

Amelia hesitated. "Can I ask something?"

"Of course."

"How do we make sure we don't overinterpret everything?" she asked. "I don't want to read meaning into things that aren't there."

Caleb considered her carefully. "That's a wise concern," he said. "Discernment isn't about finding meaning everywhere. It's about recognising what carries weight over time."

Daniel nodded. "So we don't rush conclusions."

"Exactly," Caleb replied. "We watch. We listen. We test what we sense against Scripture, against community, against character."

Amelia smiled, relieved. "That helps."

As Caleb walked away, he felt a quiet gratitude rise in him. These were not naïve questions. They were the questions of people taking their faith seriously.

That evening, Caleb returned once more to the sanctuary. He sat alone again, letting the stillness hold him.

He thought about the seasons of his ministry when discernment had meant making hard calls quickly. When clarity had been demanded on short notice. Those seasons had shaped him.

But this one was different.

Here, discernment was communal.

Shared.

Slow.

And perhaps that was exactly what Willowend needed.

As he stood to leave, Caleb paused midway down the aisle, looking around the familiar space. This church was no longer asking him to decide everything. It was learning how to listen together. And as he turned off the lights and stepped outside into the quiet evening, Caleb felt a steady assurance.

This was not confusion.

This was depth.

And depth, he knew, would carry them faithfully into whatever came next.

As the days unfolded, Caleb became increasingly aware that discernment was shaping not only conversations, but choices.

Small decisions were being approached with care. Not caution born of fear, but attentiveness born of responsibility.

People asked not, just *can we?* But, *should we?*

And more importantly, *Why?*

It surfaced during a discussion about expanding one of the midweek gatherings. Numbers had grown steadily, and space was becoming an issue.

"We could add another night," someone suggested.

Or move venues," another added.

Caleb listened as the ideas were offered. Each one was sensible. Each one had precedent. Yet the group did not rush toward any of them.

Mary spoke again, her voice calm. "Before we decide how, perhaps we should ask what this gathering is meant to be."

The room quietened.

Daniel nodded slowly. "It started as a place to listen."

"And to pray," Amelia added. "Not to teach."

"So if it grows," Mary continued, "we need to be careful we don't turn it into something louder just because it's larger."

Caleb felt a quiet gratitude. These were not the words of people afraid of change. They were the words of people attentive to essence.

"So what are we listening for?" someone asked.

"Peace," Mary replied. "Not excitement."

No one argued. They agreed to wait another week. Not as avoidance, but as faithfulness.

Later that afternoon, Caleb reflected on how often leadership meetings elsewhere were driven by urgency. By the pressure to act, to demonstrate progress, to respond visibly. Here, restraint was being valued. That was discernment at work.

At home that evening, Rachel listened as Caleb described the conversation. "It sounds like people are learning the difference between momentum and movement," she said.

"Yes," Caleb replied. "And that difference matters more than we usually realise."

Rachel smiled. "Especially in seasons of renewal."

The next morning, Caleb received a phone call that stayed with him. It was from a pastor he had met briefly through the retreat work. They spoke politely at first, then more openly.

"I'm struggling to know what to encourage in my church," the man admitted. "People are hungry. But I'm afraid of pushing them into experiences they're not ready to interpret."

Caleb listened carefully.

"What are you sensing?" Caleb asked.

The man hesitated. "That I need to slow us down. But everything in me wants to capitalise on the energy."

Caleb nodded, even though the man could not see him.

"Discernment often asks us to protect what's forming, not accelerate it."

There was a pause.

"That's helpful," the man said quietly. "I've been afraid that slowing down would look like failure."

"Not here," Caleb replied. "Here, it looks like trust."

After the call ended, Caleb sat still for a moment. He had not given advice. He had not offered solutions. He had simply named what he was seeing.

And it had been enough.

Later that week, Caleb met with Howard again. They walked the familiar path along the edge of town, the paddocks open beside them.

"I'm noticing something," Howard said. "People are starting to ask harder questions."

Caleb nodded. "That's usually a sign of depth."

"They are not questioning faith," Howard continued. "They are questioning their assumptions."

"Yes," Caleb said. "That's discernment sharpening."

Howard frowned slightly. "It can be uncomfortable."

"It should be," Caleb replied gently. "Comfortable faith rarely grows."

At the servo, Amelia experienced the same tension. A customer she had known for years lingered after paying, clearly unsettled. "I feel like God's been nudging me about something," the woman said. "But I don't know if it's conviction or imagination."

Amelia listened, resisting the urge to reassure too quickly.

"What does the nudge lead you toward?" she asked.

"Honesty," the woman replied after a pause. "With myself."

Amelia nodded. "That sounds like something worth paying attention to."

The woman exhaled. "That's what I thought. I just needed to hear it out loud."

When Amelia later mentioned the exchange to Caleb, he smiled.

"You didn't tell her what to think," he said.

"No," Amelia replied. "I just helped her listen."

"That's discernment in practice," Caleb said.

As the week drew on, Caleb noticed how the tone of sermons had shifted too. Not in content, but in emphasis. Less instruction. More invitation. Less certainty. More space for reflection.

On Sunday morning, Caleb spoke briefly again.

"Discernment," he said, "is not about hearing God more loudly than others. It's about learning to hear God together, with humility."

He paused.

"And humility requires time."

After the service, a young couple approached him.

"We're trying to decide something important," they said. "We thought maybe you'd tell us what to do."

Caleb smiled. "I could," he said. "But I think you already know what questions you need to ask."

They looked uncertain.

"What if we get it wrong?" the woman asked.

Caleb considered her carefully. "Then we learn. Discernment doesn't eliminate risk. It just teaches us how to walk faithfully through it."

They nodded slowly, thoughtful.

That afternoon, Caleb walked alone again, letting the quiet of the town steady him. He reflected on how discernment had once felt like a solitary burden in his ministry. A weight carried privately.

Now, it was being shared. Not diluted. Strengthened.

At home that evening, Caleb returned once more to his notebook.

Discernment grows best where humility is practiced together.

He closed it gently. This season was asking much of Willowend. Patience. Courage. Restraint. But it was also offering something rare. A faith that listened before it acted.

A community willing to wait for clarity rather than manufacture it. And as Caleb prepared for rest, he felt a deep sense of alignment.

This was not a church losing momentum.

This was a church learning how to hear God without haste.

And that, he knew, would shape everything that followed.

As the weeks passed, discernment began to show itself not only in what Willowend pursued, but in what it chose not to pursue.

Ideas still surfaced. Good ones. Well-meaning ones. Some carried genuine potential. Others arrived wrapped in urgency, as though they needed to be acted upon immediately or risk being lost. What changed was the community's response. There was less eagerness to seize and more willingness to hold.

Caleb noticed it during a conversation after a Sunday service. A man he had not spoken with often approached him, animated and hopeful.

"I've been thinking," he said, leaning forward slightly. "What if we organised a big regional gathering? Invite churches from all around. Speakers, music, the lot. People are hungry right now."

Caleb listened carefully, nodding. "They are."

"I just don't want us to miss the moment," the man continued. "It feels like something special is happening."

Caleb smiled gently. "It does."

"So… should we move quickly?" the man asked.

Caleb paused, not to delay, but to consider. "What do you think would happen if we waited?"

The man hesitated. "I don't know. Maybe nothing."

"Or maybe something would become clearer," Caleb replied. "Discernment doesn't ask us to ignore hunger. It asks us to notice what kind of nourishment is needed."

The man nodded slowly. "I hadn't thought of it that way."

"Keep paying attention," Caleb said. "If the idea carries weight, it will still be there."

Later that afternoon, Caleb reflected on how often momentum was mistaken for guidance. How easily enthusiasm could be baptised as direction.

Willowend was learning something quieter, and harder - how to remain attentive without becoming inert.

At the servo, Amelia experienced this tension in a different way. A group had begun meeting informally on Thursday mornings, as she had mentioned earlier. They gathered quietly, prayed briefly, and then talked about the week ahead. There was no plan to formalise it, no desire to grow it intentionally. And yet, others began asking to join.

"We could make this a thing," someone suggested one morning. "Advertise it. Get numbers."

Amelia listened, then said carefully, "What if we let it stay what it is for now?"

Someone frowned. "Why?"

"Because it's helping people breathe," Amelia replied. "And sometimes breathing gets harder when too many expectations are added."

The group considered that. No one argued.

Later, Amelia mentioned the exchange to Caleb.

"You're exercising discernment," he said.

"I didn't feel particularly spiritual," she replied. "I just didn't want to rush."

Caleb smiled. "That's often how it works."

That same week, Daniel found himself in unfamiliar territory. A conversation he had been having regularly with a couple took an unexpected turn. They shared something deeply personal, something unresolved, something painful.

"I didn't know what to do," Daniel admitted later, speaking with Caleb as they walked slowly through town. "I wanted to help, but I also felt out of my depth."

Caleb nodded. "And what did you do?"

"I asked if they were safe," Daniel said. "Then I asked if they'd thought about talking to someone qualified."

Caleb smiled. "That was wise."

"I was worried it might feel like pushing them away," Daniel said.

"Discernment sometimes knows when to refer," Caleb replied. "It's not abandonment. It's care."

Daniel exhaled. "That's a relief."

As the season deepened, Caleb noticed how often discernment expressed itself as restraint. People were learning when to speak, and when not to. When to act, and when to wait. When to offer insight, and when to simply remain present.

This did not make life simpler.

In fact, it made it more demanding.

Waiting required patience. Listening required humility. Not acting required trust.

One evening, Caleb sat again in the sanctuary, alone but not isolated. He thought about how discernment had once felt like something he carried privately - a responsibility he bore quietly, often without affirmation.

Now, it was shared. Discussed. Tested in community.

He thought of Mary, whose words often landed without fanfare but carried lasting weight. Of Howard, whose steady questions kept the church grounded. Of Amelia and Daniel, learning to trust what they sensed without assuming authority.

This was not chaos. This was formation.

The following Sunday, Caleb spoke briefly once more.

"Discernment," he said, "is not the ability to predict outcomes. It is the willingness to walk faithfully without them."

He paused.

"And that kind of faith grows slowly, but it endures."

After the service, a woman approached him quietly. "I used to think hearing God meant clarity," she said. "Now I think it might mean courage."

Caleb smiled. "Courage to stay present, even when the way forward isn't obvious."

She nodded. "Yes. That."

That evening, Caleb and Rachel sat together, the house calm around them.

"Does it feel fragile to you?" Rachel asked.

"Sometimes," Caleb replied. "But not unstable."

Rachel smiled. "There's a difference."

"Yes," he agreed. "Fragile things require care. Unstable things require control. This feels like the first."

Rachel nodded. "Then it's worth protecting."

Later that night, Caleb returned once more to his notebook.

Discernment is not about certainty.
It is about faithfulness over time.

He closed it gently.

The church in Willowend was not rushing toward a future it could define. It was learning how to walk attentively into one it trusted God to reveal.

And as Caleb prepared for rest, he felt a deep peace settle in him. This season was not asking for bold declarations.

It was asking for steady listening.

And that, he knew, would shape them more deeply than any moment of urgency ever could.

34. WHEN WEIGHT IS FELT

Caleb realised something was changing when responsibility began to feel heavier again. Not heavier in the old way - not the weight of doing everything himself - but the weight of *holding space* for what others were now carrying.

Shared trust had redistributed leadership, but it had also widened awareness. More voices meant more stories. More insight meant more exposure to quiet burdens that had long gone unnoticed.

He felt it one Tuesday afternoon when Daniel sat across from him in the office, unusually quiet.

"I think I need to tell you something," Daniel said at last.
Caleb nodded, attentive but unhurried.

"I don't regret stepping into things," Daniel continued. "I'm grateful. But I didn't expect how much people would bring with them."

Caleb leaned back slightly. "What do you mean?"

"Once people sense they can speak honestly, they don't just share questions," Daniel said. "They share pain. Some of it feels... old."

Caleb nodded slowly. "That's often how it begins."

Daniel rubbed his hands together. "I'm not overwhelmed. Not exactly. But I'm realising that maturity carries its own weight."

"Yes," Caleb said gently. "And discernment doesn't remove that weight. It teaches us how to bear it together."

Daniel exhaled. "That helps."

Later that day, Caleb walked through town, noticing how many conversations now paused when he approached - not out of secrecy, but awareness. People no longer felt the need to funnel everything through him, yet they still seemed to recognise his role as one who could *hold* what emerged.

At the servo, Amelia waved him over.

"Can I run something past you?" she asked.

"Of course."

"I've been having more conversations lately," she said. "Not just about faith. About grief. Regret. Things people haven't said out loud before."

Caleb listened.

"I'm not worried," she added quickly. "But I'm starting to feel how much is underneath the surface of this town."

Caleb nodded. "That's a sign of trust."

"It also feels… sobering," Amelia said.

"Yes," Caleb replied. "Renewal often is."

She frowned slightly. "I thought it would feel lighter."

"It can," Caleb said. "But first, it often brings weight into the light."

Amelia absorbed that quietly.

As Caleb walked on, he reflected on how easily renewal could be romanticised. People spoke of freshness, movement, life. Rarely did they speak of exposure. Of the way spiritual attentiveness brought hidden things into clearer view, not dramatically, but persistently.

At home that evening, Rachel noticed his quiet.

"You're carrying more today," she said.

"Yes," Caleb replied. "Not because I'm doing more. Because I'm seeing more."

Rachel nodded. "That's a familiar season."

"Yes," he said. "But it feels different this time."

"How so?"

"I'm not meant to resolve it," Caleb said. "Only to help hold it."

Rachel smiled gently. "That's a harder task."

"Yes," Caleb agreed. "But a truer one."

The following Sunday, the service unfolded calmly. Nothing remarkable happened. No moments that would later be retold. And yet, Caleb sensed a collective attentiveness beneath the surface. People listened closely. Prayers were offered with care. Silence was allowed to remain.

Afterward, an older man approached Caleb quietly.

"I've been carrying something for years," he said. "I don't know why, but this week I felt like it might finally be time to say it out loud."

Caleb nodded. "You don't have to rush."

"I know," the man replied. "That's what makes it possible."

They stood together for a moment, not speaking.

Later, Caleb met briefly with Howard. They sat on a bench near the edge of town, watching the light shift across the paddocks.

"I'm sensing some fatigue," Howard said.

"In whom?" Caleb asked.

"In the church," Howard replied. "Not burnout as such. Just the tiredness that comes from honesty."

Caleb nodded. "That's real."

Howard frowned slightly. "Is it dangerous?"

"It can be," Caleb said. "If we mistake weight for failure."

Howard considered that. "So what do we do?"

"We remind people that maturity isn't effortless," Caleb replied. "And that shared burdens don't need to be carried quickly."

Howard smiled faintly. "You're good at reframing things."

Caleb shook his head. "I'm just learning again."

That evening, Caleb sat alone in the sanctuary once more. The building felt familiar, but not comforting in the way it once had. It felt attentive. Like a place that now *listened back*.

He thought about how trust, once shared, required continual care. How discernment, once deepened, revealed layers that could not be unseen. How growth, once begun, carried responsibility as well as joy.

He did not feel discouraged.

But he did feel sober.

And that, he knew, was appropriate.

As he turned off the lights and stepped outside, the air was still. The town lay quiet around him, unchanged on the surface. Yet beneath that stillness, something was being asked of them all.

Not urgency.

Not performance.

But endurance.

Caleb breathed deeply.

Renewal was not a season to be celebrated and passed through. It was a way of walking. And Willowend was learning what that truly meant.

As the week unfolded, Caleb became increasingly aware that weight, when carried well, altered the pace of everything. People moved more slowly now - not from reluctance, but from care. Conversations that once would have been hurried were allowed to linger. Questions were asked with less urgency and more sincerity. There was a sense that some things could not, and should not, be rushed through.

Caleb noticed it during a meeting that had not been scheduled, but simply happened. A handful of people gathered one afternoon in the church hall, drawn there by no particular invitation. Someone made tea. Someone else opened a window.

Chairs were pulled into a loose circle, then rearranged again when it felt too tight.

Caleb arrived quietly and took a seat without comment.

No one asked him to begin.

After a moment, Mary spoke, her voice low and steady. "I think we're learning how to sit with things we once tried to tidy away."

The words settled gently into the space.

Daniel nodded. "I've been thinking that too. People are telling the truth more often now. And truth is rarely neat."

Amelia leaned forward slightly. "It's strange," she said. "I used to think honesty would feel relieving straight away. But sometimes it feels heavier before it feels lighter."

Caleb watched the way the group held the tension. No one tried to resolve it. No one softened the words to make them easier to hear.

"That doesn't mean something's wrong," Mary said. "It means something's being trusted."

Caleb felt a quiet affirmation rise in him. This was not collapse. This was formation.

Later that day, Caleb met with a man who had rarely spoken much in the church. They sat together in the small office, sunlight falling across the desk.

"I don't need answers," the man said quickly. "I just need somewhere to put this."

Caleb nodded. "You're in the right place."

The man spoke slowly, carefully, as though testing each word before releasing it. There were long pauses. Caleb did not interrupt them. He had learned that silence often did more work than reassurance.

When the man finished, he sat back, visibly drained.

"I'm not sure what happens next," he said.

"That's all right," Caleb replied. "You don't have to know yet."

The man looked relieved. "Thank you for not trying to fix it."

Caleb smiled gently. "That wasn't my role today."

That evening, as Caleb walked home, he reflected on how often he had once felt responsible for moving people forward. For helping them progress, resolve, heal. Now, his role felt different. He was helping people *stay*.

Stay present. Stay honest. Stay open.

At home, Rachel listened as he spoke about the day.

"It sounds tiring," she said.

"It is," Caleb admitted. "But not in the way exhaustion used to feel."

"How so?"

"It's a weight that feels worth carrying," he said. "Because it isn't mine alone."

Rachel nodded. "Shared weight settles differently."

"Yes," Caleb replied. "It does."

The following morning, Caleb received a call from a pastor he had met through the retreats.

"I don't know how to name this," the man said. "But things feel heavier lately. People are opening up. And I feel unprepared." Caleb listened.

"Is that normal?" the pastor asked.

"Yes," Caleb replied without hesitation. "It's one of the signs that trust is growing."

The man was quiet for a moment. "That doesn't make it easier."

"No," Caleb said. "But it helps us understand it."

As the call ended, Caleb realised how often pastors were taught to expect growth to feel energising, exciting, affirming. Rarely were they prepared for the sobering responsibility that came when people entrusted their deeper stories.

Later that week, Howard stopped by again. "I've been thinking," Howard said, leaning against the fence near the church. "We might need to remind people that rest is still important."

Caleb nodded. "Yes."

"There's a risk," Howard continued, "that people feel obligated to carry more than they're ready for."

"That's true," Caleb agreed. "Weight shared well still requires boundaries."

Howard smiled faintly. "You're saying that more often lately."

Caleb chuckled. "Because I'm learning it more deeply."

On Sunday morning, Caleb spoke briefly again, choosing his words carefully.

"There are seasons," he said, "when faith feels light and joyful. And there are seasons when faith feels weighty and sober. Both are holy."

He paused.

"We don't rush either."

After the service, a woman approached him with tears in her eyes. "I thought something was wrong with me," she said quietly. "Everything felt heavier after I started praying again."

Caleb met her gaze gently. "Sometimes prayer brings weight to the surface before it brings release."

She nodded slowly. "That makes sense."

That afternoon, Caleb walked alone again, letting the stillness of the town steady him. Willowend looked unchanged. The same shops. The same streets. The same unhurried rhythm.

But beneath the surface, something was being carried more honestly now.

That evening, Caleb returned once more to his notebook.

Weight is not the enemy of renewal.
Avoidance is.

He closed the book and sat quietly for a long moment.

This season would require patience. It would require rest. It would require leaders who knew when to step forward and when to step back. It would require a community willing to carry one another without rushing toward resolution.

As night settled over Willowend, Caleb felt neither anxious nor triumphant.

He felt grounded.

Renewal was no longer something to be observed from a distance.

It was something to be carried carefully, together, for the long road ahead.

And that, he knew, was sacred work.

As the weight settled more deeply into the life of the church, Caleb began to notice a subtle shift in himself as well. He was sleeping differently. Not less, but more lightly. He woke earlier than usual, his mind not racing, but attentive. Thoughts arrived gently rather than insistently, as though something within him had learned a new posture - alert without anxiety.

One morning, he rose before dawn and stepped outside. The town lay quiet, the sky still holding the deep blue of night. A faint breeze moved through the trees, carrying the familiar scent of eucalyptus and dust. Nothing felt urgent. Nothing demanded his attention.

And yet, he felt awake in a way that surprised him. He realised then that weight, when carried honestly, did not crush. It clarified.

Later that morning, Caleb met briefly with Daniel again. They sat on the low stone wall behind the church, mugs of coffee cooling between them.

"I've been thinking about something," Daniel said.

Caleb nodded, waiting.

"I'm realising that when people trust you with something heavy, it doesn't mean they expect you to carry it for them," Daniel continued. "Sometimes they just need someone to hold it with them for a while."

Caleb smiled. "That's an important distinction."

Daniel exhaled. "I wish I'd understood that sooner."

"We all do," Caleb replied. "But it tends to arrive only through experience."

Daniel looked thoughtful. "It makes me more careful about what I say."

"Yes," Caleb agreed. "And more patient with what remains unresolved."

That afternoon, Caleb found himself at the Webster's place again. They sat together on the veranda, watching the slow movement of clouds across the sky. Conversation came easily, then paused, then resumed.

At one point, Mrs Webster said quietly, "I used to think faith meant having things sorted out."

Caleb nodded.

"Now I think it might mean being willing to sit with things unsorted," she continued.

Caleb smiled. "That sounds right to me."

She looked relieved. "Good. Because that's where I am."

As he drove home, Caleb reflected on how often people apologised for uncertainty, as though doubt or unresolved pain were failures rather than invitations to deeper trust. Willowend was learning something gentler now - that honesty could coexist with faith, and that weight did not disqualify anyone from belonging.

That evening, Rachel noticed the change in him.

"You're quieter lately," she said as they sat together after dinner.

"Yes," Caleb replied. "But not withdrawn."

She nodded. "I can see that."

"I think I'm learning to listen differently," he said. "Not just to people. To myself."

Rachel smiled softly. "That's usually a sign that something's settling."

"Yes," he agreed. "Even when it feels heavy."

The following Sunday, Caleb chose not to speak at all. Others led the prayers. Others read Scripture. The service unfolded without interruption or awkwardness. Caleb sat among them, attentive, present, unneeded in the best possible way. As the final hymn ended, people remained seated longer than usual. No one rushed to leave. No one seemed unsure of what to do next.

Eventually, conversations began again. Quiet ones. Gentle ones. Caleb noticed Amelia standing with a woman near the back, listening closely. Daniel was seated with an older man, heads bowed slightly as they spoke. Mary sat alone, hands folded, eyes closed, as though holding the space in prayer.

Caleb felt something settle in him then.

This was what shared weight looked like.

After the service, Howard came to stand beside him.

"You all right?" Howard asked.

"Yes," Caleb replied. "Just noticing."

Howard nodded. "It's a lot, isn't it?"

"Yes," Caleb said. "But it's right."

Howard was quiet for a moment. "You know, years ago, I would have been nervous about this kind of season."

Caleb smiled faintly. "Me too."

Howard glanced around the room. "Now it feels like something we can trust."

"Yes," Caleb said. "Because it's not resting on any one of us."

That afternoon, Caleb walked home alone again, the town quiet around him. He passed familiar places - the bakery, the servo, the post office - each carrying layers of story now deeper than before.

At home, he opened his notebook once more.

Weight reveals what matters most.
And what matters most is rarely light.

He closed the book and set it aside. This season would continue to ask much of Willowend. It would require care, patience, and humility. There would be moments when people stumbled under the weight, when rest was needed, when clarity took longer than expected. But there was no sense of retreat. Only endurance.

As evening settled and the lights came on across the town, Caleb felt a steady peace take hold. Renewal was no longer something they were discovering. It was something they were learning to live with. Carefully. Faithfully. Together.

And that, he knew, would carry them further than any season of ease ever could.

Caleb had learned, over the years, to recognise the difference between resistance and inquiry. Resistance closed in on itself. It hardened quickly, drew lines, demanded certainty. Inquiry, by contrast, stayed open. It asked without accusation. It lingered longer than was comfortable. And it often arrived not as a challenge, but as a quiet unease that refused to be ignored.
He sensed that unease beginning to surface now.

It appeared first in conversations that ended with unfinished sentences. In people who hesitated before speaking, then continued anyway. In questions framed carefully, almost apologetically, as though the act of asking itself might be dangerous.

Caleb noticed it one morning when a woman approached him after the service.

"I hope this doesn't sound wrong," she said.

He smiled gently. "Go on."

"I'm grateful for what's happening here," she continued. "I really am. But sometimes I don't know what to do with the things I'm feeling. It's like… faith is closer now, but also less tidy."

Caleb nodded slowly. "That's a good observation."

She looked relieved. "So it's not just me?"

"No," Caleb said. "It rarely is."

Later that week, the questions began to find voice more openly. A small group gathered one evening, not formally, not with an agenda, but with a shared sense that something needed to be said aloud. Chairs were pulled into a loose circle. Tea was poured and left to cool. No one rushed to begin.

Daniel spoke first, his voice thoughtful rather than confident. "I'm noticing that people are asking deeper questions lately," he said. "Not about doctrine exactly. More about how faith actually works in real life."

Amelia nodded in affirmation. "I've heard that too. Questions about disappointment. About unanswered prayer. Also about whether spiritual growth always feels this… unsettled."

Mary folded her hands gently. "Those are honest questions."

"Yes," Daniel said. "But they can sound dangerous if we don't handle them well."

Caleb listened, letting the weight of the moment settle. "They're only dangerous," he said finally, "if we pretend we don't have room for them."

The group was quiet for a moment.

"I don't want us to lose our grounding," someone said.

"We won't," Caleb replied. "But grounding isn't the same as certainty. Sometimes it's the willingness to stay rooted while the questions do their work."

Amelia exhaled. "That makes sense. I just worry about where it leads."

Caleb smiled faintly. "Questions usually lead somewhere. But not always quickly. And not always where we expect."

That evening, as Caleb walked home, he reflected on how often churches feared the questions, mistaking them for doubt or rebellion. Yet what he was seeing now felt different.

These questions were not pulling people away.

They were drawing them deeper.

At home, Rachel listened as he spoke about the gathering.

"It sounds like trust is widening," she said.

"Yes," Caleb replied. "But trust brings questions with it."

Rachel nodded. "That's always been true in our own faith."

"Yes," he said. "I just forget sometimes that communities grow the same way individuals do."

The following Sunday, Caleb decided not to avoid the tension.

"Faith," he said gently, "does not grow by pretending we have no questions. It grows by learning how to carry them honestly." He paused.

"There is a kind of certainty that resists growth. And there is a kind of questioning that deepens it."

He did not elaborate further.

After the service, reactions were mixed. Some people nodded thoughtfully. Others looked unsettled. No one argued.

That afternoon, Caleb received an unexpected phone call.

It was Ruth.

"I hope this isn't a bad time," she said.

"No," Caleb replied warmly. "It's good to hear your voice."

"I've been thinking about something," she continued. "About the way you talk about church lately. It sounds… different."

"How so?"

"Less about answers," Ruth said. "More about listening."

Caleb smiled. "That's probably accurate."

There was a pause.

"I like that," she said quietly. "Even if I'm not sure what I think about everything yet."

Caleb felt a warmth rise in him. "You don't need to be sure."

"I know," Ruth replied. "That's what makes it feel safer."

After the call ended, Caleb sat for a moment, letting the words settle. He thought about how many people longed for permission to question without being pushed to conclusions.

Perhaps that, too, was part of renewal.

Later in the week, Howard stopped by briefly. "I've noticed something," he said.

Caleb nodded. "So have I."

Howard smiled. "People are asking questions they used to keep to themselves."

"Yes," Caleb replied. "And they're still showing up."

Howard leaned back against the fence. "That feels important."

"It is," Caleb said. "It tells me they trust the space enough to be honest."

Howard frowned slightly. "Do you think it will unsettle some people?"

"Yes," Caleb said. "Almost certainly."

Howard waited.

"But I also think avoiding those questions would do more harm in the long run," Caleb added.

Howard nodded slowly. "Then we keep listening."

"Yes," Caleb replied. "That's the work right now."

That evening, Caleb returned once more to his notebook.

Questions are not the enemy of faith. Silence is.

He closed it slowly and thoughtfully … letting that truth sinker deeper into his spirit.

Willowend was not becoming a place without conviction. It was becoming a place where conviction could breathe.

Where doubt was not shamed.

Where uncertainty was not rushed.

Where faith was allowed to stretch without tearing.

And as Caleb prepared for rest, he felt a quiet assurance settle in him. Allowing questions did not weaken the church.

It strengthened its honesty. And honesty, he knew, was a foundation strong enough to carry whatever came next. As the questions began to surface more openly, Caleb became aware that not everyone experienced them in the same way.

For some, questions felt like relief - a release of pressure that had been quietly building for years. For others, they felt unsettling, even threatening, as though something familiar was being loosened without a clear sense of what would replace it. Caleb saw both responses in the weeks that followed.

One afternoon, a long-time member stopped him outside the church. "I'm struggling," the man said, not unkindly. "I've always believed faith was about standing firm. Lately it feels like everything's becoming… negotiable."

Caleb listened carefully. "What feels negotiable to you?"

The man hesitated. "Certainty. Answers. Clear lines."

Caleb nodded. "Those things can feel like anchors."

"Yes," the man said. "And anchors matter."

"They do," Caleb agreed. "But sometimes anchors are meant to hold us steady, not keep us from moving at all."

The man frowned slightly. "I don't want us drifting."

"Neither do I," Caleb said. "But asking questions doesn't mean we've lost direction. It often means we care enough to examine where we're going."

The man considered this quietly. "I hope you're right."

"So do I," Caleb replied honestly.

Later that week, Caleb sat with a younger woman who had only recently begun attending regularly. Her questions came quickly, almost tumbling over one another.

"I didn't know faith could include this much uncertainty," she said. "No one ever told me that."

Caleb smiled gently. "It doesn't always start that way. But it often grows into it."

She laughed softly. "That's oddly comforting."

"What are you most uncertain about?" Caleb asked.

She paused. "Whether God is as patient with me as people here seem to be."

Caleb met her gaze. "God's patience usually exceeds ours."

She nodded, her shoulders relaxing. "That helps."

As these conversations accumulated, Caleb became more aware of the quiet work required to hold space for them. Allowing questions did not mean encouraging endless doubt. It meant cultivating an environment where honesty could surface without fear.

And that required restraint.

During one gathering, a man spoke forcefully, eager to answer a question that had been posed tentatively. His words were confident, polished, and well-meaning.

But the room grew tense. Caleb intervened gently.

"Let's pause for a moment," he said. "Not to dismiss what's been said, but to make room for others."

The man looked surprised, then thoughtful. "I didn't mean to shut anything down."

"I know," Caleb replied. "But sometimes answers arrive too quickly to do their best work."

The room softened.

Later, Mary leaned toward Caleb and whispered, "You are now guarding the questions."

Caleb smiled faintly. "They're fragile."

"Yes," Mary agreed. "And precious."

That evening, Caleb reflected on how easily churches slipped into patterns where the most articulate voices dominated. Questions were often answered before they were fully formed. Curiosity was resolved prematurely.

Willowend was learning something different.

Not every question needed an answer.

Some needed time.

At home, Rachel noticed his weariness.

"It's a different kind of tired," she said.

"Yes," Caleb replied. "Holding space takes more energy than giving answers."

Rachel smiled. "But it also builds something deeper."

"Yes," he said. "Trust."

The following Sunday, Caleb chose his words carefully again. "There are questions that seek answers," he said. "And there are questions that seek permission."

He paused.

"Permission to wonder. Permission to wrestle. Permission to remain present even when clarity feels distant."

He did not say more.

After the service, Daniel approached him.

"I think I understand something now," Daniel said. "People aren't asking because they want us to tell them what to believe." Caleb nodded. "They want to know they're not alone while they're figuring it out."

"Yes," Daniel said. "That."

As the week went on, Caleb noticed that questions began to shape prayer as well. Prayers grew less declarative and more attentive. People named uncertainty without apology. Silence was allowed to stretch longer before words emerged.

One evening, during a small gathering, someone prayed simply, "God, help us stay honest."

Nothing more was added.

And it felt complete.

Caleb sensed that allowing questions was not weakening faith. It was stripping it of performance. It was making room for something quieter and sturdier to take root.

Later that night, Caleb returned to his notebook again.

Questions do not erode faith when they are
held in trust, they refine it.

He closed the book and sat quietly.

This season would require courage. Not the courage to defend answers, but the courage to remain present when answers were slow to arrive.

It would require leaders willing to resist the urge to tidy what was still forming.

As Caleb prepared for rest, he felt both the weight and the privilege of that task. Allowing questions was not an abdication of leadership. It was one of its most faithful expressions.

And Willowend, he sensed, was growing strong enough to carry it.

As the questions continued to surface, Caleb became aware of another quiet shift taking place beneath them.

People were no longer asking simply, *What do we believe?* They were asking, *How do we live with what we believe?*

The difference mattered.

It showed itself in practical ways. In conversations about forgiveness that lingered uncomfortably long. In decisions postponed because someone sensed that acting quickly might cost more than waiting. In moments when people chose restraint over certainty, humility over explanation.

Caleb noticed it one afternoon when a woman approached him hesitantly near the back of the church.

"I think I've been asking the wrong question," she said.

Caleb waited.

"I keep asking whether something is right or wrong," she continued. "But lately it feels like the better question is whether I'm willing to stay faithful when it's unresolved."

Caleb nodded slowly. "That's a deeper question."

She sighed. "It's also harder."

"Yes," he said gently. "But it's often the one that shapes us most." That evening, a small group gathered again without planning. The pattern had become familiar now - chairs drawn together, tea poured, silence allowed.

Someone spoke about disappointment. Another spoke about confusion. No one tried to connect the stories into something coherent.

They did not need to.

At one point, Daniel spoke quietly. "I used to think faith was about moving forward. Now I think it's also about not running away."

Amelia nodded. "From God. From ourselves. From each other." Mary smiled softly. "From the work that questions are doing in us."

The room held the moment without comment.

Caleb felt a quiet gratitude rise in him.

These were not rehearsed insights. They were the fruit of attentiveness, formed slowly in the soil of shared trust.

Later that night, Caleb and Rachel sat together, the house quiet around them.

"Do you ever worry," Rachel asked gently, "that allowing so much questioning might unsettle people who need certainty?"

"Yes," Caleb replied honestly. "I do."

She waited.

"But I worry more about what happens when people feel they must silence their questions to belong," he continued. "That kind of certainty doesn't last."

Rachel nodded. "It becomes brittle."

"Yes," Caleb said. "And brittle things tend to break under pressure."

The following week, Caleb received a message from someone who had not been present for months.

I've been watching from a distance. I heard things were changing. Not dramatically. Just honestly. That made me feel like I might be able to come back.

Caleb read it twice.

He replied simply.

You're welcome whenever you're ready.

At the servo, Amelia noticed a similar pattern.

People lingered longer. Conversations deepened unexpectedly. Someone admitted they had stopped praying years ago and were unsure how to begin again. Amelia did not rush to reassure. She listened.

"I don't think God's offended by where you are," she said quietly. "I think He's just glad you're speaking honestly."

The woman nodded, eyes bright. "That's what I hoped."

As these stories accumulated, Caleb became increasingly aware of how fragile this season was. Questions could deepen faith, but they could also fracture it if handled carelessly. Cynicism lurked nearby. So did fear.

Leadership, he realised, now required a particular kind of vigilance. Not the vigilance that guarded doctrine aggressively, but the vigilance that guarded posture.

Curiosity needed humility. Inquiry needed patience. Freedom needed responsibility.

During one Sunday gathering, a man spoke openly, expressing frustration with parts of his faith journey. His words were raw, unfiltered.

The room tensed.

Caleb watched closely.

Before he could respond, another voice spoke gently. "Thank you for trusting us with that."

The tension eased.

Caleb did not need to intervene.

Later, Howard approached him quietly.

"That could have gone badly," Howard said.

"Yes," Caleb replied. "But it didn't."

Howard nodded. "Because the room knew how to hold it."

"Yes," Caleb said. "That's new."

That afternoon, Caleb walked alone again, letting the rhythm of the town steady him. Willowend looked as it always had. Unremarkable. Familiar. Quiet.

Yet beneath the surface, something resilient was forming.

A faith that could tolerate ambiguity without dissolving.

A community that could host questions without rushing to answers. A church learning that maturity did not mean having fewer questions, but carrying them with integrity.

That evening, Caleb returned once more to his notebook.

*Questions do not threaten faith when they are
met with patience - they become pathways.*

He closed the book and set it aside.

The season ahead would not be easy. There would be moments of discomfort. Times when clarity would feel distant. Instances when old habits would tempt them to retreat into certainty.

But Willowend had begun to learn something rare.

That faith, at its strongest, was not brittle.

It was supple.

Able to bend without breaking.

Able to hold questions without fear.

Able to trust that God was present not only in answers, but in the honest asking itself.

And as Caleb prepared to sleep, he felt a deep, quiet assurance.

Allowing questions had not loosened the foundations of the church.

It had revealed how deep they truly were.

And that depth, he knew, would carry them faithfully into whatever lay ahead.

36. WHEN WISDOM IS SHARED

Caleb had always associated wisdom with distance.

Not detachment, exactly, but perspective - the ability to step back far enough to see what others could not yet see.

For most of his ministry, that perspective had been expected of him. People came looking for it. They assumed he carried it by virtue of role and experience.

What he was discovering now unsettled that assumption.

Wisdom, in this season, was not arriving from the centre outward. It was emerging among them. He noticed it during a conversation that unfolded slowly one afternoon near the church entrance.

A small group had gathered, not intentionally, just drawn together by timing and presence. Someone mentioned a decision they were wrestling with. Another offered a reflection rather than advice. A third added a Scripture quietly, without explanation.

No one dominated the space.

Caleb stood nearby, listening.

What struck him was not the content of what was said, but the restraint with which it was offered. People spoke tentatively, as though aware that wisdom was something to be handled carefully, not asserted.

After a while, the conversation paused.

"Well," someone said softly, "that gives me enough to sit with."

And the group dispersed.

No conclusions. No directives. No sense of unfinished business.

Caleb felt something shift in him.

This was wisdom.

Not certainty delivered whole, but insight offered with humility and received with care.

Later that day, Daniel came by, his expression thoughtful. "I had a moment today," he said.

Caleb gestured for him to sit. "Tell me."

"I was talking with someone who asked what they should do," Daniel continued. "And for once, I didn't feel the pressure to answer."

Caleb smiled. "What did you do instead?"

"I asked what they were noticing," Daniel said. "What felt heavy. What felt light."

"And?"

"They figured it out for themselves," Daniel replied, a note of surprise in his voice. "Or at least, they found the next step."

Caleb nodded. "That's often how wisdom works. It surfaces when space is made for it."

Daniel leaned back. "I used to think wisdom meant knowing more."

"And now?"

"Now I think it means listening longer," Daniel said.

Caleb felt a quiet affirmation rise in him.

At the servo, Amelia experienced something similar. A regular customer mentioned a conflict that had been weighing on them. Amelia listened, asked one or two gentle questions, then fell silent. The customer spoke again, slower this time, as though hearing their own words more clearly.

"I think I know what I need to do," they said at last.

Amelia smiled. "Then you're already on your way."

When Amelia later mentioned the conversation to Caleb, she looked uncertain.

"I didn't say much," she said. "It felt almost… too simple."

Caleb shook his head gently. "Simple doesn't mean shallow."

She considered that. "It felt like something settled."

"That's wisdom," Caleb said. "It often feels like that."

As these moments all accumulated, Caleb became increasingly aware that his role was changing again. Not disappearing, not diminishing, but refining.

He was no longer expected to be the primary source of insight.

He was being asked to *recognise* it when it appeared.

That required attentiveness of a different kind.

One evening, Caleb and Rachel sat together, the house quiet around them.

"I'm noticing something," Rachel said.

Caleb looked at her. "So am I."

She smiled. "People are growing into wisdom without being told they are."

"Yes," Caleb replied. "And that's important."

Rachel nodded. "It protects them from pride."

"And from dependence," Caleb added.

The following Sunday, Caleb chose to speak about wisdom briefly.

"Wisdom," he said, "is not the ability to make decisions quickly. It is the ability to remain faithful when decisions take time."

He paused.

"And wisdom grows best when it is shared."

After the service, a woman approached him.

"I've always thought wisdom belonged to people with more experience than me," she said.

"Experience helps. But wisdom often grows wherever humility is practiced," Caleb said.

She nodded slowly. "That gives me courage."

Later that afternoon, Caleb met with Howard. They walked along the edge of town, the familiar paddocks stretching out beside them.

"I'm seeing something new," Howard said.

"So am I," Caleb replied.

Howard smiled. "I think people are beginning to trust their own discernment."

"Yes," Caleb said. "And to test it gently in community."

Howard frowned slightly. "Is that risky?"

"It can be," Caleb replied. "If humility is lost."

Howard nodded. "And if it's not?"

"Then wisdom multiplies," Caleb said.

That evening, Caleb returned once more to the sanctuary. He sat quietly, listening to the familiar sounds of the building settling around him. He thought about how often wisdom had been treated as a commodity - something to be acquired, displayed, defended.

Here, it was being treated differently. It was being shared.

Not diluted, but strengthened.

Not broadcast, but offered.

Not enforced, but recognised.

Caleb felt a quiet gratitude rise in him. This kind of wisdom would not draw attention. It would not impress outsiders. But it would sustain them.

As he stood to leave, he paused midway down the aisle, a familiar place of reflection. For years, people had come to him seeking wisdom. Now, he was learning to see it rise among them.

And that, he realised, was not a loss of calling.

It was its fulfilment.

As Caleb turned off the lights and stepped outside, the evening air was cool and still. Willowend lay quiet around him, unchanged on the surface, yet deeper than before.

Wisdom was no longer something carried by one.

It was something held together.

And he was confident that would carry them faithfully through whatever lay ahead.

As wisdom continued to surface quietly among the people of Willowend, Caleb became increasingly aware of how easily it could be misunderstood.

There were those who assumed wisdom would announce itself clearly - with confidence, clarity, and decisive direction. Others expected it to feel reassuring, even comforting. But what he was witnessing now rarely felt like either.

Wisdom, in this season, often felt tentative.

It spoke very softly. It waited to be invited. It left some room for disagreement without insisting on resolution.

Caleb noticed it during a meeting that began with a sense of unease. Several people had gathered to talk through a difficult situation involving someone on the fringe of the church community.

Opinions differed. Emotions were present but restrained.

"I don't think we should step in," one person said carefully. "Not yet."

Another shifted in their seat. "But if we wait too long, they might feel abandoned."

The room grew quiet.

Caleb watched closely, resisting the instinct to intervene. This was not confusion. It was discernment stretching toward wisdom.

Mary spoke at last. "Perhaps the question isn't whether we act or wait," she said. "Perhaps it's whether we're willing to stay attentive either way."

The words did not resolve the tension. They reframed it.

Daniel nodded slowly. "That changes how I'm thinking about it."

Others murmured agreement, not just because the answer had become clear, but because the posture had.

Caleb felt a familiar stirring. This was wisdom taking shape - not by eliminating complexity, but by teaching them how to hold it faithfully.

Later that afternoon, Caleb walked through town, reflecting on how often leadership was measured by decisiveness. Yet here, decisiveness was being tempered by humility. People were learning that not every situation required immediate action, and that restraint could be as faithful as intervention.

At the servo, Amelia waved him over briefly.

"I had an odd moment today," she said.

"Tell me," Caleb replied.

"Someone asked what they should do about a family situation," Amelia said. "I listened, asked a few questions, and then said nothing."

Caleb smiled. "And how did that feel?"

"Uncomfortable," she admitted. "But also right."

"What happened next?" Caleb asked.

"They talked themselves into clarity," Amelia said. "Not a solution, exactly. But a next step."

Caleb nodded. "Wisdom often reveals itself that way. Not as a map, but as a direction."

Amelia frowned slightly. "Do you think it is always supposed to feel that uncertain?"

Caleb considered the question. "Quite often, yes," he said. "Because certainty can sometimes short-circuit reflection."

She smiled faintly. "That explains a lot."

As the days went on, Caleb became more aware of the internal work this season required of him. Recognising wisdom in others meant releasing the subtle need to be the one who named it first.

It meant resisting the urge to clarify prematurely.

It meant trusting that the Spirit was at work beyond his direct involvement.

That trust was not effortless.

One evening, Caleb sat alone in the sanctuary again, the familiar stillness settling around him. He thought about the years he had spent honing his ability to respond quickly, to offer insight when others hesitated. That skill had served him well. But it was no longer the primary need.

Now, the work was slower.

He was learning to watch.

To listen for what was emerging rather than impose what he already knew. That shift required humility.

The following Sunday, Caleb noticed how wisdom shaped the service in small but significant ways. A Scripture reading was followed by a longer silence than usual.

No one rushed to fill it. When someone prayed, their words were simple, unembellished. There was no sense of performance.

After the service, an older woman approached Caleb quietly.

"I used to think wisdom meant having peace about everything," she said. "Now I think it might mean being willing to live without it sometimes."

Caleb smiled. "That's a wise insight."

She laughed softly. "It doesn't feel impressive."

"Wisdom rarely does," Caleb replied. "But it endures."

Later that week, Caleb met with Howard again. They sat beneath the familiar gum tree, the afternoon light soft around them.

"I've been thinking about leadership," Howard said.

Caleb nodded. "Me too."

"I used to think that leadership meant guiding people toward answers," Howard continued. "Now it feels more like helping them learn how to ask better questions."

Caleb smiled. "That's an important shift."

Howard looked thoughtful. "It's also slower."

"Yes," Caleb agreed. "But it forms something deeper."

Howard sighed. "I suppose that's worth the wait."

"It is," Caleb said. "Especially if we want something that lasts."

As the week drew to a close, Caleb felt both encouraged and sobered. Shared wisdom was not easier to manage than centralised leadership. In some ways, it was more demanding. It required patience, discernment and a willingness to tolerate ambiguity. But it also carried promise.

People were growing more confident in their ability to listen. Less dependent on external affirmation. More attentive to the subtle movements of the Spirit.

That evening, Caleb returned once more to his notebook.

Wisdom does not announce itself loudly,
it invites attentiveness and waits to be recognised.

He closed the book and sat quietly for a long moment.

Willowend was not becoming a place known for its answers.

It was becoming a place known for its care.

Care in speech. Care in action. Care in restraint.

And as Caleb prepared for rest, he felt a steady assurance.

This kind of wisdom would not draw crowds.

But it would shape lives.

Quietly.

Faithfully.

Over time.

As wisdom continued to be shared and recognised, Caleb began to notice a quiet strengthening in the fabric of the church.

It was not obvious at first. There were no visible milestones, no announcements marking progress. Instead, it showed itself in steadiness. In the way people stayed present when conversations became difficult. In the way disagreements were handled without urgency or withdrawal. In the way silence was allowed to do its work without embarrassment.

Caleb sensed it most clearly during a gathering that could easily have gone poorly.

Two people spoke about the same situation from very different perspectives. Neither was wrong. But neither was entirely right.

Their words landed with weight, and for a moment the room felt tense. No one rushed to smooth it over.

Daniel shifted in his chair, clearly ready to speak, then stopped himself. Amelia folded her hands and waited. Mary watched quietly, her expression attentive rather than concerned.

Caleb felt the familiar instinct rise again - the urge to step in, to reframe, to offer a synthesis that might relieve the tension. He let it pass.

After a long pause, one of the speakers said quietly, "I think I need more time with this."

The other nodded. "So do I."

That was all.

No resolution. No conclusion yet. But the tension softened, not because it was removed, but because it was honoured.

As people stood to leave, the mood was calm. Thoughtful. No one seemed unsettled by the lack of closure.

Later, as Caleb was walking home, he reflected on how rarely churches were taught to live with unresolved differences. How quickly disagreement was labelled as division, rather than an invitation to deeper understanding.

Here, something else was forming.

Wisdom was not being used to settle arguments.

It was being used to sustain relationship.

At home, Rachel noticed his quiet again.

"You're carrying something again," she said.

"Yes," Caleb replied. "But it's not heavy in the way it used to be."

She waited.

"I'm realising that wisdom doesn't always make things simpler," he said. "Sometimes it makes us more careful."

Rachel nodded. "Carefulness is not weakness."

"No," Caleb agreed. "It's attentiveness."

The following week, Caleb received a message from Ruth.

I was thinking about what you said last time we spoke. About listening more than explaining. I tried it at work this week. It changed the conversation.

Caleb smiled as he read it.

He replied simply.

That sounds like wisdom finding its way into practice.

She responded a moment later.

I wouldn't have called it that before.

Caleb set the phone aside, feeling a quiet gratitude. Wisdom, once recognised, had a way of travelling beyond its place of origin.

In the days that followed, Caleb noticed how people began to reference one another's insights. Not quoting, not attributing, but building gently on what had been shared before.

Someone would say, "I've been thinking about what we talked about last week." Another would add, "That helped me see something differently."

Wisdom was becoming communal memory.

Not owned by anyone.

Not controlled.

But carried.

One afternoon, Caleb met with Howard again, sitting together beneath the familiar gum tree.

"I think we're past something now," Howard said.

Caleb looked at him. "Past what?"

"The need for you to be the one who knows," Howard replied. Caleb smiled faintly. "I hope so."

Howard nodded. "People still look to you. But not for answers. More for permission."

"Permission for what?" Caleb asked.

"To trust what they're sensing," Howard said. "And to take responsibility for it."

Caleb considered that quietly. "That feels right."

Howard smiled. "It also feels risky."

"Yes," Caleb agreed. "But all wisdom requires risk. Otherwise it remains theoretical."

That evening, Caleb returned once more to the sanctuary. He sat alone again, the familiar stillness wrapping around him. He thought about the many seasons of leadership he had walked through. Seasons of building. Seasons of conflict. Seasons of fatigue. Seasons of renewal.

This one felt different.

There was no sense of urgency. No sense of arrival. Just a steady deepening.

He realised then that wisdom, when shared, did not move quickly. It moved faithfully.

It did not demand attention.

It earned trust.

The following Sunday, Caleb spoke briefly once more.

"Wisdom," he said, "does not always tell us what to do next. Sometimes it teaches us how to remain faithful where we already are."

He paused.

"And that is often enough."

After the service, no one rushed to speak with him. People lingered, talking quietly among themselves. Small groups formed and reformed. Conversations drifted and deepened.

Caleb stood near the doorway, greeting people as they passed. He felt no need to insert himself.

This was not disengagement.

It was confidence.

As the building slowly emptied, Caleb remained behind for a moment. He walked once more down the centre aisle, stopping halfway as he had so many times before.

The space felt different now.

Not quieter.

But fuller.

As he turned off the lights and stepped outside, the evening air was cool and steady. Willowend lay very calm around him, unchanged on the surface, yet strengthened beneath.

Wisdom had not arrived as a moment.

It had arrived as a way of being.

Shared.

Practised.

Trusted.

And as Caleb walked home, unhurried and at peace, he knew this was the kind of formation that would endure.

Not because it was impressive.

But because it was faithful.

And faithfulness was wisdom's truest companion.

Courage, Caleb was learning, did not always announce itself with resolve.

More often, it arrived quietly - as a decision not to retreat, a willingness to stay present when withdrawal would have been easier, a commitment to keep walking forward even when the ground felt uncertain beneath his feet.

He sensed that kind of courage being asked of Willowend now.

Not because something had gone wrong, but because something had gone *deep*.

As wisdom was shared and questions were allowed, as trust was carried by many and discernment was practised patiently, an inevitable tension began to surface. Not conflict exactly, but resistance of a subtler kind. The kind that appeared when change, even healthy change, began to touch long-held assumptions.

Caleb noticed it first in tone rather than words.

A hesitation before agreement.

A tightening in posture during certain conversations.

A careful distancing when unfamiliar language was used, not dramatic, not hostile, but cautious.

It showed itself one Sunday after the service, when two people stood near the doorway speaking in lowered voices. They stopped when Caleb approached, then resumed with polite smiles.

He did not confront it. He noted it.

That afternoon, Caleb sat alone on the veranda, watching the light move slowly across the yard. He thought about how renewal was often spoken of as an arrival - something that came, settled, and was celebrated.

Rarely was it described as something that demanded courage long after the initial excitement faded.

Yet here it was.

Renewal was now asking people to decide whether they would trust the work unfolding among them, or quietly resist it.

Not through opposition, but through caution.

That evening, Caleb met with Howard again. They sat together in the familiar place beneath the gum tree, the air warm but steady.

"I think we're entering a more testing season," Howard said.

Caleb nodded. "I think so too."

Howard hesitated. "Not everyone seems comfortable with how things feel now."

"No," Caleb agreed. "Comfort has shifted."

Howard sighed. "Some people are even worried we're losing something."

Caleb considered that carefully. "We might be," he said. "But not the things that matter most."

Howard looked at him. "That takes courage to say."

"Yes," Caleb replied. "And more courage to live."

The next morning, Caleb received a phone call that confirmed his sense of what was forming. It was from a member who had been part of the church for many years.

"I need to be honest with you," the man said. "I'm uneasy."

Caleb listened without interruption.

"It feels like we're moving away from what we know," the man continued. "I'm not against growth. But I cannot recognise everything anymore."

Caleb paused before responding. "Thank you for trusting me with that."

The man exhaled. "I didn't want it to sound like criticism."

"It doesn't," Caleb replied. "It sounds like care."

There was a pause.

"I don't want to leave," the man said quietly. "But I don't want to feel lost either."

Caleb nodded, though the man could not see him. "Courage isn't always knowing where things are heading," he said. "Sometimes it's choosing to stay while you're still orienting yourself."

The call ended without resolution.

But it did not feel unfinished.

Later that day, Caleb spoke briefly with Amelia at the servo. She looked thoughtful.

"I think some people are nervous," she said.

"Yes," Caleb replied. "That's understandable."

"They're not angry," Amelia added. "Just… unsure."

Caleb smiled faintly. "That's often when courage is needed most."

Amelia hesitated. "What if they decide it's all too much?"

Caleb met her gaze. "Then we bless them. But we don't retreat from what we know is faithful."

She nodded slowly. "That feels hard."

"Yes," Caleb agreed. "Because courage always costs something."

That evening, Caleb sat with Rachel at the kitchen table, the house quiet around them.

"I think the season is changing again," he said.

Rachel looked at him attentively. "How so?"

"Depth is asking for resolve now," Caleb replied. "Not force. Not argument. Just steadiness."

Rachel nodded. "People will feel that."

"Yes," he said. "And some will struggle with it."

Rachel reached for his hand. "You don't have to harden to be steady."

"I know," Caleb replied. "That's the kind of courage I'm praying for."

The following Sunday, Caleb chose his words with care.

"There are moments," he said gently, "when faith asks more of us than enthusiasm. Moments when it asks for courage."

He paused.

"Not the courage to be loud. But the courage to stay faithful when things feel unfamiliar."

He did not expand on it.

After the service, the atmosphere was subdued but thoughtful. Conversations were quieter. Some people left quickly. Others stayed longer than usual, lingering as though unsure which direction to go.

Caleb did not try to manage the mood.

He trusted it.

That afternoon, as he walked home, Caleb reflected on how often leaders felt pressure to smooth over tension quickly. To reassure, to explain, to convince.

But courage, he was learning, was not about eliminating discomfort.

It was about remaining present within it.

That evening, Caleb opened his notebook again.

Courage is not the absence of fear,
it is faithfulness that refuses to retreat.

He closed the book thoughtfully.

The season ahead would certainly not be simple. There would be conversations that required clarity. Decisions that required resolve. Moments when the misunderstandings could not be avoided.

But Willowend was no longer fragile.

It was rooted. And roots, Caleb knew, were formed not in ease, but in endurance.

As night settled over the town, Caleb felt a quiet steadiness take hold. Courage was not yet being demanded loudly. But it was being asked for. And when the moment came, he sensed Willowend would be ready to answer - not with noise, but with faithfulness.

As courage began to be quietly required of the community, Caleb noticed that it did not express itself uniformly.

Some people leaned into it instinctively. Others hovered at the edges, uncertain but attentive. A few withdrew slightly, not out of rebellion, but out of self-protection. None of it surprised him. Courage rarely arrived as a shared emotion. It emerged as a series of individual decisions, made privately before they were ever visible publicly.

He became aware of this one evening during a gathering that felt more restrained than usual. The room was full, but subdued. Conversation moved cautiously, as though everyone sensed that something important was being navigated beneath the surface.

No one named it directly, yet it shaped the space all the same.

Mary spoke first, her voice gentle but steady. "I think we need to acknowledge that this season is asking something of us."

No one interrupted.

"Not something dramatic," she continued. "But something that will be costly."

Daniel nodded slowly. "Staying present feels harder lately."

"Yes," Amelia said. "It would be easier to step back a little. Let things settle without us."

Caleb listened closely.

"And yet," Mary added, "this is very often the moment when stepping back costs more than staying."

The words landed quietly, but firmly.

Caleb felt the truth of them settle in his chest. Courage, he realised again, was not about advancing the work. It was about refusing to abandon it when familiarity gave way to uncertainty. Later that night, Caleb sat alone for a while, reflecting on how often people misunderstood courage as confrontation. As standing firm against opposition. Yet what was being asked here was subtler.

It was the courage to trust formation rather than control.

The courage to resist retreat when reassurance was unavailable. The courage to remain generous when suspicion crept in quietly. The following morning, Caleb received a message from someone he had not spoken with in some time.

I'm not sure where I fit anymore.
I don't disagree with what's happening.
I just don't know how to participate.

Caleb read it slowly.

He replied simply.

You don't have to rush to find your place.
Staying present is participation.

There was no immediate response.

Later that day, Caleb met with Howard again. They walked together along the edge of town, the paddocks open and quiet beside them.

"I'm hearing concern from a few people," Howard said. "Not anger. Just… hesitation."

Caleb nodded. "That's to be expected."

Howard frowned slightly. "Some are worried that if they speak up, they'll be seen as resistant."

Caleb stopped walking and turned to face him. "That would be a failure on our part."

Howard raised an eyebrow. "How so?"

"If courage is only celebrated when it aligns with momentum," Caleb said, "then it becomes coercion."

Howard considered that. "So, courage also looks like making room for dissent."

"Yes," Caleb replied. "And for uncertainty."

Howard sighed. "That's complicated."

"Yes," Caleb agreed. "But necessary."

That afternoon, Caleb found himself unexpectedly tired. Not physically, but inwardly. He recognised the feeling. It was the fatigue that came when leadership moved beyond clarity into patience. When outcomes were no longer visible enough to motivate easily.

He resisted the temptation to interpret the tiredness as failure. Instead, he rested.

That evening, Rachel noticed the change in him.

"You're quieter again," she said gently.

"Yes," Caleb replied. "But not discouraged."

She waited.

"I think courage is being asked of me too," he said. "Not to push forward. But to hold steady."

Rachel smiled softly. "That's always been your harder work."

"Yes," he admitted. "Because it doesn't look like leadership from the outside."

Rachel reached for his hand. "It looks like trust from the inside."

The next Sunday, the atmosphere in the church was thoughtful rather than celebratory. Caleb did not try to lift it artificially. He allowed the weight to remain.

In his brief remarks, he said only this: "Courage is not always loud. Sometimes it is simply the decision to remain faithful when things are no longer clear."

He paused.

"That kind of courage is rarely applauded. But it is deeply formative."

After the service, reactions were mixed. Some people thanked him quietly. Others avoided conversation altogether. A few lingered, uncertain.

Caleb welcomed all of it.

Later that afternoon, he stopped by the servo again. Amelia looked up from the counter, concern in her eyes.

"I think I upset someone today," she said.

Caleb listened as she explained.

"They said things felt too uncertain now," Amelia continued. "I didn't know what to say."

"What did you say?" Caleb asked.

"I told them I was still learning how to trust what God was doing," she replied. "And that I wasn't sure either."

Caleb smiled. "That was honest."

"It didn't fix anything," Amelia said.

"No," Caleb replied. "But it didn't betray the work either."

She exhaled slowly. "I'm realising that courage doesn't mean knowing what to say."

"Yes," Caleb agreed. "Often it means refusing to pretend."

As the week unfolded, Caleb noticed that courage began to ripple quietly through the community. Not as confidence, but as commitment.

People continued to show up. Conversations continued, even when they were uncomfortable. Disagreements were no longer avoided, they were now handled with restraint.

The church did not fracture.

Nor did it surge forward dramatically.

It held.

That evening, Caleb wrote once more in his notebook.

Courage is faithfulness without applause.
It is presence without certainty.

He then sat quietly for a long moment.

This season would not reward urgency. It would not produce quick affirmation. But it would form something durable.

Willowend was learning that renewal did not only require openness and wisdom.

It required courage. Not the courage to advance. But the courage to endure.

And as Caleb prepared for rest, he felt a steady confidence settle in him.

They were not retreating. They were being refined. And that refinement, though quiet, would shape them for whatever lay ahead.

As the season pressed on, courage began to show itself less in what people said and more in what they chose to *keep doing*.

People kept coming.

Not everyone, and not always cheerfully. But steadily. They continued to show up every Sunday, they continued to gather midweek, they continued to sit in conversations that did not resolve neatly. The absence of certainty no longer drove them away as it might once have done.

Caleb noticed it one quiet evening when only a handful of people arrived for a gathering that had once been full.

No one apologised for the smaller number.

No one tried to compensate.

They simply sat, prayed briefly, and listened.

At one point, a man spoke who rarely contributed. His voice was hesitant, but clear.

"I don't have much to say," he began. "I just want you to know I nearly stopped coming a few weeks ago."

The room stilled.

"I didn't disagree with anything," he continued. "I just felt exposed. Like faith was asking more of me than I was ready to give."

No one interrupted.

"But I realised," he said after a pause, "that leaving would have been easier than staying. And I didn't want my faith to be shaped by what was easiest."

The words hung in the air.

Caleb felt something steady settle in his chest.

This was courage.

Not loud. Not persuasive. Simply honest.

Afterward, as people began to leave, no one rushed to comment on what had been said. A few nodded. One person quietly thanked the man. The moment did not need explanation.

Later that night, Caleb sat alone again, reflecting on how courage often went unnoticed precisely because it did not announce itself. It did not seek validation. It did not demand reassurance. It endured.

The following week brought a conversation Caleb had been expecting. A couple asked to meet with him, their posture careful, their words measured.

"We're not sure where we land with everything," one of them said. "We don't want to disrupt what's happening. But we also don't want to pretend we're comfortable."

Caleb listened.

"We're trying to decide whether to step back for a while," the other added. "Not leave. Just… breathe."

Caleb nodded slowly. "That sounds honest."

They looked surprised. "You're not disappointed?"

"No," Caleb replied. "Courage doesn't always look like staying in the same place. Sometimes it looks like naming your limits without withdrawing your trust."

The couple exhaled together.

"That helps," one of them said. "We didn't want to feel like we were failing."

Caleb smiled gently. "Faith is never measured by proximity. It's measured by integrity."

As they left, Caleb felt both the weight and the privilege of the moment. Courage did not require uniform response. It required faithfulness in the place each person truly stood.

At home that evening, Rachel listened as he spoke about the meeting.

"You're giving people permission to remain human," she said.

"Yes," Caleb replied. "I think that's part of what this season is asking."

Rachel nodded. "And you?"

He smiled faintly. "It's asking the same of me."

The next Sunday, Caleb noticed a change in himself.

He was less vigilant.

Not careless. But less watchful for signs of failure. Less alert to who was leaving or staying. He realised that some of his earlier attentiveness had been driven by fear - the fear that courage might falter if not continually reinforced.

Now, he trusted the work more deeply.

During the service, someone prayed simply, "God, help us stay when it would be easier to go."

No one added to it.

Afterward, Caleb stood near the doorway as usual. People passed with quiet smiles, brief nods, occasional conversation.

There was no sense of momentum.

There was commitment.

That afternoon, Caleb walked alone again, the familiar streets steady beneath his feet. Willowend looked unchanged. The same shopfronts. The same unhurried rhythm. And yet, he knew the town was different now.

Not transformed beyond recognition. But strengthened. Courage had not removed tension. It had made space for endurance.

That evening, Caleb returned once more to his notebook.

Courage is not the decision to move forward quickly,
it is the decision to remain faithful when progress cannot be measured.

He closed the book gently.

The season ahead would continue to test them. There would be misunderstandings. Moments of weariness. Occasions when retreat would seem appealing.

But Willowend had learned something essential.

That faith did not need constant reassurance to survive.

That renewal was not sustained by enthusiasm alone.

That courage, when practised quietly and consistently, shaped communities more deeply than any moment of excitement ever could.

As night settled over the town, Caleb felt no urge to summarise what had happened or predict what would come next.

He felt content to trust what was forming.

Not because it was safe.

But because it was faithful.

And that, he knew, was enough to carry them forward.

The first thing Caleb noticed was not the sound, but the absence of it. The town was quieter than usual that morning, the kind of quiet that was not empty but attentive. Willowend had learned, over time, to listen differently. Not just for danger, as it had during the fire season, but for meaning. For the subtle signals that something was being asked of it.

Caleb walked the familiar route into town without hurry. The bakery door was open, the smell of bread drifting onto the footpath. The servo forecourt was quiet, though Amelia's car was already there. The post office window reflected the pale blue sky, steady and untroubled.

Nothing dramatic announced itself.

And yet Caleb felt the weight of the moment.

He had been feeling it for weeks now - the sense that the season was not ending so much as settling.

The sharp edges of uncertainty had now softened. What remained was not clarity, exactly, but coherence. The church was no longer bracing itself for change. It was learning how to live within it.

He unlocked the church doors and stepped inside. The building greeted him with its familiar stillness - the faint creak of timber, the quiet smell of old hymn books, the light filtering through the narrow windows and settling gently across the pews.

He stood for a moment, hands resting on the back of the nearest seat.

This place had held so much.

Fear. Prayer. Waiting. Awakening. Courage.

And now, something else.

Responsibility.

Caleb moved to the front and sat, not to prepare a sermon, but simply to be present. He had learned that some mornings did not require productivity. They required attentiveness.

As he sat, he thought of the people who now carried the life of the church with him, not as helpers, but as participants.

Mary, whose discernment had steadied the community more than once.

Amelia, whose faith had grown not from certainty, but from honesty.

Daniel, learning how to integrate belief with adulthood, no longer sheltered, no longer cynical.

Others too. Quiet ones. Faithful ones. People who would never be named in a report or noticed beyond Willowend, but whose obedience shaped the ground beneath the church more surely than any strategy.

Caleb realised that somewhere along the way, leadership had shifted.

Not away from him.

But outward.

The thought did not unsettle him.

It relieved him.

Later that morning, he met briefly with Howard. They sat on the church steps, the sun warming the stone beneath them.

"I've been thinking," Howard said. "About what happens next."

Caleb smiled slightly. "So have I."

Howard hesitated. "There's no obvious next step, is there?"

"No," Caleb replied. "And that's probably the point."

Howard nodded slowly. "I don't feel like we're meant to build something bigger."

"No," Caleb said. "But we are meant to tend what's here."

Howard looked out at the street. "That feels less impressive."

"Yes," Caleb agreed. "And more faithful."

They sat in silence for a moment.

"I think," Howard said finally, "that what we've learned is how to stay."

Caleb glanced at him. "Yes."

"Stay present. Stay humble. Stay open."

"Yes."
Howard smiled faintly. "That might be enough."

By midday, Caleb found himself at home, sitting at the table with his notebook open but untouched.

Rachel moved quietly around the kitchen, the rhythm of the space familiar and grounding.

"You're not writing," she observed.

"No," Caleb said. "I don't think I need to."

Rachel smiled. "That's new."

He returned the smile. "I think the story is living now. It doesn't need recording every day."

She poured tea and sat opposite him.

"You're not restless," she said.

"No," he replied. "I'm settled."

She studied him for a moment. "Then you're ready."

"For what?"

"For whatever comes next," she said. "Even if it doesn't look like progress."

Caleb nodded. He had learned that readiness did not always announce itself as excitement. Sometimes it arrived as peace.

That afternoon, his phone buzzed briefly. A message from Ruth.

Just wanted you to know I was thinking about you both today. I'm proud of the way you live what you believe - even when it's quiet. Love you.

Caleb read it twice, then smiled. He did not reply immediately. He let the words sit, grateful not for affirmation, but for connection.

Later, he walked again, as he so often did now, through the town. He stopped briefly at the servo. Amelia waved.

"Everything okay?" she asked.

"Yes," Caleb said. "Everything's steady."

She nodded. "It feels like that."

As he continued on, Caleb realised that Willowend had become something rare.

Not a place defined by revival.

Not a church defined by growth.

But a community shaped by faithfulness.

The kind that did not need constant explanation.

The kind that endured.

As evening approached, Caleb returned home. The light softened across the paddocks, the sky wide and unhurried.

He stood on the veranda and looked out across the land he had come to love not because it was extraordinary, but because it was entrusted to him. He thought of all the small churches scattered across the country. Weathered buildings. Faithful leaders.

Small communities holding hope quietly, week after week.

Not unseen.

But often unnoticed.

Caleb knew now that God did some of His most careful work in places like this.

Not at the centre.

But at the edges.

Where trust was learned slowly.

Where obedience was practiced without applause.

Where faith was lived, not performed.

As the sun dipped lower, Caleb felt no urgency to move.

The work was not finished.

But it was grounded.

And that was enough.

The story of Willowend would continue - in lives shaped, in faith practised, in courage chosen again and again.

Not because it was dramatic.

But because it was faithful.

And in that quiet faithfulness, Caleb knew, God was still at work. As night settled more fully over Willowend, Caleb found himself thinking less about what had happened and more about what had been *held*.

There had been no defining moment to point to. No single decision that had changed everything. Instead, there was a layering of faithfulness - small choices made repeatedly, often without certainty, always without spectacle.

He realised that this, perhaps, was the truest measure of the season they had come through. Not what had been gained. But what had been *kept*.

Trust had been kept when fear would have been easier.

Presence had been kept when withdrawal would have been justified.

Hope had been kept when answers were incomplete.

Caleb sat at the small desk near the window, the lamp casting a soft circle of light across the timber surface. He opened his notebook, not with urgency, but with care. He no longer felt the need to capture everything. Just enough to remember.

We did not rush, he wrote. *We did not force. We stayed.*

He paused, then added another line.

And staying changed us.

Outside, the town moved quietly into evening. A car passed now and then. A dog barked briefly, then settled. Somewhere down the road, laughter drifted and faded.

Ordinary sounds.

Holy ground.

Rachel joined him after a while, carrying two mugs. She placed one beside him and leaned against the doorway.

"You're thinking again," she said.

"Yes," Caleb replied. "But not searching."

She smiled. "That's different."

"Yes," he said. "It feels like the difference between steering and trusting the current."

Rachel sat opposite him. "You've let go of needing to define the season."

"I think the season defined us," he said quietly.

She nodded. "It always does."

They sat in warm silence, the kind that had grown between them over so many years of shared vocation and shared restraint.

Their marriage had been shaped, like the church, not by dramatic turning points, but by endurance.

Rachel broke the silence gently. "You've noticed, haven't you?"

"Noticed what?"

"How little people look to you now for permission."

Caleb considered that. "Yes."

"And how much they look to one another."

"Yes."

Rachel smiled. "That's not loss, you know."

"I know," Caleb said. "It's fruit."

Later, as the house grew quieter, Caleb stepped outside once more. The stars were beginning to show, clear and steady above the darkened paddocks. The air had cooled, carrying the faint scent of grass and dust.

He thought of the questions he used to ask himself.

Are we doing enough?

Are we leading well?

Are people responding?

They felt distant now. Not irrelevant, but incomplete.

Better questions had taken their place.

Are we faithful?

Are we listening?

Are we making room for God to work without needing to manage the outcome?

Those questions did not demand constant answers. They asked for posture.

Caleb leaned against the veranda railing and let his thoughts drift beyond Willowend. He imagined other pastors standing in similar places at similar hours. Unlocking small buildings. Preparing sermons that would be heard by a few dozen people at most. Carrying concerns they could not always name.

He felt a quiet solidarity with them.

Not because their work was heroic.

But because it was hidden.

And therefore precious.

He knew some would never see what they hoped for. Some would labour faithfully and leave without visible fruit. Others would watch communities change slowly, almost imperceptibly, and wonder if it was enough.

Caleb had learned that it was.

Not because success was guaranteed.

But because obedience mattered more than outcome.

The next morning, Caleb rose early again, as he so often did. Not because he needed to, but because he wanted to greet the day before it gathered momentum. He walked briefly through the town, nodding to a few early risers, exchanging simple greetings.

At the church, he unlocked the door and paused.

He had unlocked this door thousands of times.

And yet it never felt routine.

Each turning of the key was an act of trust. That God would meet His people again. That the work of faithfulness would continue, even when unseen.

Inside, the sanctuary was still. Sunlight filtered gently through the windows, touching the pews and the worn carpet.

Caleb stood for a moment, then prayed simply.

"Thank You for what You are growing here. Teach us to tend it well."

He did not ask for protection from difficulty.

He did not ask for expansion.

He asked for steadiness.

Later that day, a small group gathered without any fanfare. No firm agenda. No program. Just people sitting together, sharing honestly, listening attentively. There were pauses. Moments of uncertainty. Quiet laughter.

Nothing to report.

Everything to treasure.

Caleb watched from the edge, not directing, not interpreting. Just present.

He realised then that the greatest gift of the season had not been renewal.

It had been release.

Release from needing to carry the church alone.

Release from measuring faith by momentum.

Release from mistaking noise for life.

Willowend had not become extraordinary.

It had become faithful.

And faithfulness, Caleb knew, had a long reach.

It shaped lives quietly.

It prepared people for seasons they could not yet see.

It left room for God to move in ways that defied planning.

As the afternoon light shifted, Caleb felt a deep, reassuring sense of completion settle in him.

Not an ending.

But a fullness.

The story of Willowend was not finished.

But it no longer needed to be driven.

It would be lived.

One gathering at a time.

One conversation at a time.

One quiet act of courage at a time.

And in that slow, faithful unfolding, Caleb trusted that God would continue to do what He had always done best.

Work patiently.

Work gently.

Work deeply.

Often unseen, but always present.

Morning returned to Willowend without ceremony. There was no sense of conclusion in it, no signal that anything had ended. The light rose as it always did, touching the paddocks first, then the roofs, then the quiet streets where people would soon begin their day. Life resumed, steady and unremarkable.

And that, Caleb realised, was precisely the point.

He stood again on the veranda, hands resting on the railing, watching the town wake. A ute passed slowly. A dog barked once, then fell silent.

Somewhere nearby, a kettle clicked off. The ordinary sounds of a place that knew how to carry its own weight.

Caleb no longer felt the need to interpret these moments.

Once, he might have asked what they *meant*. What God was *saying*. Whether there was a lesson to be drawn or a direction to be named.

Now, he simply received them.

Faith, he had learned, did not always announce itself through insight. Sometimes it arrived as consent - the willingness to live fully within the life God had already given.

Rachel joined him, slipping her arm through his.

"You're thinking again," she said.

"Yes," he replied. "But not about what's next."

She smiled. "Good."

They stood together for a while, neither needing to speak. They had reached a place where words were no longer required to affirm what had been learned.

Eventually, Caleb said quietly, "I used to think the goal was to lead people somewhere."

Rachel glanced at him. "And now?"

"Now I think the calling is to walk with them while God leads."

Rachel nodded. "That sounds right."

Caleb thought of Willowend Baptist Church - its modest sign, its weathered walls, its familiar pews. He thought of how easily such places were overlooked, and how rarely they featured in conversations about growth or innovation or influence.

And yet, he knew what had been formed there.

He had seen people learn to pray honestly.

He had watched courage emerge slowly, not as confidence, but as perseverance.

He had witnessed genuine faith deepen without any spectacle, without urgency, without fear.

This was not failure.

This was fruit.

Later that day, Caleb unlocked the church once more. He moved through the familiar space slowly, touching the back of a pew, straightening a chair, opening a window to let the breeze move freely. These were such small acts, barely noticeable, yet full of intention.

Tending was holy work.

A few people arrived early, greeting one another quietly. No one rushed. No one asked what the plan was. They simply took their places, trusting that what was needed would emerge as it always had.

Caleb did not begin with announcements.

He did not frame the moment.

He simply invited them to pray.

The prayer was unpolished. Brief. Honest.

"God," someone said, "thank You for being patient with us."

There was no need to add anything.

Afterward, Caleb stepped back, allowing the gathering to find its own rhythm. People spoke when they needed to. Silence was not filled. Tears were not hurried away.

This was church as it was meant to be.

Not a performance.

Not a strategy.

A people learning how to remain faithful together.

As the gathering ended and people drifted out, Caleb lingered near the doorway. He exchanged nods, brief words, quiet smiles.

Nothing needed to be said.

One by one, the space emptied.

When he finally closed the door, Caleb paused with his hand resting on the handle.

He had closed this door many times before.

But today, it felt different.

Not final.

But complete.

Later, walking home, Caleb thought again of the countless small churches scattered across the country. The pastors who unlocked doors each week without knowing who would come. The leaders who prepared faithfully without certainty of outcome. The congregations who gathered not because it was easy, but because it was right.

He hoped they would recognise themselves here.

Not in the details.

But in the posture.

He hoped they would hear this quiet assurance:

That faithfulness mattered.

That obscurity did not diminish significance.

That God's work was not just confined to the visible or to the impressive. That renewal did not always arrive as fire or noise or momentum.

Sometimes, it arrived as steadiness.

As courage.

As a people who learned how to stay.

As evening settled again over Willowend, Caleb returned home.

The light softened across the land, the sky wide and open, holding more promise than explanation.

He felt no need to define the future.

The work ahead would come, as it always had, one step at a time.

One conversation.

One prayer.

One quiet act of obedience.

And that was enough.

Because God was still at work.

In Willowend.

In small churches.

In faithful lives lived far from attention.

Not rushing.

Not forcing.

But patiently shaping hearts that were willing to listen.

Caleb did not know what Willowend would look like in five years' time.

He did not know who would still be there, or what challenges would come, or how faithfully the next season would be lived.

But as he stood there, the town quiet around him, he knew this much: God had been present in the ordinary days, in the slow conversations, in the prayers that did not sound impressive, and in the people who stayed when leaving might have been easier.

Nothing here had been rushed, and nothing here had been wasted. The work of God had not announced itself, but it had endured.

And perhaps that was the truest hope of all - not that churches would become extraordinary, but that they would remain faithful, attentive, and open, trusting that God still delights to do His deepest work in the places that rarely make headlines.

And as Caleb stood there, the day gently closing around him, he knew this with certainty:

The story did not end here.

It simply continued - wherever faith was practiced, courage was chosen, and God was trusted to do His deepest work in the quiet places.

So, dear reader, we come to the end of a very long journey. Of course, Willowend is a fictional town, and the Baptist Church there is not real. There is no Pastor Caleb Merritt, and neither he nor his church are based on any real people. And yet, by now, I trust you will have been drawn into this story to the point where you feel you truly know this man of God and his people. Not because this is a remarkable work of fiction, but because the story itself is deeply familiar and instantly relatable.

The Willowend story is special because it reflects the reality of hundreds of small country Churches and their communities. Every character, every conversation, and every chapter in this unfolding journey has already taken place in so many small churches and communities just like Willowend. That is why I think every reader – whether you are a pastor, church leader, elder, long-time member, or the person who runs the local servo – will find yourself somewhere in these pages, recognising both the ordinariness and the quiet beauty of such places.

My ministry has been devoted to helping people grow in a real relationship with Jesus Christ and to live faithfully as His disciples in their own context – at work, at church, and in the wider world. So, in that sense, Willowend is not simply a story I made up. It is a teaching tool. If you, as a reader, have learned even a portion of what I learned while writing this, then the deeper purpose of these two books has been fulfilled.

You may wish to return to this story again someday, perhaps with a notebook of your own, and reflect on what God might be teaching you about your life, your faith, and your calling. For me, the brief notes Caleb kept jotting down captured the essence of this story. As I went back and read his many entries in that notebook, I realised how foundational his observations were to all Christian ministry. I am sure I will read them all many more times in the days ahead, and I hope you might too.

Thank you for joining me in Willowend. May God hold you and bless you in your journey.

9 781764 263573